The Christmas Postcards

Karen Swan is the *Sunday Times* top three bestselling author of twenty-three books and her novels sell all over the world. She writes two books each year – one for the summer period and one for the Christmas season. Previous winter titles include *The Christmas Party*, *Together by Christmas* and *Midnight in the Snow*, and for summer, *The Spanish Promise*, *The Hidden Beach* and *The Secret Path*.

Her five-book historical series, called 'The Wild Isle' and starting with *The Last Summer*, is based on the dramatic evacuation of Scottish island St Kilda in the summer of 1930.

Previously a fashion editor, she lives in Sussex with her husband, three children and two dogs.

Follow Karen on Instagram @swannywrites, on her author page on Facebook, and on Twitter @KarenSwan1.

Also by Karen Swan

The Christmas Postcards

Karen Swan

PAN BOOKS

First published 2022 by Macmillan

This edition first published 2022 by Pan Books
an imprint of Pan Macmillan
The Smithson, 6 Briset Street, London EC1M 5NR
EU representative: Macmillan Publishers Ireland Ltd, 1st Floor,
The Liffey Trust Centre, 117–126 Sheriff Street Upper,
Dublin 1, D01 YC43
Associated companies throughout the world
www.panmacmillan.com

ISBN 978-1-5290-8425-2

1 3 5 7 9 8 6 4 2

A CIP catalogue record for this book is available from the British Library.

Typeset in Palatino by Palimpsest Book Production Ltd, Falkirk, Stirlingshire
Printed and bound by CPI Group (UK) Ltd, Croydon, CR0 4YY

Visit **www.panmacmillan.com** to read more about all our books
and to buy them. You will also find features, author interviews and
news of any author events, and you can sign up for e-newsletters
so that you're always first to hear about our new releases.

For Michael Georges, for digging all the holes

The Christmas Postcards

Prologue

'I can't do it.' Natasha's grip tightened around the cable, knuckles blanched white as she tried not to look down.

The walkway swayed slightly as Hels jumped off and onto the platform at the other end. She had practically skipped her way across, more like a Disney squirrel from *Snow White* than a trainee dentist from Somerset. She whirled back to find Natasha frozen mid-step between the two wooden stepping stones. Her expression of free-spirited delight turned into surprise, then cackling mischief. 'Oh, don't tell me you're stuck!' she laughed, clapping her hands. 'That's too funny!' She reached for her phone and took a few pictures of Natasha's rigid stance.

Natasha looked at her in panic. She would have said she was rooted to the spot if only it weren't so blindingly obvious that she wasn't rooted to anything whatsoever. She was thirty feet above the ground with just a cable to keep her safe. 'I can't do it,' she said again, trying to project her voice.

'Hon, if you can walk, drunk, over cobblestones in your vintage Jimmy Choos, then you sure as hell can walk this. Eyes up, chop-chop. You're holding everyone up.'

Natasha looked back down trepidatiously at her own feet,

1

trying to focus on her trainers and not the gaping chasm beneath them. She willed her legs to walk but, as if prodded by the devil's imp, her gaze went straight to the drop. The pine-cone-speckled ground seemed to rise up and then fall again. With a whimper, she dropped into a straddled half crouch – ungainly, undignified, uncomfortable. Her thigh muscles began to burn.

The aerial walkway swayed again as Sara, behind her, took another step closer. They were supposed to keep three stepping stones clear of the person in front at all times, that was what the guy who'd harnessed them up had said. Was she the only one who'd been listening? Had the rest all been distracted by Hels's dirty dancing behind his back?

'Come on, Nats!' Sara called from behind her. 'Get a shift on. It's chilly when you stop.'

'I . . . I . . .' Natasha hesitated, trying to stand tall again, but her body felt set in concrete. 'I'm really stuck.'

'Natser,' Hels called again. 'Just think of the margaritas we'll have after this. Mmmm.'

That was easy for her to say, from the safety of the solid platform encircling the tree trunk. Natasha eyed it desperately. There were thirteen steps between there and where she had stopped. Why had she stopped? If she had just kept on moving, she'd be there already and everything would be fine. The problems always started when her brain engaged.

Voices began to heckle and shout from further back in the line: *What's the problem? Get a move on!* She was creating a log jam. The cable system meant no one could overtake on the walkways, and she could only be unclipped at one of the platforms. For as long as she was stuck, they were too.

'I can't, I can't, I can't,' she whispered, knowing no one could hear. She dropped her head, realizing she was shaking.

She couldn't go back but nor could she go forward. She was suspended in mid-air, just waiting to fall.

'Hey!'

The shout intruded past the fog that had descended upon her. She looked down to see the instructor who had buckled them up and given them their safety briefing – taking the premixed passionfruit martini can from Hels's hands – staring up at her. His hands were on his hips. 'Are you okay?'

'Can't you get her to shift on?' someone shouted further back.

She shook her head. 'I can't. I can't move.' She couldn't even project her voice.

'She's been like that for five minutes now!' someone else pitched in.

The man blinked for a moment, taking in her awkwardly crouched posture across the two stepping stones. No one would willingly hold themselves in that humiliating, frankly painful position. '. . . Okay. I'll come up.'

She watched him, daring only to swivel her eyes, as he climbed the ladder to the platform on the tree ahead of her. Within moments he was standing beside Helena, who said something to him that made him nod. Natasha gasped as the walkway tautened beneath his weight as he stepped out, walking casually towards her like he was in the pub. 'Nats, is it?'

She nodded.

'Are you feeling okay? Are you unwell?' he asked, stopping in front of her. Natasha, still in her half crouch, looked up at him.

'You . . . you haven't clipped on,' she whispered in disbelief, gripping the cable even more tightly. He might die at any moment.

3

'Oh! Shit!' he exclaimed, looking down and seeing that he was standing there completely untethered. 'I keep forgetting.' He clipped the buckle on his harness to the cable. 'Don't tell my boss, will you?' he grinned.

Natasha didn't reply. His devil-may-care attitude wasn't doing anything to make her feel better, or safer.

He crouched down in front of her, elbows resting on his splayed knees. 'So you're really stuck, huh?'

'I can't do it,' she whispered. 'I'm sorry.'

'Don't be. We'll get you back. You're perfectly safe, I promise.'

She glanced at him and saw that his eyes were kind, that despite his infinite ease up here in the treetops, he wasn't mocking her for her cowardice. He rose to standing again but the motion made the bridge swing and her grip tightened on the cable as she whimpered again. She felt like she was falling, like she might die, her chest felt tight, her breathing shallow.

He put a hand out to steady her, his skin warm against hers; she was gripping so tightly, she was restricting her own blood flow. 'So Nats, my name's Tom. I won't let you fall, I promise. Do you trust me?'

She didn't reply – he was a stranger! Of course she didn't trust him! – and he gave a low laugh. 'I'll take that as a no, then.'

She swivelled her eyes to him again, still the only part of her that could move.

'That's fine. Fair enough. I can still work with your condemnation and suspicion.'

She smiled in spite of her terror.

'Ha, good. There we go. She smiles!' He grinned back, and even amid her rigid terror she could see he was good-looking: one of those happy-go-lucky, smiley, athletic guys who could do anything and make it look easy. 'Okay, so then the first thing we're going to do is try to get you to stand. No sudden movements. You're just going to slowly straighten up.'

Stand? He might as well have said *handstand*. She felt the smile fade, her breathing shallow. 'No.' She had to stay low, hidden, small.

There was a pause and she could tell he was assessing her, that it was beginning to dawn on him this was no ordinary freeze. She was well and truly stuck fast, as though welded there.

'Okay, then we're going to do standing up for beginners. You keep holding onto the sides and I'm going to put my hands under your arms to help guide you up. It'll keep you feeling stable—'

She shook her head. 'No.'

There was another pause. If she couldn't even stand, what hope was there for her to walk? She saw him twist round, no doubt looking for one of his colleagues, but the nearest one was several trees away and fully involved with a little boy's birthday party. To her mortification, the children were bouncing and jumping on the walkways: no hands, no fear.

Tom turned back to her. 'Okay, let's try this, then. With your permission, I'm going to come in close and hold you. Then you'll close your eyes and I'll guide you to standing so you won't even have to see where we are.'

'No.' Her voice was barely even a breath.

'. . . Well, it's basically that or a tranquillizer dart.'

Her head whipped up in alarm but he just gave a shrug. 'I'm only half joking.'

She swallowed.

'Close your eyes. Go on, just close your eyes for me. I won't do anything. Just close your eyes and allow yourself to feel the sensation of being up here.'

'But that's exactly what I don't want to feel,' she muttered.

He grinned, like she was the one who'd told a joke now. 'I know, but if you can "feel" the sense of space around you and also recognize that you're not actually falling, it will help your instincts unlock. Your body may not like it up here, but your mind will be reassured you are safe. Just try it. I'm right beside you, I won't let anything happen to you.'

Warily, she closed her eyes. It had the effect of heightening her other senses and she became acutely aware of the breeze, not just around her but below her too. She felt the twist of the cable handrail in her tightly gripped palm, the solidity of the oak stepping stone beneath her feet, the burn in her thighs. She had a sense of her own body in this space – precarious, but stable.

When she opened her eyes again, he was looking at her. 'Okay?'

She nodded.

'Can you stand on your own?'

Quickly she shook her head.

'Then can I step into your space and hold you? No funny business, I assure you, but it will calm your nervous system, which, right now, is having quite the party.'

She gave a small half smile at his joke again. 'Fine.' Anything to get off here.

'Good. So then I'm going to step onto the same blocks as you. The bridge will move slightly but we won't tip or fall—' And before she could even hesitate, he stepped onto the very blocks supporting her. The walkway shifted at the transference of weight and instinctively, as he moved into her personal space, her hands flew to him as if he were the steady object. No sooner had she released her death grip of the cable than he wrapped his arms around her and clasped her tightly to his chest. She couldn't see over his shoulder so she was peering into the blackness of his North Face fleece, unable to see anything, but she realized she was now standing at least.

'Are you okay?' he asked, but she heard the question mainly as a rumble through his chest.

'Uh-huh.'

'Good. Now step on my feet.'

'. . . Huh?'

'Step on my feet.'

'I can't do that. I'll crush you.'

She felt his laughter as another rumble against her ear. 'I hardly think so,' he chuckled. 'Go on, step up. Don't worry – there's method in the madness.'

Tentatively, she placed her feet on his. This was ridiculous, but also seemingly the only alternative to a tranquilliser dart.

'Now hold on tight.'

'What are you going to do?' she asked, gripping him tightly.

'Think of it as a dance.'

'A *dance*?' she gasped in horror.

'Yes. We're going to—' He suddenly pivoted on the balls of his feet and spun them both round 180 degrees. '—turn.'

It was done before she could even protest. She felt his hand lift off her back and fiddle quickly with a buckle on his harness between them and she realized he was detaching and re-attaching himself to the walkway, to stop the cable from twisting around them. Then he did something to her harness too.

A few moments later, his hands were on her back again. He moved so quickly, not even having to look. Fear seemed an alien concept to him. 'Still okay?'

She could scarcely nod now. She was standing on a stranger's toes, clasping him like a limpet, thirty feet off the ground, waiting to die.

'Can you waltz?' he asked, but left her no time to reply. 'It's really very simple. Step, step, close. Step, step, close.' His feet moved in time with the instructions, walking her backwards, one of his hands on the cable rail, the other looped around her waist, until moments later, she felt him take a bigger step. She gave a small gasp and clung to him even more tightly.

'You can open your eyes now,' he said after a pause.

Huh? They had stopped moving. Tentatively, one eye opened, she drew back – but only so far. He had somehow buckled their harnesses together, linking them so that he was tugged gently by her movements. He released her again with a single flick of the clasp.

'Terra firma, of sorts,' he grinned as she saw that they were on the platform.

Natasha staggered backwards off his feet onto the deck. 'Oh God, it's over, it's over,' she breathed, pressing a hand to her chest as she looked down at the solid platform. Not sure she could trust herself to stand unsupported, she sank to her knees, letting her head hang. It was over.

'*I'd* be weak at the knees after that display of heroism too!' Hels laughed coquettishly. She would flirt with the postman, the postman's dog. 'How can she *possibly* thank you?'

'No need. It's all in a day's work,' Tom chuckled, unclipping his harness from the line and crouching in front of her again. 'You okay?' he asked, dropping his voice.

She looked up, feeling her stomach curl with mortification as she saw him properly now, without the veil of terror over her eyes. He was tall, she already knew that; brown hair, strong brows, blue eyes, yes; but there was something in his smile, the kindness in his voice, that made her want to reach her arms out and press her face into the crook of his neck

8

again. He felt . . . familiar, somehow, as though they'd met before.

'Thank you so much. I feel so pathetic.'

'Don't. It happens – a lot,' he said. 'We see it all the time. Don't beat yourself up. You did good.'

She knew he was just being kind. That the toddlers were braver than her.

He must have read the scepticism on her face because he chuckled. 'Still suspicious of me, huh?'

'No, I . . . no.' She shook her head wanly, wanting him to believe her, but words wouldn't form, adrenaline rendering her dumb. She felt like her mind and body were only just coming back under her own control again. What had happened back there? She remembered how expertly he'd distracted her with jokes, how safe she'd felt the moment his arms had closed around her, the confusion that came from standing on his toes, dancing through the trees—

'I mean it, Nats, you did good.' His words forced her to hold his gaze and she felt a charge, as if something other than mere kindness zipped between them. He seemed to sense it too, as he frowned slightly and the look between them held for a few moments longer than was polite. His mouth opened, but there was a slight delay before the words came. '. . . Let's get you standing, shall we?'

He rose to standing again, putting a hand out to her. She slipped her hand into his, feeling the size of his palm against hers, the grip of his fingers as he effortlessly pulled her back up. There was another pause.

'So . . .' He smiled, shaking his head slightly and breaking the eye contact. 'Uh . . . so, I know you've paid for the full treetops experience and it's completely up to you, but my advice would be to cut yourself some slack and leave it here for today. You've had a pretty bad shock and this is supposed to be fun – not ritual torture.'

'Exactly. This is a hen party. The torture is supposed to come after you're married, Nats, not before!' Sara said, joining them as she stepped onto the platform now too and unclipped herself.

'You're getting married?' Tom asked, taking a step back as he planted his hands on his hips.

'Is it that shocking?' Hels asked wryly, watching his reaction.

'She just looks so . . .' He looked back at Natasha. 'You look so young.'

'Yeah, well – true love doesn't give a stuff about age,' Hels drawled. 'Romeo and Juliet were teenagers.'

'I'm not a teenager,' Natasha said quickly.

He nodded slowly. '. . . Well . . . congratulations.'

'Thanks.' She looked down at the boards again.

She could see the feet of all the people who had been stuck behind her, walking quickly past, desperate to get onto the next platform and ahead of her, lest she should try her luck again.

'And don't worry, I have no intention of putting myself – or anyone else – through that again,' Natasha said, pushing her hair back. 'I am really sorry for putting you out.'

'You didn't put me out.'

She looked back up to find him still watching her, but without the cheeky grin from before. The air seemed to crackle between them and in her peripheral vision, Natasha could see Hels's mouth and eyes widen with scandalous delight, as if she could see it too. Natasha knew she wouldn't be hearing the end of this unexpected flirtation.

'Um, the others will be wondering where we are, I guess.' She glanced at Sara, who was the emcee of the trip.

'Oh, they're fine,' she said dismissively. 'I texted Rach while we were waiting around and told them to meet us back at the treehouse. They finished a while ago.'

Natasha rolled her eyes, pressing her hand to her forehead in embarrassment that she'd caused all this fuss. 'Ugh, I'm such an idiot.'

'No, it's actually very helpful. It gives them time to hide the stripper.'

'*What?*' Her hand dropped down again.

Hels cracked up. 'Your face!'

'I said no—'

'No vegetarians, I thought it was,' Sara finished for her, frowning thoughtfully and tapping a finger to her lip.

Natasha caught sight of Tom's bemused expression at their jokes. His smile seemed to fade as their eyes met again. 'Well . . . it sounds like you've got an interesting weekend ahead of you. I'm glad we were able to keep you alive for it.'

'I think I'd rather have fallen,' Natasha groaned. 'I'd choose a night in the ITU over a stripper gyrating in my face, any day.'

'You wouldn't say that if it was Channing Tatum,' Hels drawled.

'You're sure you're feeling better?' Tom asked her.

'Yes. Just incredibly stupid.'

Tom looked at the others. 'Is she always this hard on herself?'

'Don't get us started,' Sara groaned. 'She's not called Little Miss Perfect by accident.' She wrinkled her nose. 'Let's just say she has high standards.'

'Oh?'

'Perfect hair, perfect flat, perfect body, perfect fiancé—'

'I'm standing right here!' Natasha protested. 'I can hear you!'

'See? Perfect hearing.'

Tom grinned just as the radio on his belt clip crackled into life. 'Duty calls,' he sighed. 'Back to it.'

'Oh, but aren't you on duty now, with us?' Hels enquired. 'Can't you stay? You did just save her life!' she said in a dramatic voice.

'I think it would be hard to argue I was working after the conversation moved on to strippers,' he quipped. He looked at them, his gaze finishing on Natasha again. 'Well, it was nice meeting you all . . . Nats, enjoy your hen weekend.'

'Thanks. For everything.' She was aiming for levity but her voice sounded strained.

'Anytime you want to dance in the trees . . . I'm your man,' he shrugged, his gaze lingering for a moment longer even as he began to turn away.

'I bet he says that to all the girls,' Hels muttered as they watched him walk back towards the ladder, pulling his radio from his belt clip and talking into it. Was he off to save someone else now? He made it look so casual.

'Earth to Nats.'

'Huh?' Natasha switched back to find Hels clicking her fingers in her face.

'Yeah, you have a good old look, girl. You didn't see how easily he just scooped you up out there. It was sexy as hell.'

'If you say so. I was too busy trying not to have a heart attack,' she muttered, trying to push away the feeling of desolation that was beginning to sweep over her. Adrenaline comedown?

Sara put a hand on her shoulder. 'What happened, anyway? One moment you were fine, the next you were like a deer in headlights.'

Natasha shook her head, just as baffled. 'I honestly don't

know. I was having a great time, I really was. It just came on from nowhere.'

Sara frowned, looking over at Hels.

'Don't ask me,' she said, shrugging. 'I didn't know anything about it till I got over here and found she wasn't behind me. One minute we were talking about her vows, the next it was *brace, brace*; practically blue lights.'

'But you're feeling okay now?' Sara asked, looking concerned.

'Fine. It was just a . . . freak thing.'

'Well, I think we can safely say it raised *all* our heart rates,' Hels laughed, giving her a nudge and a wink. 'He certainly made up for the fact that we're henning in a Center Parcs.'

Sara's mouth opened in panic but Natasha put a calming hand on her arm. 'I'm having a fabulous time!'

'You're sure?'

Natasha nodded. Poor Sara looked so terrified at the prospect of letting her down. It really ought to have been Hels – as her very oldest and best friend – organizing the weekend, but they all knew that would go rapidly off the rails. Strippers would have been the least of it.

'Well, let's find the others and have some lunch,' Hels said. 'I'm starving. Lust always gives me an appetite.'

'But don't you two want to complete the course?' Natasha asked. 'I'm perfectly happy to find a bench and wait for you to do the other aerials. I'll feel so bad if you miss out on my account.'

'Tash, we're here to get you trashed, not to go bird-spotting,' Hels drawled, pulling out her vape from her jeans pocket and sucking on it as they climbed down the ladder and back onto the pine-strewn ground.

'You haven't really got me a stripper, have you?' Natasha

asked as they retrieved their bikes from the racks and began cycling along the smooth roads that wound through the forest.

'I'm afraid we can only promise no vegetarians,' Hels shrugged, flanking her on one side, Sara on the other. Natasha felt more like a prisoner than a bride-to-be as they escorted her towards their weekend cottage, where the others would be waiting with warm wine and potentially a man in a thong. She gave a laugh, ignoring the dread still lurking in the pit of her stomach, and cycled on anyway. Moving ever onwards, towards her future.

Chapter One

Vienna, Saturday 26 November 2022

'Which one is it?' Natasha asked, looking up at the townhouse, desperate to get in as quickly as possible. They had been travelling for over thirteen hours now and skipped four time zones. Little wonder the toddler now sleeping in her arms had screamed for half of it.

'Fourth floor,' Rob replied, paying the cab driver and over-tipping as usual. 'Host's name is Huber, should be by the buzzer.'

'Didn't you say the host was going to be away this weekend?'

'Yes.' He picked up their bags and climbed the steps to join her by the locked door. She was standing in her usual maternal stance, swaying gently, one hand on Mabel's head as she slept upon her shoulder.

'So then did he say he'd leave the key somewhere for us?' she asked. 'Another neighbour, perhaps?'

'No, the key's in a strongbox outside his apartment door. Don't worry, I've got the code.' He shoved a hand in his pocket to reach for his phone.

'But no mention of how to get into the *building*?'

She watched the dilemma dawn over his handsome face. 'Ahhh . . . Bugger. No. He didn't mention that.'

'Right.' She gave another shiver. It was already dark, the city twinkling prettily in its early Christmas lights, and there was a cold wind. She wrapped her arms tighter around Mabel. They were still dressed in their island clothes – light cotton dresses and bare legs, with just a cardigan thrown on as a nod to their return to the European winter. They couldn't stand out here for long. It was certainly below freezing already. 'Well, just try one of the neighbours then. I'm sure they get it all the time.'

Rob stared at the list of names. Huber's apartment was number eight. 'Reckon Slesinski in number seven gets fed up with random Airbnb-ers pressing his bell?'

'I don't know, Rob. I just want to get our daughter into the warmth and into bed.'

He wrinkled his nose. 'Pluta.' Number four. 'They're less likely to get hit up. I'll try them.' He pressed the button for number four and waited.

'*Ja?*' a female voice asked after several moments.

Natasha watched as he leaned forward and spoke to the woman. He always described his German as 'passable', but he sounded pretty fluent to her. She could only pick up the word *Huber* as he conversed with the woman, even ending the conversation with a cheery laugh.

A moment later the buzzer buzzed and the heavy front door unclicked.

'You see?' Rob smiled, holding it open for her. 'She was happy to help. I bet Slesinski would have hung up on us.'

'You have absolutely no way of knowing that,' she said wearily, stepping onto the old marble floor and waiting for him to bring in the bags. The lobby was wide and spacious, with an old green velvet chaise pressed against one wall and a long stick stand holding several umbrellas. There was a

16

wooden cabinet with pigeonholes, some of which were empty and others completely overstuffed with letters.

They shuffled into the small lift. It was mirrored and Natasha gazed at her sleeping daughter's reflection as they moved sedately up through the floors – flushed, chubby cheeks and a rosy pout, dark hair that naturally fell in duck curls. The poor child was completely exhausted and Natasha couldn't bear the thought of having to get her on another plane again tomorrow. Perhaps it would have been better to push through after all and just deal with the five-hour transfer at the airport. Still, she told herself, they would all feel better after a good night's sleep in a comfortable bed.

The doors opened and Rob shuffled out backwards, pulling the bags with him and knocking his shins with the travel cot for the umpteenth time. Apartment eight was easy to find. Rob entered the code he read from his phone and retrieved the key easily. Triumphantly.

He had just slid it into the lock when someone called up – seemingly to them. Surprised, Rob walked over to the staircase and looked down. He gave a wave and immediately slipped into his passable German again, talking easily and gesticulating enthusiastically. Natasha wandered over too and saw a young woman two floors below, leaning on the hand-rail. She was barefoot, in workout gear with her hair pulled into a scruffy ponytail. She called something up to Natasha that she didn't remotely understand.

'This is the resident in number four who let us in,' Rob explained. 'She's telling us to just knock if we need any information.'

'That's kind,' Natasha said coolly, giving the woman a polite smile and holding her daughter a little bit tighter. 'I'm going to put Mabel down.'

She pushed on the open door and walked into an airy apartment with high ceilings and three-quarter-height windows, gauzy curtains protecting them from the curious gazes of neighbours across the street. The rooms were narrow and furnished in the fashionable mid-century look, with brass lamps and a 1970s-style bouclé wool sofa. It wasn't Rob's usual kind of place – he preferred an English country house vibe – but it was only for one night, and well located for an easy return to the airport tomorrow morning.

The bedroom was navy with baroque plasterwork and a neon sign that spelled *Lovers* in fluorescent pink. Mabel stirred in her arms, as if disturbed by the silence. It was only just after six here but for her body clock it was gone ten – well past her bedtime, and Natasha needed her to stay asleep. If she awoke now, it could be hours before they got her off again.

The problem was, the travel cot was still out in the lobby with Rob. For a moment Natasha deliberated going back out there and telling him to come in with it, but she didn't want to be the nagging wife; it wasn't Rob's fault he made friends wherever he went, he just had 'one of those faces'. She pulled back the duvet instead and threw the top pillow onto the floor, then laid Mabel down, seeing how her little body sank into the bed's soft embrace. Carefully, she positioned Moolah, Mabel's beloved soft cow toy, in her arms and tucked the duvet around her. The toddler sank a stage deeper into her sleep, her thumb automatically finding her mouth in spite of their best efforts to wean her off, but Natasha didn't have the heart to stop her now. They were all tired and there was comfort in old habits. Natasha lay on the bed beside her, gently stroking her cheek and feeling the same strong pull towards oblivion as her daughter. Jetlag was always such a bitch.

Her eyes were closing when she heard the sounds of Rob coming into the next room – drawing the curtains and switching on lights, the low mumble of chat-show hosts starting up on the TV. He wandered through a moment later with the travel cot and suitcase, pausing as he took in the sight of the two of them. He raised an eyebrow as he saw Mabel, curled up in the middle of their bed like a hibernating hedgehog and clearly not going anywhere.

Natasha gave an abashed smile. 'I'm afraid you took too long. I needed to put her down.'

'I was getting directions for the best bakery in town,' he murmured, going over and staring down at their daughter before kissing her tenderly on the cheek. 'Voted best for pastries on Tripadvisor, apparently.'

'Oh. Well then.'

Rob Stoneleigh always liked to have the best, be it pastries, cars or shoes. 'You're not going to sleep already, are you?'

'I'm so tired, Rob. I didn't get a wink on the flight – unlike some of us.'

He held his hands up. 'Hey, it's not my fault if she'll only settle on you.'

'No.' Natasha smiled as she looked down at their toddler again. It was exhausting, but she secretly liked that she was so irreplaceable to her daughter. So needed.

Rob watched her for a moment, before leaning over the bed and kissing her lingeringly. 'It was a good holiday, though, wasn't it?' he murmured.

'The best.'

He kissed her again. '*You're* the best. I don't know what I'd do without you.' His pale grey eyes settled upon her, a flash of anxiety running behind them like a shadow.

She pressed a hand tenderly to his cheek. 'And why would

19

you ever need to know? I'm not going anywhere,' she whispered. They had done a lot of talking in the past week, frank words pressing on bruised hearts, but they had come through it and were in smooth waters again.

'Not even to the other room with me?' His eyes had that particular gleam in them. 'That sofa looks comfy.' He winked, making her smile with his lack of subtlety. 'We could make an evening of it, the last night of our holiday – I'll go get us some wine, a takeaway . . . Viennese paradise.'

She put a hand to his cheek, stopping him before he was carried away. 'It sounds lovely, but I'm not sure anything can compete with a fluffy pillow and eight hours' sleep right now.'

There was a pause as he checked to see whether she was joking. 'You do realize it's not yet seven? If you go to sleep now, you'll be up in the middle of the night. You know you should adapt to local time when you come off a long-haul flight.'

'*I* know that, but Mabel doesn't, and she's going to wake me whenever she likes. Maldives time, Austrian, it won't matter. Which is why I want to sleep while I can. I am dropping.'

The glint faded in his eyes and he pulled back off the bed, straightening up. Mabel stirred at the movements on the mattress, a tiny baby snore escaping her dribbly lips.

'I'm sorry,' Natasha whispered. 'I'll adapt tomorrow.'

'Fine. Sure,' he said casually, pulling his shirt over his head and tossing it on the chair. He walked across the room. 'So shall I put this up or not?' He indicated to the travel cot.

'May as well leave it. She'll be in with us for the night now, and it'll only be one more thing to pack again in the morning.'

'Okay.' He hauled the suitcase onto the luggage stand and unzipped it, almost sighing out loud at the sight of the damp swim shorts and bikini from their last swim in the Indian Ocean. But it was back to reality tomorrow.

'Can you pass my pyjamas?'

He rifled through their neatly packed dirty laundry, finding her white linen PJs with the navy piping, and tossed them over to her. Natasha undressed lying on the bed, throwing her clothes on the floor and climbing under the duvet beside her baby girl a few moments later.

Rob watched in astonishment. 'You're not going to brush your teeth?'

'Nope. Not tonight.'

'But you always brush your teeth. Even after the Parkers' barbecue when you threw up five times and called Lauren a stuck-up cow, you still brushed your teeth.'

'That's how tired I am,' she replied, closing her eyes and wishing he wouldn't keep reminding her of that one terrible night; Lauren had sulked with her for weeks and only a spa voucher had pulled her out of it.

She heard him unzip his jeans and step out of them. 'Well, I'm going to have a shower and change, then I'll pop out for some food. You're sure you don't want anything?'

'Positive,' she murmured, his voice sounding distant. 'Remember to set the alarm.'

'Yeah. I'll set it for eightish. That way we've time to get those pastries for breakfast and have a short walk. We'll need to be out of here by ten at the absolute latest.'

''Kay,' she mumbled, almost asleep already and hearing the shower go on. 'Ten.'

*

'Mumma.'

Natasha groaned, opening one eye but unable yet to lift her head. Mabel was kneeling beside her, sucking her thumb and twirling a strand of Natasha's long blonde hair.

'I'm hungry.'

'Mmm?' Natasha murmured, trying to gather consciousness. Her body felt like lead, pressed deep into the mattress. Beside her, Rob was snoring. Natasha hadn't heard him come to bed last night. Usually he spooned her, but their little girl sleeping between them had kept his body away from hers. She was vaguely aware of having slept better because of it.

Mabel patted her cheek with sticky fingers. 'Hungry, Mumma.'

Natasha frowned. 'What's that on your . . . ?' She took hold of her daughter's little hand and inspected it. Her fingers were covered in a grainy, pale-blue goo.

Natasha was instantly awake. She sat upright. 'Mabel, what did you do? What is this stuff?'

Mabel blinked back at her.

'You're not in trouble. Just show Mummy what you were doing. Were you playing?'

Mabel crawled over the bed and slid off the end of it. Natasha watched with a growing sick feeling. She must have crawled out of bed without either of them stirring. If they'd just put her in the travel cot, with its high sides . . .

Natasha threw back the duvet and followed her daughter through the sitting room into the kitchen she'd been too tired to even glance in last night. It was supposed to be a minimalist's dream – dead matt anthracite-grey cupboards offset with a black soapstone worktop, with only an expensive coffee machine on display – but instead it was every mother's nightmare; Mabel had opened the cupboard under the sink and emptied the contents all over the floor. Red and yellow dish-washer tabs were scattered like marbles; a bottle of washing-up liquid was on its side, green liquid oozing slowly from the uncapped nozzle; and an open box of dishwasher salt had tipped over, the spillage mixing with the washing-up liquid.

Natasha understood suddenly what her daughter had put her fingers in. In the next instant she had scooped her up and was running her hands under the tap. 'Mabel, did you put your hands in your mouth?'

Mabel blinked back at her, looking surprised by the sudden rush to action, her mother's switched sleepy-to-stern voice.

'Mabel, open your mouth, let Mummy see.' Natasha opened the little jaw and peered in. There was no froth she could see, no odour to suggest she had ingested any of it. Natasha clasped her wet fingers and pressed them to her cheek. 'Mabel, sweetie, just tell Mummy if you put your fingers in your mouth?'

Mabel blinked.

'Did you eat any of the things on the floor?'

'. . . No, Mumma.'

'You're sure? Because it would make you feel poorly if you did. And Mummy doesn't want you to feel poorly.'

'I'm hungry.'

'I know, but . . .' She sighed. Where even was the nearest paediatric A&E department to here? This was no way to end their holiday, or start her day. 'Rob!'

Carrying Mabel, she hurried back through to the bedroom. Rob was still spread-eagled on the bed, sleeping soundly on his back.

'Rob!' she barked.

He startled, almost cartoonish. 'Huh? What's happening? What's wrong?' He blinked to see his wife and daughter standing above him. He groaned, one hand automatically going to his head.

'Mabel got into the kitchen cupboards and tipped all the cleaning products on the floor. Her hands are covered in washing-up liquid and dishwasher salt and I can't tell whether she's ingested any!'

There was a perplexed pause as Rob tried to process this deluge of information. He gave another groan. He looked pale beneath his tan.

She frowned. 'How much did you have to drink last night?'

He ignored the question, beginning to rally. 'If she'd swallowed any salt, she'd be throwing up, surely?' he queried, propping himself up on his elbows. Natasha's eyes fell to the dip that ran between his defined abs. His hair was sticking up and he had the dopey look of the newly woken, but he still looked better than most men on their A game. 'Has she been sick?'

'No. But she's hungry. I'm worried she might have put some of it in her mouth.'

He wrinkled his nose. 'Well, if she did, I'm sure she'd have spat it out again immediately. Imagine what that would taste like. You wouldn't be able to swallow it down.'

'Never underestimate what a toddler will put in their mouth,' she said, hoisting Mabel up her hip again and stroking the child's cheek, assessing her again for signs of poisoning. 'You don't think we should take her to A&E, just to be sure?'

'Nats, we wouldn't be in any doubt if she'd swallowed dishwasher salt. If she had, she'd be running a rinse cycle by now.' He laughed gently at his own joke.

'That's not funny!' she chided, even though he had a point.

'Besides, we have a plane to catch. Let's just get home and we'll ring 111 if she displays any symptoms. What time is it?'

He reached for his watch, flashing another impressive scene of suntanned latissimus dorsi and transverse abdominis muscles. Was it any wonder Mabel had been a honeymoon baby?

She watched as his entire body flinched and for a moment, she too froze as if in unified recognition of an impending disaster. Rob looked back at her with wide eyes. 'Tasha! It's five to eleven!'

What? She took a step back. It couldn't be. The room was still dim. She ran over to the curtains and pulled them back, looking out. It was snowing, low grey skies filtering out any brightness, lights glowing from the rooms across the street.

'Fuck! That means our car's been and gone!' he said, throwing his phone back down and leaping out of bed.

'But how can we have overslept? Didn't you set the alarm?' Natasha asked as he stepped into his jeans and put on last night's shirt that he had pulled off over his head. It was still buttoned up and in under a minute, he was in his shoes, ready to go. Meanwhile, she was still holding the baby. In her pyjamas.

'I thought I did,' he said, scratching his head. 'My phone must have been on silent or something. Look, I'll go down and try to catch a cab off the street. You get dressed and I'll see you both down there.'

'But—'

He zipped up the suitcase and picked up the still-packed travel cot. 'I'll take these with me.'

'But our clothes.'

'Just put on what you had on yesterday and carry your PJs. We can stuff them in our hand luggage.' He ran from the room before she could get another word out. He hadn't even seen the state of the kitchen! They couldn't possibly leave it like that. On the other hand, if they wanted to make their flight . . .

'Oh my God,' Natasha cried, putting Mabel down on the bed and picking her clothes up off the floor. She pulled them on without any of her husband's fluency or ease, her knickers inside out and her dress incorrectly buttoned.

'Why are you sad, Mumma?' Mabel asked as Natasha sat on the edge of the bed and untied the laces on her plimsolls. They had been so easy to slip off last night but needed Houdini to undo them now.

Natasha gave a fraught rictus smile. 'Mummy's not sad. I'm just a bit rushed, darling. We've got to hurry or the plane will go without us.'

'I'm hungry.'

'I know, sweetie. And we'll get you something at the airport, I promise.'

'Hungry *now*.'

'I know, baby. But we'll have to wait just a few more minutes, okay?' Her mind frantically rifled through what snacks she might have in her handbag – a Babybel? Box of raisins? Some sesame snaps?

She whisked Mabel off the bed and ran through with her to the bathroom, plonking her on the toilet. 'Now do a wee-wee as quick as you can, darling. Quick as you can. We won't be able to stop in the car.'

'But I don't need to.' Mabel's voice was beginning to slide into a wail as her parents' stress took its toll.

'No? Did you go already?'

Natasha couldn't see how. There was no step for her to use and no potty. That didn't bode well . . . 'Mabel? Tell Mummy where you went.'

Mabel's bottom lip wobbled.

'No, don't cry. Mummy's not cross, darling. I just need to know if I need to clean anything up before we go.' They couldn't leave the apartment like this, they just couldn't.

She lifted Mabel off the toilet and sat on it herself. She could see Rob's toiletry bag on the counter, his razor, toothbrush and toothpaste beside it. She flushed, washed her hands and stuffed everything into the bag.

'Okay,' she said, hoisting Mabel back onto her hip and running back to the bedroom. She threw the washbag onto her pyjamas on the bed. 'Now where did you do a wee-wee, darling, hmm?' she asked in her best sing-song, not-stressed-at-all, happy-go-lucky voice. They went into the sitting room and this time Natasha saw immediately the small shining puddle near the curtains. Perilously near the curtains.

'Oh! Right. Righty-ho,' she said, putting Mabel back down and running to the kitchen in search of a mop, trying not to go flying on the slick on the floor. 'Where's the freaking mop?' she asked as she heard her mobile begin to ring in the bedroom. Rob, she knew. He must have a cab. 'Shit. Shit. Shit.' She looked around, then grabbed the wad of kitchen roll and ran through with it, mopping the puddle as best she could, drawing the curtains back to keep the urine from seeping into them.

Mabel was crying now.

'It's okay, darling,' Natasha said as sanely as she could. 'It's all done now. All done.' She ran back to the kitchen and threw the used towels in the bin. She righted the box of dishwasher salt and the washing-up liquid and put them back in the cupboard. She grabbed a few handfuls of dishwasher pods and threw those in too, but that was all she could manage. Her phone was ringing back to back, a clear sign Rob was stressed downstairs.

Scooping up Mabel, the pyjamas and washbag, she hit 'answer' on her phone as she flung open the front door and headed for the lifts. 'Yes, yes, I'm coming! I'm going as fast as I can, Rob!' she cried as he warned her their plane would be leaving without them.

The lift doors closed at the same time as the apartment door swung shut. Natasha clasped Mabel's head and began shushing her as they travelled down through the floors. It wasn't the chic city-break finish they'd envisaged for their trip, but she wouldn't let it detract from what had been a dream holiday. Everything had been perfect. Just perfect.

Chapter Two

Four hours later

Duffy stood on the street and looked up, the whirling snow blowing into his eyes and sticking to his lashes. The building was a pale mustard and gave the impression of having been watered down by over a century of rains. Half capitals ran between the tall windows, the steeply pitched roof hiding attic rooms. It felt both grand and aged, like an old general still wearing his medals.

This had to be the one. He checked the email on his phone again. *There's a bus stop opposite* – he turned and saw it, an old lady sitting on the bench in the shelter with her shopping trolley beside her, seemingly oblivious to the cold. *A parking bay for bikes immediately outside.*

This was it. He went up the steps and referred back to the email. Directions, done. Instructions for getting in . . . There was a code for a security box to get the apartment key but – he looked around at the plain old walls – there was no keypad here. And the owner, Otto Huber, was out of town for the weekend.

He stared at the list of names beside the buzzers. Perhaps the neighbour at number seven – Slesinski – would let him in? He went to press it, just as the front door suddenly opened and a pretty young woman in leggings and boots stepped out. She had dark hair and startlingly light hazel eyes, a smattering of freckles on her nose. The unexpectedness of her beauty made him feel like he'd been punched in the guts.

'*Danke*,' he said in his patchy German, walking over as she held the door open for him. She gave a slow smile and he realized he was staring.

'Huber?' she asked, looking him up and down.

Did he look like a tourist in his jeans and down jacket? '*Ja*.'

'Fourth floor,' she replied in flawless English.

'*Danke*.'

'You're very welcome.' She made as if to move off but then turned back to him. '. . . Your first time in Vienna?'

He gave up the pretence of having any further German. 'Actually, yes.'

'How long are you here for?'

'Just tonight. I fly out again tomorrow.'

'Hmm. What a shame,' she said evenly, tipping her head to the side. 'Vienna has so much more to offer than can be seen in one night.'

Was she flirting with him? 'Well, if I could stay longer, I would.' For sure.

'But you can't.' She gave a small shrug of her eyebrows, as if she'd heard that line before. There was an air of suggestion in all her words, knowingness in her eyes.

'Do you live here?' he asked, looking for ways to engage her, now it was apparent she wasn't in any rush to escape.

'Apartment four,' she shrugged.

She could have just said 'yes' and he felt a smile climb into his eyes. 'You must be tired of all these people coming and going from the fourth floor?'

'Usually. Not always.' She held his gaze, seeming to know the spell her beauty cast. She gave a secretive smile as she began to turn away. 'Mind the cat. He scratches.'

Duffy tried to think of something else to say to keep her talking but it had been an age since he'd flirted with anyone and his mind blanked as she walked off. Where would she be going on a Sunday afternoon? To the gym? The supermarket? Would she be back shortly?

He watched her for a few moments, feeling a small bolt of victory as she turned back once, with an enigmatic smile. He stepped into the lobby, vaguely forming an impression of faded grandeur – shabby antiques sitting uncomfortably with the functional furniture needed to run a building with multiple occupants. There was a lift but he unthinkingly took the stairs, his mind still on the beautiful neighbour as he went two steps at a time.

Now inside, he retrieved the key easily and let himself into the apartment, padding through as silently as a cat. There was a strong smell of cleaning products and he regarded the highly stylized decor with bemusement. It looked to him like a Doris Day film set.

He shrugged the rucksack off his back and set it down as he wandered through the rooms. The bedroom was navy blue with a neon light that was supposed to be arty but just seemed clichéd. He peered through to the bathroom – marble-effect tiles, walk-in shower, no bath – but it was big and clean with thick towels. The kitchen, on the other side of the sitting room, was one of those that had everything hidden and made making a meal feel like navigating an escape room. He opened the nearest cupboard and found an ironing board and mop. There was a coffee machine on the counter but no kettle; clearly Mr Huber wasn't a tea drinker. No toaster either, that he could see. Which was a shame as he'd brought a small jar of Marmite with him, especially. His only creature comfort from home.

His phone rang in his jacket pocket.

'So are you in?' the lightly accented voice in his ear immediately asked, no introductory preamble.

'Yeah, I'm in,' he replied, a small smile on his lips as he wandered back through to the living room.

'And?'

'And I'm living every 1950s American suburban housewife's dream,' he said, brushing a hand against a marabou-feathered lampshade. The brass base was fashioned as flamingo legs.

'Switch to video,' the woman commanded. 'I want to see.'

He obeyed, scanning the room with his camera to give her a panoramic view. There was a loud tut. 'Ugh, it's beautiful. Even better than the pictures.'

'It's wasted on me, you know that. I told you a studio would do me fine.' He went and stood by the window, looking down onto the street below. It was snowing heavily, the old lady still waiting for the bus, a teenager in a North Face puffer and beanie walking past, head nodding to the sounds from his airpods. No sign of the woman from number four coming back, though. 'I'm only here for one night, remember.'

'Which was why I thought it would be nice for you to have a last night of comfort and luxury,' she protested.

He turned back into the room. Even just by sitting in it, he would make the place look untidy. He did it anyway. Propping the phone against a ceramic pineapple vase on the coffee table, he bent down to unlace his boots and shrugged off his featherweight down jacket, lying on the sofa with a heavy sigh.

'Anya, it was very nice of you to reserve this for me. And I do appreciate the sentiment,' he said politely, looking back at the frustrated blonde on his screen.

The unspoken 'but' hovered as her sigh whistled into the room. 'No wonder we broke up.'

'It's true. You deserve a man who can tell his Pratesi from his . . . pappardelle.' He gave a bemused frown. Did that work?

'The very fact you even know Pratesi tells me you're not as clueless as you'd like everyone to believe.'

'No comment. Besides, if I hadn't been so infuriating, you wouldn't have dumped me, you'd never have cried into your Jägerbomb and met Henrik, moved back here, started living happily ever after . . . and I wouldn't be talking to you right now from this beautiful apartment.'

'I want *you* to live happily ever after too, Duff.'

He lay back on the sofa and stared up at the ceiling rose. 'I know.' He flashed her a smile. 'And I intend to, don't worry.'

But she did look worried. 'I hope so.'

She always worried about him and he turned away again; she scrutinized him like a mother. 'Have you put on weight?' she asked, peering closer to the screen.

'Been trying to. Can you tell?'

'A little.' There was a pause. 'I'm so sorry we're not there. I can't believe the timing of it all.'

'It can't be helped. How is she?'

'Oh fine. The fall wasn't as bad as we first feared but Henrik was so worried.'

'Of course. Listen, she's his mum. It's the right thing to do.'

'But now I'll miss you.'

'We'll always have Paris. I mean, WhatsApp,' he crooned, giving a lazy laugh.

'I just wish I could see you in person before you go. We'll be back tomorrow afternoon. Can you really not stay an extra night?'

'Nope. I'd miss my connection at the other end.'

His gaze roamed the room, taking in the smaller details now: the Bose speakers in the ceiling, the Diptyque candle on the coffee table, the oversized photography books that were supposed to betray an aesthetic sensibility. His eyes caught on a small bulge pushing from behind the curtain.

'Well, will you promise to stay in better contact? Send me emails any chance you get. Let me know how you're getting on. You know how I worry when you go quiet.'

His gaze went back to the mystery item behind the curtain. Curiosity got the better of him and he wandered over. '. . . Huh? Oh yeah, of course. Where technology allows.' He pushed the curtain back to reveal a small black and white stuffed toy.

'Good. That's something,' Anya said, sounding placated.

He picked it up, unable to ascertain what it was supposed to be. '. . . But don't panic if I do go quiet for a while, okay?' He turned it over. Was it a cow?

He felt a jolt of recognition, something distant within him unlocking as he held the toy in his palm. Emotions trickled over him like a sweat.

'Define "a while".'

It was another moment before he registered the question. He looked back at her distractedly, trying to keep his mind on the conversation. ' Oh . . . um, a few weeks or so. I'll be in and out of range so don't freak out.'

'You still want me to send you the Chelsea results?'

He was still looking at the toy. It was so familiar, so very nearly what he remembered. 'Yeah,' he mumbled distractedly. 'Although if we lose to Liverpool, don't bother. Spare me the pain.'

'And did you call your father yet?'

He looked back reflexively at the screen. There was a voice in the background. 'Is that Henrik?' he asked hopefully.

'Don't change the subject. Did you call him?'

He sighed. 'No, not yet.'

'But you're leaving tomorrow!'

'I know. I'll call him at the airport.'

'That's too late.'

'Nonsense. I'll be stuck there for hours. It'll give me something to do.'

'Promise me you'll call him.'

'Ugh—'

'Promise me,' she said firmly.

He rolled his eyes. 'Fine. I promise.'

She didn't reply and when he finally looked back at her, the worry was written all over her.

'*You* call him if you're so concerned,' he shrugged. 'He always liked you more than me anyway.'

'That's not true and you know it,' she said in a quiet voice.

Henrik called her again. It was her turn to roll her eyes.

'Sounds pressing.'

'Yeah. I'd better go.' He saw her catch her breath as their eyes met. 'Listen, Duff—'

'I know.'

'But—'

'I know. Don't worry, I will. I've got a lucky mascot now, look.' He held up the toy cow.

'What is *that*?' she laughed. She leaned forward, her face almost pressed to the screen from trying to see better. 'It looks like a cleaning cloth!'

'Thank you! I'll have you know this is . . . this is very nearly Moodle.'

'Very nearly Moodle?' she repeated slowly.

'Yeah.'

'Duffy, I have no idea what that means.'

He laughed. 'It was Lottie's childhood toy. She took it everywhere with her. And I mean everywhere!'

'And what did you have? An imaginary friend?' she laughed.

He laughed too, then shrugged. 'I had her, I guess.'

'Where did you get it?'

'Right here. I just saw it poking out from behind the curtain.' He looked back at her. 'Serendipitous, don't you think?'

'Not really,' she demurred with a look of distaste. 'I'd say there must be a child out there looking for it but from the state of the thing, it looks more like a dog's toy.'

Was it? It was certainly worn, the pile almost rubbed bare in places. He held it gently in his hand, realizing he didn't care either way. It was so close to being the toy of his childhood memories, forever in his sister's hand as they had walked to school or the playground, always sharing a pillow with her . . . What were the chances of finding it, here of all places? A city he had had no reason to visit after Anya's mother-in-law's fall and which he was only in now because logistics were in place. It felt auspicious, like some kind of sign. 'He can be my talisman.' He flashed her a grin but it only seemed to make her sad.

'I love you, you know that, right?' she asked.

'I do. And I love you too.'

She arched an eyebrow. 'More than you love Margot Robbie?'

'No, don't be ridiculous.'

She laughed and he smiled at the familiar sound, knowing there was fear that lay beneath it. 'I'll email when I get there, okay?'

'Okay.' Her eyes were shining with unshed tears. She was trying so hard to be stoic. 'Bye, you.'

'Bye, Anya.' He pressed disconnect and quickly squeezed his own eyes shut too. '. . . Bye.'

The rest of his one day in Vienna passed slowly. Unremarkably. He wasn't interested in sightseeing or shopping and it was all he could do to stop himself from watching the clock. This was just a stopover, he reminded himself, a necessary holding station while he waited for all the different elements of his forthcoming adventure to align. He tried to make the most of the luxuries and rituals he would be leaving behind – he showered, consciously enjoying the feel of hot running water; he made coffee with frothy milk – not because he liked it but just because he could. He ordered a chicken arrabbiata from Uber Eats and ate it at the table, feeling the weight of the stainless steel cutlery in his hand. He knew the coming months would bring countless meals in the backs of trucks or perched on his lap; he knew he would go weeks at a time without being able to bathe; he knew he would only drink from rivers and that any booze the locals gave him would make him either pass out or hallucinate. And when he lay on top of the bed, he spread out like a starfish, feeling his skin brush over the silky cotton and knowing that such extravagantly open movement would be impossible in a sleeping bag.

He stared at the *Lovers* sign that glowed on the wall opposite. It seemed to mock him, a taunt of the one thing he did not have on his last night in civilization; the thing that mattered most of all – someone to wrap himself around, to lose himself in.

The memory of the flirtation on the steps earlier buzzed more loudly. It had been in the back of his brain all afternoon, an itch he couldn't quite scratch. He jumped off the bed and went over to the window, watching snowflakes whirl past the glass. Several inches had fallen since he'd arrived. It was quarter to ten, the evening already dying. He should have another shower, he told himself. Go to sleep. Watch a film in bed. His bag was already packed by the bedroom door. He had just one sleep, one phone call and one flight to get through and he would be on his way.

That was what he *should* do. And besides, hook-ups weren't usually his thing. But what about any of this was usual?

He stood motionless for several moments, then walked through the apartment, swiping the key from the console table and letting the door swing shut behind him. He jogged down the two flights of stairs and stopped at the brass number 4 on the door. He knocked before he could stop himself and she opened almost immediately, as if she'd been waiting on the other side.

She saw his bare feet on the carpet and a light came into her eyes, as if the fact that he hadn't even stopped to put on shoes betrayed his crisis of the soul. 'What is your name?' she asked, looking back up at him.

'Duffy.'

She looked at him more closely. 'You have sad eyes, Duffy.' She stepped forward and pressed a hand to his cheek, boldly intimate.

He didn't stir, though he was as much taken aback by her words as her actions. 'What's your name?' he asked instead.

'Klara.' She stared at him, so sure of herself, of him. Had he done exactly what she'd expected? She gave another of her enigmatic smiles. 'You're late,' she added, as if in reply, stepping back to let him in. 'I had almost given up on you.'

Chapter Three

Frome, Somerset, Monday 28 November

Hels's black Audi was already parked on the drive by the time Natasha drove through the gates, Hels herself sitting on the front step with what was left of a smoothie in her hands. Beside her was a large knotted freezer bag with Mabel's gold-fish in it.

'Sorry,' Natasha panted, jumping down onto the gravel and hurrying over, car lights flashing as she pressed lock, the gate whirring shut. 'It's been a morning.'

'It's been a week! Look at that tan!' Hels said admiringly, standing up and giving her a hug.

'Ha! Don't. Paradise is already beginning to feel like a distant memory.' She sighed as she slid the key into the lock and opened the front door. 'Mabel's lost Moolah and when I say she's inconsolable . . .' She rolled her eyes. 'She screamed for the whole flight home, refused to eat and as for sleeping . . . We've had maybe two hours of shut-eye? So we all overslept this morning because we're still jetlagged to hell, putting Rob in a furious mood because he was supposed to leave early for some important meeting—'

'Course he was. Important man,' Hels shrugged.

'Then Mabel wouldn't let me leave at nursery drop-off. The teacher had to distract her with feeding the chickens.'

Hels snorted. 'And people ask me why I don't have kids.' She saw Natasha's expression. 'Although obviously I *adore* my goddaughter. But perhaps you should have some vodka with your coffee? I'm stressed just listening to that and I'm about to perform a root canal.' She looked about her. 'Where's Bella?'

'Still at Hattie Pinkham's.' Their beloved golden retriever was being looked after by a widowed lady in the village who spoiled her with constant treats. Natasha knew even without seeing Bella that she would need to put her on a diet immediately.

'Hmm. It feels odd not being attacked by a cold wet nose and a strong case of halitosis on arrival.'

Natasha laughed as she shrugged off her coat and threw it over the newel post at the bottom of the stairs. 'How long have you got?'

'My first patient's at ten, so . . .' Hels whistled as she checked the time. 'Twenty minutes? Twenty-five if the gossip's particularly juicy.'

Natasha grinned. 'What gossip? It was a family holiday!'

'Uh-uh-uh. You distinctly said to me this trip was make or break for you guys.' Hels followed Natasha into the kitchen. It was an impressive space – pale cappuccino Shaker cabinets, white Silestone worktops and a slate floor. One whole wall was given over to French windows that opened onto the terrace and the rectangular lawn with long views over the rolling fields beyond. Sometimes horses were grazed there but more often it was sheep, bundling about in the distance like blown balls of cotton wool. If Rob worked every hour he could, it certainly wasn't for nothing. There were definite rewards.

'So?' Hels prodded her with a bony finger as Natasha reached for the cups. 'Which was it?'

Natasha couldn't keep the smile from her lips. 'Make, of course.'

'Of course! Never doubted it!' Hels said, throwing her arms in the air in solidarity.

'It was wonderful,' Natasha sighed. 'Finally, some time to ourselves – that was all we really needed, you know. And Mabel absolutely loved it.' She stood at the boiling tap and made their drinks.

'Well, you're certainly looking better – and I don't just mean on account of the tan. You're bright-eyed and bushy-tailed again.'

Natasha threw her a nervous glance. 'You will just forget the things I said before, won't you? I should never have said them.'

Hels pulled an imaginary zip over her mouth. They knew all – or almost all – of each other's secrets; Natasha had kept only one from her in seventeen years. 'I don't listen to half of what you say anyway.'

Natasha chuckled softly. 'Good. I had just let everything get on top of me. Honestly, I look back now and . . .' She shuddered as she remembered her tears and the slammed doors in the weeks before they'd gone. 'I think I was becoming paranoid. Any woman that looked at him, I just assumed the worst – and that's not me! I've never been the jealous type!'

'Ha, the other way round, if anything. So, how did he talk you off the ceiling, then?'

'He gave me his phone and told me to go through it.'

Hels gave a shocked laugh. 'Wow! Okay! Brave man.'

Natasha nodded. 'He's got absolutely nothing to hide. I

feel so stupid now, of course.' She handed Hels her coffee with a pained look.

'Listen, the hours he works, anyone would get suspicious from time to time. I get it,' Hels shrugged. 'And don't underplay how tough it's been on you both with you-know-what. There's been some days I've seen more vitality in my washcloth than in you. You've had a shitty run of it. Cut yourself some slack . . . I take it there were plenty of baby-making opportunities out there?' Hels gave her a cheeky wink.

'Yes. But even if I'm pregnant right now, this very minute, there'll still be a four-year gap between Mabel and the baby.'

'Oh my God, *stop* trying to micro-manage Mother Nature! Mabes will be a most excellent big sister whether it's a four-year gap or fourteen.'

'Fourteen?' Natasha winced.

'I know. Let's hope it's not that for all our sakes,' Hels agreed.

Natasha went through to the pantry and came back a moment later with the biscuit tin. 'Choccy digestive?'

'I shouldn't.'

'No, neither should I,' Natasha said with a shrug, reaching in for one anyway. Hels copied her, before jumping off the counter and following her over to the soft linen check chairs by the French doors.

'So,' Hels said, settling into the cushions and looking back at her intently. 'Do you think you *are* preggers?'

Natasha held up her crossed fingers and raised her face heavenwards, as if asking for a blessing. 'Honestly, if it hasn't worked in those conditions, I don't know when it would. We were both really relaxed, really rested . . .'

'Then I'll drink to that,' Hels said with a wink, toasting her with her mug of coffee.

Natasha toasted too. 'And if we're not, then Rob's agreed we can see a specialist in the new year, so that's progress too.'

'Good. About time. Although you doubtless won't need it now.' Hels ate her biscuit in two bites. 'Most importantly, did you see any sharks?' she asked, spraying crumbs.

Natasha smiled. Sharks were far more interesting than babies to her friend. 'Dozens. But they were all the little reef ones.'

'Manage to talk Rob into trying scuba?'

'No, he still didn't fancy it,' she sighed. It had been her only disappointment out there. Having qualified as a diver in her late teens, she had really hoped to introduce him to the sport so they could explore the coral reefs together; but he wouldn't be budged.

'Shame!'

'I know, but we did do some snorkelling safaris. There was a good creche, so Mabel was happy to be in there for a bit while we went out on the dive boats. Other than that it was mainly swimming, making sandcastles and a lot of sleeping. Well, a lot of sex and then sleeping.'

'Ugh, stop, it's nauseating. Snorkel safaris. Sex. Baby sharks.' Hels batted her hand. 'You know too much happiness makes me nervous.'

Natasha grinned. 'Did I miss anything here?'

'Here? In roaring Frome? Oh yes, it was kicking in your absence.'

'Did you see that new vet again?' Hels, perennially and determinedly single, had gone on her second date with the new partner at the veterinary practice the night Natasha had left.

A coy smile climbed upon Hels's mouth. 'Might've done.'

'I want details.'

44

'We went riding.'

Natasha shot her a bemused look. 'That's very wholesome of you. But you don't ride.'

'Tell me about it! For three days afterwards, I was walking into clinic like John Wayne! My nurse got a nasty paper cut from laughing so hard.'

Natasha laughed. Hels already cut an imposing enough figure, at five foot ten with a curly auburn mop of hair and bright green eyes. 'You must like him, if you're prepared to do that to yourself.'

'He's nice,' she shrugged non-committally.

'Nice?' Natasha scoffed. 'Oof, damnation by faint praise!'

'He's *suspiciously* nice. I'm just waiting for his freakery to come out.'

'He's a vet. How freaky can he be?'

Hels rolled her eyes. 'You sound like a Jewish mother about doctors.'

'Well, we've got to find you a good man. Remind me of his name again?'

'Dave. David Trenchard. He even *sounds* like he should be a vet, doesn't he?' she asked, eyes narrowed as if looking for ammunition against him.

'Are you going to see him again?'

'Again?' Hels chuckled. 'You've been gone a whole week, my dear. A lot can happen in that time.'

'How much a lot?'

'Well, he's already texted me twice this morning. From my own bed.'

'Ooh! You really do like him! So how many times have you seen him then?' And when Hels didn't immediately reply, she answered for her. 'Every day? You've seen him every day since we went?'

Hels shrugged carelessly, but her leg was jigging nervously as she saw the excitement on Natasha's face.

'You know we'll have to meet this one then. You can't keep him hidden away like all the rest and just use him for sex!'

'He's hardly hidden away. His practice is half a mile from here.'

'Yes, but he's a big animal vet. I'm hardly likely to have to call on his services for Bella. Or Goldie.'

'Ah, yes . . . about that.' Hels shifted position and gave an apologetic grimace. 'I meant to tell you . . .'

'Oh no,' Natasha groaned, looking over at the bagged gold-fish on the counter. 'That's not Goldie?'

'I think my radiators were too hot.'

'You *boiled* him?' Natasha almost threw coffee over herself.

'No! The tank wasn't actually on the radiator, dummy, but I think I overestimated the cooling effect of the windows and underestimated the heat of my radiators. The water was distinctly tepid when I found him floating upside down.'

'Tepid.'

Their eyes met across the upholstered ottoman. 'Nats, Mabel's three, the fish is orange. If *I* couldn't tell them apart, I doubt she will.'

'You killed her pet. You are an abysmal godmother,' Natasha tutted.

'Ach, it's just this sweet, cuddly bit where I'm terrible. Just you wait till she's a teenager, then I'll earn my crown. There's nothing she can do that I didn't do first. I'll be a step ahead at every turn.'

'You always were.' The two women had been friends since middle school, when Hels had joined midway through year five and Natasha had been charged with looking after her. It hadn't been 'like at first sight'. Natasha was form captain and Hels had wasted no time in telling her that she'd been expelled from her previous school for 'persistent disruptive behaviour' – throwing paint in the art room, disconnecting the microphone in morning assembly, sticking a banana in the headmaster's car exhaust, among other terrors which no one had ever thought to trace back to her parents' current and nasty divorce.

Natasha had been both aghast and awed at the sheer daring of this tall, lanky creature with spiky hair (no one else was using product aged nine) – her instinct was to steer well clear and watch on from a distance, but she was a dutiful girl. As an only child she was her parents' pride and joy, and if something was asked of her, she would do it. Brilliantly. So she had obediently showed the new girl every classroom, identified the strict teachers and warned her of their pet hates – no dotting an 'i' with a heart for Mrs Holmes-Neeld; no writing in the second person for Mr Wilkins – and sat with her at lunch, advising her to always dodge the macaroni cheese; all while Hels had glowered back at her with angry eyes and a sneer on her lips. They each implicitly understood they would never cross paths again once the day was through. There had been less than an hour till the school bell when the two boys who ruled the playground with Chinese burns had followed them into the girls' bathroom and demanded Hels show them her knickers. She had shown them a *Kuchiki-taoshi* – or single-leg takedown – instead. It turned out she had a judo green belt, not to mention one of her father's darts in her blazer pocket. Natasha had never seen anything more dazzling in her life and the door hadn't even swung shut behind the scarpering boys before friendship had broken out.

Natasha's gaze caught on the large kitchen clock. 'Oh, it's quarter to ten.'

47

'Bugger, must dash then.' Hels downed the rest of her coffee and sprang up. 'By the way, we've got dinner at Lauren's on Friday night.'

'Right.' Natasha was used to having her social diary organized by her best friend.

'Rob'll be around, won't he?'

'Yes, he'll be back by then.'

'Where is he this week?'

'Leeds. Some pharmaceutical company, I think.' Rob owned an IT consultancy which, as well as providing standard on-site training, infrastructure support and data protection solutions, specialized particularly in cloud backup and disaster recovery.

'Ah, the glamour!'

'And will you be bringing Dave?' Natasha asked, following her into the hall as Hels shrugged on her coat.

'I've not decided yet.'

'Oh, do! Otherwise I'll have to buy a donkey just to have an excuse to meet him.'

'Why a *donkey*?' Hels spluttered.

'I love donkeys!'

'They're grumpy, like me.'

'Poor Dave. I feel I need to meet him just so I can give him some sort of user's manual for operating you.'

'Oh, he can operate me just fine,' Hels chuckled, her voice laden with innuendo. She hugged Natasha hard. 'Anyway I'm glad you're back and looking perky again. Call me if you want me to drink some of your wine after work. You know I don't like thinking of you here alone all day.'

'I'm fine. Between Mabel and Bella, I won't get a minute to myself.'

Hels looked unconvinced. 'Uh-huh. So what are you going to do today while I'm happily performing ritual torture?'

'Collect Bella from Hattie's, finish that charcoal of Sue Chelford's Weimaraner and then collect Mabes at twelve. But before any of that, I need to see if Rob's got hold of the Airbnb host in Vienna. The cleaners must have found Moolah after we left.'

'You're certain it was left there?'

'Absolutely.'

'What if they threw it?'

Natasha's blood chilled at the very thought. 'They wouldn't throw a child's toy . . . Surely?' she asked weakly.

Hels's pause made it clear she would have thrown it. 'Well, you went back to them quickly, right?'

'Yes. When we got home yesterday, but the guy's been out of town for the weekend. We didn't hear back.'

'It'll be fine. And if it's not, just trawl the internet for another. There's nothing you can't get nowadays.'

'Hmm, I hope you're right.'

'Good luck, babe. Me? I'd rather pull teeth.'

Natasha laughed. 'You're not funny, you know.'

'So you're always telling me,' Hels grinned back as she sauntered to her gleaming car. She gave a wink and reversed, sending a spray of gravel into the hydrangea beds, and slipped through the gates that opened and closed automatically with a low whirr. Natasha waved till she was out of sight before stepping back inside the beautiful house Rob had worked so hard to give her. She leaned against the door for a moment and tried to see it through fresh eyes.

It had been her wedding present from him, and everyone always admired it when they visited. It somehow commanded admiration, like a salon blow-dry. It sat proudly in its four-acre plot, atop a hill and set back from one of the roads that led into the village. In theory she could cycle there; she had said she would when he'd first carried her over the threshold; she'd had fantasies of cycling in for leafy-topped carrots and fresh eggs. But then she'd had Mabel almost immediately, and it was far too dangerous to put her on a bike seat when the cars roared past at sixty miles per hour.

The house itself was a new build, only fifteen years old, and built in mellow Cotswold limestone with green oak beams strapping the walls and ceilings inside. The colour palette they had used was all bluey-greens – 'England in the drizzle', Rob had said as they stood in the queue at the Farrow & Ball shop. There were some fruit trees and a swing set for Mabel in the garden. The lawn at the back gently sloped towards the horizon and at night, the lights from the local towns glittered in the distance, like bygone campfires of other tribes. It was all wonderful . . . and yet she never felt quite satisfied with it. Somehow the shelves were always a bit too bare or there were never quite enough paintings on the walls; the blinds were wrong or a room needed repainting. She couldn't ever pinpoint exactly what it was that stopped her from really *loving* their home. Rob would roll his eyes and gently deplore her profligacy, all while indulging it. He called it her nest and loved how she fussed, mistaking her dissatisfaction for perfectionism.

She made herself a herbal tea and took it through to her studio. Her artist's easel was bare, the commissions she was working on kept safe in large leather portfolios in drawers. Switching on the laptop and allowing it several minutes to download all her emails, she checked her phone for WhatsApps.

She had several – one from Hels telling her she was freezing her tits off on the step; one from Sara reminding her about book club tomorrow and asking where the bikini was from in her last Insta post; one from Rob. She clicked on it and her heart gave a small leap as she saw it was a forwarded message.

The Christmas Postcards

Hey Robert, I am happy you and your family enjoyed the apartment this weekend. I have asked the cleaners about the toy but they have not found no cow. They will let me know if it turns up. In meanwhiles, please leave a review and I hope you will come back again to beautiful Vienna. Many regards, Otto.

Oh God. Oh God . . . She felt her stomach lurch as Moolah's status switched from *missing* to *lost*. She had been clinging to the belief that it would have been found there; she remembered positioning the toy cow in Mabel's arms in the bed. She'd gone over and over it in her head and that was definitely the last time Natasha recalled seeing it. She hadn't allowed herself to believe the toy was anything other than mislaid. This wasn't like when it went missing in the house – even that could involve hours of searching behind the sofas, in the garden, the prams, the car. But to have lost it somewhere between Vienna and Somerset . . . that was really . . . that was properly . . . gone.

Oh God. She rubbed her hands down her face. How would she tell Mabel?

Immediately she tabbed onto Google and began to search. She tried myriad search threads – toy cow; cloth cow; baby cow toy; black and white cow toy – but eBay had nothing. Facebook marketplace, nothing. Etsy, Gumtree, Preloved – nothing. There were plenty of toy cows to be had, just not their cow. Not Moolah. If Natasha could only remember the brand, that would be something. She could see, in her mind's eye, the label on the side that she had never thought to read. Why hadn't she read it?

Were there any photos, she wondered, showing it? She could zoom in . . .

51

Forty minutes later, she gave up again. In every photo she could find that had Moolah in it, the label was crumpled or covered by a baby's hand.

She stared at her now-cold tea that she'd forgotten to drink. She had bought Moolah in a supermarket in France, she remembered it clearly; Rob had thought it was ridiculous to buy Mabel yet another soft toy, but there was just something about it Natasha had been drawn to. What was the name of the supermarket? Perhaps if they had a website, they might list the toys they carried. She'd bought Moolah three years ago, but even if they didn't have the actual toy, they might have the brand and then she could contact their head office . . . ? She wouldn't be the first desperate mother, surely, to contact them in desperate need of a beloved toy replacement.

She tried to remember every French supermarket she'd ever seen. There was Monoprix, Intermarché, Géant, Carrefour, Hyper U . . . oh God, who else?

Twenty minutes later, she was looking at a particularly good Reblochon when the phone rang.

'Yes?' she murmured.

'Nats? It's Lauren.'

'Lauren, hi.' Natasha tried to inject some cheer into her voice.

'I was just checking you're back. I'm about to order the cheesecake for Friday and I want to be sure of numbers.'

'Well, we're both around and I can bring a very nice Reblochon if you like,' Natasha said, rubbing her face in her spare hand. This quest was hopeless. Moolah was gone. Her child would never sleep again.

'Ooh, now there's a thought! Could y—?'

'No. Ignore me. I was just getting lost in French supermarket websites.'

There was an astonished silence. 'French supermarkets? But what's wrong with Waitrose?'

'Nothing. Absolutely nothing.' She gave a sigh, realizing she would have to explain. 'It's just that Mabel's lost her cow toy, you know, Moolah?'

Lauren gasped like someone was pointing a gun at her. She had twin girls, just under two. She knew exactly how calamitous this loss really was. 'Oh Natty, no!'

'Yeah, I'm afraid so. I bought it in France, in a supermarket, when she was a few months old and it's been her treasure ever since. She can't sleep without it, it has to sit at the table with her when she eats. You can imagine.'

'Darling, I absolutely can. How horrendous. And you're getting no joy on the websites?'

'Nope. But I do know where to go now for linen bedsheets and expensive cheese.'

'Can you go back to France and look on the shelves directly? In fact, go back to the very store. Do you remember where it was?'

'Yes. Pézenas, in Languedoc. And honestly, if I thought there was a chance they still had them, I actually would!' Natasha laughed. 'But it was three years ago.'

'But you never know, they could have one kicking about in the stock room. It's really not beyond the realms of possibility that one fell behind the shelves.'

Lauren was an eternal optimist, probably because she was the sort of person to whom that *would* happen; her life fell like her hair – artfully put together. 'Hmm. It's a long way to go just on that infinitesimal chance, though. And I'm not sure any of us wants to get back on a plane this week.'

'I suppose. Besides, I don't want you missing dinner on Friday. We're meeting Hels's new man. Dave. *The* Dave.'

'*The* Dave? So he is going, then? She just told me she wasn't sure.'

'I know, she's trying that on with me too but I've told her I'm insisting. We all want to meet the new vet anyway and I think she's mad about him. She's being a lot more sarcastic than usual.'

'Always a good sign,' Natasha sighed, still distracted. 'Listen, will you mind if we have to bring Mabel with us on Friday? I'd normally ask Rosie to babysit, but I honestly don't think I can leave her with Mabel at the moment. It's impossible putting her down. Last night was dreadful.' Rosie was a professional dog-walker in the village and could be seen each morning walking along the pavements come rain or shine, with up to eight canine charges on leads, heading for the fields. The nature of her job, with its early starts, meant her afternoons were often free and she and Natasha had slowly built up a light babysitting routine that suited them both. Mabel adored her and Rosie was both cheerful and highly capable but this current situation was a whole other level; sometimes, only blood ties would do.

'Of course, of course. We'll make it work. Poor little thing, although hopefully she'll have settled by then. Or you never know, you might have found it. You've double-checked the bags, I assume?'

'Of course.'

'Do you know where you lost it?'

It was the sort of question that would usually elicit an irritated response from Hels – *if I knew where it was, it wouldn't be lost, would it?* – but the fact was, Natasha did know. She was certain it had been left in the apartment. She'd replayed every moment of that morning in her mind ever since she'd first realized they were 'a man down', as Rob had put it, apologizing with his usual smiling charm to the other passengers on the flight.

'Yes, that's the most irritating thing about it! We stayed in Vienna for a night on the way back from the Maldives, you know, to break the journey up for Mabel. We went to this Airbnb and I know for sure she had it when I put her to bed that night. But then we overslept the next morning – jetlag – and almost missed our flight. We practically flew out the door carrying our pyjamas in our bare hands, and the first time I realized we didn't have Moolah with us was as we were taxiing down the runway.'

'Well, have you tried contacting the host? Isn't that what they call them?'

'Yes, already done. He said the cleaners found nothing.'

'But it *has* to be there.' Lauren sounded indignant, as if she was being told the fish counter was out of wild sea bass. 'If you're absolutely certain that was where you had it last – perhaps it fell behind the bed? Can't they look again?'

'Hard to insist.'

'Hmph. You know what these Airbnb places are like; cleaner, my arse. They probably just flicked a Flash wipe over the toilet, smoothed the sheets and that was it.'

'Ew!'

'I'm sorry to say it, but it's true. If you were to go in there right now, I bet you'd find it in under two minutes.'

'Maybe I should go back to Austria, then,' Natasha sighed.

'It's definitely an option,' Lauren agreed, missing the sarcasm. 'Logic dictates it's there, unless . . .' She stopped.

'Unless what?'

'Well, unless someone else stayed in the apartment after you, and they found what the cleaners missed.'

Natasha gave a snort. 'Trust me, no one would willingly

take Moolah. *We* love her, but to anyone else, she's just a rag.'

'Even to another child? If it was a family that stayed there?'

'It wasn't exactly a family-oriented place.'

'But you stayed there.'

'Only because it happened to be available. Everything was so last-minute. But there were no child locks in the kitchen or anything.'

'Heavens.'

Natasha rolled her eyes. Her friend approached motherhood with a formidable professionalism. 'Yes, I was shocked.'

Lauren gave a sudden gasp. 'I've got it! Put out a Missing alert on social media.'

Natasha hesitated for a moment. 'You mean like people do when their dogs run off?'

'Exactly!'

Natasha laughed. 'Lauren, I can't put up a post alerting people to a missing toy!'

'Of course you can! She's as important to Mabel as Bella is!'

That was true.

'I've seen plenty of mothers do it. One posted on Mumsnet that her DD lost a glove in the park and they were reunited with it *the same day*!'

'But this is a sophisticated Airbnb in Vienna. The potential net I'd have to cast to reach their visitor base is much wider than the mums in the local park.'

'You'll never get anywhere with that attitude. I say it's worth a try and you should stick something on Facebook. Let's face it, you have nothing to lose.'

'Mmm, that's true. I'm absolutely dreading picking her up later and having to say Moolah's still missing.'

'Just do it, Nats. And if that fails, I'd personally be getting on a plane to France. Or Austria. Maybe both.'

'Yes, because you're a lunatic,' Natasha grinned.

'Type A, I think you mean,' Lauren chuckled, pleased with the label. 'Right, so I'm all good to go on the cheesecake, then?'

'Yes, yes, count us in. We can't wait to see you and meet The Dave.'

'Great, well, must get on. Come for seven thirty, before Hels has a chance to get smashed. You know, last time she used my Airwrap as a wind machine for her karaoke?'

Natasha laughed – how could she forget? – as they disconnected. The peace of the Maldivian beaches already felt very far away as she felt herself pulled deeper back into the fold of their daily lives: dinner parties, nursery runs, work meetings. It was noisy, chaotic and frenetic. Rob was already over two hundred miles away and she wouldn't see him again till Friday evening, but she felt closer to him than she had in months, and she placed a hand to her still-smooth belly, knowing just how lucky she was. Life was very nearly perfect; she just needed to sort out this one little storm in a teacup.

Her finger tapped on the keyboard as she looked back at the wheel of Reblochon. Lauren was right, she had three choices open to her: France, Vienna or Facebook.

She opened a new tab and logged in.

Chapter Four

Vienna, Monday 28 November

Duffy sat at the gate, one foot slung across his knee, watching as the plane was being refuelled. The snow had turned to sleet, banks of grey slush piled against the terminal walls. The sky was a solid grey, only the whirling orange lights of airport buggies providing any brightness as suitcases were ferried to and from the aircraft. He had been staring out mindlessly for forty minutes now, watching without seeing, the phone lying inert in his palm.

A little boy – no more than seven or eight, he guessed – was sitting cross-legged on the floor next to him, trying to learn a card trick. A magic book was splayed open in front of him, breaking down the sleights of hand. Duffy watched for a few minutes as the boy's frustration grew; he appeared to be a card out each time he repeated the trick.

The boy's father, sitting beside Duffy, was engrossed in a film on his iPad, headphones plugged in; the mother had fallen asleep sitting upright, her chin pressed into her chest and a plastic bag rolled on her lap, her hands gripping it as though it contained rolls of cash.

'Do you want to try it out on me?' Duffy asked the boy, leaning forward so his elbows were on his knees.

The boy twisted and looked back at him. Duffy blinked and gave a smile.

'Really?'

'Sure.' He put his phone back in his jacket pocket.

The boy swept up the deck of cards and swivelled around on his knees to face him. Duffy waited patiently while he shuffled and reshuffled the deck, fingers fumbling as he arranged the cards. He pulled up and spread out three kings at the back of the deck.

'Choose a card.'

'Any card?' Duffy asked, but it was mainly a joke to himself.

'Yes, any of those three,' the boy replied earnestly, his brown eyes wide.

Duffy pointed to the king of spades on the right.

'Okay.' The boy slid the cards back in and went to turn the deck over, but Duffy put a hand out to stop him. He took the top card and slid it around to the others at the back. 'Now try.'

The boy hesitated, then squared the deck and turned it over. He supposedly inserted the three displayed cards into the middle of the pack, waved his hand theatrically above the deck and clicked his fingers. When he turned over the top card, the king of spades peered back at him.

The boy gasped, looking delighted.

'It's all about the "indifferent" card, see?' Duffy whispered, waiting as the boy thought through what had been done differently this time. His mouth opened, his eyes widened as he realized the trick. Duffy held his hand up for a high five and the boy slapped it.

The father, distracted by their exuberance, looked up from his film to find his son celebrating with a stranger. Nudging his wife awake, he rose from the seat, pulling the boy up by the arm. 'Come. They will be boarding soon. You must go to the bathroom.'

The child looked crestfallen, shooting Duffy a shy look as he put his cards back in the box and picked up his book from the floor. Duffy gave him a shrug and a wink as his parents briskly whisked him off to the toilets.

He went back to looking out of the window again. The refuelling had finished and the last of the bags were being loaded. He saw his own rucksack on the conveyor belt, wending towards the hold. It looked different to all the other bags with easy-glide wheels and robust padlocks, identifiable ribbons and packing tape. His was bright orange ripstop nylon, 50-litre capacity with buckles fastened and all straps tied up, every last cubic millimetre accounted for now the talismanic toy cow, Moodle, had been squashed into the lid too.

A tannoy sounded, followed by a throat being cleared, and Duffy looked over to find a steward leaning over the microphone at the gate desk.

'We are now ready to begin boarding for Qatar Airlines flight QR184 to Doha. Would all first class and business class passengers please come forward with their passports and boarding cards ready.'

Duffy remembered his promise to Anya. He reached for his own phone again and stared at the screen. He was running out of time to get this done and it wasn't like he'd not had the opportunity. His day had been slow, measured and calm. He'd woken late, in his own bed – Karla, it transpired, wasn't one for overnight guests – and lain there savouring the comforts of a coil-sprung mattress; he'd drunk good coffee and stood at the window, people-watching the commuters on the street below; he'd taken a half-hour shower and gone for a walk along the river, before finding the coffee shop she had recommended for breakfast and feasting on blueberry pancakes in a caramel sauce. It had been a slow morning, full of indulgence; there had been countless times when he could have made the call.

'This is Qatar Airlines flight QR184 to Doha. We are continuing boarding and now invite all passengers in rows one to twenty to please come forward to the gate. Please have your passports and boarding passes ready for inspection.'

Everyone at the gate seemed to rise as one, even though clearly they couldn't all be seated in the first twenty rows. Duffy sat back, went into 'contacts' on his phone and brought up the number. He felt the familiar flinch in his chest as he saw the name but this time he pressed dial and put the phone to his ear.

It rang seven times and was about to go to voicemail when it was answered. 'Hello?'

'. . . Hey Dad, it's me.' There was a pause and he dropped his weight forward, his elbows on his knees, pinching his temples. '. . . It's been a while. How are you?'

A sigh whistled down the line. 'The usual. Except my hip's still giving me gyp.' His father said it as though they'd spoken last week, not eight months ago.

'Still? Well, have you seen a doctor about it?'

'What for? There's nothing they can do. It's old age.'

'You're not old – and hip replacement surgery is an everyday procedure now. You'd be in and out in a couple of days and it would be life-changing. You'd have more mobility, be pain-free. How are you sleeping?'

'Fine.'

'It doesn't bother you at night?'

'Not as much.'

Duffy looked up as a pair of legs passed within inches of him. He leaned back again and looked over. Seemingly the entire plane, and not the first twenty rows, was now waiting to board. Duffy was in Row 9.

He realized there was a growing silence.

'But other than your hip, all is well?' Duffy asked with forced brightness. 'Bridge club?'

'Same old duffers. Nothing ever changes.'

'Golf?'

'After all the rain we've had? The course is waterlogged.'

'Oh, yes, of c—'

The tannoy sounded again. 'This is Qatar Airlines, flight QR184 to Doha. Boarding is now in progress. Would passengers in rows one to forty please come to the gate with passports and boarding passes ready.'

'Who's that . . . ? Where are you?'

'Uh, Vienna airport.' Duffy felt his blood pressure spike as he heard the immediate suspicion in his father's voice.

'*Vienna?*' Confusion clouded the word. It wasn't Duffy's usual sort of destination. 'But I thought you were in Buenos Aires! What in blazes are you doing there?'

Duffy swallowed. His body felt heavy, his heart sluggish. *Say the words*, he told himself. *Just tell him.* He dropped his head in his hands. He felt like there were rocks in his stomach. *He has the right to know.*

'Hello? Hello? Are you th—?'

'Sorry, Dad, the line dropped out for a moment there.'

'What's going on? Why are you in Vienna?'

Duffy squeezed his eyes shut. 'No reason, I just came out to see the sights.'

'A city break? You?'

'Why not?'

'Who are you there with?'

He swallowed. '. . . Do you remember Anya?'

'The German one that dumped you?'

'Yeah. Well, she's married now to an Austrian guy. She lives out here.'

'Don't tell me – you went to the Schönbrunn Palace?'

'Yes,' he lied.

'And St Stephen's?'

'Naturally.'

There was a small grunt. 'Full of tourists. Worst possible time to go, too, this time of year.'

Duffy pinched his temples again. This had been a mistake. 'Yeah, well, the opportunity came up so I took it.'

'Of course you did.' Disapproval chimed through the words. 'So I suppose you're on your way back here, are you?'

'Well—'

'Because if you're calling me begging for a bed over Christmas, you should know I won't be here. I've got a house-sitter coming in while I do a cruise down the Nile. A posh job, not one of those floating city monstrosities.'

'Right. That sounds . . . great.'

'Yes. Well, I can't bear this bloody country at Christmas. The damp. It gets into my bones.'

But they both knew that wasn't why he hated this time of year. The blood in Duffy's veins suddenly ran hot. He clenched a fist and stood up, walking over to the window and pressing his head against the glass. 'Um, so look, I really have to go, it's final boarding. I just wanted to say hello, see how you're getting on . . .' Ahead, walking across the tarmac to the plane's stairs, several steps behind his parents, he could see the boy with the magic trick still shuffling the deck of cards and trying to finesse his technique. 'It's nice to hear everything's okay with you . . . Enjoy the Nile.'

There was a hesitation and he got that feeling he often had with his father, those pregnant pauses that contained entire worlds of pain, frozen solid. '. . . I've got to go. There's someone at the door and Bertie needs his walk.'

The line went dead.

'. . . Bye, Dad.' His father had never been one for 'protracted goodbyes' and Duffy stood motionless for a few more moments, trying to process the emotions that were always unleashed during their interactions: anger, bitterness, disappointment, frustration. Rage that they couldn't say what really sat between them. Why had he let Anya pressure him into this? She didn't know how bad things were between them, not really. It was just theory to her, a story to which she had attached misplaced sentiment, but not every estrangement had to be a tragedy. Sometimes it was necessary for growth, or survival, and both he and his father were far more comfortable letting the scabs thicken over their wounds.

Duffy closed his eyes and took a few deep breaths, forcing himself to let it go. At least it was done. He had kept his promise and made the call but he had offered nothing more than that; telling his father the full story had never been part of the deal. Telling Anya the whole truth wasn't either. It was better this way for everyone. He needed to keep things clean and uncomplicated, for his sake as well as theirs.

He slid his phone into his pocket and joined the queue, becoming a face in the crowd, just one of the hundreds waiting impatiently, with somewhere else to be.

Chapter Five

Whinfell, October 2018

The door swung shut behind them and Natasha looked up. 'We're climbing *that*?'

The blue wall rose twenty metres high, knobbled with brightly coloured handholds, a couple of eight-year-olds scrambling up like Spider-Man. The noise inside the sports centre was deafening, the smell of rubber mats reminding her of school. It wasn't exactly . . . the spa experience she had said she'd like for her hen.

'You'll be fine!' Sara said, looping a long, skinny arm through Natasha's and squeezing it. 'Look at those kids.'

'I am. That's what's making me nervous.'

'You'll be fully roped at all times,' Sara said.

'She was fully roped last time and look what happened.' Rachel rolled her eyes as she pulled her wild red mane into a ponytail.

'*That* was just a . . . freak spasm,' Natasha protested. 'I've done indoor rock climbing before. I'm actually not bad.'

'We'll see.'

Natasha felt rattled by the scepticism. She still couldn't understand what had happened to make her freeze like that earlier. Heights had never bothered her before, although she had had this feeling once as a child – on a school skiing holiday when she was eleven, she had found herself at the top of an icy slope and she hadn't been able to move. She had been gripped by the utter certainty that if she continued forward, she would fall and slide, but she knew that turning back was impossible too. There had been no other option – short of being airlifted off the mountain – and she had been paralysed with fear knowing she had to go on, even though she *would* fall, even though she *would* get hurt. It had been an extraordinary thing, to have to act against her own best interests and simply put herself at the mercy of gravity. Momentum.

They saw the others coming back over. Lauren and Hels had left lunch early and gone ahead to get them booked in and sign all the paperwork. Hels was holding their soft-soled, grippy climbing shoes and began handing them out. 'Right, put these on. We've got our own instructor who's going to take us on that wall over there. It's the adults' wall.' She pointed to a dark grey wall that looked no different to the blue one.

'There's a difference?' Lizzie asked dubiously. Vertical was vertical, wasn't it?

They went over to a bench and began pulling on the shoes; they fitted snugly, more like rubbery socks.

'Right then,' a male voice said, approaching behind them. 'Is this the Larson party? Sara Larson?'

They turned to find their instructor walking towards them with six harnesses looped over his forearm. He stopped in his tracks. 'Oh, hello again,' Tom smiled, clearly recognizing at least some of their group. Certainly her. Natasha felt herself blush. Why did it have to be *him* instructing them, of all the staff they must have here? After the way she'd humiliated herself in front of everyone, in front of him, she would have happily settled for never having to see him again.

A smile climbed into his eyes. 'How was lunch? Any . . . vegetarians?'

'Nope. No vegetarians,' Hels grinned. 'Not yet, anyway.'

'It sounds like you had a lucky escape then, Nats.'

'Yes.' He remembered her name. Of course he did. She would be forever scorched on his brain as the fool he'd had to walk backwards off the course! She looked away, There was a directness to his gaze that unnerved her, as if he could see beyond the masks they all wore. She wore. 'And how are you feeling about this activity?' he asked, seeing her diffidence. 'Harnesses, ropes, height?'

'Fine,' she replied quickly.

'She was just telling us she's rather good at indoor climbing – apparently,' Sara said.

'I am! I honestly don't have a problem with heights.'

'Is it the bridesmaid dresses, then?' Hels asked, eyes narrowing. 'Is mine too low-cut? I did ask her to go lower. Quite a lot lower.'

'I have . . . no issue with your dress, Hels,' she said, feeling baffled by the turn in conversation.

'Well, it's just, that's one of the things we were talking about when you did your Covent Garden human statue impression.'

'Funny!'

'And if it's not the height or the dresses that spooked you . . . ?'

'Can we just move on?' Natasha asked impatiently. 'It was just a weird freak thing, okay? Tom said it happens all the time, didn't you, Tom?'

He looked surprised. 'Oh . . . uh, yeah. All the time.'

It wasn't the most convincing backup. She jerked her chin in the air, determined to show them all this time. She would redeem herself in front of this man if it was the last thing she did.

Tom looked around at their small group. All of them were dressed in gym kit – leggings and Sweaty Betty long-sleeved yoga tees – except Lizzie, who was permanently cold and was instead bundled up in an Eminem hoodie and blue trackies. 'So, have you all climbed on a wall like this before?'

'Yes!' Sara said eagerly, shooting her hand up like a pupil in school. 'And I loved it.'

Tom grinned. 'Great. How about the rest of you?'

'No, but I'll give it a shot,' Lizzie said with a shrug. As a trainee chef at their local Harvester back home, she was well accustomed to adrenaline rushes.

Hels, standing beside Lauren, suddenly put her hands upon the other woman's shoulders. 'Lauren's an expert social climber,' she proffered sweetly.

'Helena!' Lauren gasped, swiping her on the arm as everyone laughed. Even Lauren.

'Right, well you've all signed your disclaimers, so we can get straight on with it,' he grinned, leading them over towards the grey wall. 'For those of you who don't know me, I'm Tom. What are your names?'

'It's Hels,' Hels said, pressing a hand to her own chest. 'Sara, Lizzie, Rachel, Lauren and Natasha. But I see you remembered *her*.'

'Well, she did make herself rather . . . memorable,' Tom said lightly, before flashing Natasha an apologetic smile.

He had a nice smile; it was impossible not to smile back.

They stopped at the base of the grey wall and instinctively looked up as Tom laid the harnesses out on the ground. 'Now, if you'd each like to stand by a harness and step into the leg loops, like this . . .' He demonstrated with his own one and waited for them to copy him. 'Then bend down, shrug your arms through like this.' He waited again. 'And then click in front here.'

Lizzie dropped into a few comedy pliés and waved her arms about. The thick sweatshirt fabrics billowed unflatteringly where the harness cinched at her arms and legs. 'Do I look like a Ghostbuster? Or like I'm about to jump out of a plane?' she joked.

Tom grinned. 'You can take turns climbing in pairs. Can I just check – is everyone happy with belaying? Lowering yourself on the ropes?'

'*Love* it,' Hels said with a girlish swish of her head.

'If you're not sure about it, you can just climb back down as you went up. Belaying's quicker but there's no rush; just find your legs for the first few climbs. There's no set path, you can choose your line, take your time and try to get to the top. Lizzie, if you go last, just so you can see what the others do and I'll give you some tips while you wait.'

'What's the big red button for at the top?' Hels asked, staring right at it, her hands on her hips.

Tom gave a slow smile. 'Well, that's an incentive, for those who want it.'

'So you mean this is a race.'

'It doesn't have to be. You can just take your time.'

'But it's really a race,' Hels said, pinning him with a challenging look.

He chuckled, knowing she wouldn't let it drop. 'Fine. Yeah. It's a race. Go like hell.' He glanced worriedly at Natasha. 'But take your time. Getting to the top is optional, but getting down again is mandatory.'

She laughed. He sounded like her mother used to. *Be assertive. But kind. But assertive.* 'I'll be absolutely fine.'

'Oh yeah? How fine?' Hels asked, adjusting her harness straps like a pro.

Natasha arched an eyebrow. 'Finer than you.'

'It's on, bee-atch! We'll go first. Rope us up, Tom!' Hels said triumphantly, punching a fist in the air.

Dammit. Natasha had the distinct feeling she had walked straight into one of Hels's traps.

'Yessir!' he quipped, taking them over to the ropes and fastening Hels to one of the lines dangling down the simulated cliff face. Natasha looked up at it as she awaited her turn. From this angle, at the bottom of the wall, it looked very high and very vertical. There was no clear route that she could make out; she would have to make her decisions on the spot.

'Okay,' Tom said, turning to stand before her now and looping the rope through the clip on her harness. She stood very still, watching him expertly thread a complicated knot, his hands sure and swift. His eyelashes were very long, she noticed as she waited, her body swaying a little as he tugged on the rope to check the knot.

'Good, you're all—' he said, looking back at her and catching her staring, 'set.' He stared back. Was he assessing her for signs of panic again? He had seen at her at her absolute worst – cowering and pathetic – and she felt another burst of resolve to win this; to show him that she wasn't a complete loser.

He stepped out of her orbit. 'Right, well then, ladies, you're all good.'

'Oh, but I'm really, really not, Tom,' Hels quipped, giving him a wink. 'I'm all bad.' She burst out laughing at his expression and Natasha saw how he looked almost bashful, glancing over at her. Natasha looked up to the red button instead.

The two women moved forward, reaching their hands up and feeling the holds.

'Will you give us a ready, steady, go?' Hels asked.

He grimaced. 'I'm more of a ready, *set*, go man, to be honest.'

'Fine. You say potato.'

Natasha looked up the full height of the wall, all her focus on the big red button.

'Ready.'

She searched for her first handhold.

'Potato.'

She reached for it, laughing.

'Go!'

They were off, chuckling as they went. Natasha moved with a dexterity she didn't know she had, quickly finding a rhythm between hands and feet. Hels was tall and more easily able to make the grabs, but Natasha was supple from a childhood spent dancing and it was level pegging between them for the first yards.

'Go on, Nats!' she could vaguely hear the others calling. As the bride – and official VIP of this weekend – they had to support her, she knew, but Hels had never been one to be discouraged by being the underdog. In fact, it only spurred her on. Natasha could hear her laughing and cursing as they climbed, enjoying the challenge.

'Come on, Nats! Hurry up!' Hels taunted, half a move ahead. 'Just imagine Rob's the red button!'

Natasha looked for the next hold – a thick pink grab immediately above her head. She reached up, looking for where to place her foot, noticing they were high up off the ground already. She was aware she was breathing heavily, muscles beginning to burn as she pulled and reached, lifted and held, her body balancing on narrow ledges. Some parts of the rock face bellied out in places, making it harder to cling on and forcing them round on longer but flatter routes.

'*I'm getting married in the morning . . .*' Hels sang breathlessly, climbing higher and higher, beginning to pull away. 'Poor Rob . . . I thought you'd put up more of a fight than that.'

Hels reached for the next handhold but missed it, swinging slightly on the rope to the side and having to scrabble with her foot for a few moments until she could balance herself. It was an opportunity for Natasha to close the marginal gap between them—

'Whoa!' Hels laughed and in the next instant she was off again, moving even faster as the adrenaline rush super-boosted her.

But the opposite was happening to Natasha. Something in her body was changing. She was becoming heavier, it seemed. Or were the handholds spaced further apart up here? The red button wasn't even ten metres above her – just a few more moves; Hels was about to slap it – but Natasha knew it was happening again. 'Oh no, no, no,' she whispered, as she felt the icy creep in her veins. '*No*.'

She tried to force herself to move but everything felt sluggish and remote, as though she was climbing in oven gloves. Above she heard the red button *buzzzz*, followed by Hels's jubilant whoop and seconds later, Hels herself freewheeled past her back down the rope, bouncing off the wall with her feet. 'So long, sucker!' she cried, pulling a face and giving her the double birds, looking exactly as she had aged twelve.

Natasha didn't stir. She couldn't. It had actually happened again, the freeze sticking her down to one place like she was a fly caught in a web. She knew better than to look down again. She squeezed her eyes shut, tears sneaking out at the edges. Why? Why was this happening? She was aware her breathing was coming fast, too fast, her heart pounding like a jack-in-the-box. She was beginning to feel dizzy.

Distantly, she could hear the girls below, calling up to

her – Tom too – but she didn't move a muscle. She must not stir. Instinct told her to keep very still. She just had to wait and breathe, wait and breathe, but her hands and feet were beginning to tingle and she realized she wasn't breathing well enough.

She tried not to think about the people on other walls turning around and watching her, picking up on the fuss; Tom looking on and shaking his head again with dismay, rueing his bad luck of being landed with them – *her* – today.

The sports centre began to spin, sounds fading to silence, her world narrowing down to a square of the moulded grey plastic in front of her— Oh God. She closed her eyes again and started to count. She would be fine once she got to a hundred. *One, two, three* . . .

She was at thirty-six when she felt a warm hand press firmly on hers. She opened one eye. Just one.

Blue eyes smiled back at her. 'Guess who?' Tom asked. He was on Helena's side of the wall, holding on casually to a grab above his head, not even seeming to notice how lightly he was perched. Like Peter Pan. 'You okay?'

'I don't know what the hell is happening to me,' she whispered, her knuckles still blanched white as she gripped the handhold with all her strength.

He seemed to read the depths of her fear, for it wasn't irritation she saw in his eyes. 'It's okay, Nats, we'll get you down.'

'I don't know why this is happening,' she repeated, her voice rising with panic.

'It's okay.' His hand squeezed harder upon hers, his thumb rubbing lightly over her skin.

'But you don't understand. This isn't who I am. This doesn't happen to me. I'm not usually this . . . pathetic. I'm not.'

73

'I know you're not.'

But he didn't. He was just being polite. Pitying. 'I'm not scared of this. Heights don't scare me. I'm not scared of this wall.'

'I know.'

'. . . So why can't I move?'

He held her gaze and she could see thoughts passing through his mind. 'I don't know,' he said finally. 'But I could see as you were going up, you're technically very able. You're strong and supple, more than capable of scaling this wall. You can definitely do this.'

She knew he was trying to convince her, a mind game to get her back down. 'No. I can't. I thought I could but I can't,' she whispered, shaking her head, terrified he was going to make her move. She knew, logically, that no harm could come to her – even if she let go, she wouldn't fall but simply dangle like a spider on its own thread – but her heart rate was accelerating once more. Everything was beginning to spin again, a tightening at her ribcage making it hard to breathe.

'Nats? Nats, look at me.'

His voice sounded far away even though she knew he was right there. She felt the pressure lift off her hand and then, in the next moment, pressure at her stomach as he threaded something through her harness and tugged her towards him. She was back in his orbit again.

'I've attached a sling to connect your harness to mine. You're safe. Just hold onto me, Nats.' His voice sounded like it was underwater, wobbly and losing shape. She felt a hand moving her arms up off the wall and then she was leaning against him. She smelled a smell she knew; his smell. It made her feel safe, even as the world began to bounce and drop. Bounce and drop. He was still saying words – she could feel the reverberations through his chest – but it was hard to catch them and they drifted past like bubbles. Her hands felt tingly, her head so heavy—

The bouncing stopped suddenly and she felt something solid beneath her feet . . . voices . . . heat. She felt the tension between her body and his release, and then her feet left the ground again and she felt herself carried over to a bench.

'Sit forward, Natasha, that's it. Try to get your head between your knees and breathe slowly and deeply.' She felt a hand on her back, warm and comforting, slowing down her startled heart. 'That's it. Breathe slowly and deeply.' His voice was low beside her. 'You're okay, I've got you. This will pass. Just focus on your breathing.'

She could see feet. Lots of feet.

'Move back, please. Let her have some air. She's fine.' His brisk voice sounded further away again, even though the warm pressure was still on her back.

'. . . ambulance?'

'No, she'll be fine. It's passing. Just give her some air, please. And some privacy . . . Thank you.'

The feet moved, revealing purple interlocking rubber tiles.

'Natasha, I want you to tell me three things you can hear. Can you do that for me? Three things.'

She didn't reply immediately. It felt an impossible task.

'Three things you can hear.'

'. . . You,' she began.

'Good. What else. Two more things.'

'Wind.'

'. . . Okay, yes, the air con. What else?'

'. . . Laughing.'

'Okay. Now I want you to move three parts of your body for me. Any three.'

Slowly, she stretched her fingers, which were curled on her lap. Then she wiggled her toes. Finally she shrugged her shoulders. She could feel the oxygen beginning to reach her lungs again, sensation coming back into her hands. The hand was still warm and heavy upon her back.

'Great. You're doing brilliantly. Now finally, tell me three things you can see.'

She stared at the floor. 'Purple.'

'Yes.'

'. . . Feet.'

'Go on.'

She felt exhausted.

As if reading her energy, she felt his head dip down, towards her. He drew back the curtain of hair that obscured her face from his. She turned her head slightly. '. . . Blue eyes.'

The blue eyes smiled. 'How are you feeling now?'

Safe. 'Better.' She realized her breathing was under control again, her heart no longer racing – but she felt utterly drained.

'Has that happened to you before? Before earlier, I mean?'

She shook her head, seeing how he frowned slightly. She dropped her head again, feeling like she'd failed.

'Nats?' a voice whispered. Hels was crouching in front of her on her hands and knees, peering up through the halo of Natasha's hair. Her eyes were wide with worry.

Natasha tried to smile but her body still felt out of whack, as though her gears were in the wrong position.

'I'm so sorry.'

'Not your fault.'

'I feel like such a bitch.'

The comment made Natasha shake her head feebly. 'No.' She closed her eyes and took a deep inhale, trying to suffuse her body with strength. 'I'm pathetic.'

'Stop that.' She felt the pressure increase on her back.

She slowly straightened up so that her hair fell away from her face and she could see the room again. Almost everyone was watching. Lauren, Sara, Rachel and Lizzie were standing in a crescent a few paces behind where Hels was kneeling. Lauren's hand was over her mouth, Lizzie biting her nails anxiously. They all looked aghast.

'I'm sorry. I'm fine,' she said, trying to reassure them. 'I don't even know what just . . . I mean why . . .'

'You had an anxiety attack,' Tom said gently. 'It's a rough thing to go through.'

She frowned. 'But why . . . ?' She couldn't understand it.

'It's a sign of overwhelm. Your body's trying to tell you something.'

'Like what?'

He shrugged. 'I don't know.'

'But I'm not scared of climbing,' she said in a quiet voice. 'Or heights.'

'It's not that.'

Then what? she wanted to ask, but she couldn't muster the energy. She wished he wouldn't stare at her like that.

'You really need to go and lie down,' he said finally. He looked over to the others. 'Where are you all staying?'

'The treehouse,' Lauren said, stepping forward quickly.

'Okay, I'll get a buggy for you,' he said, unclipping his walkie-talkie from his waistband.

'I don't need a—'

'You do,' he said firmly, looking straight at her as he began talking into it. '. . . Okay. They're on the way. They should only be a few minutes.'

'Thank God you knew what to do,' Sara said, coming over to crouch by Hels.

Tom gave a shrug. Natasha could feel it through his hand still on her back, heavy and warm. She wished everyone else would go. Their attention felt like another draw on her reserves.

'She's been working really hard lately. Pulling mad hours before the wedding and the honeymoon. D'you think it could be that?' Sara asked in a lowered voice.

'Possibly. What does she do?'

'Structural surveyor.'

Natasha felt a small laugh through the planted hand.

'What?' Sara asked.

'I dunno. I guess when I hear "structural surveyor", I imagine someone a lot less . . .'

'What?'

He seemed to be struggling to find the word. '. . . Glamorous.'

'Ha!' Hels quipped. 'You should see her in a hard hat and a boiler suit!'

'I can hear you, you know,' Natasha said, lifting her head again and trying to joke, but all she really wanted to do was sleep.

People had drifted away and were beginning to move about more naturally, attaching themselves to the ropes again now that it was apparent she wasn't going to need CPR on the floor or defibrillation, or anything else dramatic. She watched blankly as some children – no doubt the ones who'd been scampering squirrel-like through the treetops earlier – began to scramble the wall as though gravity didn't apply to them.

Tom's walkie-talkie crackled into life; she couldn't make out the words that came over the line. '. . . Thanks, Kim. Coming out now.' He clipped the radio back on his belt. 'They're outside,' he said to her. 'Think you can stand?'

She nodded.

'Are you dizzy?'

'No, I'm fine.'

She felt his hand lift off her back; the warm heavy weight of it had seemed to centre and still her, as though rooting her to the ground. Slowly she got up and the girls rushed forward, as though readying to catch her should she fall.

'My colleague Kim is waiting for you right outside the doors,' Tom said as they began to walk her off.

Natasha looked at him. 'Wait. You're not coming?' He was her safety, didn't he see that?

Apparently not, for he seemed surprised by the question. 'Uh . . . I have another lesson after this one. I'm sorry.'

He was working and she was just another client, of course she was. She wasn't sure why that should feel so crushing. 'Oh . . . Thank you.'

He shrugged. 'No worries.'

No worries. She was off his hands now, at least.

'Come on, you'll be right as rain as soon as you've had a rest. And *then* we can get back to this weekend being a lot more hen and a lot less chicken, what do you say?' Hels cackled, trying to rally her.

'More hen. Less chicken,' Natasha mumbled. 'Got it.'

Chapter Six

Frome, Tuesday 29 November

'Sara, I'm so sorry, I've had to bring her ladyship with me, I hope you don't mind?' Natasha asked. She stood on the pavement proffering a wine bottle with her free hand as Mabel sat on her other hip, dressed in her pyjamas, thumb in. The toddler looked pale, with dark moons cradled beneath her eyes. It was her third night on the trot of trying to sleep without Moolah and it wasn't getting any easier; the days were simply becoming more fractious as exhaustion set in.

'Of course! Is everything okay? Is she poorly? She looks so washed out.'

'She's fine, honestly. But I can't really put her down; she's lost her favourite toy, the one that helps her go to sleep, and it's made her so clingy. I may well have to eat dinner with her sleeping on my lap.'

'Oh, the poor thing!'

It was trying to sleet, and pale whiskery flakes shot through the haloes of amber light from the streetlights. Natasha's hair was streaming in the wind, her cold hand pressed protectively against Mabel's tousled curls.

'Quick, come through, come through, it's so chilly out here.'

The small seventeenth-century oak door was shut behind

them and Sara took her coat as Natasha shrugged it off awkwardly, Mabel clinging to her like a baby koala. The house was already filled with noise, sounds of conversation and laughter spilling through the narrow doorways, so different to the airy quietness she'd left at home. Bella had given her sad eyes at the door as they had left her alone but Natasha really couldn't have turned up here with both her child *and* dog in tow. They couldn't all have attachment issues!

'Everyone's here and dinner's just about ready,' Sara said excitedly.

'What feast are you delighting us with tonight?' Natasha asked as they walked past worn velvet curtains, antique bobbin chairs and threadbare rugs, Natasha's hand automatically reaching out to touch as they passed. This house always felt so rich with history, as if she could feel the energy of the lives that had been lived here. It was chaotic, untidy and very dusty, but she loved it. The house had a pulse and the kitchen was its beating heart.

'Just lasagne.'

But Natasha knew there would be no 'just' about it. Sara – a bronze sculptor by day – was a superlative homely cook, excelling in bakes and cakes and the sort of 'school night suppers' that comforted everyone from toddlers to city CEOs weary of nouvelle cuisine. Her lasagne would have some secret ingredient in it that would have everyone purring.

The house always made Natasha feel a bit drunk as she walked through it, with its sloping ceilings and uneven flagged floor. Following her friend to the kitchen felt like crossing a ship's deck in a storm.

'You are looking *amazing*, by the way!' Sara said over her shoulder. 'That tan! Were you really only gone a week?'

'Yeah, I wish we could have had longer. It's such a long

way to go for just seven days but Rob couldn't get any more time away from work.'

'He really does put in the hours, doesn't he?' Sara asked. 'Still, look at your house. And at least you get to go on these lovely holidays. It'll be staycations for me and Marty for the next few years. I suppose the weather was good?'

'Yeah, only one storm the entire time.'

'I'd love a winter tan. Look at me – I'm like porridge. And lumpy porridge at that,' she bemoaned, smacking her own backside with a garrulous laugh.

They walked into the kitchen. It was everything Natasha's wasn't: long and narrow Eighties orange pine, often in shade and with views only to the end of the garden. And yet, the garden was a mini jungle with bushy azaleas screening the fence and a stepped cluster of rangy potted pelargoniums and agapanthus; the kitchen was cosy, with sheepskins thrown over the bench seats and stubby red candles stuck into the necks of old wine bottles. Perhaps it was because the seventeenth-century building was so historic that it often had the conviviality of a medieval tavern; either way, what it lacked in square footage and open aspects it made up for in atmosphere and location. As a townhouse on the middle of the historic high street, everyone passed the front door, meaning Sara got to see and hear everything first. Hels called her the Town Crier, and she was always the first person to call if a scandal or secret broke.

'Nats!'

'You made it!' the others cheered as she came through. 'Oh!' The rowdy tenor changed as they saw what – or rather who – she was carrying.

'Ohhh. Is she okay?'

'What's happened?'

Hels simply winked in greeting, holding her arms out for her goddaughter to be passed over to the table.

'She's fine, honestly, she's just having trouble settling at the moment,' Natasha said, reluctant to explain it. The whole situation bordered on the ridiculous. All this upheaval on account of an old toy cow?

'Rob not around?' Sara asked, questioningly holding up a bottle of red and a bottle of elderflower.

Reluctantly, Natasha nodded for the cordial. 'Leeds this week. Back Friday.' Sara poured her a glass and handed it over. 'Thanks.'

'Your stories on Insta were amazing! Did I see one of you actually swimming with a turtle?' Ros Whiteman asked.

'Yes, it just came right up to our villa on the house reef,' she shrugged. 'A family we met later on were so cross when they heard; they'd paid especially for a turtle diving expedition and didn't get to see a single one! It was pot luck.'

'*Your* luck, you mean!' Hels quipped.

'Ugh, I so need a winter getaway,' Rachel said, in full knowledge there was no chance; she was the village florist and as such, Christmas was one of her busiest times of year. Extravagant bunches of mistletoe were already bustling in her windows and the first of her wreath-making courses started next week.

'I reckon I need it more!' Emma Bingley scoffed. 'I've not had a day out of jeans for over . . . eleven years?' Eyes rolled. No one could out-work or out-moan Emma. Her family had owned the dairy farm and surrounding three hundred acres for over a hundred and fifty years and very little disrupted the farming routine – not weather or anniversaries; certainly never holidays. Come Christmas Day she would be knee deep in wellies, pushing cows through the mud; she would not be

KAREN SWAN

sinking her toes into golden sand anytime soon. Possibly ever.

Natasha watched as Mabel sat on Hels's lap, her thumb in her mouth, sleepily, curiously pulling on a strand of her godmother's twisty hair. Hels was looking down at her with an almost maternal expression, stroking her cheek softly. She hastily rearranged her features when she realized Natasha was looking over, but it was too late; Natasha had seen, and besides, she'd known for years that this ice queen had a warm heart.

'Here, come and sit down, Nats,' Ros said as bums shuffled along and a space was made for her on the bench. Ros was the village hairdresser and lived in the flat above the salon at the other end of town. She had a pet snake, a white-blonde pixie cut and tattoo sleeves, and it amused Natasha no end that she spent most of her days doing blue rinses and soft perms for the village's largely mature population.

'My God, if only this could be wine,' Natasha groaned, drinking half the glass in one.

'Tough day?'

'Certainly a long one.' She sighed. 'It started at four thirty this morning, after four hours' fitful sleep, and Mabel's scarcely let me put her down since.'

'She can't still be teething, surely?'

'No, she lost her beloved toy while we were away. She's always slept with it but we hadn't realized until now that her sleep is actually *dependent* on it.'

'Ah, yes, my niece has a toy like that and it's always the end of the world when it goes missing. My sister literally lives on her nerves worrying it'll get lost in the park or at someone's house.'

'Well, I am living your sister's worst nightmare. And it

84

really is a nightmare. I know we've just had a dream holiday and I'm so lucky, blah blah blah – but honestly, three nights of practically no sleep and full-on days where I can't even put her down has undone all the holiday's R&R, for sure. Rob's been away all week so I'm flying solo. My shoulders are right back up here again.' She indicated to her ears and took another glug of her elderflower, pretending it was wine.

'Can I help? I'd be happy to take her to the swings one morning.'

'You're an angel, but she won't leave my side. Every day at nursery so far this week, they've had to call me to pick her up early. She won't stop crying.'

'God, poor you, that's rough. When's Rob back?'

'Friday evening. He's on site all this week. Honestly, I don't think he believes me when I tell him how unsettled she is.'

'You can't replace the toy?'

Natasha shook her head. 'I'd have more luck finding the Holy Grail than another Moolah.'

There was a collective murmur of coos as Sara opened the oven and pulled out a bubbling dish of lasagne, the aroma falling over the group like a mist and breaking up their various conversations. Natasha looked around at all the familiar faces. Not everyone here was a close friend – some, like Julia Canford and Caroline Somerville, who were much older, were more acquaintances – but she could feel her tension easing as she sat among them. It felt good to be around other adults. Her weeks were often long and lonely, but this one was extreme and there was only so much solitary time and baby talk she could take.

The book club had been going for thirteen years now, set up originally by Julia and some of her direct neighbours on the high street, but membership had gradually opened up to other streets as people moved away or dropped out for various reasons. The group met every other month and everyone took it in turns to host, although Sara seemed to host more frequently than the others. Their club's rules were strict – no more than ten members, and new people had to be proposed and seconded by existing members; members had to live in the village (Natasha, living on the very outskirts of the village, had got in by dint of her postcode and the fact that Hels wouldn't accept 'no'). But there was no age restriction, and currently the group ranged from twenty-three to sixty-six. The club dates, once agreed, were set in stone – no crying off at the last minute allowed, except for real emergencies like a lost child or birthing cow – and the book they were discussing had to have been read by everyone. Right to the end. It meant the conversations were always lively and engaged – to put it mildly – and very often their laughter could be heard out on the street. The meeting for *Fifty Shades* had proved particularly raucous, prompting Marty, Sara's husband, to take refuge in the Three Feathers.

'How are you, Jo?' Natasha asked, patting the hand of the woman on her other side and seeing how the seamstress was staring wanly at her drink. She looked like she might fall asleep in it. 'You look almost as tired as me.'

'Worse. I guarantee it.'

'Why? What's going on?'

'I have a bridezilla on my books and now my life is not worth living.'

Natasha smiled at the melodrama, casting another glance along the table towards her daughter. In spite of the noise as everyone chatted and caught up, Mabel's eyelids were drooping. She looked minutes away from sleep. Hels had one arm cradled around her, the other on her glass of wine as she laughed at something Lizzie was saying.

'Who is this bridezilla?' Ros asked, delighted by the foray into gossip and leaning forward on the table.

'I really shouldn't say,' Jo said reluctantly, but she looked put out by her own discretion. 'It wouldn't be professional.'

Ros's eyes narrowed thoughtfully. 'Is it Becky Morrison?' She hooked an eyebrow. 'It is, isn't it?'

'I can't say.'

'Is it a December bride, though? Tell us that. You can tell us that. It's not gossiping, it's a legitimate question from us wondering when your work stress will lift.'

Natasha chuckled, enjoying the girl talk. This was what she needed.

'Fine. Yes. The wedding's in December,' Jo admitted.

'And is she getting married in Saint Mary's? Or All Saints?'

'. . . All Saints,' Jo said suspiciously.

'It's Becky Morrison,' Ros said triumphantly, sitting back. 'I knew it was.'

'How do you know?' Natasha laughed, her hand cupped around her drink, her gaze falling every few moments to her almost-asleep child.

'I saw the vicar in the post office earlier and asked if he was feeling ready for the festive season; he said it was helped by the fact there's only one church wedding there this month. I'm already doing Amy Barker's wedding but hers is at Saint Mary's, so it has to be Becky.' She looked back at Jo. 'What's she asked for, then?'

'She wants a dress with an outer skirt that comes off to reveal a hand-beaded lace catsuit for the reception.'

A silence met her words and Jo's head collapsed into her hands. 'I know! That's what I said when she first said it.'

Natasha laughed and shook her head. 'Where does she think this is? The Vegas Strip?'

'She came to me for her hair, asking for a waterfall braid threaded with crystals. I turned her down on the spot.'

'You didn't want to do that?'

'Oh, I could do that in my sleep, but don't think I've forgotten the time she left me a two-star review because I gave her a shag cut like Miley Cyrus but somehow she didn't miraculously look like Miley Cyrus.'

Natasha could see that Mabel had finally fallen asleep on Helena's lap. Her mouth was parted, bottom lip drooling, her hands limp at her sides.

'Excuse me a sec,' she said, getting up. 'The princess finally sleeps.'

She went over and mouthed 'thank you' to her friend as she lifted the little girl up. Mabel stirred, but only very slightly. Oblivion had finally claimed her and she was a dead weight in Natasha's arms.

'Sara, is it okay to put her down in the snug?'

Sara, serving up the lasagne in giant squares, looked up. 'Put her in one of the beds upstairs if you like.'

'The snug's probably better, in case she wakes. I wouldn't hear her up there.'

'Good point. Just shove Daisy off the sofa if she's lolloping on it; she's convinced it's hers now.'

Daisy was Sara and Marty's wolfhound, a gentle giant with no sense whatever of her own might.

Carrying Mabel in her arms, Natasha walked through to the burnt-orange snug. There was a bushy Christmas tree in the corner with multicoloured fairy lights, claret velvet tub chairs and a large, sagging yellow sofa with blue repair patches on it. Sure enough, Daisy was stretched out asleep in front of the log fire. She looked so blissful, it felt as unfair to wake her as to wake Mabel.

Natasha looked at the tub chairs instead – they were high-sided on three sides, with a deep seat cushion. Mabel could curl up with her back to it and feel perfectly 'held'. There'd be little to no chance of her rolling off, but the footstool would provide a good security blanket. It had a tiny frilled gingham cushion on it, too, that was nicely flattened from years of bearing the weight of Marty's outstretched legs. Just perfect. Tossing it on the chair, she gently set Mabel down into the curve of the back, her cheek resting on the cushion. Then, grabbing a stitched suzani off the back of the tub chair, she tucked it tightly around her sleeping child. She had already decided she would bring Mabel straight into bed with her tonight when they got back. Rob, a naturally confident father, was strongly opposed to their daughter sleeping in their bed 'at this stage' – as though she was nineteen and not three – but no doubt the journey home would wake her, and Natasha wasn't prepared to spend another night walking up and down the hallway trying to settle her. Not when she was having to do this all on her own. Rob could enforce his rules when he was around and living this too, not from the peace and quiet of a fancy four-star hotel room.

She walked back into the kitchen a few moments later. Sara was setting down the steaming plates of pasta and a large green salad was being passed around. Hels was seemingly holding the bowl of garlic bread hostage.

'Is Mabel okay?' Rachel asked.

'Fast off – for the moment anyway. I should have a window of opportunity now but you never know, so I'll eat fast just in case,' she grinned.

'Poor you,' Emma said as she took her place again. 'Hels was just bringing me up to date on what's happened.'

'Well, all advice greatly received. Lauren Tennant said I should fly back to Vienna, where we lost it, or back to France, where we bought it – three years ago.'

'Fly around Europe on a wild cow chase? She would say that!' Rachel scoffed. 'More money than sense, that one.'

'She did also suggest putting out a post on Facebook or Mumsnet, but that was a waste of time too. It's a really ragged old toy. If it was in the next room, you'd probably confuse it for old socks and chuck it in the bin.'

'It's a good idea though,' Caroline said, halfway up the table. She had worked in marketing for Sainsbury's before her sons were born and was considered the group's tech genius. 'If you can get enough reach, anything's possible. Likes mean shares, which mean a potentially limitless web.'

There was nothing limitless about Natasha's web. 'Well, last time I looked – at lunchtime – it had eleven likes.'

Caroline winced. 'When did you put it up?'

'Yesterday morning.'

'Ouch.'

'Yeah. I had more responses showing off my morning coffee.'

'So then you have to make it go viral,' Hels shrugged, reluctantly relinquishing her hold on the garlic bread.

'Oh, because it's that easy,' Sara laughed, checking everyone was tucking into their dinner.

'Well, if teenagers in their bedrooms can do it . . .' Hels shrugged. 'I mean, how hard can it be? One of my patients is TikTok famous and her posts get tens of thousands of likes, just for doing these little dances and mimes.'

'I'm not sure Natasha doing a dance is going to help get

the toy back,' Caroline said apologetically. 'Especially if she can't hold said toy in the video.' She looked at Natasha. 'You've obviously got pictures of it?'

'Hundreds. Mabel never put her down.'

Julia Canford, matriarch of the book club and grandmother to eight, cleared her throat. 'Well, I'm not going to pretend to understand *half* of what you're talking about, but even I know that if you want make this go virus—'

'Viral!' Rachel laughed.

Julia shrugged. 'Don't you need someone famous to help? Isn't that how it works?'

'Yes, but that's easier said than done too! I certainly don't know any celebs,' Lizzie said wistfully.

'Me neither,' Emma chimed. 'Unless we're encompassing livestock too, in which case, I do know the owner of the prize heifer at this year's Agricultural Show.'

Everyone laughed.

Julia tore off a piece of the garlic bread. 'Well, it's probably no help at all, but my eldest granddaughter works for a terribly successful singer. English boy, but he lives in America now. He was in that band off the telly.'

'Oh?' Ros asked. 'What's his name?'

'Harold or Harry something. Or is it Henry? Always struts about like he's Mick Jagger.'

'Mick . . . ? You mean, like . . . Harry Styles?' Ros asked.

'Yes, that's the one! That's him!' Julia beamed. 'Thank you. Harold Styles.'

Jo, Rachel and Lizzie's mouths dropped open in unison. As the youngest women of the group, this revelation hit deeper.

'Your granddaughter works for Harry Styles?'

'Yes, Lily. She's twenty now. Don't ask me doing what. She

told me once and even when she explained it, I still didn't understand.' Small frown lines crinkled Julia's brow. 'All I remember is she said something about "content". I don't know what it means, but apparently he's doing well for himself anyway. She's in America with him at the moment, on tour.'

'Your granddaughter is in America right now, on tour with Harry Styles?' Rachel almost whimpered.

'Yes. She's coming back at Christmas, and not a moment too soon, frankly. She's worn out, all that packing and unpacking, plus it's hard to eat well when you're on the move like that. Her mother has been cooking bone broth for weeks and freezing it so that she can feed her up again.'

Everyone shared amused looks except Jo, who was tapping frantically on her phone, her delicious supper forgotten. She looked up a moment later. 'He's got forty-two million followers.'

'Well, that would do it!' Hels laughed. 'Harry will bring Moolah home!' She raised her glass as if in a toast.

Natasha shook her head, laughing too. 'Honestly.'

Caroline got onto her phone as well. 'Mmm, his grid is stylized though. It's all agenda – his tour, his album. There's nothing personal on there. His team must post for him.'

Hels almost spat out her wine. 'Oh my God, Caroline, we're not being serious! Of course he won't put up a post about Mabel's lost toy!'

'I don't see why not, if someone he knows asks. He could put it on his stories if nothing else.' She looked at Julia, explaining for her benefit, 'That means it'll only be up for twenty-four hours; it's not a permanent post like the grid. It won't affect his optics.'

'Optics . . . ?' Julia murmured, still looking baffled. 'Well, look, I'm very happy to ask her to ask him. Nothing ventured, nothing gained, that's what I always say.'

'No chance,' Hels said with a dismissive shake of her head. 'He'll never do it.'

'Not with that attitude. I admit it's unlikely, but if the poor child can't even sleep, why wouldn't you at least try?'

'It's certainly cheaper than a round ticket through Europe,' Jo said, eyes bright at the prospect of being only two degrees removed from Harry Styles.

Natasha watched on, amazed by the debate. Somehow her domestic drama had hijacked book club – and Sara's incredible lasagne. Everyone was too busy talking to eat.

'Mmm, this is *so* good, Sara,' she said enthusiastically, trying to change the subject. 'What's that slightly fiery ingredient?'

'A dash of red pe—' Sara began, but Caroline talked over her, clearly stirred to action by Hels's wholesale dismissal of the proposal. 'You said you posted on Facebook, Natasha, yes?' Caroline asked.

'Well yes, but—'

Caroline got her phone out too and began tapping the screen. '. . . Ah yes, right, there it is.' She glanced over at Natasha. 'You've got fifteen likes now.'

'Wow,' Natasha smiled. 'I'm so well connected! We'll have her back in no time.'

'Okay, Julia. I've shared it, and as you and I follow each other on Facebook, it should show on your timeline now too. Can you share it with Lily and ask her to ask him if he can do anything? We're just asking for a share, not a kidney.'

'Of course. Lily's always been such a sweet girl,' Julia smiled.

'You're very kind to even think of asking him, but honestly, I don't think Harry Styles is going to trouble himself over our small calamity,' Natasha said, at pains not to cause further fuss. 'Even if you just share it on your own pages, that would be more than enough. In all likelihood, Moolah's already been binned, but I do appreciate your support.'

'Why's she called Moolah?' Julia enquired curiously.

Natasha rolled her eyes. 'Rob named her – Moo for a cow, obviously; moolah—'

'Because he's got plenty of it?' Emma quipped.

Natasha blushed, embarrassed by her husband's jokey wordplay. She never thought about it now; the word had become a beloved name to her child, but out of context here, the obvious reference – devotion – to money felt crass.

'Well, if that's all sorted, shall we move on to the reason for being gathered here tonight?' Sara asked, relieved everyone was eating again. 'What did we all think of the book? Because I for one thought it was atrocious. Turgid, dull . . .'

At once their voices clamoured, ten women gathered in both unity and dissent, and loving every moment of it.

Natasha lay in bed, stroking her daughter's head, still humming a tune from *Frozen* and trying to keep awake. It was almost three and the moon was drifting around the earth's curve like an untethered silver balloon. She could hear foxes screeching in the nearby copse, their barks piercing an otherwise pristine silence.

Beside her, Mabel slept fitfully, her breath still coming in tremulous sighs from the latest bout of tears. As predicted, she had woken while being carried to the car as the frigid night air smacked her rosy cheeks. Natasha had tried to settle her back to sleep but her bewilderment upon waking, not knowing why she was in the car in the dark of night, added to her panic as she remembered once more that Moolah was gone. Eventually, just after midnight and following two hours of pacing with the child in her arms, Natasha had run the bath and they had climbed in together, Mabel dozing on her chest, bubbles popping quietly all around them. Natasha had had the presence of mind to light a candle before they climbed in, not just to cast a gentle, glowing light, but to give her something to watch as her child slept.

Now back in bed – she had managed to transfer Mabel this time without disturbance – the dead of night ticked slowly on. Her hair was still damp on the pillow, Mabel's already dried into tight little curls. Rob had rung during dinner but she had missed the call, unable to hear over the noise as differences in opinion were noisily debated. He had sounded tired as he'd left a message, the slight pique in his voice suggesting he'd completely forgotten about her book club date with the women of the village. She tried not to feel resentful that he would be getting a full night's sleep while she blinked, owl-like, through the twilight hours, soothing their baby daughter. She knew he would take the lion's share of it this weekend when he got home again; it wasn't easy for either one of them with the amount of travelling he had to do and after a long week on site with clients, having to slip into full-time parenting to give her a break wouldn't be easy on him either. Perhaps by then, Mabel would have adjusted and she'd be sleeping through again. This would be forgotten. It couldn't last forever . . . surely?

She watched a satellite blinking in the sky, wondering if the same would ever be true again for her. She never seemed to sleep well. Every night she would fall into sleep like a stone thrown into a well, worn out by her days running after a toddler, but after a few hours she would be torn from her rest by a racing heart, anxiety coursing through her limbs and her arms aching for a baby not yet growing. She desperately wanted a sibling for Mabel, someone who would test and stretch her, love and mould her. It was good for children to be challenged and not always believe they were right, to have to learn to share, wait their turn, listen to others, make space . . . As a child herself, Natasha had yearned for a little brother or sister, but her father – believing they couldn't afford two children or rather, couldn't afford their lifestyle with two children – had 'put his foot down'. It had broken both her and her mother's hearts and no amount of toys or pretty things he bought to compensate had ever made up for it.

Wanting a large family – noisy and sprawling, full of chaos – had been one of the first things she had told Rob. Things had moved fast between them and by their second date, he was telling her he saw them having a future together. Far from being spooked by her desire for lots of kids, it had seemed to draw him closer to her. He wanted the same and when Mabel had been conceived on their honeymoon, it felt their dreams were coming true. So why wasn't it happening for them now? What had changed? Was it down to her, or Rob? They were both eating less meat and cutting back (largely) on alcohol. Perhaps they had to go harder? Start taking supplements? She'd been on folic acid for a year already.

Rob's laissez-faire approach – 'It'll happen when it's supposed to' – didn't give her the comfort he anticipated. Her pain was twisting into paranoia that perhaps he was more like her father than she had thought, her quiet bafflement turning into a fury that he wasn't as destroyed as she was by an absence that felt like a loss. They were failing to consolidate their family and, to her, that felt like they were failing *as* a family. Mabel needed siblings, couldn't he see that?

She had a sense of them being finely but precariously balanced. The holiday had helped them both to relax – it was the longest stretch Rob had gone without working that she could remember – and for the first time in a long time, sex hadn't solely been about dates, times and latency peaks. Her paranoia that something was fundamentally broken between them had dissipated and they had been happy again, but it felt fragile still, like a protective shell that needed to harden. That sense of connection was hard enough to maintain when he was working away; coming together again on no sleep would do them no favours.

She reached for her phone and tapped the screen, opening the Facebook app, even though she knew it was stupid.

Twenty-two shares.

She groaned and let it drop onto the sheet, blinking up at the ceiling and waiting for the morning to come.

Chapter Seven

Nepal, Friday 2 December

Duffy sat by the side of the road, arms splayed over his knees, waiting for the bus. It had been due fifty minutes ago but he wasn't concerned; there was no rush. He was glad of the rest, having been travelling most of the week – flying from Vienna to Doha on Monday, and from there catching a transfer to Kathmandu on Tuesday. After a fitful night in the capital trying to sleep in a hotel with chapati-thin walls he had hitched a ride to Pokhara, where he had rested for a couple of days, biking around the lake and sorting out some administrative requirements while allowing his body to adjust to the new time zone.

Already the sumptuous comfort of Vienna felt like a distant memory as he sat in the noise and dust, his hands growing cold. He stared into the distance, remembering Klara's clean, scented skin, her easy laugh and provocative look—

'Hey, man.'

He looked up to find a shaggy-haired guy with a nose ring looking down at him.

'You speak English?' The man was American.

'Yep,' he replied with an easy nod and a smile.

The American beamed. 'This is the bus stop, right?'

'In theory. Where you heading?'

'Khande. Only we've been hanging here for an hour and there's been no sign of no bus.'

'Yep, welcome to Nepal. That's how it is here. It'll come when it comes. You're in the right place though.'

'Right. Okay. Just thought we better check.'

'This your first time here?'

'Sure is.' The man beckoned to another guy who was leaning against a bent handrail that looked like it had had a disagreement with a bus. 'I'm Jay, and this here is Stevie.'

Stevie had an impressive dark blonde mohawk and the edges of a tattoo of eagle wings inched past the collar of his jacket.

They all shook hands. 'Good to meet you. I'm Duffy.'

'We saw you sitting here but you looked so chill . . . You've got the look of someone who's been here before.'

'It's true, I have.' Duffy noticed that the Americans were dressed in almost identical clothing to him – lightweight trek trousers, down jackets and beanies. It was a uniform in these parts. He could easily guess where they were going. 'Where are you from in the States?'

'Portland, Oregon. And you're British, right?'

'Yup.'

'London?'

'Cumbria actually, further north. Although I'm probably only classed as an honorary Brit now. I haven't been home in nearly four years.'

'Where've you been?'

'Mainly travelling through the States and South America – Peru. Bolivia. Chile. I flew here from Argentina.'

'That's some miles you're clocking up. Gotta be expensive.'

'Depends how you live, I guess,' Duffy shrugged. 'I don't need much. A bit of bar work here and there, some gardening occasionally, is usually enough to tide me over.'

'So how many times you been here, then?' Jay asked, unzipping his jacket pocket and pulling out some Rizla papers and a wad of tobacco.

'This is my third time.'

'And where you headed to?'

'Khande, like you.'

Jay's eyebrows went up. 'Oh yeah? You doing the ABC too?'

'Yep.' The Annapurna Base Camp trek was one of the most popular in the Himalayas, although the big commercial groups tended to leave from Nayapul.

'So will this be your third time doing it?'

'Yep.'

'You sound as bad as us.'

'Yeah? What've you been doing?'

'Well, we got here five weeks ago and did the EBC.'

Duffy pulled an impressed face. Everest Base Camp was the dream for every hill walker, trekker and climber across the planet, but as such, with all the sherpas and pros too, it was vastly overcrowded and commercial. 'Like Glastonbury in the snow,' someone had said to him once. He had no desire to ever go there himself. 'And how was it?'

'Busy.'

'Mmm. Although probably quieter than most other times of the year,' he said optimistically.

Jay pulled a face. 'That I would not like to see.'

'Nope. I guess it's why we're all out here now, right? Avoiding the crowds?' Duffy asked them.

'I'm telling you, half the so-called climbers we saw leaving Base Camp to go up to Camp One – they didn't even look like they deserved to be trekkers at Base Camp; the help they needed just getting there? It was insane. It was scary thinking they were going further on.'

Duffy sighed. 'That's the problem with Everest. All those fixed ropes and sherpas and canned O – they'll get anyone up. It's big money.'

They all tutted and shook their heads, staring out into the traffic.

'Well, we're glad we did it anyway,' Stevie continued. 'We practically ran up compared to some of the others. You ever do Everest?'

'Me? No. But I've seen it from Lhotse.' He had been able to see the crowds through his binoculars.

'You should give it a go. Everest is the Big Daddy, a feather in our caps, I guess. But we've got another six weeks here, doing the ABC – that's a week, as you know – then the circuit trek, which is another three.'

'Man, I am looking forward to the two weeks' downtime at the end,' Jay quipped. 'This next month is gonna be brutal.'

'Yep,' Duffy said. 'That's pretty hard on the body, doing all that back to back. But at least the ABC is lower altitude.'

'Yeah,' Jay nodded, offering him a puff of the cigarette. 'What's after this for you?'

Duffy politely declined. 'I'm just taking it a day at a time. I don't have any plans past Annapurna at the moment.'

'A true hobo, huh?'

Duffy glanced down the road and saw the bus approaching. Traffic was heavy and there had to be at least thirty mopeds and motorcycles buzzing around it like some sort of consort, the roar of Royal Enfield engines flanking either side and weaving in front of it, horns honking constantly. 'Looks like we're up.'

He drew his legs in and rose, the Americans following suit and stubbing out the cigarette as they slung their backpacks over their shoulders.

'How long you think this'll be?' Jay asked as they stepped

back for the bus to draw alongside. People swarmed around them, high voices calling for children, old men spitting out their *paan*.

'Should be just under an hour,' Duffy replied. 'Then again, my transfer from Kathmandu to here should have been six, seven hours and it was closer to ten in the end.'

'You drove here?' Jay looked amazed. 'But you know there's a flight from Kathmandu to Pokhara? It's like thirty minutes! Goes several times a day.'

'Yeah, I know.' Duffy grabbed the loop on the top of his orange backpack and lifted it off the street.

'And you still chose a ten-hour coach ride?'

'Actually, it was the back of a truck. With three goats. The journey's the destination though, right?'

Jay and Stevie threw back their heads and laughed.

The doors opened and there was a rush to board – as with the flights – people clamouring to get on with their journey, as though sitting down quickly would make the bus leave any sooner. Duffy walked over to the hold where the driver was loading up the bags and swung his pack in himself.

'*Namaste*,' he said to the driver.

'*Namaste*.'

Jay and Stevie were already seated up front by the time he embarked a few minutes later. Their backpacks were in the shallow racks above their heads and he feared they would regret it; the roads were in poor condition and rutted with potholes, not to mention the shocks on the bus were most likely shot too. They would feel every last bump, and he bet those bags would end up on their laps.

Duffy walked slowly down the aisle, checking each row for a single seat, smiling as he went. When he got to the end, he turned back and showed the driver his ticket with a shrug. It wasn't uncommon for these journeys to be overbooked.

With an easy shrug too, the driver motioned for Duffy to follow him and they walked over to his cab at the front. It wasn't large, but there was a narrow seat behind the driver's, and the windscreen afforded a wide-angled view of the road ahead. The cab was decorated with a large laminated image of a Hindu goddess, with a string of bells wrapped around the rear-view mirror and a stick of incense poking out from a jar glued to the dash.

Soon enough, they pulled away and Duffy stared out placidly at the road ahead, his body bobbing and swaying with the bus. There were no road markings to keep the oncoming traffic an official distance away; everything was simply judged with lightning reflexes and enthusiastic horn-honking, sudden sharp braking and wild swerves all par for the course. Electricity cables hung slackly in a loose lattice as they passed through the streets, past crudely built apartment buildings stacked like Lego blocks. Almost every one had a balcony, lines of washing strung along them, neighbours chatting across the voids.

They passed a man pulling along helium-filled foil balloons, the pink cluster like a bubble cloud behind him; a child pedalling furiously and chasing after a dog; a man sitting on a stool repairing bikes. Duffy looked at faces, heard the cadence of voices. They passed by a river, the meander winding inwards as though to kiss the road, water buffalo grazing peacefully on the banks; the riverbed was dry but for a narrow channel of icy meltwater, and sharp, shattered rocks were scattered messily along its length like black confetti. In the distance, as he twisted back, he could still see Lake Phewa, its fishing boats painted their distinctive cornflower blue and aquamarine and tied to wooden poles that stuck out of the water. He saw a monkey swing in a tree . . .

There was so much life here, in so many different forms. Everything was both familiar and yet also new to his gaze. The sky was a cold grey with low-lying clouds, but bright colours blazed everywhere – padded jackets, flags, boats, cars, balloons, houses – and he could feel the energy of lives being lived in this wild place, people scratching a living, seeking adventure, escaping themselves, finding themselves. Which was he doing, he wondered? Escaping or finding himself?

The driver braked sharply as a moped swerved for a goat. A moment later Duffy heard a loud thud behind him, followed by a distinctly Western cuss.

He smiled to himself, knowing the Americans' bags were down, feeling his phone buzz in his pocket. Signal? He pulled it out quickly. This area was remote, but even in deepest Asia there was connectivity. He checked the screen and winced as he saw Anya's name, remembering too late that he had promised to call her when he arrived. He'd been in Nepal three days now.

Call me when you get this!

He smiled. Typical Anya. Never one for formality, politeness or sweetness, her messages were always direct and to the point, tinged with a hint of alarm. He slid the phone back into his pocket and went back to watching the road. He would contact her when they arrived at Khande. They definitely had wifi there and she had waited this long already.

It could wait a little longer.

His phone rang when he was halfway through his press-ups. He strained to see if he could see the caller ID from here, but he already knew who it was. There was only one person in the world who cared about his whereabouts, who would check in on him and pray for him to pick up. He pushed on through several more press-ups – his training regime was vitally important – but it was too late, his focus had gone. He knew that if he didn't pick up now, she'd only ring again. And again. And he had promised he would call.

Jumping his feet towards his hands and springing up, he picked the phone up off the bed.

'Yuh hello?' he panted. 'Hey, Anya.' His heart rate was elevated. He never worked out for long but he went hard and fast when he did: push-ups, crunches, hill climbers and pull-ups – if the door frame would take it.

'Where are you?' Straight to the point, as ever.

He wasn't entirely sure he should tell her. This wasn't the sort of place she would ever have seen. The room was small, with just enough space for a single bed, a window at one end hung with unlined oyster satin curtains. The bed consisted of a thin mattress on a trestle and his sleeping bag was already rolled out, his hiking shoes off and left politely at the door. The roughly plastered walls were painted half pink, half green but there were no pictures, no books, not even a view – not today, at least; the low-lying clouds had grown thicker during the afternoon, bumping just above their heads. He could have been in Croydon for all he could see out there. The bathroom was shared, but it had a Western toilet and hot running water – his last luxury for a while – and he had been lucky to secure a single room; another benefit of trekking out of high season. He was planning on getting some dinner shortly and then an early night. He wanted body and mind to be fresh for tomorrow.

'I'm at the lodge in a place called Khande. It's an hour from Pokhara if you want to look it u—'

'You have wifi there?'

'Well, some. Connection comes and goes.' He frowned as he picked up the impatience in her voice. She was always brisk, but this was clipped even by her standards. 'Why?'

'I need you to send me a photo of that toy you found.'

There was a pause as he replayed her words in his head, trying to make them make sense. '. . . What?'

'The toy cow! Moodle.'

In truth, he'd almost forgotten about it. In the course of unpacking and repacking his bag in Pokhara – he had left half his belongings in a locker in the city – the toy had slipped deeper into the rucksack, his mind on other things. '. . . Why?'

'I need to see it.'

'*Why?*'

'Just send me the picture. I'll explain in a sec. I want to see if I'm right first.'

'Anya—'

'Just do it.'

He groaned. Now he remembered why they'd broken up. 'Right now?'

'Right now. I'll call you back when it comes.'

She hung up, leaving Duffy staring at the phone in bewilderment. He had never fully understood his ex, but this was downright disorienting. With a sigh, he sat up and rifled through the pack, obediently looking for the toy.

'Hey, little fella,' he said as his hands found it and he pulled it out. He felt the peculiar mix of thrill and dull ache in his chest that came any time he set eyes upon it. 'Ready to do some travelling?'

The toy did not reply.

He held it up to the light and took the photo. Within a minute he had shared it with Anya – already braced for her querying of the dubious satin curtains in the background –

although how long it would be before she received it, he couldn't tell. Coverage was always patchy and it might be a few days before it even sent.

He sat on the edge of the bed and began doing some tricep dips, enjoying the feeling of his muscles beginning to burn.

She rang again.

'Fuck's sake,' he muttered, sitting back on the bed and answering, his elbows on his knees.

'I knew it!' she gasped.

'Knew what?'

'You've got that little girl's toy! It's the same one! It's identical to the one in her post, plus she lost it here in Vienna and you found it here!'

Duffy stared at his socked feet, trying to make sense of this rabble. 'Anya, what the hell are you talking about?'

'Duffy! Don't you ever check your socials?'

'I'm in Nepal, not New York!'

She tutted disappointedly. 'Honestly, you miss everything, even when you're at the centre of it!' She gave a long-suffering sigh. 'A little English girl has lost her favourite toy, and when I say favourite toy, I mean, she can't sleep without it, she's lost her appetite. Her mother's beside herself. She's only three.'

'And you're saying I've got her toy?'

'Yes! She lost it in an Airbnb in Vienna, last weekend. They were there on Saturday night and you stayed Sunday night, right?'

'Yeah,' he muttered.

'And you found the toy in the apartment?'

'You know I did. I was talking to you when I found it.'

'Right. So it's hers. You've got to send it back to her.'

He gave a laugh. 'Anya, I'm not sure which part of "I'm in the Himalayas" you don't understand? I assure you, I am

107

nowhere near a DHL office right now.' He ran a hand through his hair, exhausted by the drama. 'How the hell do you even know about this, anyway? Do you know them?'

'Duff, the whole thing's blown up on social media. It's gone viral. The mother put out a post on Facebook and Harry Styles shared it! Then Jennifer Lawrence! Then Justin Bieber! And then – wait for it . . . Margot Robbie!'

'Oh, no fucking way!' he laughed.

'Yes way! It's had sixteen million likes and over a million shares. There's even a hashtag trending: findmoolah!'

'Moolah?'

'The toy!'

'You mean Moodle?'

'His name's Moolah. And he's a she.'

Duffy looked at the toy in his hand. 'No. He's definitely a he.'

Anya laughed from six thousand kilometres away. 'Fine. Whatever you say. But you've got to give him back. This thing has exploded and you can't be the monster who took her teddy.'

'I'm a monster now?'

'You will be if anyone finds out you took a little girl's toy, discovered all this fuss and then kept it anyway. Are you heartless?'

'I didn't do anything. It was lost behind a curtain and you know what they say – finders keepers.'

Anya gave a gasp of mock horror. 'You *are* a monster. I knew it,' she quipped, seeming to be enjoying all this immensely. 'Honestly, Duff, you don't stand a chance of keeping it. This little girl is cuter than Bambi. There's not a person in the world who'd deny her her toy. Any judge would rule against you.'

It was his turn to laugh. 'Oh, it's going to court now too, is it?'

'For sure.'

'But isn't possession nine-tenths of the law?'

'I'm going to send you the post so you can see that cute little face and understand exactly what you're up against.' Her voice became distracted and Duffy could picture her in her Viennese apartment, scrolling on her phone as she chatted to him in cashmere socks and her husband's sweatshirt (well, she'd always worn his, so he figured . . .). 'You'll have to bear with – the mother posted about a million photos, all pulling at the heartstrings.'

'Oh God no, don't jam my inbox,' he said quickly. 'There's nowhere near enough bandwidth for downloading a file that size out here. It'll be buffering in the ether for eternity.'

'Too late, it's already gone,' she said with a tone of satisfaction.

He gave a weary sigh, already knowing it would never get here. 'Fine, I concede defeat; I'll send the toy back first chance I get, okay?'

'But when will that be? She's so little. She won't understand if it's weeks and weeks away.'

'Well, that's the best I can I do,' he shrugged. 'If it bothers you so much, you can . . . you can find some way to get in touch with the mother and explain. Tell her the toy is safe with me till then.'

Anya gave a sudden excited gasp. 'Say you want a ransom! Seriously!' she laughed. 'I don't think there's anything that mother wouldn't do to get the toy back. You want a house? Done! A Porsche? Sure! Take two!'

'A date with Margot Robbie?'

'Easy!'

They laughed together. They'd always been best as friends. Duffy knew he'd been a difficult partner – too angry and broken to accept her love – but saving their friendship in spite of that was one of the things he was most proud of.

'God, this is the most exciting thing that's ever happened to me,' Anya said, almost gushing. 'I'm a hero. The woman who found Moolah!'

Duffy rolled his eyes at the prospect of being known as the guy who'd *taken* Moolah.

'Perhaps they'll want to interview me on the breakfast TV shows,' she giggled.

'Well, don't mention me,' he said quickly. 'Keep my name well out of it.' He pinched his temples, all amusement gone. The last thing he wanted was for his name to end up in the press. 'Just tell the mother I'll send it when I'm back in civilization, okay?'

'Okay, fine. But you owe me dinner with your ransom millions when you get back.'

Back. There was a short silence.

'. . . Duff?'

'Yeah, I'm here. Sorry, the line dropped for a sec,' he lied. He stared out of the window into the clouds. Everything was grey and amorphous; he felt in the middle of nowhere. Vienna – its vibrancy, solidity, weight of history – seemed an impossibility here, where everything was airy and intangible, ready to drift away. He pulled himself back to the conversation. 'Look, I'd better shoot. It's time to get a drink and some food. I want to get an early night. Big day tomorrow.'

'Well, stay safe,' she said, in the motherly warning tone she seemed to reserve just for him.

'I'm trekking, Anya – basically walking through a national park.'

'Nothing's basic at four thousand metres,' she shot back. 'Remember, I know you.'

They sent each other kisses and hung up, Duffy falling back on the bed and looking up at the ceiling. The phone call had unsettled him. Anya's megawatt energy was often a drain, but particularly now, when they were worlds apart; her easy vivacity, her unquestioning belief that there would always be a tomorrow, was an emblem of everything he'd left behind. She was rooted in a world that he no longer belonged to.

He felt something staring at him and turned to find the toy cow tipped forward on the mattress, eyeballing him. He picked it up. 'Well, Moodle. Moolah. Whoever you are. This is a right mess. You never said you were a VIP. I hope you're not going to be this much trouble for the rest of the trip?'

Silence echoed in reply.

'Not much of a talker, huh?'

Chapter Eight

Natasha was working in her studio, trying to capture and perfect the expression in the eyes of Sue Chelford's Weimaraner, when she heard Rob's key in the lock, followed by a soft thud as his bag hit the floor. His sigh was weary as Bella skittered over the oak parquet to greet him, groaning happily and wagging her tail so hard she almost hit herself in the face. 'Hey, girl,' he whispered to her, patting her flank like she was a bag of flour. They were the sounds that told Natasha everything was restored again, the sounds of a happy home, a bustling one. It felt so quiet and still when it was just the two of them (three, counting Bella); but Mabel's joy and Natasha's relief at his homecomings almost made up for it.

'How are my favourite girls?' Rob asked a few seconds later, poking his head through the doorway and finding a scene of domestic contentment. The log fire was crackling quietly, a Christmas candle scenting the room with notes of cinnamon, clove and spices. Mabel was sitting on the floor on her plastic playmat, playdough spread around her with various blunt plastic cutting implements and stencils.

'Daddy!' she yelled, scrambling to her feet and running over with her arms outstretched, ready to be swung.

Rob duly obliged, laughing as she squealed delightedly, before pulling her in close and blowing raspberries on her neck. 'Have you been a good girl for Mummy?'

She nodded.

'Have you?' he asked in a sing-song voice.

'Yes,' she said solemnly, her chubby face a portrait of butter-wouldn't-melt innocence that betrayed no sign of the mental trauma they had endured in his absence. For four nights, they had had midnight baths and storytimes told by torchlight under the covers – anything to make their wakefulness feel chosen and fun, rather than imposed and wretched. It meant the tear storms weren't so violent, but Natasha was now beginning to wonder if her daughter was enjoying the wakeful nights a little too much.

'Good girl.' He gave her a noisy kiss on the cheek and set her down, walking over to where Natasha was sitting at her easel. 'Hey, you,' he said, in that low, sexy voice that invited forgiveness when forgiveness was due, other things at other times.

'Hey yourself,' she said, moving only her eyes to look at him as he leaned in to kiss her cheek.

'Has it been awful?'

She nodded.

'You look tired.'

'Thanks,' she said sarcastically, feeling resentful that he looked well rested. His expression fell and she immediately felt bad. 'Sorry,' she said quickly. 'I'm not trying to make you feel guilty. It's been getting better, slowly. It's fine.'

Rob kissed her quickly again, his arm tight around her shoulders. 'I'm sorry,' he murmured. 'I got back as soon as I could. I even got away early – a meeting ran short – but then I hit traffic on the M5 so . . .' He gave a hopeless shrug.

'It's fine. You're here now.'

He looked at the charcoal she was finishing. She didn't think it was her best work; she kept working on it, finessing details, but now she felt it was overworked and stiff.

'Wow.'

She wrinkled her nose, having heard the slight – ever so slight – hesitation that preceded the word. 'I can't get the eyes right.'

'They look like eyes to me. Round; blacky bits in the middle.'

'Ha ha.' She sighed. 'No, I can't capture the look in them.'

'Do dogs' eyes have looks?'

She was amazed he would even ask. 'Because Bella's look the same when you come home as opposed to when you're going out?'

'Touché.' He kissed the tip of her nose. 'I still don't know why you insist on torturing yourself like this, though.'

She watched him walk over to the stove and throw on another log. 'Because I enjoy it – even if it doesn't always look that way. Besides, what else would I do otherwise? Mabel's only going to be at nursery more and more, and with the hours you pull, I'd be rattling around here on my own.'

'I thought it was every woman's dream to spend her days putting her feet up, lunching with her friends and going to spas and shopping.'

She frowned, not entirely sure whether he was joking. 'My friends work too, you know.'

'Well, so long as you're not toying with the idea of going back to the office. Mabel needs you.'

'No, I know.' Her fledgling career as a structural surveyor had barely had a chance to get off the ground anyway. Falling pregnant on their honeymoon had meant she'd worked for only seven months after the wedding and even though Mabel was starting at nursery now and Natasha had more free time, she already felt left behind, the friends she had qualified with now in junior management positions with several years' experience behind them. All Natasha had achieved in that time were nappy-changing skills, a full nursery-rhyme repertoire and the ability to function without sleep. Besides, if her prayers were answered, she'd only be back on maternity leave again soon – and it wasn't like the job had fed her soul. It had been a means to an end, a good job to fund a nice lifestyle and even if getting married and pregnant at twenty-two had never been in her plans, she'd ended up in the same place, hadn't she? At least the pet portraits allowed her to make money from doing something she loved. She didn't feel quite so much of a sponge.

She saw Rob frown. 'Mabes, what did we say about sucking your thumb?' he asked, going over and gently pulling it from her mouth. Almost immediately the child started to cry. Peace popped like a bubble in this house at the moment.

Rob looked back at Natasha, almost confused by the regression. It had taken them months to wean her off.

Natasha could only shrug. 'And she sleeps in our bed now, too.' He might as well know all of it. This was no time for postulating the merits of good and bad habits. They were doing whatever it took to just get through.

'. . . Right.' He ran a hand through his hair, the Friday feeling look that had been on his face as he first peered through fading fast. 'Christ, all this on account of a lost toy.'

'Yup,' she sighed. It was her turn to sag. She looked back at the Weimaraner's flat gaze. What would bring them to life?

'Would a bottle of red and a takeaway help?' Rob asked,

knowing how to brighten hers. 'Leave that. Go have a bath. I'll take over here with the Dark Mistress of the Night.'

She chuckled. 'That would have been so perfect – but we're due at the Tennants' tonight, remember?'

She saw his body tense up. 'Please tell me you're kidding.'

'No.' She gave a puzzled frown. 'You can't have forgotten, surely? I literally told you last night.'

He gave a groan and straightened up, rubbing his hands over his face. 'Yes, yes – you probably did, it just slipped my mind. It's been a hell of a week.'

She watched as he shrugged off his suit jacket with jerky, frustrated movements. 'Is everything okay at work?'

'It's fine.' He sighed, sounding weary to his bones. 'Just the usual – too much on and too few people to do it.'

'You *have* to hire new staff, Rob. It can't just be you who's constantly saving the day. You are chronically overworked.' How many times had she told him this? Last Christmas morning, certainly, as he'd flown out the door when Amazon's cloud network had gone down; and again in August when he'd had to leave their Devon holiday early because the university's internal server had crashed the day before A-level results came out. It placed a strain on them as a family, there was no doubt about it. But more than that, Natasha worried about how hard Rob pushed himself. Men his age had heart attacks from half the amount of stress. She had said over and over again that they didn't need such a big house, nor such a fancy one – but he was such a driven man, always wanting the very best for his family.

'It's just this stage – we've got more work than we can handle, but till the contracts earn through . . . We're getting there, though.' He ran a hand through his hair, tired but still handsome. 'Besides, it's better to be too busy than not busy enough.'

'Hmm,' she disagreed. 'Well, I think it's you who needs the bottle of wine and a bath.'

'Uh-uh, it's definitely the other way round. I want to see if you've still got your tan lines.' He winked at her, the gleam never long out of his eyes, and she grinned as he came back over, kissing her lingeringly on the mouth for a moment.

'What time are we expected?' he asked, when she'd pulled back. Mabel was back on the floor mixing the pink and blue dough into an unappealing purple.

'Seven thirty. I've already flagged up that Mabel will be coming with us.'

'Really? Isn't Rosie free?'

'Oh, Rosie's free, but if Moolah isn't around to comfort our girl to sleep, then apparently it can only be me . . . Although I'm hoping she might switch her attentions to you now you're back.' She flashed a smug smile.

'Of course she will,' he cooed, scooping up the toddler again and tickling her in the ribs, making her squeal with delight, before swinging her onto his shoulders – the cue for bathtime. 'She's a daddy's girl, isn't that right, my chickaboo?'

Natasha listened to the two of them disappearing down the corridor and across the hall, climbing the stairs, chattering all the while. The sounds of a happy home, filled once more.

'Grayshott Manor' was picked out in relief when the head-lights swung onto the stone pillars as they turned onto the drive. The electric wrought-iron gates were different beasts to the Stoneleighs' five-bar gate; around them, ancient spe-cimen trees were picked out with spotlights in the dark, as if to light up a performance by the creatures living within their boughs.

The large house was handsome and imposing, sometimes

even a little austere, Natasha thought – early Georgian and blocky in form, built in chilly grey stone, it had yawning windows and attic room dormers that peeped over a parapet ledge like naughty children. In the summer there was a pink rose that bloomed against the wall, majestic for a minute, but at this time of year, the bare thorny vines crept over the facade like broken capillaries. There was an antique Ayres bow rocking horse in the front centre upstairs window – lovely in principle, but its wild, staring eyes and toothy grin always made Mabel cry.

Rob had changed into dark jeans, a fresh shirt and navy velvet smoking jacket; Natasha was in a teal silk midi dress with a bracelet stack and slouchy heeled boots. Mabel was in her pyjamas, but Natasha had jokingly put a velvet bow slide into her hair because 'smart casual' at the Tennants' always meant silently dropping the 'casual'.

'You made it!' Lauren cried as she flung open the door. 'Our local celebrities!'

'. . . Our local what now?' Rob asked, looking baffled, Mabel sitting on his hip.

Natasha laughed, shaking her head as she and Lauren glanced cheeks. 'Oops, he doesn't know. I haven't told him yet.'

Rob frowned. 'Told me what?'

Lauren looked delighted. 'Oh, that's hilarious. I can't believe you don't know, Rob! *Sixteen million* likes about your own family's crisis and you're blissfully unaware! I love it!'

'Nats, what's going on?' Rob's voice had changed, the sense of levity gone.

'Relax,' Natasha said, putting a hand on her husband's arm. It was unlike him to be defensive. 'The post I put on Facebook about Moolah has gone viral, that's all.'

'Viral?' He said the word in the same tone he always said 'virus'; it meant calamity in his world.

'Sixteen million likes, Rob!' Lauren repeated, leading them down the flagstone corridor past yellow candles flickering in bronze sconces, Victorian landscapes dusty in their gilded frames. 'It's insane. Honestly, we've all been so excited—'

Rob caught Natasha by the elbow, allowing Lauren to go on ahead, gesticulating wildly and tossing her long hair, unaware she had lost her audience. 'Why didn't you tell me about this?' he asked in a low voice, no trace of amusement in his gaze.

'I was going to tell you when you got in, but I forgot,' she shrugged. It made no difference to her if sixteen or sixteen million people liked the post – Moolah was still missing.

'You *forgot*? After all the grief we've had this week?'

She arched an eyebrow. 'We?'

He stiffened, hearing the rebuke: *he'd* had a working week of eight-hour sleeps in a corporate hotel. '. . . It was the first thing we talked about, Nats,' he hissed. 'I don't understand how you could fail to mention that sixteen million people are talking about us? What did you put in this post?'

'Rob, relax. Jesus,' she hissed back. 'No one's *talking* about us. People are just sharing the post. They're trying to help.'

'But what did it say?'

'Just that Moolah's missing – where we lost her and when. Some photos—'

'Photos?' he snapped.

'Of course! People can't recognize her without first seeing what she looks like.'

'What photos? Is Mabel in them? Are we?'

She swallowed, realizing the cause of his agitation. He was hot on cyber security – well, he would be – and was forever telling her why she shouldn't be posting selfies: identity theft was big business. Crooks would take a holiday photo and use it to compile a fake account that might be used for anything from trolling to full-blown hacking. 'They do show Mabel, yes,' she admitted. 'But then, I wouldn't just have a photo of Moolah on her own, would I? She would only incidentally be in photos I took of Mabel. I couldn't separate one from the other.'

The truth was she had tried to find photos that showed her daughter's bond with – and dependence on – Moolah. She had to make people understand what a loss it was; this was no mere *toy*. It was a nanny, a sibling and a pet, all rolled into one.

'How many pictures did you post?'

'Five? Six?' If she'd had any idea the population of a small country was going to be privy to their domestic crisis, she would have chosen fewer photos.

'And us?'

'Not of you. Just one of me and Mabes.' That one had been an indulgence, she could admit that. Her favourite photo ever, it was a close-up of her and Mabel, cheek to cheek, with Moolah clutched tight to Mabel's chest.

He closed his eyes, looking weary. 'Well, I guess that's something,' he muttered, pinching his temples. 'My clients?' he added, in reply to her questioning frown as he looked up again. 'It hardly looks good to have *me* at the centre of a viral post when they're hiring me to contain their data!'

'I know. And I'm sorry. I never thought for a moment it would kick off like this.' She glanced up to find Lauren standing in the doorway to the drawing room and watching them bicker, her eyebrows raised, mouth parted, her arms held mid-air as if frozen in beckoning them towards the drawing room.

'Sorry, I couldn't remember if we'd locked the car,' Natasha smiled, hurrying after her.

'I was just saying, Rob – do you want to know *how* it all went viral?' Lauren asked, biting her lip as though holding back her excitement.

'Every fibre of my being wants to know,' he deadpanned.

Lauren threw her head back and laughed as they walked through into the drawing room where everyone was congregated. Immediately the ambient noise levels went up, old friends turning to see them as though they really were celebrities.

'Harry Styles shared it,' Lauren said proudly, stopping by a console table and pouring some champagne into a couple of flutes. 'Then Justin Bieber picked it up, saying the same had happened to him as a boy and how it had broken his heart. Well, the Beliebers went into hyperdrive. You can *imagine*.' She rolled her eyes.

'Oh yes, I'm imagining all right,' Rob said, catching Natasha's eye as she took Mabel from his arms, both of them a little sore from the disagreement in the hall.

She went over to the small group standing by the fire – Hels and Sara were being entertained by their host, Zach Tennant.

'How is she?' Sara asked, chucking Mabel on the cheek as though she'd been in some terrible accident.

'Stubborn! And entirely oblivious to the drama.' Natasha handed Mabel over to her godmother, who was reaching for her again.

'Do you know the fuss you've caused, young lady?' Hels asked her with mock sternness. 'Do you? You've triggered long-repressed trauma in Justin Bieber!'

Mabel kicked her legs excitedly, not understanding but sensing it was thrilling.

Natasha's eyes grazed the room, looking for Hels's date.

The Dave. Had she been persuaded to bring him along after all? She saw Marty, Sara's husband, standing by the twelve-foot Christmas tree, deep in conversation with a man she didn't recognize. He was blonde, tall and looked like he played rugby.

'Honestly, I can't *believe* how it's all gone off since book club,' Sara said, bringing the conversation back to the drama again. Natasha had a sense it was all they'd been talking about that evening. Hollywood names weren't often dropped into dinner-party conversation in Frome. 'Is it true Amal Clooney shared it too?'

'I'm not sure. Maybe.' Natasha shrugged. 'To be honest, I don't really care. I just want someone to actually *find* Moolah.'

'Still lost?' Hels commiserated.

'Yeah.' The vast amount of worldwide attention was only serving to spell out how hopeless it all was. If sixteen million people couldn't find their beloved lost toy . . . Did they have to accept Moolah was gone for good?

'How's Rob coping with his new celebrity status? I must say, he's not looking best pleased,' Zach frowned.

'Well, he's only just heard,' she grimaced. 'I may have forgotten to tell him when he got in.'

'He didn't know?' Sara asked, looking as delighted as Lauren had done.

She shook her head, watching her handsome husband nod benignly to Lauren's excitement. He had that air of bemusement he often wore. She put it down to his decade of seniority on them, as though permanently surprised to find himself here, with all of them.

'Hmm. Well, if you'll excuse me, ladies, I'll have a quick word with him before he hits my wine cellar. Trouble's afoot with the Christmas Eve meet,' Zach said sombrely.

'Oh?'

'Yes. Frank Watson's saying we can't cross his land. He's still irked about the state of his blackthorn hedge from last time.' He drained his glass of Bollinger like a commando readying to storm a building. 'Be right back.'

'Well, this isn't so shabby,' Sara said as the three women clinked champagne glasses, pleased to be alone together. Hels put Mabel down on the ground and watched as she toddled off towards the Tennants' spaniels, who were sleeping in a large tweed bed in a corner.

The room was grandly furnished with yellow silk curtains and chintzy sofas, a huge old Ziegler rug and lots of brown furniture from Zach's family. His parents had owned this house, and his grandparents before them. Their friendship group very often celebrated New Year's Eve here; as the biggest house it comfortably accommodated even five families, as numbers of kids were gradually added to year on year.

'So come on, give us the goss,' Sara said, lowering her voice. 'Did Harry Styles slip into your DMs? Or Mr B?'

'And why would they do that?'

'Well, I thought they might've sent you a personal message of support. Justin did that post talking about how it's the little things that can matter the most. I thought he might have . . . reached out.'

'I think he's done quite enough already,' Natasha said, sipping her drink and feeling decidedly less excited about it all. Once she had got over the shock of discovering Julia's granddaughter had come good, and had woken up the morning after book club to find Harry Styles's post had garnered over a million shares as she slept, she'd had to turn off all notifications. Her phone felt ready to explode, and she could spend every waking moment of the next month reading through the comments and still wouldn't get through them all.

Sara's eyes narrowed. 'Have you actually checked, though? I know what you're like. You leave me on unread for days.'

'Sara, I'm surviving off an average of three hours' sleep a night. I really haven't got the time to read all their comments. There's over thirty thousand. I couldn't get past the first two hundred!'

'I'm not talking about comments. I'm talking about messages. DMs. There's a difference, Nats. The Beliebers will just be commenting on Justin's sweetness, but if anyone actually *has* Moolah, they'll DM you, not leave a comment.'

'Oh.'

Sara slapped a hand out. 'Jesus, y'are useless. Utterly useless. Pass me your phone.'

Natasha did so without protest. Unlike almost everyone she knew, her phone was not the Holy Grail and it was not the centre of her world.

'Hey.'

They looked up to find the blonde rugby-playing vet coming to join them.

'You must be Dave,' Natasha said, smiling brightly at her oldest friend's new boyfriend. 'I'm Natasha Stoneleigh.'

He smiled back, and she immediately liked the softness in his eyes. On first impressions, she gauged that he had a steady manner, placid and understated – everything Hels didn't know she needed. 'I know. I've heard a lot about you. You've been best friends since primary school. I'm under no illusions that it's you I've got to impress tonight.'

'Oh, trust me – you save animals on a daily basis. We're all already impressed.'

'You might say differently if you'd seen me this afternoon, up to my elbows in a cow's uterus—'

Sara spluttered on her drink.

'There's more than a few moments of farce in my job.'

Seven years of veterinary school but none of the ego of their doctor friends? Natasha was sold already. 'So how are you finding it here?'

'Busy. I've been here almost two months and I've not stopped.'

'I'd have come to introduce myself before, only, we have a dog and a goldfish,' she shrugged. 'So there wasn't much natural opportunity.'

'I was with Hels when the goldfish sadly . . . passed. I tried CPR, but it was too late.'

She chuckled, pressing a finger to her lips. 'Shhh. Mabel still hasn't noticed.' Her eyes scanned the room for her daughter, finding her sitting in the dogs' bed now and tapping their heads as she talked to them with a very earnest expression. The spaniels didn't seem remotely perturbed by this.

'And what do you do?' he asked.

'Well, funnily enough, I work with animals too,' she said. 'But my work's less hands-on.'

'Oh yes?'

She grinned. 'I'm an animal artist; I do portraits of people's pets.'

He laughed. 'I see. I wasn't quite sure where you were going with that description.'

'She's properly brilliant at it,' Hels said. 'You should see them. In fact . . .' She pulled her phone from her trouser back pocket and brought up Natasha's Instagram page. 'Look at that. Amazing, right?'

Dave took the phone and peered closer. 'Hm, they really are good. That border collie.'

'Rona, yes. She's a sweetie.'

'You've got the look so well. And the fur, how do you make it look so real?'

'Just detail. A-lot-a-lot-a-lot of teeny tiny brushstrokes.'

'And you do oils as well as sketches?'

'I do all mediums – watercolours, oil, acrylics, charcoal and pencil. It all depends on the person's budget, the animal, the look they want.'

He handed the phone back to Hels with a thoughtful look. 'Hmm.'

There was something in his contemplation that stirred Natasha's attention.

'I had a client at my previous practice, I'm just trying to recall her name,' he murmured. 'She's got a few horses I used to treat; her husband hunts and he owns a particularly fine stallion. At my last appointment, she said she wanted to commission a fine portrait of the horse and asked if I knew of anyone. I didn't, sadly. It's a shame, as I think she'd have loved to see your work.'

'I imagine she'll have found someone by now,' Natasha murmured, thinking a stallion hunter would have been a distinct step up from poodles and budgies.

'Yes, this was back in the summer. But if you're happy for me to give her your details, I can try to get in touch with her and ask. You never know, she might still be looking!'

'Where does she live?'

'Snowshill, near Broadway.'

'Worcestershire?'

'I think it's Gloucestershire, actually. Right on the border. But it's about sixty-odd miles from here.'

She wrinkled her nose. 'Mmm, that's quite far. It'd be a lot of driving, and my hours are pretty constrained by Mabel's nursery pick-ups.'

'Sure, of course,' Dave shrugged.

'Not impossible, though,' Hels said quickly, glancing at

her. Unlike Rob, she was always on at Natasha to take on more work. Hels saw the restlessness that fizzed through her limbs, as though her energy field was compressed by village life.

'Who's Anya Ebner?' Sara asked suddenly, looking up. She had been scrolling through Natasha's phone all the while.

'Huh?'

'Anya Ebner. You've got twenty-three messages from her. In caps lock!'

Hels scowled. 'Sounds like a lunatic, then. Steer clear.'

But Natasha reached for the phone. 'Let me see that.' She clicked on the name.

I know you must be receiving thousands of messages but PLEASE PLEASE READ THIS . . .

Natasha's mouth parted into a small 'o', her eyes growing wide as she read and then reread the words. She took a step back as if she'd been pushed, a hand going over her mouth. 'Oh my God! I don't believe it! She's found Moolah!'

The words seemed to carry through the room, the other conversations stopping mid-sentence. She looked across at Mabel but the child had fallen asleep beside the dogs, the three tiny mammals curled like autumn leaves in the tweedy bed.

She turned to face Rob instead, her eyes shining. 'They've found her!' she laughed, but more quietly now, not wanting to wake Mabel. Even this good news could wait for sleep.

'Moolah's alive?' Lauren gasped, with typical melodrama, prompting disdainful looks from Rob and her own husband.

'Yes! They've found her! They've got her!' She gave a laugh that seemed to come from the very centre of her, the stranglehold of angst of the past week beginning to loosen like an axed vine.

'Where? Who are they?' Sara asked.

'She says . . .' Natasha's heart was beating at triple time and she pressed her hand to her chest, as if to keep it in. She couldn't believe this was happening. They had actually found the needle in the haystack? '. . . She says her friend found Moolah behind a curtain in the apartment in Vienna while she was FaceTiming him . . . She says she lives in Vienna and that she booked the apartment on behalf of this friend, who stayed for a night en route to Asia. She says he's travelling in Nepal now.'

Hels's eyes narrowed. 'Wait – so the toy's with this friend in Nepal? Or she's got it?'

Natasha read the message again, the words swimming before her eyes as adrenaline took over. 'It looks like . . . hmm . . . I think it's in Nepal.'

'*Nepal?*' Hels had to laugh. 'So pretty much the most remote place on the planet?'

'Remote doesn't mean desolate,' Rob said quickly, coming over and placing a hand on Natasha's shoulder. He squeezed it warmly and she looked back at him with bright eyes – feeling their closeness on the Maldivian beaches return again like a fresh tide, their bicker in the hall all forgotten now. 'Kathmandu's a modern city like any other. They'll have logistics companies.'

'Yeah, but people don't travel to Nepal for the *nightlife*, Rob,' Hels argued. 'The guy's not in Kathmandu. He'll be up a mountain somewhere.'

Lauren gasped again, excitedly. 'Do you think he's going up Everest?'

'I doubt it, if he's packing random children's toys,' Zach said. 'Weight is everything at that level of mountaineering.'

'Hmm, maybe he is up a mountain, though. Anya says he isn't somewhere where he can post it at the moment.' Natasha bit her lip anxiously, reading and rereading the words. Moolah was somewhere in Nepal? Was that any better than somewhere in Vienna? Now she was even further away.

Sara stepped forward and gently put a hand on her arm. 'You know, you have to be careful with things like this. Take it all with a pinch of salt; there's a lot of pranksters out there.'

'Prankster?' Natasha shook her head at her pessimism. This was real, not a joke. It had to be. No one would be so cruel as to taunt a young girl. Would they?

'Seriously. I wouldn't rush into telling Mabel yet – not until you're sure. This woman's saying a friend of hers has got it and taken it to Nepal.' Sara winced. 'That's rather convenient, isn't it? They raise your hopes, keep you dangling . . . People pull stunts like this all the time.'

Natasha gave a small strangled laugh as she looked around and saw the growing caution on all her friends' faces. 'But why? Why would they do that?'

'Power? For the lols?' Sara shrugged. 'Sad lonely keyboard warriors.'

Natasha felt reality begin to bare its teeth again, her heart pounding harder as that beam of sudden dazzling hope began to shimmer and fade into bitter, crushing disappointment. She looked back at Mabel, double-checking the child was still asleep. Perhaps her friends were right – it was better that she hadn't overheard. Until they knew for certain, they couldn't afford to raise her hopes too. 'But . . . this Anya . . . she says he'll send it to us when he's next back in civilization.' Even as she said it, though, she heard how the words sounded. Vague promises. Distant strangers.

'So he is doing Everest!' Lauren exclaimed triumphantly.

'There's more to Nepal than Mount Everest,' Zach sighed.

'Like what?'

Zach couldn't think of a reply.

Lauren looked back at Natasha. 'Well, if he can't post it over to you . . .'

'I am not flying out to Nepal!' Natasha laughed, knowing exactly what her friend was about to suggest, but the sound was brittle. She looked back at the group, seeing their sceptical expressions. 'Oh God . . . it's a hoax, isn't it?' There were too many ifs and buts, too many not-quites.

There was a silence and Natasha knew she mustn't buckle as she felt her hope wither and die as quickly as it had come. This was a dinner party; she couldn't dissolve in a puddle of tears because her daughter's toy was still lost, as lost now as it had been when they'd walked in.

'Well, how has she signed off, this Anya?' Lauren asked hopefully.

'Just that this friend has said he'll send it back when he can.'

'No, not good enough,' Hels said decisively, seeing how Natasha's face had fallen. 'Flush her out!'

'How?'

She watched as Hels narrowed her eyes, her brilliant cunning mind beginning to plot. 'Tell her . . . tell her to give you the address of the apartment where you all apparently stayed. That's not public knowledge, is it? You didn't put it up anywhere?'

Natasha shook her head. 'No. I just said it was lost in an Airbnb in Vienna.'

'Okay. So then that's the first test – she needs to confirm the apartment address.'

'Yes!' Sara cried, warming to the detective theme, champagne flying in an arc out of the top of her flute as she leaped forward excitedly. 'And then tell her you want proof her friend has got Moolah. Demand this mate's email and tell him he needs to send you a photo himself.'

'If he's halfway up Everest, though . . .' Lauren began.

'He's not up Everest, darling! How many times must we say it?' Zach said exasperatedly.

'You can probably still get connection standing on the top of Everest. Most mountaineers use satellite phones now,' Dave shrugged.

Hels glanced adoringly at her new boyfriend, as if this nugget about satellite phones confirmed her suspicion of his all-round brilliance. 'Exactly. Message her back right now and tell her we want proof of life.'

'Proof of life?' Rob laughed.

But Hels wasn't laughing. 'We need to know for sure.' She pointed a finger silently towards his sleeping daughter, her goddaughter, curled up in the dog bed, thumb in her mouth and stroking her cheek with the dog's ear as she dreamed childish dreams. 'Proof. Of. Life.'

Chapter Nine

Whinfell, October 2018

'I'm fine,' Natasha sighed.

'She's fine,' Hels echoed.

'Stop fussing.'

'Y'all need to stop fussing.'

'Hels?'

'Yes?'

'Stop fussing.'

'Oh.'

Natasha sighed and pushed herself up to sitting. 'I don't need to lie down. I'm not sick. I'm not hurt.'

'But you were paralysed. *Again*,' Sara said. 'That's the second time today.'

'I am aware. And I don't know what's going on,' she sighed, feeling drained by it all. 'But I feel absolutely normal now, so please . . . chill.'

'Is it vertigo?' Lauren asked, looking pleased to have thought of the prospect. 'If it keeps happening every time you climb high up, it might be vertigo.'

'It's never been an issue before, but . . .' Natasha shrugged. 'Yeah. Maybe it's that.' Why not? It was as plausible a reason as any.

'Are you worried about anything?' Rachel asked through slitted eyes.

'Rach, she's organizing a wedding,' Hels snapped. 'Of course she's worried. Have you ever had a sane bride? Answer honestly.' A finger was pointed at her accusingly.

Rachel hesitated for a moment. 'No. Never. They're all nutters.'

'Thank you. She's stressed, but that is normal in these circumstances, so we're not going to start panicking,' Hels said, sounding distinctly panicked.

'I'll tell you what is going to make me panic,' Natasha said, watching closely.

'What?' they answered as one, concern on all their faces.

'Being sober for my hen weekend. It's bad enough that I've made an idiot of myself in front of hundreds of people—'

'And the hot climbing instructor,' Lizzie interjected.

'. . . Thanks, Lizzie.' Natasha really didn't want to be reminded of that. 'But if we don't start having some fun, this is going to go down in history as the worst hen do ever—'

Sara looked like she might cry. The 'outdoor activities' idea had been hers, after Natasha had said she didn't want anything involving a club or a stripper. Hels had been incandescent that *not* wanting those things had been translated to mean she must, therefore, want to 'become a tree hugger and swim with toddlers'. No one had had the heart to tell Sara that going to Center Parcs, instead of London or Paris, was an atrocious idea, and it was only the revelation that Sara had managed to book them into one of the luxury treehouses that had kept the weekend on track.

'—And that is all completely my fault,' Natasha said

quickly, pressing a hand to her chest. 'I take full responsibility for the failure. In Hels's own words, I am a chicken and not a hen. So, I think drinking ourselves to oblivion is the only way to rescue this once and for all.'

'Agreed!' Hels said, jumping up off the floor, one arm held aloft like a Roman general as she marched into the kitchen. 'And on this point, I have come prepared.' They heard the sound of glass clattering, and she returned a moment later with a box of bottles in each arm.

'Six bottles of prosecco, three bottles of Stoli and three bottles of Bombay Sapphire.'

'For six of us?' Lauren looked concerned.

'She stipulated oblivion. Oblivion I have brought,' Hels said staunchly.

'Did you bring any mixers?' Lizzie asked.

'Huh?'

'You know – Coke, orange, tonic? Or are we drinking neat?'

Hels winced. 'Mixers. Fuck.'

'I brought crisps,' Rachel said, holding up a large bag of Doritos.

'Anything else? Any olives? Pretzels? I said you were in charge of all snacks,' Sara said sternly. 'You know I hate Doritos.'

Rachel reached into the carrier bag and pulled out a bag of Hula Hoops instead. 'Dinner.'

'You do know it's only three o'clock?' Lauren asked nervously, as crisps bags rustled and wine bottles clinked.

Hels scowled as she pulled the foil off one of the prosecco bottles. 'What's your point?'

'I'll get some glasses.' Lizzie got up and went to the kitchen. 'Nats, while we're getting ourselves sorted, you can stop sitting there looking pretty and go and see the special surprise we've brought especially for you. It's on your bed,' Hels said with a wicked look.

'Oh *no*!' Natasha groaned, falling back into the sofa cushions. 'You said you wouldn't!'

'We lied!' Sara giggled.

'What is it?' A tutu and neon-pink tiara, no doubt.

'Go through and see,' Sara shrugged.

Rachel took Natasha by the wrist and pulled her up to standing. 'Go on!'

A few moments later, Natasha shrieked from the bedroom. 'You have got to be kidding!' she cried. 'I can't wear that!'

'Oh yes you can! And *don't* come back through till you've got it on!' Hels ordered in her most authoritative voice.

'Oh my God,' she wailed. 'It's hideous! . . . It's disgusting . . . Where did you find this? . . . Oh my God . . .' Her distant voice modulated through the stages of undressing. 'It's giving me electric shocks . . . It's making my hair static!'

Several minutes passed in silence, but for low groans coming from the bedroom.

'What are you doing?' Rachel asked finally.

'I can't do up the zip! It's rusty!'

Several moments later, Natasha wandered back into the living area – it was more of a shuffle really, her legs getting tangled in so much fabric. She was clutching a 1980s satin wedding dress to her body, so shiny it was practically mirrored. The bodice plunged to a point and was covered in artificial-looking pearls, with lacy sleeves that voluminously puffed at the shoulders and tightly tapered down to the wrist. The skirt was gathered in rococo Bo Peep swags and on her head was a band of silk roses, an explosion of stiff tulle attached to it that could have taken someone's eye out.

The others collapsed on the floor laughing.

'Oh God, it's even worse than I'd hoped!' Hels cried, clutching her sides.

'What is *this* for?' Natasha queried, pulling on a fabric loop at the cuff.

'I think that goes over your middle finger, so it goes down over the back of your hand,' Sara said helpfully.

'Morticia Addams style, you mean?' Natasha grimaced as the lace sleeve was pulled into a sharp point. '. . . How nice.'

'I found it in the charity shop,' Sara said, looking very pleased with herself. 'I was instructed to find the very worst one I could. I went all around Bristol before I came across that!'

'Well, all I can say is mission accomplished,' Natasha smiled, giving a cheesy double thumbs-up. 'Ritual humiliation is go!'

'Listen, it could be a lot worse,' Hels said with one of her 'be grateful' looks. 'We could have made you *go out* in that.'

Natasha gave one of Lauren's signature horrified gasps.

Lizzie was filling their prosecco glasses. 'Right, everyone, neck that.' A glass was put in Natasha's hand and she – along with the others – downed it, feeling the burn and liking it.

'And again.' Lizzie held the bottle out.

'What, already?' Lauren asked. She wasn't a big drinker.

'This is a hen party that has already required medical assistance today. Now it's in cardiac arrest. No quicker way to shock it into life again than by downing some drinks. Now neck it.'

'Yes, sir,' Lauren muttered, doing as she was told.

'Shall I put some music on?' Sara asked, wandering over to the Sonos and connecting her Bluetooth.

'Before this gets any messier, I'm going to nip down to the supermarket,' Hels said suddenly, pulling on her boots.

'What? No!' Natasha cried. The supermarket was in the centre of the village complex, an eight-minute cycle ride away.

'I'll be right back, don't worry. I'm just going to get some mixers for the spirits.'

'But you've just downed two glasses of prosecco! You can't get on a bike now. You could run over some poor kid on his way to the bouncy castle!'

'Which is why I have to go right now. Later will be too late. I've got twenty minutes before the booze enters my bloodstream. Time me!' And she shot out the door, running down the treehouse steps only to return twenty seconds later for her purse. '. . . Time me,' she panted, staggering back out again, racing the clock.

'That's the prosecco done!' Lizzie hollered over the music, shaking the upended bottle for the very last drops.

The others, dancing in the middle of the room, didn't stop. They'd had a bottle each and were already feeling the happy effects, waving their arms in the air and singing badly at the tops of their voices. Natasha had almost forgotten she was dressed like Elton John's bride and was standing on the arms of the sofa, belting out the lyrics to Justin Bieber's 'Baby' as though she was Meatloaf.

'Vodka, then!' Hels yelled back, her glass already empty. She wove a path over to the kitchen and unsteadily helped pour monster shots of Stolichnaya into the water tumblers as Lizzie opened the Coke. She was carrying them back between splayed fingers when she saw the group standing at the door.

Natasha had her back turned and was swooping and diving

as she sang, completely lost in the moment, but one by one the others noticed, falling still and silent, amusement dancing in their eyes as she rocked on.

'. . . What? . . . What is it?' Natasha panted, pink-cheeked and bright-eyed, eventually noticing as the song ended that she had been alone in her raptures. Feeling a breeze at her back, she turned, and was so surprised to see the group of men standing there, she stepped backwards off the sofa arm and fell back into the cushions. White satin billowed around her like a parachute.

'Sorry! We did knock,' the guy nearest said, laughing. 'Great singing, by the way!' he grinned, looking directly at Natasha.

'Ben, you made it!' Hels said delightedly, rushing forward and giving them the vodka Cokes instead, even though they were carrying beers. 'Quick, down those. You'll have to play catch-up.'

'Who . . . ?' Lauren looked at Hels questioningly as the four men downed their drinks without hesitation.

'We met down in the supermarket earlier, when I went to get the mixers. Ben here was working on the till and about to clock off. Then Nats's lovely rescuer Tom came in and we all got chatting, and I told them to find a few mates and come join us! Livens things up a bit.' Hels gave a flirty wink.

'It looks pretty lively already,' one of the guys said, seeing all the empty prosecco bottles lined up on the side table. He had a goatee and his long dark hair was pulled back in a ponytail.

'Oh, trust me, we're only just getting started,' Hels said with another wink. 'What's your name?'

'I'm Jack. I work in the bike hut, doing all the repairs. And this is Andy, he's a chef.'

'Ooh, good to know,' Rachel said. 'If we get munchies later.'

Andy grinned. 'Yeah, I'm the one you want hanging around. Short order's my thing.' He had strawberry blonde hair and a nasty-looking burn mark on his hand, as if to prove his culinary credentials.

'Long order's Lizzie's,' Hels said, linking an arm through her friend's proudly. 'She's just got the lease on her own teashop.'

'Yeah?' Andy grinned as Lizzie stood a little taller.

'Tom you already know, of course,' Ben said, stepping aside to let his friend further into the room. 'He's a climbing instructor—'

'And paramedic,' Hels added.

Natasha gave a feeble laugh, but she wasn't feeling at all amused. She had been reassured that no one was going to see her in this ridiculous get-up, least of all *him*, the man she had already humiliated herself in front of several times today.

'So you're the bride,' Ben said, grinning at the sight of her costume.

'What makes you think that? I always dress like this,' she deadpanned.

'Nats is our bride but she's not a very good hen. She's been self-demoted to chicken,' Hels joked. 'This is a chicken party now.'

'Oh! Poor Nats! But she's making up for it now, though,' Sara said loyally, squeezing Natasha around her shoulders and puffing up her satin skirt, as if trying to make her look more bridal.

'You look pretty young to be getting married,' Jack said, casually smacking his hand down to open a beer bottle on the edge of the windowsill. Natasha immediately knew Hels would find that devastatingly attractive.

'Twenty-two,' she shrugged. 'Not so young.'

'It is pretty young,' Tom contradicted, swiping the freshly opened beer from Jack's hand without asking and swigging it.

'Oi!' Jack protested.

Natasha watched. Tom had changed out of his all-black climbing gear and was wearing jeans and a hoodie. He was broad-shouldered and tall, she already knew that, but the switch to off-duty clothes seemed to have changed his energy too, as though he was a completely different man to the one she had met earlier. There he had been a professional, a helper, an employee. Somewhat anonymous. A guy with nice eyes just doing his job.

But he wasn't working now and, standing in their treehouse with a beer in his hand, it felt strange to know how it had felt holding onto him as she stood on his feet, his muscles moving against her; his arm clutching her tightly as he brought her down the wall . . . Even through her paralysing fear, that awareness of his physicality had broken past, surfacing like bubbles before they sank into the depths again.

'It's because Tash's fiancé is an older man,' Rachel grinned as Lizzie handed back round some refilled vodka tumblers. 'He's getting on a bit. He can't afford to wait to get her down the aisle.'

'Yeah? How much older?' Andy asked.

Natasha brought her mind back to the present. 'Only ten years. She's exaggerating, as usual.' She rolled her eyes, but the raised eyebrows of the group of guys appeared to contradict her again. Andy started coughing, as if his beer had gone down the wrong way.

'How did you meet him?' Ben asked.

Natasha saw that Tom was staring at the ground, holding his beer. He looked bored. 'He drove into me.'

'*What?*'

It was the typical response. No one ever expected this. 'Yeah. He T-boned me at a junction. We swapped details and then . . .' She shrugged. 'He rang an hour later asking if he could take me to dinner. To say sorry.'

'Sorry my arse!' Ben spluttered.

That was also a typical response.

'Oh! So it was the thunderbolt, was it then?' Jack quipped. 'Love at first sight and all that?'

Natasha didn't reply. She didn't want to say that it hadn't been, at least not for her. When she and Rob had swapped numbers, she hadn't for a moment thought about him in that way. Yes, he had nice eyes – sexy eyes – but as far as she was concerned, he was too old for her. But then he had been so charming and attentive; he'd chased her so hard and talked about their future together in a way that no one had ever spoken to her before, and she had felt herself fall. All the guys she'd met at university were just driven by lust – hook-ups, sexts, Tinder – but Rob was beyond all that. He was a mature man who wanted what she wanted: a big family and a home. She had instinctively sensed that with him she would never be alone again.

Like her, he was orphaned. His parents were dead, but they had died not drawn-out deaths in hospital like hers, but together in their sleep, killed by carbon monoxide poisoning from a faulty boiler in their holiday villa in the Caribbean. Unlike her, Rob had siblings – an older sister and a younger brother – but they were estranged following a dispute over his parents' estate. His sister had claimed for herself pieces of jewellery which their mother had specifically told Rob she was keeping for him to give to his future wife. The brother had sided against him too, pulling a similar stunt with their father's beloved sports car, and Rob had seen neither one of them since the funeral.

Natasha still hadn't met them, though she had tried countless times to talk him into brokering peace. She knew what it was to be alone in this world and she didn't want it for him. They had each other, it was true, but that still wasn't enough – not if he actually had options. But it was still too soon and Rob's lingering pain was such that his body almost folded inwards any time she tried to bring up the idea of inviting them to the wedding. He was adamant he wouldn't have their day 'soured' by simmering feuds. The wedding was going to be tiny, sacred and intimate, just them and a few friends as witnesses – his best man James, and of course Hels as her chief bridesmaid. It was going to be *bijou*.

But none of that could be explained quickly to complete strangers and when they heard the story of how they met – making assumptions about an irresistible attraction – it felt somehow disloyal to contradict them. It seemed brittle and graceless to correct fantasy with fact.

'When's the wedding?'

She swallowed, feeling the familiar pitch in her stomach. 'Next weekend, actually. In Devon.'

'Jeez. How mad is that? Here you are tonight, in Cumbria, partying with us,' Jack said. 'And this time next week you'll be a Mrs!'

'In a *much* nicer white dress, though,' Lauren said, looking pleased by the prospect. Though Natasha's wider friendship group couldn't attend the ceremony – the tall, round folly where they were saying their vows could only accommodate six people and a table – still she had been at pains to include them as much as she could. Rachel was doing her flowers; Lizzie had made the cake. Sara had organized this weekend and Lauren had been the Chief Dress Inspector, arranging Natasha's various boutique appointments and fittings, and having the last word on everything from shoes to nail colour to 'something blue'.

'So what's the groom doing tonight, while you're partying with the likes of us?'

Natasha wished he hadn't asked that. She bit her lip. 'He's playing golf at Wentworth with his best man.'

There was a silence and she knew she couldn't have made him sound more middle-aged if she'd tried. Andy, Ben and Jack held their amusement in check for all of three seconds, before almost spraying beer everywhere. She doubted any of them had ever picked up a golf club. She certainly couldn't see them in the shorts and long Argyle socks.

'Well, he's a lucky fella, this old bloke who plays golf but can't drive . . . But he's not sealed the deal *just* yet!' Ben laughed, holding his beer bottle aloft. 'Let's assume nothing! So in that spirit, I propose a toast to the chicken here!'

'To the chicken!' everyone yelled. Everyone except Tom, who just lifted his bottle in silence. 'Down the hatch!'

They all obliged, gulping down beer or vodka, whatever was in their hands. Natasha watched Tom, seeing how he looked back at her as he put his empty bottle down on the windowsill and took another. She felt the room give a little spin as he held her gaze, even as he tipped his head back and drank that beer down too. He was on a mission to get wasted. They all were. She was a bottle of prosecco ahead of him.

Someone – Sara – turned the music up, the songs shuffling through a Y2K playlist. Natasha already knew she would never hear 'Baby' again and not remember the mortification of being caught in full performance mode wearing this ridiculous dress.

She looked away. She was already drunk but she needed to be a lot drunker. She needed to dance, not get melancholy. She got up and swished into the kitchen, knocking an empty bottle from a side table with her voluminous skirt. She found the vodka bottle on the worktop and poured herself a hefty dose, reaching for the orange juice when someone came and stood beside her. She knew who. She could tell from the scent of his shower gel.

'Hey.'

She turned to find Tom leaning against the counter. 'Hey,' she breathed, feeling a sudden rush through her blood. Adrenaline? Did she associate him with danger now? Did that make him her safety?

She held up the Stoli bottle in one hand, waggling it questioningly, but he held up his fresh beer. He held her gaze and she felt suddenly shy, as though they'd skipped ahead a few steps and met each other the wrong way round, going straight to full-body contact before even a handshake. Or a conversation.

'So how are you feeling now?'

'Oh fine,' she said dismissively, not wanting him to linger on her crises. 'Clearly my day dramatically improved after leaving you.' She playfully pinched the skirt of the dress and splayed it out, showing off the full shininess.

He grinned. 'Clearly. If your fiancé could only see you now.'

Natasha realized she was glad he couldn't. 'And you? How was the rest of your afternoon? Next lesson went well?'

'Yep. A bunch of nine-year-olds racing about like lunatics

and not listening to a word I said.' He shrugged his eyebrows and took another swig of his beer. 'Same old, same old.'

'Well, at least it was uneventful. No more dramas of the wrong sort.'

'Who says your drama was the wrong sort?'

'Ha! I'm sure you've got much better things to be doing with your time than rescuing the likes of me.'

'It was the best thing to happen to me all day, actually. Rescuing a beautiful woman not once but twice.' He grinned. 'I feel like a superhero now.' He puffed up his chest and thumped it once.

He thought she was beautiful? She laughed, feeling skitterish.

'So have you worked here long?' She sipped her drink, looking at him over the rim of the glass. He was rolling the cap of a beer bottle along on its side. He had a good profile – straight nose and full lips . . .

He glanced up, caught her looking and smiled. 'Just a few months. I'm saving up for my next trip.'

'Oh? Where are you going?'

'The States.'

'Wow.'

'Yeah.'

'Whereabouts?'

'Yosemite.'

'Climbing?'

He nodded.

She bit her lip nervously. No wonder he'd forgotten to clip on his harness standing on that little rope bridge. It must have been like climbing the stairs for him. 'How long will you go for?'

'Until the money or the visa runs out, whichever is first.'

He shrugged and she watched him roll back his shoulders, as though the mention of it was enough to trigger his body into action; he didn't seem aware he was doing it. Her eyes travelled over him.

She realized she was staring again. 'It's your thing, is it?'

'My first love and probably my last. I grew up doing it. My mum was really into it, and she used to drag me and my sister along.'

'Your sister climbs too?'

'Oh yeah. She's the best of all of us.'

'Really?' She liked his lack of ego in admitting it. 'How old is she?'

'Twenty-three. She's my twin, actually.'

'Stop it!' Natasha gasped, pressing a hand to her chest in earnest. 'You're a twin? I always wanted to be a twin!'

'*Don't* ask if we're identical,' he grinned, pointing his beer bottle towards her warningly.

'As if!'

'Oh, you wouldn't believe the number of people who ask it.' He laughed, shaking his head and taking another swig of beer.

'Who's older?'

'Lottie. By three minutes.'

'So you're the little brother,' she murmured, watching him, building up a picture of him and his family. 'Any other siblings?'

'No, it's just the two of us.'

'Does your dad climb too? I've got this image of you all now – ruddy cheeks, climbing trees.'

'Nah, he's a physics teacher. He's always telling us he knows too much about the laws of gravity to do anything so dumb as try to defy them.'

146

'Oh dear! It doesn't sound like he approves.'

'That's putting it lightly. He thinks I'm a complete bum.'

She frowned. In spite of his casual tone, she could hear the pain in his words. 'Oh. I'm sorry. That's sad.'

He shrugged. 'Different strokes. Different folks.' He took another swig of his drink, but there was a slight hardness in his tone now. 'I don't care. I just do my own thing and live my life on my terms. My mum always had this mantra – *Do today what must be done, for who knows? Tomorrow, death comes.*'

'Oh, that's morbid!'

'Is it? I think it's the opposite. It makes me live in the moment and go for what I want. It's a Buddhist thing, I think.'

'You're a Buddhist?'

'No. I'm just a guy who believes in seizing the moment.'

His gaze was steady upon her, and she felt all the words leave her head. It suddenly felt as if he might seize her. It was the drink befuddling her, she knew that. Their social interactions had been hijacked by their premature physical familiarity, their manners dislocated now that she knew what it felt like to have him hold her and press her against him . . .

'And you? I understand you're a structural surveyor.' He grinned. 'Really wouldn't have guessed that.'

'No? What would you have said?'

'Hmm.' It was as if she'd given permission for him to scrutinize her at last. He put his bottle down and looked at her intently, narrowing his eyes and letting his gaze travel up and down her slowly, deliberating. He may as well have been trailing his fingers over her bare skin; it made her want to shiver, but she knew she had to suppress it.

'I'd have said an artist.'

What? She fell still. How could he have known . . . ?

He reached forward, and she startled a little as he picked

up her right arm. He looked at her for a moment before he turned her arm gently, exposing the underside of her wrist, slowly rubbing his thumb over a smudge of dark green paint. He looked back at her with a slow smile.

She swallowed. How had he even seen that? It was tiny; she'd been painting minutes before Hels had come to pick her up yesterday and bring her here. 'Well, in my dreams perhaps,' she said quietly, aware that her pulse was rocketing beneath his fingers and betraying the invisible effect he had upon her.

'Didn't you know dreams can come true?' A flicker of laughter danced in his eyes, but something else too.

'For you, maybe. You can go away and climb for months at a time.'

'And you can't paint?'

'I have rent to pay. Very few artists are lucky enough to make their rent.'

'Anything's possible if you want something enough.' He looked down, seeing he was still holding her arm. '. . . Would you like your arm back?' he smiled.

'Why, thank you. So kind.' It felt warm from his touch and she wished she could press it to her cheek. She caught herself mid-wish and stiffened. He took another swig of his drink, but the preliminary chit-chatty conversation that had seemed so easy between them suddenly felt stiff. The room seemed smaller, as if they were growing in it, becoming bigger and filling it up.

He looked at her again. 'So, the lucky man – what does he do?'

He. She realized she hadn't mentioned Rob's name and that Tom wasn't asking for it either. Instead he hovered undefined and formless between them – an idea rather than the flesh-and-blood man she would share her life with. She knew she should say his name, bring him into the conversation more fully. Her mouth parted. '. . . He has his own business. An IT consulting and data protection company.'

Tom gave a small snort. 'Yeah. Of course,' he said after a moment.

'Of course?'

'Well, it had to be something like that.' He shrugged.

'Did it?' She stared at him, sensing an undercurrent flowing beneath their words. 'What does that mean?'

'Just that a woman like you wouldn't settle for . . .' His voice trailed off.

'What? A bum?' she finished for him, catching his eye and wanting to challenge his assumption. She felt offended. Did he think she was a snob? A gold digger? 'How do you know what I would settle for?'

'I just do. It's how it goes. You'll marry him and live a really nice life, and you'll get to paint after all, and that's . . .' He stopped talking abruptly, as if catching himself.

'That's what?'

He shook his head. 'No, forget it.'

'I can't forget it!' she laughed, but feeling panicked too. She had to know what he thought. 'Finish what you were saying. You can't make a half statement like that and just leave it hanging! I'll marry him, live a nice life, get to paint and that's – what?'

He looked down at her. 'That's the trade-off you'll make for not really loving him.'

Natasha felt as though he'd slapped her, taking a step back and away from him. 'Why . . . why would you even say something like that?' she asked, her voice a half-croak.

'Because I think it's true.'

'But you know nothing about me.'

'I know.'

'So then you can't say things like that. You have nothing to base that upon!'

'Don't I? You didn't answer Jack's question earlier about the thunderbolt.' He shrugged.

He'd picked up on that? 'So? That doesn't mean anything!'

'Most women fall over themselves to tell you it was love at first sight. You looked like you wanted to run from the room. Which tells me either you just don't believe in love at first sight, or you didn't fall in love at first sight with him.' He put the bottle to his lips. 'Which is it?'

'. . . I don't believe in love at first sight.'

'Oh.' He offered nothing more, and she watched him drink his beer with a rising sense of indignation.

'What do you mean, *oh*?'

'Nothing. You're entitled to your opinion.'

'Well, that's good of you,' she said sarcastically. 'Am I to take it you disagree?'

'Yeah. I think you can meet someone and not know them – but still somehow *know* them. You know what I mean?' His words seemed to settle upon her like snowflakes.

'Well, I agree there can be a connection, but it's not a foundation for anything real. It's just a physical thing. That's just lust.' She felt argumentative. Wasn't that the basis of every one-night stand she'd had in the past three years? He was just like every handsome stranger she'd met in a club, drunk and lonely. She reminded herself of the way Rob would draw a bath for her at the weekends and fill it with her favourite salts; how he'd put a ramekin of brown sauce on the plate when they had salmon because she – like her father used to

150

do – loved it; even though it was a culinary abomination. *That* was knowing someone. *That* was intimacy.

'Can't it be more than that? Spirits colliding? Hearts and minds, as well as bodies?'

She swallowed, remembering again her arms around his neck, his hands on her waist, a careless waltz upon a rope bridge. 'I don't think so, no.'

'Huh.' He took another swig of his beer, rolling the bottle cap absently between his fingers. 'Interesting. So then, I'm guessing, you've never lost anyone close to you?'

'Why would you guess that?'

He smiled, coming down to lean on his elbows, eyes upon her. 'Just answer the question.'

'. . . Actually, my parents.'

He looked surprised. 'Oh. I'm sorry.'

She shrugged. Everyone was always so sorry. It didn't change the fact. She felt his stare deepen upon her, like the sky at golden hour making everything glow with intense radiance.

'Any—?'

'Only child,' she said quickly, heading him off at the pass. 'Lots of cousins, though.'

'Ah.' His mouth pulled down at the corners as he kept rolling the bottle cap. 'Was it sudden? Losing your parents?'

She shook her head. 'Cancer for my mum. Emphysema for my dad. They both suffered.'

He nodded, looking thoughtful. 'So then that's it. That's why you're in such a rush to get married. You want to make him your family.'

'Would there be anything wrong in that? Aren't we all looking for security?'

His head whipped up. 'Not me. I want the very opposite of that.'

They were both quiet for a moment, chastened by the sudden sharpness in his voice as they took in their polar stances, the strange, instinctive familiarity between them receding as if for the first time, giving them both air. 'Well, that's fine,' she said quietly. 'I want security and you want adventure. No one's stopping either of us.'

She took a swig of her vodka, wondering why she felt so edgy. Pushed.

'Well, you're not stopping me,' he said after a long pause, his words seeming to hang upon a cliff edge. Natasha looked back at him, aware of a silent *but*. '. . . But maybe I should be stopping you.'

She gave a startled laugh. 'I'm sorry?'

'I'm serious. You're twenty-two. Your life's only just getting started. Why are your friends letting you go through with this?'

'*Letting* me?' She had to laugh. He had some nerve. 'Well, unlike you, they know I'm happy.'

He watched her as if he was a psychologist, reading her body language, deaf to her words. She made herself look back at him, challenging his stare; but to her surprise, it wasn't cockiness she saw; like a porcelain cup held up to the window, she glimpsed shadows beyond the brightness.

She frowned. 'Have you lost someone close to you, too?'

It was his turn to be on the back foot. 'Yes. But it was different.'

'How?'

'It was sudden.'

'Does that matter? Surely loss is loss.'

'No. Because unless you've been through that, unless you know what it is to lose someone in a moment' – he clicked his fingers, making her startle – 'you can't believe you can find them in a moment, too.' She saw his jaw pulse as the air between them seemed to thicken. 'But I went to work this morning and did my job, only to find myself holding you. Twice.'

Natasha felt her heart pounding too fast. The music was turned up in the next room, someone – Lizzie? Sara? – squealing with laughter.

'And the difference between you and me is that I know, now, that when life gives me something, I have to take it. Because there will be other days when it takes away. I have to recognize the opportunities to be happy and take them, even if on paper it doesn't make sense.' He grinned, dazzling her with a sudden smile again. 'Even if she's getting married to another guy in a week.'

'You're outrageous,' she laughed. He was joking – he had to be – but there was something in the way he looked at her, so direct . . . 'We should probably go back through,' she said, turning away, but he pressed his hand upon hers on the counter, stopping her.

'Do you think it's too late to back out now? Is that it?'

'What?'

'It is, isn't it? You're going to marry him out of obligation—'

'. . . Where do you get off coming out with these statements?'

'I'm just telling you how I see it.'

'But you know nothing about my relationship. You've not even met him—'

'I know!' he said, suddenly alive. 'I met *you*. I met you, Natasha, and shall I tell you what I saw? I saw a woman literally paralysed with fear. Twice.'

'I'm . . . scared of heights.'

'No, you're not. You told me you're not and I saw that

you're not. You went up that wall fine. Instinctively. And that's where you keep coming unstuck – because every time you tap into your instincts, you freeze. Your body is literally trying to stop you from taking another step forward.'

'No.'

'Yes. Your body is telling you what your mind doesn't want to face. That's what's been happening out there. But you're not listening. You don't want to marry him.'

'That's a lie!' she cried.

Every word was the truth – how could *he* have seen it and no one else? – but what was she supposed to say? That this was all a terrible mistake but it had all gone too far, too fast? That every night she woke up with a sob as she dreamed the registrar had said *I now pronounce you . . .* ? It was already too late. Rob had picked up his suit. She'd had her yellow fever shot for the honeymoon. She couldn't admit her doubts to anyone, not even Hels – so why on earth would she bare her soul to him?

He looked down at her. 'I think you're making a mistake. And I think you think it too.'

'I don't!'

'No? So are you also going to deny, then, that there's something between us?'

She stared back at him, jolted with shock that he'd actually said it. 'I hardly know you.'

'That doesn't mean it's not there . . . And I don't think that this charge, buzz, whatever it is between us, could happen if it was completely right between you and him.'

'Us? There is no us! You have no right to say these things.' She turned away. For as long as she was looking at him, she couldn't think straight. She was drunk, in a treehouse, wearing a hideous wedding dress and falling for the smooth lines of a stranger. 'I love my fiancé and I can't wait to marry him.' Her voice was small and flat.

He leaned towards her. 'Sorry, what was that?'

She turned back again, feeling bolder. 'I said, I love my fiancé and I can't wait to marry him.'

He winced at the words, his eyes grazing over her, scratching her skin and rooting out her lies. 'So then, I'm imagining it?'

She shrugged defiantly. 'I don't even know what "it" is.'

He took a step closer suddenly, his body almost touching hers, and she gave a small gasp, catching her breath. '. . . It's that.'

He stared straight down at her and she felt like he was holding her again, like she was standing on his toes, his arms around her, her face pressed to his neck—

'There you are!' Sara peered around the door. 'Hurry up with the drinks. We're going to play a game!'

'A game?'

But Sara had already disappeared again.

'Nats—' Tom reached for her arm but she was too quick, panic making her mercurial and whip-fast. She ran after her friend, leaving him standing there.

'I'm not playing strip fucking poker,' Lauren was saying as she came back through. Natasha almost stopped in her tracks. Lauren never swore; only when she was off her head. Rachel was dancing on one of the sofas with Andy. How much had they all had to drink out here? Had they been doing shots?

'If you think I'm bloody well stripping off . . .' Lauren staggered sideways a few steps, looking utterly aghast, although Natasha wasn't sure why; she was almost certainly the only one among them to be wearing a matched lingerie set. 'I'm engaged too, you know!'

KAREN SWAN

Ben laughed, catching her by the elbow and steadying her. 'That's fine, chill. I'm not even wearing undies, so . . .' He shrugged. Hels was almost crying with laughter as she watched Lauren's face.

'How about Spin the Bottle, then?' Jack asked, picking up one of the empty prosecco bottles.

Natasha frowned. 'Excuse me! Is this a hen party or a Sweet Sixteen?'

'Oh no. I'm not fucking kissing anyone either!' Lauren said quickly, slurring her words. 'That wouldn't be appropriate.'

Jack rolled his eyes. 'Fine. We'll play it with dares as an option, then, as well as kisses.'

'Damn right. I like kissing,' Hels said bullishly. 'This *is* a hen night, after all, and it's only those two getting married.' She laughed, taking a sip of her drink and leaving everyone to do the maths that there were, coincidentally, four single women here and four single men.

They were all sitting down in a circle when Tom wandered back through, carrying a fresh beer. Natasha kept her gaze down, still shaken by what had happened between them in the kitchen. Had he just been trying his luck? Perhaps it was a bet, or a dare they'd all agreed on the way over – who could seduce the hen? A game of chicken, perhaps? She kept her gaze well away from him.

'You know, I always wanted to see what it was like up here,' Jack said, sitting beside her and nodding appreciatively at the decor. 'It's cool.'

Natasha didn't reply. She was aware of Tom's trainers coming into her peripheral vision as he sat down opposite her between Lizzie and Rachel.

'Well, there had to be something to redeem the weekend,'

Sara said on Jack's other side. 'Nats made it very plain she didn't want a stripper, or clubbing.'

'Or vegetarians,' Hels quipped, looking over at her.

'And so that only left Center Parcs?' Ben scoffed.

'Thank you!' Hels cried. 'My sentiments exactly!'

'Listen, I thought this was a halfway house between that sort of Magic Mike thing and a spa weekend! I thought she wanted something . . . wholesome, but exciting too!' Sara said defensively.

'And obviously I wanted to wear a full polyester meringue, too. I really wanted that,' Natasha added.

'Well, the day wasn't entirely without thrills,' Hels said in a tone Natasha knew only too well. 'She did manage to get up close and personal with Tom not once but twice today.' She looked across at Jack. 'You should have seen how he got her off the rope bridge. It was hot!'

Natasha's head whipped up. Had her friend seen the two of them in the kitchen just now? Had she clocked that something was off – or rather, distinctly on – between them?

Jack and Andy looked surprised. 'Yeah?'

'It wasn't like *that*,' Natasha said quickly. 'Don't listen to Hels. She's a wind-up merchant.'

'Hmm, I'm not so sure,' Ben grinned, kicking at Tom's foot across the circle. 'Tom was pretty keen to get over here.'

'Don't be ridiculous, Natasha's the chief hen!' Lauren protested.

'Chicken!' Hels interjected.

'She's off limits.'

'Actually, I read that the bride-to-be is five times more likely to cheat on her fiancé on her hen night than the groom is on his stag do,' Sara piped up, holding up both hands. 'Five times!'

'I don't believe that!' Lauren gasped.

'It's true. Saw it on Insta,' Sara shrugged.

'Oh well, there you go then,' Rachel laughed. 'Facts.'

'Right.' Lizzie held up an empty prosecco bottle. 'I'll go first, shall I?'

Everyone fell silent as she spun it, the heavy green bottle whirling in fast revolutions before slowing to a spot and pointing at . . . Jack.

'Kiss or dare?'

'Kiss!' Lizzie shot back, no hesitation.

'Oh yes! Starting strong,' Jack laughed with a punch to the air, leaning forward as Lizzie provocatively crawled over to him on all fours. Natasha glanced at Tom, to find him already looking at her; she wanted to look away but she couldn't, and as Lizzie leaned in to kiss Jack, she felt like *she* couldn't breathe. Tom's directness troubled her. His proximity bothered her.

'Go, Lizzie!' Hels cried, clapping excitedly.

'Woo-hoo! Attagirl,' Sara cheered as she sat back again. 'Right. Jack, your turn,' she said, jogging him with her elbow.

'Right.' He stirred into action, spinning the bottle with a careless twist of his wrist. Natasha watched it like it was a knife, not sure how she felt as it landed on the gap between Tom and Rachel.

'Rachel!' Hels yelled, just as the guys hollered, 'Tom!'

'It's definitely me, definitely!' Rachel said, getting up on her knees and meeting Jack halfway, planting a long kiss on his lips.

'I definitely saw tongues!' Lauren protested.

'So?' Hels cried. 'She's single, isn't she? She can lick him all over if she bloody well wants!'

Lauren looked stunned by the very idea. Natasha took

another gulp of her drink, trying not to think about any of it. The alcohol had well and truly hit her now. It was barely seven o'clock but she felt out of control, rattled by Tom's words and unsettled by the predatory tone of the room. She should go to bed, she knew, and put a stop to today once and for all. The sense of danger that had lurked over her all day felt stronger than ever.

She watched as Rachel reached for the bottle, spinning and somehow managing to break a nail. 'Ow!' She sucked on her finger as she waited for it to come to a stop. 'Natasha!' She laughed. 'Oh well, this will be like old times,' she said, crawling over and kissing her. It was just a peck on the lips, but it didn't stop the men cheering like it was the golden goal in a World Cup final.

'Now wait a minute, just wait a minute!' Jack cried, holding his hands up as Rachel sat back. 'I think we need an explanation of what exactly "old times" means? Are we to believe that you two . . . ?' His eyebrow was arched questioningly, waiting for a scandalous secret to be revealed.

'We were eleven, practising how to kiss,' Natasha said quickly. 'We practised on our arms and on the mirrors in the changing rooms too, so don't start getting carried away.' She reached forward and spun the bottle quickly. She wanted her turn to be over and done with.

'Tom!' Lizzie yelled.

What? No! Natasha stared at the bottle in disbelief. 'No!' The word burst from her before she could stop it. 'I'm the bride. I can't—'

'You just kissed Rachel!' Andy cried.

'But that was different!'

'How? You either have to kiss the person the bottle points to, or do a dare.'

She hesitated, feeling Tom's gaze upon her, her heart pounding at double time. 'Fine. Then I'll do a dare instead. Let's shake things up a bit.'

'There she is! Hen not chicken!' Lizzie cheered.

'All right, a dare!' Hels looked delighted. 'Okay then, Tom, what do you dare Natasha to do?'

'Wait, Tom chooses?' Natasha swallowed. 'I thought you . . . pick it out of a hat, at random or something.'

'Do you see a hat here?' Hels spread her arms wide. There were lots of empty bottles and crisp packets, but no hat. 'No, if you forfeit his kiss, he gets to choose.'

Everyone looked at Tom. He was sitting very still, his back against the sofa, his knees up and arms loosely laced around his legs, beer bottle almost empty. What was he going to do? He could ask her to do anything, say anything, reveal the secrets she wanted to keep hidden – because she knew he could read her; he could see in her – somehow – things that others couldn't. Not even her best friend. Not even Rob.

'Ooh! Do a blind tasting of something in the kitchen,' Lizzie stage-whispered as Tom stared over at Natasha, hidden thoughts and possibilities streaking through his mind.

'Hurry up!' Lauren moaned. 'A good game is a quick game!'

Tom clasped his wrist in his hand suddenly, focusing on her with an intent look. Everyone waited for him to speak. '. . . I dare Natasha to kiss the person in the circle she really wants to kiss.'

Natasha swallowed. She should have just kissed him and been done with it in the first place, when there had been no conditions attached; when it had been random bad luck and nothing more. But now . . . She looked around at the others waiting expectantly, faintly hopeful looks on their faces.

'Well, I'm sorry, but there's *no one* here I want to kiss—'

'Chicken.' The word dropped from him like a stone.

She stared at him, feeling the silence begin to blow up as the tension between them tightened. The others would notice if she didn't stop this before it started. '. . . Fine. I'll kiss you, then.'

'Because I'm the one you really want to kiss?' he teased, not teasing at all.

'Because the bottle pointed to you in the first place. So let's just be done with it.'

'Ha! Dead romantic, isn't she?' Jack laughed.

But Tom was already smiling. He crossed to the middle of the circle and waited as she tried to move her voluminous skirts out of the way so that she could get up. He reached out a hand, ever her rescuer.

'Thank you,' she huffed, as he pulled her up onto her knees and she felt her breath catch in her chest again as she caught his scent, remembering once more how he had carried her to safety earlier.

They were kneeling before one another but she didn't dare lift her eyes to look at him. 'You can kiss my cheek,' she said, turning her head.

'No. *You* have to kiss *my* cheek,' he said evenly. 'Your spin. You kiss me.'

Ben, Andy and Jack laughed at the gameplay as Tom pointedly looked away.

'Fine.' She reached up to peck his cheek, but in the next instant he turned back, clasping her head in his hands and kissing her full on the lips. Everyone cheered with delight at his trick, the boys giving a whoop as the kiss lingered and he even dipped her a little. She could feel the pressure behind his lips, wanting more, knowing he wasn't going to get it.

'Whoa! What the fuck was that?' Hels yelled, laughing, as

he finally pulled away, his hands warm against her cheeks. 'You almost made *my* clothes fall off!'

Tom's eyes glittered with triumph as he stared back at Natasha. 'Well, she's getting married next week,' he murmured. 'I figure if I'm the last guy she kisses as a single woman, I'd better make it count.'

Chapter Ten

Nepal, Saturday 3 December

Duffy walked into the kitchen area, enjoying the sounds of spoons clinking against china bowls, conversations drifting from the trestle tables. No one slept late here; not like in Vienna or London, where lying in bed was considered an indulgence, here the luxury was in getting up and getting out, breathing in air that felt filtered and pink-tinted, sitting beneath a quiet sky. He had slept well, barely stirring through the night, his body attuning to the new frequency of the mountains that sat a few miles from here like granite emperors. Already he could feel the shift in himself, as if his own body and mind were hardening in response too. It was a necessary adaptation; like a snake shedding skin, he needed to leave behind the parts of himself that were a liability in a place like this – emotion, comfort, softness, nostalgia.

'*Namaste*,' said the man standing beside a vast stock pot. He was wearing a padded jacket and an apron and when he smiled, his front tooth was missing.

'*Namaste*,' Duffy said as he approached.

The man filled his bowl with porridge and apple, then handed him a mug of hot lemon, honey and ginger.

Duffy took it to a table by the window and looked out.

They were still low here, in the foothills of the foothills of the Himalayas, but by the time he went to bed tonight, he would be at an altitude of seventeen hundred metres and the terrain would be vastly different. And then different again the next day, too. It was like stepping into a new world each time: here green, over there brown, up above white. Sticks to stones to snow; abundance to asceticism over the course of a few thousand metres.

'Hey Duffy.'

He looked up as Jay and Stevie walked in. They made a beeline for the porridge too, coming to sit beside him a few moments later.

'How you doing, man? Didn't see you in here last night,' Stevie said, beginning to eat.

'No, I got caught on a call.'

'Not your mom?' Jay joked.

Duffy kept smiling. 'Worse – my ex. She fusses about me way more.'

'Yeah. I had one of those,' Jay replied. 'She meant well and all, but *damn*. There was nothing she couldn't worry about.' He shook his head as he shovelled his food.

'You, Stevie?'

'Nah,' he shrugged. 'There ain't nobody who cares if I live or die.'

Duffy paused mid-bite, not sure if the comment was intended to sound as bleak as it was. Jay's shoulder barge and Stevie's cackling laugh answered for him.

'I'd miss your bad jokes, for sure,' Jay grinned.

'Thanks, man.'

Duffy wrapped his hands around his mug and looked out. The lodge was situated on the very first metres of a path that led all the way up to Annapurna Base Camp. This was the last stop for civilization, although Anya might have begged to differ. There were several buildings scattered nearby, all of them single-storey wooden structures with corrugated tin roofs, sometimes tin walls too. They had hand-painted 'Restaurant' or 'Hotel' signs nailed to wooden poles, with the signature Nepalese-blue plastic tables and chairs. Some women were sitting on a stone wall, talking intently. A man was walking along the path with a small herd of goats. A cockerel somewhere kept crowing.

'So what's your plan of attack today?' Jay asked.

Duffy tuned back in. '*Not* to attack,' he smiled. 'I'm taking it easy. I want to soak it up. The other times, I was just on this mission to get up there, to blitz it.' He shook his head. 'I'm going to do it right this time.'

''Cos the journey's the destination, right?' Stevie said, echoing Duffy's own words in Pokhara, as they'd sat waiting for the bus.

'Exactly. I'm planning on stopping at Tolka tonight.'

'Oh yeah?'

'How about you guys?'

'We were thinking of pushing through to Landruk. I dunno, though,' Stevie shrugged. 'We'll see whether we've got the legs for it.'

'Did you have much recovery time from EBC?'

'Not really. Just the travelling time to here.'

'Huh.' It sounded like a mistake to Duffy, but he kept his opinions to himself. If the two Americans had done Everest Base Camp, they were experienced enough trekkers not to need his input. And everyone was different. They might be far fitter than him. Highly unlikely, but possible.

They finished their breakfast without feeling much obligation to talk, the conversation as unforced as it was unhurried.

Stevie and Jay pushed their chairs back first, eager to get on. If they were to get to Landruk today, they'd be climbing an extra two hours and that meant a race against the clock, battling the temperatures, the weather, the light, the miles and the altitude. They couldn't afford to hang back.

'So listen, it's been good to hang with you,' Stevie said, offering to bump knuckles. 'I hope we see you up there.'

'I hope so too,' Duffy agreed. 'Take it easy.'

'Oh, we won't,' Jay laughed.

Duffy watched them go. A part of him – a very small part – felt a tang of envy at their companionship. Experiencing something like this on his own was profound and isolating, and though he was largely glad to be free from distractions, he couldn't deny he was lonely too. It crept up on him at unlikely moments – seeing a cloud shaped like a dolphin and wanting to point it out; rounding a corner and stepping into a rainbow and realizing no one would ever believe him; the yearning to pose for a daft selfie and have someone to send it to; standing in falling snow and hearing the boom of silence; catching snowflakes on his tongue like he used to as a kid.

Still.

It was best this way.

He returned to his bedroom and did what little packing there was to do – rolling up his sleeping bag and sticking his wooden toothbrush in the lid of the pack. He paid for his room – all of one hundred rupees (or one US dollar) for the night. His meal had cost the same but that would increase with the altitude as food had to be portered further up the mountains.

He began walking, the path still crunchy with frost, night's breath still lingering in the low temperatures. The path was largely level at this point, moving him away from the village and civilization, bushy shrubs bellying out and trees filled with the chatter of birds. Chickens pecked the ground and a black dog with a tail that curled up and tapped its own back trotted alongside him for a kilometre or so, nosing his hand for treats until he got to the start of the steps that indicated the onset of steeper terrain. The dog turned away again without ceremony and headed back as Duffy stepped up.

It began here in earnest. The rest of the world was behind him now, a shadow at his back. It was a five-day trek to get to the ABC – four, the way the Americans were doing it. Distance wasn't the issue but altitude. He'd be climbing up to four thousand metres to his destination but, compressed into a mere thirty-five-kilometre span, almost every step would be tortuously steep. He was under no illusion that he was entering a world of pain.

He had been going for half an hour when his phone beeped in his jacket, the technological intrusion already feeling alien in this outsized wilderness. He stopped to retrieve it. Pockets of coverage were intermittent and he never knew when he might get a signal again, or even *if* he would. He had a new email, with URGENT written in the subject box, though he didn't recognize the name.

Dear Mr Duffy,

I have been given your details by Anya Ebner, who says she is a friend of yours. She contacted me in relation to a post I placed on Facebook earlier this week, regarding my young daughter Mabel's lost toy, a soft cow which we misplaced in Vienna. Anya tells me you stayed in the same apartment as us, found Moolah and took her with you and are now travelling in Asia? You'll understand why we are sceptical of this claim. The post has garnered a lot of attention and we're well aware people like to play hoaxes to get in on the action. Anya has confirmed the address of the Vienna apartment where you stayed and it is the same one. However, it still seems 'convenient' that you – apparently the person now in possession of Moolah – have left the country.

I haven't mentioned anything yet to Mabel as she has been inconsolable since losing Moolah. I don't know if you have children yourself but the impact upon our family has been profound; Moolah was far more than just a toy.

Please, if this is all a game, just come clean and don't waste our time. We cannot expend our emotional energy on a prank. It may seem a joke to you but it is nothing of the sort to our three-year-old girl. If however you maintain this is genuine, then kindly provide proof by way of a photo so that we can judge for ourselves that it is the same toy. If you really are travelling in Asia, but cannot send Moolah back immediately, it will be something at least to know that she's safe and her return can be guaranteed sometime soon. It might even be that we could show the photo to our daughter, to tide her over.

On the other hand, if this is a prank, then you should be ashamed of yourself.

Kind regards

Natasha Stoneleigh

Duffy burst out laughing as he reread the spiky email, and then twice more too. She wanted *proof*? Anya hadn't been entirely wrong about the ransom after all; this woman was behaving as though it was a hostage situation. She sounded uppity and entitled and stiff, almost brittle with tension. What did they call mothers like her? Tiger Mums?

He stepped back to allow a couple of trekkers past on their

way back down, their knees buckling, walking poles planted heavily with every step. '*Namaste*,' he said, still bemused by the woman's unreasonable demand, her ready, matronly chastisement – *be ashamed of yourself*.

'Ridiculous,' he muttered to himself, as he resumed the hike. The stone steps extended up and away from him, but he focused on putting one foot in front of the other. He wouldn't let his mind or gaze drift further than that. Left foot, right foot. It was the only way to get where he was going. There was never anything more, in life, than the next step.

He let his hands brush the rhododendron bushes as he passed, the splayed leaves like green hands slapping his. The gradient was steep and unremitting; what was bearable over ten metres felt brutal over a hundred, much less a thousand. He was fit and strong, his body could deal with this better than 99 per cent of the world's population. That still didn't make it easy. He had done it twice before, but that didn't make it easy either.

He stopped for a hot drink at a guesthouse halfway along and sat on one of the make-do benches, with tree trunks lashed together, especially for weary travellers. He looked out over the valley, fingers laced around the enamel mug. There was still nothing to suggest he was in the shadow of the planet's highest mountains: the slopes were verdant with rhododendron forests, the path a scrubby mud-and-sand track scattered with rocks. Far below, hidden from here, was a tumbling river, the Modi Khola, its milky meltwaters the only indication of their altitude. Eight of the world's fourteen mountains that sat above eight thousand metres were in Nepal – they were the biggest objects on the planet, but they could still hide behind corners and thick clouds. The metaphor of the 'elephant in the room' surely had its genesis here? He felt their presence, though; their ancient majesty and eternal immovability under-pinned every waking and sleeping moment of life here. They were as vital as the air, and as impossible to do without.

He pressed his hands together in respect as he said goodbye to the old lady who had made his drink and moved on. He wondered if Stevie and Jay were making good progress. They had set themselves a formidable challenge to reach Landruk by dark. There was no such thing as a casual decision out here; consequences were all too real. When they got to Tolka, they would have to be sure they could reach the next stopping post in time or else stay put. Sleeping out wasn't an option, obviously, and they would have to be led by sound rationale, not ego.

He was on a downward slope now; often the path went down before climbing even more steeply again further on. It was frustrating to 'undo' hard-won altitude, but mountains were neither smooth nor constant; they had chasms and crev-ices, caves and fissures, house-sized boulders that sat right in the path. And they were always shifting. The 2015 earthquake near Kathmandu had rocked even the mighty Himalayas, catastrophic rockslides burying several small remote villages at a stroke; the trekking paths that had once cut through them now continued above them, with destroyed houses lying crushed beneath the travellers' feet.

Duffy heard a local approaching. He knew it was a local, even though he could not yet see them, because of the distinc-tive sound of tinkling bells. It carried through the mountains, distinctive and effective, able to cut through wind and overlay the roar of a rushing river.

Moments later, the man appeared. He was wearing trad-itional dress: a *daura suruwal* (double-breasted shirt and pegged trousers) with a dark tweed waistcoat and a cotton *topi*; all the Nepalese men wore them, the distinctive tub-shaped cloth hat woven in a tribal brocade. This valley was the home of the Gurung tribes.

'*Namaste*,' Duffy said, smiling as the pale mules nodded past, sure-footed and eyes downcast. The pack bags across their backs were brightly woven in reds and blues, the bell reins looking like they belonged at a festival.

'*Namaste*.' The man stopped to look at him. 'Machha-puchhre?'

Duffy nodded. 'Yes.' Machhapuchhre was one of the mountains on the Annapurna Massif. Its base camp sat just below Annapurna's and he should get there in three days, if everything went according to plan.

The man pointed back the way he had come. 'Avalanche.'

'Oh.' Duffy's eyes widened. It was the last stop before the ABC. 'Is anyone hurt?' The man was calm and not seemingly in a hurry. This didn't appear to be an emergency warning.

'No. Nightfall. No people.'

'Good. That's good to hear.'

'But path is . . . full.'

'The path is blocked?' Ah. That wasn't what Duffy wanted to hear and he felt a tightening in his chest. He'd been tracking the long-range weather forecasts for weeks and there was a good window coming up. He didn't want to lose valuable time on account of a snowslide. 'How long to clear it?'

The man waggled his hands. 'Few days.'

'Okay,' Duffy nodded, feeling a bit reassured. Hopefully it would be cleared by the time he got there, then. It was in no one's interests to have a blockage at the top of one of the most popular trekking routes in the Himalayas. Climbers generally booked rooms as they went, coming up and going down the route in a constant exchange; if people couldn't get to their final destination for a few days, most likely they would sit there and wait till they could, causing knock-on reservation problems further down the mountains. There were only so many places to eat and sleep out here.

'Thanks for telling me,' Duffy said as the man nodded and prepared to go again. He would doubtless be informing everyone who was coming up behind him, but precious few would turn back. Even just getting to this point was an achievement, not to mention costly – international flights, internal transfers to Pokhara, then Khande, equipment, visas, passes . . .

The bells began jingling again as the mules stepped onwards, their musical song and bright colours anachronistic in the harsh terrain.

'Oh. I wonder—' The words were out before he had realized he was going to say them. 'Could I . . . ?' He motioned taking a picture, then pointed at the mules.

The man tipped his head side to side in the Nepalese manner, indicating 'yes.'

Duffy quickly shrugged off the backpack – a golden rule he usually never broke; the backpack didn't come off till he was in his bedroom. But everything was different this time. He was no longer living by rules. This was to be a trek full of firsts and lasts. He unclipped the lid and pulled out the toy cow that had caused an international sensation.

The man chuckled as he saw it.

'Is it okay to put it here?' Duffy asked, grinning too.

'Yes, yes,' the man replied, tapping the mule between the shoulders and holding onto its reins.

Duffy tried to balance it but the animal was too bony; or perhaps Moodle was too overstuffed.

'I do for you,' the man said, reaching to hold it for him.

'Thank you,' Duffy said, stepping back and looking through the screen. The man's brown face was deeply lined, his eyes watchful, intelligent and kind. His modest Nepali clothes contrasted with the fiesta colours and finery of the mules, the leafy backdrop betraying little – yet – of Duffy's coming adventure.

He clicked.

'Thank you. Thank you so much. *Namaskar.*' He pressed his hands together.

'*Namaskar*,' the man smiled, continuing on his path.

Duffy stared at the image captured on screen. But for the toy cow sitting front and centre, it would have made for a great travel image. As it was, it looked somewhat ridiculous.

Still, if it gave Mrs Stoneleigh the proof she so desperately needed . . . he thought sardonically, typing out a message. He had been tempted not to reply at all given her manner, but there was a child at the heart of this and he did know how important these toys could be. He knew very well.

He pressed send, watching the blue circle spin. It was out of his control now. It might never reach her, even with the best of intentions. Whatever. He put his phone away and began putting one foot in front of the other again.

Left foot.

Right foot.

The world at his back.

Chapter Eleven

Frome, Saturday 3 December

Natasha stood in her dressing gown and cashmere bed socks, staring down at the dusty boxes of Christmas decorations piling up on the landing.

'Rob, what are you doing?' she asked, her voice a croak.

'We're getting the house ready for Christmas,' Rob said, only his legs visible as he stood on tiptoes on the loft ladder and reached for another box.

She frowned. We? Christmas? Now? 'Where's Mabel?'

'Watching *Peppa Pig* in the snug,' he replied.

'What time did she wake up?'

'Sixish.'

'That's pretty good,' Natasha muttered, feeling inexplicably guilty that she had slept through. It was gone nine now, so they'd been up for hours already. Little wonder Rob was like action man, go-go-go. He twisted slightly on the ladder. 'Here, can you take that?'

She reached her arms up to take the box from him, even though movements of any kind were feeling distinctly ill-advised at the moment. Just being vertical was an achievement.

'Can't this wait till next weekend?' she asked, groaning as

she took its weight. She set it down beside the others as Rob pulled over the loft hatch and descended the ladder. 'We always get the tree the second weekend in December.'

'I know, but next weekend is looking tricky,' he said, glancing at her with a nervous grimace.

'What?' Her voice cracked midway through the word, rising an octave.

'I'm sorry. I didn't want to say anything until I was sure and I'm *still* not a hundred per cent sure yet, but . . . yeah. Possibly . . .' He sighed apologetically. 'Probably.'

'But you only just got back!'

'I know, but I'll be around till Friday, most likely.' He picked up the top two boxes and carried them downstairs.

Natasha shuffled behind him, wishing she wasn't feeling quite so broken. 'But why always the weekends?' But she already knew why. The answer was always the same. They could only get in and do the programming on the mainframes when the offices were closed.

'It's not always the weekends. I'm here now, aren't I?'

'But . . . but . . .' She couldn't make her brain work as she followed him into the kitchen. She'd drunk far too much last night; the excitement of this Anya woman's message, followed by the crushing disappointment that it was most likely a hoax, had given her a rare thirst. She winced as she vaguely recalled writing an email, fuelled by indignation and champagne.

She wasn't feeling so feisty now. With a groan, she shuffled over to the cabinets and reached for her mug. Usually she started her days with a camomile tea, but today just the thought of it made her stomach turn.

'Tea?' she asked him.

'Thanks darling.' He opened one of the boxes and stared in at the contents as if he'd never seen them before. 'When

175

did we get this?' he asked in open bafflement, pulling out an oversized felt robin as big as a beach ball.

'Rob, we've had that for years! How can you not remember it?' Bella always growled at it on the mantelpiece, perturbed by its gigantic proportions and ominous staring stillness.

'Huh.' He put it down on the kitchen table with an air of defeat and she dunked the teabag, watching him pull out the garlands that would be tied in swags on the stairs and finished with red ribbons – by her. Rob was great at starting jobs, but not so hot on seeing them through.

'Do we really have to do this now?' she sighed, sliding his tea across the island and staying stretched across it on her tummy, resting her head on her arms. 'I just don't feel Christmassy yet. It's too early,' she mumbled, closing her eyes.

'You don't feel Christmassy because you don't have any Christmas things up,' he argued, chuckling at the pathetic sight of her. 'Also because you're hung to hell; also because we've just returned from a 30-degree holiday in the Indian Ocean. What we need is a cold snap, the fire on all day and a tree with presents under it. *Then* you'll feel Christmassy. So once you're dressed we'll go and choose the tree.'

She groaned, then opened a single eye. 'Wait a minute, has this frenzy of festivity been triggered by seeing the Tennants' mega-tree last night?' she asked suspiciously.

'I would hardly call this a frenzy, darling. I'm just not quite so broken as you. You were in very high spirits last night.'

Was that Rob code for 'you embarrassed yourself', she wondered? He could sometimes inflect a certain tone of disapproval that set her on edge. But it had been so long since she'd really let her hair down. 'Well, I felt like . . . letting go for once,' she mumbled. 'Everything's been so shit.' Not just this week with losing Moolah, but the weeks and months that had preceded it of not falling pregnant. She felt like she was failing, letting both Rob and Mabel down as her body seemingly refused to conceive.

He came over and began stroking her back. 'I know, and it was good to see you laughing again. It reminded me of the old Natasha. Made me realize how long it's been since we've seen her.'

'Old Natasha?' she whispered.

'Yes, the girl I fell madly in love with, remember her?' He picked up his tea and wandered back to the boxes. Was she being oversensitive or was he intimating that she wasn't that girl now? And if she wasn't that girl now . . . ? She looked up at him sipping his tea.

He was wearing his battered jeans and a loden cashmere sweater, mismatched brightly coloured socks: fully in weekend mode. 'You need a trim,' she murmured.

'I know,' he said, automatically reaching up and pushing back his fringe. 'I'll try and get to the barber's later too.'

Bella padded across the tiled floor and began drinking noisily from her water bowl, leaving puddles everywhere as a slip hazard. Mabel was in the snug next door, sounds of oinking drifting through, followed by delighted little laughs.

Natasha smiled at the sounds, pulled out of her hangover fog for a few moments. She walked through, unable to resist. 'Good morning, my munchkin,' she smiled, reaching over the back of the sofa and kissing her daughter's plump cheek and inhaling the scent of her hair. It was funny how she could miss her even just overnight, even by being in a different room. 'And how's Daddy Pig today?'

Daddy Pig was Mabel's favourite character. 'He broke the wall.'

A dramatic crack zigzagged across a cartoon house, a nail

in the wall, a hammer in Daddy Pig's hand. 'He broke the wall? Oh dear. That sounds messy.'

'Mummy Pig is cross.'

'I'm not surprised.' She stroked Mabel's mussed hair; she always smelled of roses and sunlight. 'Are you hungry? Do you want some toast?' She tried to smooth away the dark circles under her eyes with her thumbs; the child looked bruised by exhaustion. 'With honey?'

'Wiv honey,' Mabel echoed, hollow-eyed and distant, as if she was dreaming with her eyes open.

Natasha kissed her forehead and wandered back into the kitchen. Bella was stretched out on the floor now and she thumped her tail a few times, as if calling for her morning greeting too. 'Yes, yes, and you,' Natasha murmured, stopping to stroke her head.

Rob had brought the rest of the boxes downstairs and was opening them all systematically.

'So I liked Hels's new guy. The vet,' he said, glancing up.

'Dave? Yes, he's lovely.' She dropped some bread in the toaster and went to the larder. 'Seemed very grounded. I noticed he kept looking for her.'

'Probably desperate to get away from us lot,' he joked. 'Is Hels keen?'

'I think so, but she's not saying much yet. She's keeping her cards close to her chest.'

'Well, let's hope she doesn't fall into her usual tricks.'

'What do you mean?' Natasha felt a prickle of defensiveness for her friend.

'Just that she usually jettisons the good ones, and Dave seems like a good guy.'

'I don't think she breaks up with them for laughs,' Natasha replied. 'Besides, Mark kept asking her for money and Jim cheated on her. She just doesn't put up with bullshit, that's all.'

Rob was up to his elbows rifling through a box. 'I guess, but you know what I'm saying. She's twenty-six, not eighteen. People are settling down, getting married. She shouldn't throw away an opportunity like this.'

'I don't think she sees Dave as an opportunity, Rob! She earns good money, has a great career, her own place.'

'So, what . . . he's just a good shag?'

Natasha shrugged. 'I'm sure it's a lot more than that, but even if it is, that doesn't mean she has to marry the guy. In fact, I'm not sure she'll ever get married. She doesn't believe in institutions and, frankly, you wouldn't either if you'd witnessed the fallout from her parents' divorce. It was vicious. They did everything they could to destroy each other and really only ended up fucking up her and her brother.'

'That's sad,' he said distractedly, opening the next box and pulling out a reel of lights. 'So many lights! Why do we have so many?'

'Because *you* keep buying them! – lights for the bay trees, lights for the banisters, lights for the tree . . .' She watched as he stood up with a huff. '. . . Rob, are you looking for something in particular?' she asked as he scratched his head, looking harassed.

'Yes, the wreath.'

'For the door?' Now she was perplexed.

'Yes, the one with the pheasant feathers. It looked so good last year. Made the place look Christmassy but also smart. Not tacky.'

Natasha frowned at him. 'Well, you won't find it in there. We don't have an artificial wreath and we've certainly never had one with pheasant feathers.'

He frowned. 'We haven't?'

'No. I make them fresh every year at Rachel's workshops. I'm going next week, in fact.'

'Really?' He looked puzzled. 'I swore we had one with feathers!'

Natasha rolled her eyes. She knew that if she covered his eyes right now, he wouldn't be able to tell her the colour of his own socks. 'You must have eaten too much cheese,' she sighed, catching the toast as it popped up. She began smearing it with honey.

Her phone buzzed on the counter and she opened it distractedly with her one unsticky finger. Seeing she had a new email, she frowned, thinking it was spam that had somehow got past the firewall. She didn't know any T. Duffy and her finger was already on the 'bin' button when she suddenly gasped, memories from last night breaking through the fog in her brain.

'Oh my God,' she mouthed as she clicked on it. Her hands flew to her mouth as the image opened. 'It wasn't a hoax!'

Rob looked over. 'What?'

'It wasn't a hoax! He's got Moolah! He's sent a picture!'

'Let me see.' Rob ran over, peering over her shoulder to take a look.

The photo was beautiful – Moolah sitting on some sort of pack horse, its reins threaded with brightly coloured bells and vibrant saddle cloths. An older man was holding the toy in place and smiling at the camera, looking straight at it as though he was peering past the glass and seeing into their souls.

'So is that him?'

'I'm not sure . . . Uh . . . maybe?' Her mind was racing. 'His friend said he was travelling in Nepal, but she didn't say whether he was Nepalese himself.'

'He doesn't look like a Duffy.'

'Huh.' But Natasha was less interested in the man than the toy cow anyway. She was scrutinizing Moolah, looking for anything about this toy that differed from her recollection of their own, but everything seemed exactly right. Her eyes kept scanning, looking for the clue that would confirm she couldn't believe what she saw, that she mustn't dare to believe this was real. They couldn't be this lucky, could they? Surely, after a week and a couple of continents, they couldn't have found their beloved little cloth toy again? And yet somehow, against the odds, all the evidence showed they had.

'. . . Or like he's just come back from a trip to Vienna.'

'What does that mean? How should someone look, coming back from Vienna?' Natasha protested, tuning back in. But it was true. The man in the picture looked Nepalese. He was more likely a local this Duffy had passed and got to pose for him.

She felt something in her ease as she finally allowed herself to believe. She had been so tightly wound all week, unable to comfort her daughter in the way Moolah provided. But this was the breakthrough they'd been hoping for. Proof of life. When she'd sent her email last night, she'd been so sure it was a hoax and she winced, remembering her maternal rage as she read his note back.

Dear Mabel,

   I'm pleased to tell you Moolah is alive and well and enjoying the fresh air of the Himalayas. She says hello and is sorry if you have been worried but she just wanted a little holiday. She will come home very soon, once she has seen some of the biggest mountains in the world. People come here to touch the sky but we all know the cow jumped over the moon so she is keen to give that a go. I will keep her safe, I promise.

Yours, Duffy (friend of cows)

P.S. Mabel, Moolah is asking that you get lots of sleep now please as she has lots of stories to tell you and she doesn't want you to fall asleep.

'Friend of cows?' Rob scoffed. 'He sounds like a right joker.'

'I think that's intended for Mabel, not us. Anyway, it's proof he's got Moolah, that's all that matters.' Natasha felt her hangover recede like a tide, the weight that had been pushing on her chest all week lifting from her. 'We should show Mabel,' she said, looking at her husband. 'Don't you think? He's written the note to her; there's a photo as proof that she's okay. He's even told her to go to sleep.'

Rob sighed, looking sceptical. 'It is not for some stranger on the other side of the world to tell our daughter what to do or how to feel.'

'But he's done her – *us* – a kindness.'

'Or it could unsettle her all over again. She's just beginning to adapt.'

'How many times were you up with her last night?' Natasha asked. She had slept through in her boozy haze.

'. . . Twice.'

'Right, that's not adapting, Rob. She's three, not three months. She should be sleeping through. We've got nothing to lose.'

'Fine. But on your h—'

But Natasha was already running through to the snug. 'Mabel, look! Look!' She all but jumped onto the sofa beside her and held her arm out for Mabel to snuggle into her.

'Darling, we've received a very special message from someone we all love very much. Would you like to see?'

Mabel blinked. 'Who?'

'It's from Moolah, baby. She's on holiday.'

'Moolah?' Mabel's thumb dropped from her mouth as she patted at the screen. Natasha unlocked it and showed her the image.

'That's Moolah!' Mabel cried, her eyes wide and mouth open as she stared. 'She's on a horse!'

'That's right. Doesn't she look happy? And there's a message for you too. Would you like me to read it to you?'

'She can't write, like me.'

'No, I know, so she asked her friend Duffy to write for her. He's a friend of cows, apparently.' Natasha couldn't quite believe she was saying the words, but she only had to take one look at her daughter's face to lean into the farce.

Natasha read the message slowly. 'Imagine that,' she said finally. 'Moolah's going to see the highest mountains in the world. She's going to touch the sky.'

'And jump over the moon!' Mabel's eyes were wide and shining.

'Isn't she just the luckiest?'

'I wish she tooked me with her.'

'You're just a bit too little for moon-jumping, darling.'

'When is she coming back?'

Natasha hesitated. How long did it take to trek a Himalaya? Weeks? *Months?* 'Soon, I promise.' It was the best she could offer. 'But at least now you know she is coming back.'

'Will she send me more pictures?'

'Ummm . . .' Natasha bit her lip. She hadn't thought about that. She looked into her daughter's big eyes and saw the hope shining from them. 'I'm sure she'll try her hardest.' She gave a big smile and changed the subject. 'In the meantime, let's go choose our Christmas tree, shall we?'

'Yes!' Mabel jumped up on the cushions. 'A Christmas tree! A Christmas tree!'

Christmas was the one thing Natasha could control. Moolah may no longer be lost but for as long as she wasn't here, much still hung in the balance. Nonetheless, if this man had managed to send one photo from the back of beyond, surely he could send another? *Would* he, though? Possibly the main obstacle wasn't his ability to communicate, but his willingness to interrupt his once-in-a-lifetime trip to send updates for a random little girl in the English countryside.

Not to mention, Natasha knew she hadn't exactly been friendly in their first communication. Wasn't it an intended snub that he hadn't replied directly to her but to Mabel instead? She had offended him; she sensed it.

But she could change that. She could make him like her. She would make him engage, even all the way from over there. Her daughter's happiness depended upon it. Operation Charm Offensive was on.

'No, not that one.' Natasha shook her head.

'What's wrong with it?' Rob asked, looking affronted, one arm stretched out so that he could hold the tree upright.

She wrinkled her nose. 'It's too stringy at the top.'

'Stringy?'

'Yes. What about that one?' She pointed to one behind him.

He twisted to see. 'We just looked at that one! You said it was too bushy at the bottom.'

'Oh. Oh yes.' Natasha hitched Mabel a little higher on her hip and pulled her hat down over her ears. It was fiendishly cold, their breath hanging in little clouds before them. 'What do you think?' she asked her daughter.

'I liked the pink one.'

'That one's not for sale, sweetie. It stays in the office.'

'Thank God,' Rob muttered under his breath as he returned the stringy-topped tree. 'Well, you're going to have to choose one. We've looked at all the Nordmanns now.'

'I know we have, but I do prefer a spruce. You know I do.'

'What?' He didn't look like he knew any such thing. 'A spruce? But Nordmanns are way better. They're thicker and they don't drop as easily.'

'I just think spruces are more old-fashioned looking. They're more Father Christmassy,' she shrugged.

'I don't understand you sometimes,' Rob sighed, walking over to the spruces in his jeans and wellies. He had distinctly lost his early-morning Christmas fervour now, and Natasha knew he was being driven crazy by the short loop of piped Christmas pop songs.

She put Mabel down and watched her toddle after him. Natasha looked around the yard, wishing she felt more festive than she was pretending to feel. It was reassuring, at least, to see they weren't the only ones 'starting early' this year; the car park was already filling up quickly, mainly with young families like theirs, overexcited children pulling along weary parents. People loved coming to 'cut their own' trees. The plantation had started out as just a sideline for the Bingleys' farm – Emma's idea, she had given over a few old pastures to the seasonal project – but it had rapidly taken off and now incorporated a cafe with hot chocolate, mulled wine and Lizzie's Christmas cake and mince pies. There was even a small real-life nativity area with a few reindeer, donkeys and a manger.

Her phone rang and she reached for it in her pocket, instinctively knowing who it would be. 'Morning, Dog Breath,' she groaned, walking slowly. 'Oh my God, Hels, my head's about to fall off.'

There was a pause and in that split second, Natasha felt a jolt of panic.

'Uh . . . hello? Is this Natasha Stoneleigh? The animal artist?' a woman asked. She was well spoken, sounded a bit older. She distinctly didn't sound like someone whose nickname was Dog Breath.

Bugger.

'Um . . . speaking,' Natasha said primly, watching as Rob hoisted Mabel onto his shoulders and 'introduced' her to the donkeys.

'Oh hello, your details were passed to me by a mutual acquaintance – Dave Trenchard?'

Natasha blinked as the vague impressions of another memory from last night began to form. Dave didn't hang around! She had only met him for the first time last night. Had he contacted his former client this morning? Surely any self-respecting, hungover, twenty-something man would still be in bed at this time on the weekend?

'Dave, right.'

'Dave used to be our vet before he moved. He's an excellent veterinary surgeon.'

'Yes, I've heard he's great.'

'The thing is – and I hope you don't mind me calling so early – but before he left, I told him I would like to have a portrait done of my husband's horse as a Christmas present. This was back in . . . oh, August time. He wasn't able to give me any recommendations and to be honest, I let it slide and forgot all about it until I received an email from him a few minutes ago. I don't suppose you might possibly, *possibly*, be able to do something before Christmas?'

Natasha tried to remember where he had said this woman was based. She recalled it was a fair distance away, that travel times would be an issue. 'Well . . .' The hesitation was fatal.

'It's just that I've just looked at your Instagram page and it's wonderful – exactly what I'm looking for,' the woman said quickly.

'Thank you—'

'Such a talent you have!'

'Thank you.'

'I couldn't help but notice you don't have any oils on your page, though.'

'No. They're expensive and take a lot of time. I mainly work in charcoal or watercolours. Most of my clients don't have the budget.'

'Oh, but I do,' the woman said quickly. Natasha couldn't remember her name. Had she even introduced herself? 'And an oil would be just the thing. Just the thing.'

Natasha took a breath. She could feel the woman's will – her sheer desperation – pushing her. 'The thing is, it would be difficult to complete an oil now before Christmas.'

'Difficult, but not impossible?'

Natasha had to laugh. 'Well, I guess anything's possible, Mrs . . . ?'

'Lorn. Diana Lorn. But please, call me Diana.'

'Okay Diana. The thing is—'

'Oh please don't let there be a thing,' the woman implored. 'Whatever your rate is, I'll pay thirty per cent extra. How's that?'

Natasha stood very still. 'You really do want it for Christmas.'

'Like you wouldn't believe. My husband's a beast to buy for – has got everything, wants for nothing. Oh please say you'll do it.'

Natasha bit her lip. 'Well, was it a head shot or a whole-body portrait you were after?'

'Whole body would be preferable. He's a handsome boy, but he's such an exceptional jumper. I wondered if we might get an "action shot", if you will.'

This commission was getting bigger, more costly – and more exciting – with every word. Most people wanted head shots because they were cheaper; Natasha liked them too because they could largely be done from stills. But if this lady wanted a capture of the horse jumping, then she would have to see the action for herself, and that meant being there.

'And large, too. As large as you could manage,' Diana added. 'A1?'

'Absolutely. Or bigger. Whatever you think.'

Natasha didn't know what to say, much less what to charge. An A1-scaled, full-body oil portrait was a rare beast and if she pulled it off – big *if* – it could propel the tidy little sideline which filled her days into something that tallied with her own artistic passions and ambition. She saw the fantastic bronze renderings Sara did for her clients – full-scale stags, strutting pheasants, noble sleeping lions – and it always made her pet portraits seem so amateurish. But this . . . this would be proper art. The sort she dreamed of doing.

'The thing is, I would have to make several site visits to observe the animal in motion, and from what Dave said, I think you're a fair distance away. I'm in Frome, in Somerset?'

'We're in Gloucestershire, but I'd pay for your travel costs, naturally,' Diana said quickly.

'Thank you, but the thing is, I have a three-year-old and

she's only in nursery a few days a week, so I have to work around her, which makes it tricky – especially when we're so close to Christmas.'

There was a slight pause. 'What if I were to pay double your fee?'

Natasha's mouth dropped open. 'But you don't yet know my fee.'

'I know. But whatever it is, double it.'

Natasha looked across the courtyard. Rob had taken Mabel off his shoulders and was holding her in his arms, blowing raspberries on her neck and making her squeal. He was a great dad and husband, always working so hard to provide for them and give them this life. Wouldn't it be something if, for once, she was to treat him?

'Well,' she stammered. 'That . . . that really is too good an offer to refuse. Thank you.'

'You mean you'll do it?'

Natasha couldn't believe the woman thought she might not! She laughed. 'Yes. But I'll need to start right away if it's to be done in time. I'll come to you early next week and see your husband's horse in the flesh . . . How many hands is he?'

'Arty? He's sixteen three.'

Big. 'Okay. I'll come, say, on Monday? My daughter's in nursery that day and my babysitter may be able to collect her for me.' Especially now Moolah had been found and was 'in contact' with them, Mabel should settle for Rosie again. 'I'll watch him to get a feel for his temperament. Will your husband be there to put him over some jumps?'

'Oh, no, and to be honest he must know nothing of this,' Diana said in a whispering, confiding tone. 'It must be a surprise. But I can put Arty on the rope and lunge him, get him jumping that way?'

'Okay, that would work. So then I'll come straight after dropping Mabel. I think you're about an hour and a half away from here, so it should be elevenish.'

'Elevenish is perfect. I can't thank you enough, Natasha! I'm over the moon.'

Over the moon. She thought of Moolah, trekking somewhere right this moment in the depths of Asia.

'Great. I'll see you then. If you can text me your address on this number?'

'I'll do it straight away. See you Monday.'

'Bye.' Natasha hung up. Rob was looking over questioningly and she hurried across to him, feeling a fizz of excitement at her unexpected prize. Mabel was sticking bits of hay through the fence to the donkeys, who seemed underwhelmed by her offering.

'Who was that you were talking to?' he asked.

'Who do you think?' she fibbed.

'Ha, she does love a good post-mortem,' he grinned, taking her by the hand and leading her to the spruces.

Natasha bit her lip, pleased to have her own secret. Mr Lorn wasn't going to be the only husband waking up to an unexpected surprise on Christmas Day morning.

Chapter Twelve

Nepal, Sunday 4 December

'It sounds like we are being shot at,' Ophélie, the French doctor, said, her eyes never moving from the cards in her hand.

Duffy nodded in silent agreement. It did indeed sound like that, the rain hammering the tin roof like bullets. It almost never rained here in December but the flash storm was making up in intensity what it lacked in frequency. They had met in the hot springs at Jhinu Danda earlier, after another full day's trekking. He had walked slowly, trying to prolong the journey, but his body was too fit, too fresh, and he found himself at his designated guest house in Sinuwa earlier than he had wanted. There probably would have been time to get to Bamboo, the next village on the trail, before sundown, but he had made his plan and he was sticking to it. He didn't need to arrive at ABC a day early. It was good discipline, holding himself back.

He'd had the springs to himself for at least an hour before the other travellers started arriving. There were various trails in the circuit that intersected at sporadic junctures, allowing people to take different routes; his was one of the lesser travelled. He preferred not to get swept along in the currents of large corporate tour groups all wearing the same baseball caps or with flags fluttering on their wrists. Nonetheless, people tended to arrive at the small settlements around the same times, and the tiny villages would come alive with euphoric chatter for a few hours. His mother had once asked him, as a boy, *Have you ever seen a sad trekker?* And to this day, he never had.

He had walked for the first few hours without passing anyone, partly because he preferred to take the older routes where he could – those trails weren't as well maintained as the main paths and deterred the commercial parties. In some places, the monsoons or old landslides had swept away sections and he'd had to tread carefully, using his hands to grab the banks or branches as he navigated loose earth, but that only added to the experience. As the routes were commercialized they became sanitized, with safety features – walls, handrails, rest benches, fully restored steps – everywhere. But this was a wilderness, and he wanted to feel a little wild. He wanted to tap into his instincts and that animal side of himself in which he saw and heard more keenly, in which the materialistic or egoistic fell away and it was just him and a mountain. Life, in the shadow of death.

There had only been one point when he'd regretted his decision. New Bridge was an impressive 287-metre suspension footbridge that led across the gorge to Jhinu Danda and the hot springs – its steel suspension cables were taut, the footboards secure, the open sides reinforced with mesh. But he knew there was another bridge, the original one, lower in the valley. Having dropped his pack at the teahouse, he had been able to scramble down the forested slopes unencumbered. The pitch was steep, the ground hard and cold beneath his hands, sticks and thorny vines scratching him as he went. He had felt a stab of jubilation as he caught sight of the old bridge between the trees, but that euphoria had quickly faded as he saw the condition of it. The wooden foot treads had largely rotted and in some places were missing entirely. The rope was mossed and fraying in parts. The river rushed several hundred feet below. If it was to give beneath his weight . . .

A memory had tried to surface in his mind as he stared at it and his body felt a flash of adrenaline as a feminine scent, a feeling, tantalized him, unarticulated, before sinking back into the depths again without quite catching the light. He had stood on the outer treads and tested its strength, bouncing lightly. It creaked but held, but that was scant reassurance when he knew the greatest weakness would be through the middle section. He would either have to commit or turn back. In the end, he had sat for twenty minutes on the ground, looking across at the other side. Being lower down the valley, it was only a hundred metres long or so, a third of the span of the newer bridge. Should he go slow? Fast? Or back up? He wasn't afraid to die, he knew that, but was he prepared to die for *this*? He hadn't come this far to die in the Himalayan *foothills*. Was the risk worth it, just to sit in some hot springs?

On the other hand, what was life without risk?

His mind and body went to war with each other, the calm clarity he had so consciously worked to nurture within himself to this point beginning to crumble as the scale of the place began to impress. As it always did. It seemed to awaken a primal urge in him to prove himself. He was a minnow out here. Death stood around every corner. But was he going to hide from it?

In the end, he had crossed quickly. He had stood up and half run, half walked like he was dodging buses on Piccadilly. He had to keep moving and not allow himself to freeze; he chose to trust in instinct. Adventure, not security. The body and mind were hard-wired for survival and self-preservation.

Only as he had passed through the middle section had he seen how friable the rope really was – it wouldn't survive another monsoon season – and when he got to the other side, his heart was pounding in his chest. Duffy 1, Himalaya 0.

The euphoria had fully kicked in when the French party arrived at the springs shortly afterwards. He was feeling heady with adrenaline, the warm water a snatched luxury he had fought for and earned. Perhaps that was why he'd been so convivial. For a short while at least, he had set down his mission – like his backpack – and chosen life, this moment; not what he had to do tomorrow and who he had to be.

Ophélie was beating him hands down at rummy, but he didn't care. They were drinking a local *chyang* – a cider-type drink made from fermented rice – and he was feeling happily drowsed; he'd only had one or two but he could still feel the alcohol swirling in his blood. Altitude made everything hit differently. The others in her group – also medics – had gradually retired back to their rooms, and he wondered if they had noticed that she and he held eye contact a moment longer, laughed a little harder at each other's stories. Ophélie was sharing a room with Claudie; she hadn't yet asked if he had a roommate or was sleeping alone.

'Rummy,' she said, setting down her cards with a triumphant smile. He could tell she was used to winning and achieving. Life went her way.

'You're too good for me,' he grinned, setting down his and showing her the hand that was typical of his luck. He shrugged, seeing how she caught her breath high in her chest when their eyes connected.

She was on her way back down the path. They both knew they would never see each other again after tonight.

'Are you tired?' she asked.

He gave a single shake of his head. 'No.' He held her gaze again, before slowly getting up and joining her on her side of the table. He noticed her leg jigging nervously and he watched it for a moment before he turned his head and looked at her. 'Are you?'

She shook her head. He didn't need to be a doctor to see her pupils were dilated. '. . . Non.'

He bent down and paused fractionally, before he kissed her. She kissed him back eagerly, winding her fingers into his hair; and when she pulled back, her cheeks were flushed. 'Have you got a single room?' she asked breathlessly.

He smiled. He wasn't the only one living from moment to moment. 'Yeah. I got lucky.'

It was still before midnight, but the sky had been wearing her night shroud for hours and the darkness was pervasive. Which only made the green glow from his phone all the more distinctive.

He was lying on his stomach, trying to sleep. Ophélie had just left and he was beginning to feel the fatigue in his muscles. She would be travelling downhill so gravity would be her friend, but he was facing some serious vertical climbs tomorrow and needed to recover as best he could, while he could.

He turned his head on the pillow and tried to ignore the notification that had come in, but the room was lit up and his mind was wondering now – who was it? Anya? His father? He had removed all contacts but them from his SIM, whittling everything on this trip down to just the bare bones. No excess baggage, either physically or emotionally. He wanted no distractions. No noise. No temptations to make him turn around again and leave this for another day, another year.

With a groan, he propped himself on his elbows and reached for it.

'Oh Jesus,' he muttered as he saw the name and was immediately reminded that Anya – unwitting of his plans – had shared his email. So three people had it now. Messy. Definitely distracting. He pinched his temples with one hand. 'Not again.'

He clicked on it, wishing he'd turned his phone off.

The first thing he saw was a pair of shining blue eyes; they were pale and ringed with yellow, like fiery hoops a tiger could jump through. Dark Shirley Temple curls framed a plump face, appled cheeks, ruby lips . . . this child was straight out of a catalogue. Cute as hell, a picture of innocence.

'Hello Mabel,' he murmured, taking in the sight of her clutching Moolah to her cheek, chubby fingers clenched tightly in a squeeze. Damn, she was sweet. Little wonder half the planet was twisted around her little finger.

He braced himself for the mother's less charismatic and tender words.

Dear Duffy,
   I can't tell you what it meant to us to receive your reply. When I say it made our year, I honestly mean it.

He arched an eyebrow. It wasn't the bullish start he had anticipated.

You've rescued Christmas and our little girl is so happy again, thank you so much. We've printed your photograph and taped it to her wall so she can still see Moolah as she's going to sleep, and tonight she went to sleep immediately – the first time since we left Vienna.

Thank you for the way you spoke to her directly in the email, telling her that Moolah's on a holiday and having adventures. It really made her feel comfortable knowing Moolah was with you and the idea that she's going to jump over the moon has totally captured her imagination; she made us look up at the moon tonight to see whether Moolah could jump it, but it's pretty full so I said probably not yet. Hopefully that alone will buy us the time we need to get her to wait while you travel and find somewhere you can send her back?

Also, I want to say I know I wasn't especially gracious to you in my first email and I'm sorry for that. I was exhausted and frustrated and – full disclosure – pretty drunk; we were at a dinner party when Anya's message was found and our friends were so convinced it was a hoax, I'm afraid they got me rather riled. You would have been completely justified in not bothering to reply at all, but that you did and so nicely too . . . Truly, we could not be more grateful.

I'm sure whatever you're doing in Nepal is incredibly challenging and you have many other things to preoccupy your mind, but if you were to have a moment to send Mabel another photograph of Moolah, it would mean the world to us.

With biggest thanks and best wishes,

Natasha

'Best wishes' too? They were positively best buddies. He read the message again, knowing exactly what was happening here – he was being schmoozed, which was fine; he didn't much care about her manipulations. He was beyond all that stuff now. He raised a hand and pulled back a corner of the window. The moon was bright and ripe and full, like a giant

Camembert. It was called the Cold Moon this month – definitely not suitable yet for jumping cows, he smiled to himself.

He let the curtain drop and tabbed into his picture gallery, bringing up the shot he had taken earlier when he'd photographed the toy in front of the hanging bridge, right before he'd run across (which would have been a strange 'last image' to be found on his phone if the worst had happened). He'd taken another, too, at the hot spring, before anyone else had arrived – Moolah sitting on the edge of the pool, half hidden by the wafting steam. He hadn't been quite sure why he was taking either photo. He certainly hadn't intended to make contact again. He wasn't looking to make friends out here, although . . . he glanced at the Ophélie-shaped wrinkles on his bedding, her imprint lingering even after she had gone . . . it was harder to leave people behind than he had assumed. Even the most glancing of connections could stick.

He thought again of the little girl's photo. If her mother was 'working' him, there was no faking the child's delight; her eyes shone with happiness and he understood exactly what this toy meant to her.

He began tapping a reply in the dark, the ghostly green glow incongruous in the Himalayan night. He knew he must sleep, that he needed to rest – but some things couldn't wait.

Chapter Thirteen

Snowshill, Gloucestershire, Monday 5 December

'Bella, could you sit back please? I can't see past your nose.'

The dog just panted, looking happy, the seatbelt strapped around her chest. She was an enthusiastic traveller and loved going in the front of the car, which was only ever allowed when Rob wasn't around.

'Turn right,' the automated voice said. *'Turn right.'*

Natasha indicated right at the T-junction and looked right and left. A bus was coming from the left, followed by a chain of cars.

'Ugh,' she groaned, her fingers tapping on the wheel. 'Why today? Why now? We're so late.'

The journey had been arduous, with tree-cutting work reducing traffic to single lanes outside Bourton-on-the-Water and adding fifteen minutes to the journey; plus there had been an accident on the A429; and then she'd overshot a right turn and had to drive an extra two miles before she could turn around again.

A space in the traffic opened up and she slotted into it quickly, joining the chain for a few hundred yards before turning left onto the country lanes. It had been raining up here and she sluiced through puddles, the car jolting awkwardly through some hidden potholes.

'*Destination, two hundred metres,*' the satnav intoned.

She passed the Snowshill sign and braked for a couple of horse riders just outside the village. Hills rose up steeply on all sides, the village nestling as if in a bowl. Honey-coloured stone houses bumped up against one another in untidy rows, ancient leaded windows twinkling at slight angles and catching the mid-morning light. The cottage roofs sat low like pulled-down caps, with little gables peeking up from the mossy slate tiles. Most of the front doors appeared to be painted in an agreed palette of sludgy greens, with climbing honeysuckle and roses – promising a profusion of scented, blowsy flower-heads in the summer months – clinging with bare fingers now.

It had to be said, the village was not looking at its best in the harsh winter gaze. Then again, where was? December so far had been unremittingly murky and so it was again today, the sky a stern battleship grey throwing a blanket of shade on the ground, and not a whisker of sunlight to be seen anywhere. There were no flowers, not even a cat sitting on a wall. Everything seemed to be in a slumber. There was an old Norman church up ahead, the lane looping around it like the oxbow of a river and doubling back out of the village again, almost as if the church and graveyard were an island.

'*Destination fifty metres.*'

Natasha sat forward on her seat, chin to the steering wheel. *Just past the church, on the left*, Diana had said in her text. The narrow rows of crooked cottages that studded the lane and village green came to an abrupt stop and she saw a set of gates set back from the road, almost hidden behind a vast, spreading beech tree. A high stone wall prevented her from seeing the gardens from here but 'Cressley Manor Farm' was smartly etched in gilded letters onto a slate plaque.

She swung in, relieved to only be eighteen minutes late. The drive was stubby but freshly gravelled and a handsome, boxy farmhouse fronted up to her. Off to the right was a stable with several long faces nodding over the doors. The sight made her smile.

A woman in jodhpurs and boots came out of one of the stalls carrying a bag of hay, raising her hand cheerfully as she saw Natasha parking up beside the battered old Land Rover.

'Now stay here and be good. I won't be long,' Natasha said, patting Bella and giving her a chewstick from her bag, unfastening her seatbelt so she could lie down if she wanted (even though she wouldn't; she would remain upright and watching through the windscreen for any sighting of her mistress).

'Hello! Natasha, it's so good to meet you,' Diana said cheerfully, striding over, an arm outstretched. 'Journey wasn't too hideous, I hope?'

'Only moderately. The usual fun and games on the motorway, of course.'

'Of course. *Such* a nightmare,' Diana said with a roll of her eyes. She didn't look like Natasha had expected – she had russet-coloured hair held back in a ponytail and a deeply freckled face, bright hazel eyes sparkling as she chatted easily while Natasha reached for her art kit on the back seat. 'You're very welcome to bring your dog too? We're all fenced in here so he can't get out, and the horses don't blink an eye.'

'Oh that's very kind, but she's not good with strangers, she can be quite nervy. She's a rescue dog; we think her previous owners used to keep her locked up and on her own for hours. I can't leave her for more than an hour really, or she'll start tearing up the house. But she's perfectly happy in the car as long as she can see me.'

'God it's awful, isn't it, how some people behave? Makes my blood boil. Well, you'll be in plain sight over here thankfully.' Diana started leading her towards the stable. A chestnut and a dun were watching their approach but a grey was showing them his hindquarters, as if in a sulk. 'I can't thank you enough for squeezing this in, Natasha. I'm sorry if I twisted your arm but when I saw your work, I just knew you were the person I'd been looking for and I don't think I could bear to have to wait another year for this; I've been mulling on the idea for so long.'

'So your husband has no idea?'

'None whatsoever,' Diana said delightedly. They stood before the stables. 'I imagine you can guess which of these is his horse?'

Natasha smiled. If the impressive height hadn't told her, the prima donna attitude certainly did. 'This welcoming fellow here, I'm guessing.' She clicked her tongue. It was enough to get the horse to lift his head in an inquisitive toss. 'What's his name?'

'Artemis. Arty.'

'How appropriate, for a horse about to have his portrait done,' she smiled.

'Indeed! Here, I'll bring him out. We'll get him into the field and you can get a better measure of him there.'

'Actually, would you mind if I . . . had a moment with him here first? I try to get some sort of eye contact right at the beginning. It helps with getting a connection and seeing who he really is.'

'Of course. Whatever works for you.'

'Do you mind if I give him this?' She pulled out a salt lick from her pocket.

'Give it a go. He loves them but he's still a moody brute. Behaves for no one but Simon. I'll have my hands full with him in the field, you'll see, but he does love to show off. He's vain as hell, knows he looks good over the jumps.'

Natasha chuckled. She clicked her tongue again, willing the horse to turn round. She needed to see into his eyes and read his character. Eyes were always the window to the soul, she was a firm believer in that, for man or beast.

'Hey, Arty,' she said, modulating her voice a little. 'What's this? What have I got here, hey?' She clicked her tongue again, seeing how his ears twitched every time she did it. She had his attention, even though he was pretending otherwise.

She began to hum, tapping her fingers on the door in time to the tune. Arty's ears twitched again; the confusion of different sounds was intriguing him and she knew curiosity would get the better of him.

Another minute later, he turned around.

'Impressive,' Diana smiled, watching his giant nostrils flare, catching Natasha's scent as she raised an arm to stroke him. 'Very impressive. You've got the magic touch, clearly. Do you ride?'

'Nope.' She laughed as the horse butted her arm with his muzzle as if trying to get closer to her.

'Dear God, he's determined to make a liar of me.'

'Are you secretly soppy?' Natasha asked, stroking his cheeks and gaining eye contact. He trusted her, she could see it. 'Have you been putting on an act, hey?'

'Well, I don't know what to say. My farrier calls him Lucifer and our vet – well, old vet now, Dave – he would have to sedate him just to check his teeth. This is not standard behaviour, let me tell you.'

'Beginner's luck, I guess.' Natasha stepped back to allow

Diana to slip his head collar on. She clipped on the lead rope and opened the stall.

'I suppose with you working so much with animals, you must know how to build rapport with them?' Diana began leading Artemis across the gravel, towards a gate that led onto a field. It had some low blue-and-white-poled jumps set up.

'Yes, that's true. I do my best to "see" their characters rather than just their features. They're pets, not just animals, and that's what their owners are wanting to have captured.' Natasha stepped ahead slightly to open the gate.

'Thank you. What's the most unusual pet you've been commissioned to draw?'

'Oh, that's easy,' Natasha said without hesitation. 'An eighteen-foot python.'

'What?'

'Oh yes!'

'And did you manage to capture its *character*?' Diana laughed.

'What there was of it.'

Artemis began to toss his head as he felt the grass beneath his hooves, picking up his feet and lifting his tail. Diana unclipped the rope to let him have a run and Natasha concentrated closely as she watched him in his first moments of freedom. He gave a few small bucks, then accelerated into a canter around the perimeter of the field.

'He's incredibly handsome,' she murmured, seeing the particular curve of the back of his neck, the ripple of his mane as he flew. He had strong musculature in his withers – from jumping all those hedges on the hunts, she supposed.

'Isn't he? Simon always says a hunt horse should have the head of a duchess and the bottom of a cook.'

Natasha laughed; she'd never heard that before.

'Arty's three-quarters thoroughbred and a quarter Irish Draught. According to Simes, that's the best combination – gives them plenty of heart room, strong shoulders, short legs and back, with a powerful engine behind but enough frontage to make you feel safe. Not forgetting good feet! Simes is forever saying *no hoof, no horse*. Honestly, sometimes I think he might be having an affair with the farrier; he's forever asking when he's coming over next.'

Natasha chuckled, still watching how Arty moved. He had beautiful extension and a natural grace to his form but he had a particular way of tossing his head to the left shoulder, she noticed. It had an artful, preening feel to it, as though he too knew he was special. She could see now why Diana wanted a full-sized portrait.

She reached for her phone and began taking some photos. His colouring was beautiful, too – a dappled grey like a rainy day sky, deepening into flecked steel freckles down the hind-quarters. She couldn't help but feel excited by the prospect of capturing his essence. *If* she could. This would be a test of nerve as much as skill. Rob was always telling her to take the pressure off, but maybe that was precisely the problem; there wasn't *enough* pressure on her. She felt caught in a permanent state of suspension, as if waiting for life to . . . get bigger, or grow brighter, or speed up somehow. She felt sluggish and strangely held back, as though she'd been tethered to an invisible stake in the ground and she could never rise up or take off in a sprint.

Yes, the last week had been draining, dealing with a trau-matized, exhausted toddler, but that crisis was being 'managed' now and the feeling of emptiness that constantly gnawed at her was still there. She wanted a sibling for Mabel, she wanted another baby to hold; it was an ache she couldn't put into words. But what was she going to do – stare into the abyss and just wait?

'He does hold his head in a particular way, doesn't he, towards his left shoulder,' she murmured.

'I know. He clearly thinks it's his best side,' Diana smiled.

Natasha opened her shooting stick stool and reached for her backpack, pulling out the artist's sketchpad. 'I'll begin with some pencil sketches today.'

'Good-o. What would you like me to do?'

'If you can lunge him on the rope, I'll study his legs.'

'And jumps?'

'Shortly, I think. We'll keep him fresh for the moment.'

'Arty!' Diana gave a whistle and raised her arms. Artemis looked at her and then away again. 'Here boy!' she called, striding over the grass, trying to encourage him to come over so she could rope him up again.

Natasha pulled out her pencils and checked them over, then set to work.

The temperature had dropped sharply by the time she packed up. She had filled four pages with various studies of forelegs, hindquarters, tail curvature and markings, and she was pleased with her start. Artemis seemed pleased with his day's exercise, too. Diana had relaxed into schooling him as the minutes slid into hours, almost forgetting that Natasha was there.

She watched the bolt slide back on his stable. 'See you soon, big fella,' Natasha murmured, stroking his cheek.

Diana walked back with her to the car as Natasha loaded her supplies onto the back seat. Bella jumped from the front seat to greet her, tail hitting the seats in her excitement. 'Yes, hello,' Natasha smiled. 'You've been very good.' She glanced at Diana. 'Do you mind if I just let her down for a moment to stretch her legs? It's a hefty journey back.'

'Of course, of course!'

Natasha put the dog on the lead and let her jump onto the drive. Bella immediately dropped her head to the ground and began sniffing, tail wagging wildly.

'A lot of animal smells for her to pick up,' Natasha said.

'Yes, quite—'

A gaggle of children yelling, roaring and screaming suddenly carried over the hedge from next door.

'Gosh,' Natasha said in surprise. It was like driving past a school playground with the windows open.

'Don't worry, it's our neighbours' children,' Diana said, quite unperturbed. 'They've got six.'

'*Six?*'

'Yes. At one point they had six under ten, which was fairly intense.'

'For you as well as them, I'm sure!' Natasha smiled.

'To be honest, we rather like it. Our three are the same age as their eldest ones, so the children have always been in and out of each other's houses. Emily and James are great fun too.'

'Exhausted though, surely? I've only got one and I find that a struggle!'

'Well, Emily does have quite a lot of help . . . *Family money*,' she mouthed.

'Oh.' Natasha wasn't sure what to say to that. 'Wow . . . Still. Six, though.'

'Yes. She put her foot down after Roops was born. Made James . . .' She made a scissor motion with her fingers.

'I'm not surprised,' Natasha grinned. 'I think I'd want cast-iron guarantees too.'

Bella pulled on the lead suddenly, picking up a scent of something interesting. Natasha took a few steps.

'So when would suit you best for the next visit?'

'Umm . . .' Natasha thought for a moment, trying to think through Mabel's schedule. She had Rachel's wreath-making class tomorrow. 'Probably Wednesday, if you can manage that? My daughter's in nursery Monday, Wednesday, Friday, so that does make it easier for me to get away for longer periods.'

'Wednesday's great. How old is your daughter?'

'Just turned three.'

'Adorable. That's by far the best age,' Diana nodded, looking wistful. 'They're like cherubs.'

'She has got us well and truly twisted around her little finger.' Bella stopped pulling on the lead, giving up the scent. 'Great, well, it's been a really strong start today. And such a pleasure to meet you.' Natasha opened the passenger car door again and Bella jumped up. Natasha buckled her seatbelt, making Diana smile.

'And you. Safe journey back,' Diana said, beginning to wave as she walked backwards a few steps over the gravel. 'See you Wednesday.'

Natasha turned out of the drive and back onto the country lane, where puddles were still glinting darkly, the sun a faint haze behind stony clouds. She realized she was shivering from all the hours spent sitting outside and she put on the heater, turning on the radio. Her body was cold, her mind tired, but she felt good; better than she had in months, in fact. Better even than in the Maldives (not that she would tell Rob that). Her hunch had been right; this was exactly the distraction she needed to tide her over until life got back on track again. She needed a busy life, a full one. Happy wife, happy life – wasn't that the phrase?

Chapter Fourteen

Whinfell, October 2018

'Oh, sorry!'

Tom looked up as she flung the door open, the knotted bin bag in her hand. He was sitting on the deck, his back against the wooden walls of the treehouse, arms resting on his bent knees. He looked quizzically at the bag. 'Cleaning? Really?' he asked dryly.

'Well, I have to do something . . . It's a meat market in there.'

'Don't sit here, then,' he quipped, but his demeanour was languid and the very opposite of predatory as he rested his head back and drank some more beer.

Natasha watched him, trying to ignore the excitement that came from having inadvertently found him. She had spent the past twenty minutes looking for him, pretending she was trying to find her phone as she went from room to room, and she'd thought he had gone. 'What are you doing out here, anyway?'

He shrugged. 'Same as you. Trying not to get seduced. It's a nightmare.'

She laughed. 'You're funny.'

'Funny enough to laugh you into bed?'

She laughed again. 'No chance.' She put the bin bag down and went over to the veranda, looking down over the park. The treehouse was subtly spotlit, highlighting leaves on the turn, a new season bleeding into being from the soil up. Beyond, the pedestrianized roads were lit too, bicycles propped against walls. No one was around. She stared out for a few minutes, listening to the wind, distant shouts emanating from chalets of children who should have long been in bed. It was gone ten. Natasha was so drunk, she felt almost sober again.

She glanced back at him, the silence between them strangely easy and familiar for two near-strangers. 'So you don't have a girlfriend?'

'Nope.'

She raised an eyebrow. 'Boyfriend?'

'Nope,' he smiled.

'Huh. That surprises me.'

'That I don't have a boyfriend?'

She shrugged as she turned around to face him, her elbows splayed on the wooden railings. She was long past caring that she was dressed for a 1980s brides' magazine.

'Why should it surprise you?' He looked back at her through hooded eyes, his head tipped back. He seemed . . . tired. Melancholic, even.

'Well, you're good-looking, charismatic, funny—'

'Great kisser.'

She grinned. She wouldn't even try to deny it. 'Yeah. You're a great kisser. If a little forward.'

He shrugged. 'Like I told you – tomorrow, death comes.'

'You've got to *stop* telling me that,' she said, giving a shiver.

'I can't. We should all live with the awareness that this is all we get. One shot. One day at a time. One minute at a time.'

She didn't reply. The memory of what had happened to her today still clung and she couldn't quite shake the heavy, dark feeling that had spread like a bruise through her body. She knew it was still there, a leprechaun lurking, waiting to pounce upon her again when she was least expecting it.

A breeze brushed through the grove and she gave a small shiver.

'You should go back in,' he murmured. 'The wind's picking up.'

She watched him for another moment then wandered over to where he sat instead. 'I can't go in there. I told you, my virtue's not safe.'

He turned his head and looked at her, bemused. 'And you think it's safe with *me*?' he asked, as their arms and thighs touched. She felt an impulse to be close to him. The feeling of his arms around her as he'd walked her to safety on the rope bridge – she'd never experienced that before. He had felt like . . . home.

'Yes. I feel safe with you,' she murmured, taking the beer from his hands and having a swig herself.

'Jeez, talk about friend-zoned. I really am losing my touch.'

She handed back the beer with a grin.

'So who's with who in there?' he asked, staring ahead through the slatted veranda.

'Well, Rachel and Andy are getting hot and heavy on the sofa. Jack and Hels have gone into her bedroom; Lauren's making toast in the kitchen with Ben, which is really frustrating because Lauren's engaged so he's wasting his time there, while poor Sara and Lizzie are left lying on the floor playing Would You Rather.' She looked at his profile, her gaze dragging heavily over him. 'You should go in and be his wingman.'

He turned his head again to look at her. 'Yeah? He can have Sara and I'll have Lizzie? Or vice versa?'

She shrugged. 'Why not?'

He didn't rush to answer. '. . . No.' That was all he said, staring at her for several long moments before turning away again.

'Are you mad at me?'

'It's not my place to be mad at you.'

'So then what?'

'So then nothing.'

'There's something. I feel like you're mad at me.'

He looked across at her again and this time, she could see a flicker of something darker in his eyes. 'No. You just frustrate the hell out of me.'

'Because I'm *getting married*?' She laughed softly. 'Don't you think it's a bit rich that you – a man I had never met before this morning – are hacked off that I'm marrying the man I love and have been with for the past year?'

'*Year?* Tch.' He tutted. 'I've got older socks.'

'I thought you said it's not about that. You said you can find someone in a moment.'

He shrugged his eyebrows. 'So you were listening.'

'It was pretty hard not to.'

'But you're not going to do anything about it.'

She gave a soft snort. 'There's nothing *to* do.'

'Because there's nothing between you and me? I think we debunked that myth back in there, didn't we?' The memory of their kiss still made her body tingle. No one had ever kissed her like that before.

'Tom, I don't know what you expect me to say,' she laughed. 'You must see that it's utterly outrageous to tell a complete stranger that her upcoming wedding is a mistake?'

'It would be outrageous *not* to tell you. And you're not a complete stranger. I know I don't know where you grew up, or what your favourite colour is, or if you're allergic to cats – but something in me recognizes something in you. Deny it.' His eyes caught hers, so clear and challenging.

'I do deny it.'

'Liar. That kiss in there told me otherwise.'

She didn't reply. That kiss in there had floored her, there was no pretending otherwise. '. . . It was just a game. Everyone was going for it.'

'So then kiss me again out here, where no one's watching, and show me there's nothing between us.'

'I'm not falling for that!' she scoffed, but her heart was pounding as she tucked her legs in and wrapped her arms around them. She rested her cheek on her knees, looking back at him as his eyes roamed over her; a dark amusement shone from them but she could see the frustration in his jaw too, the strong clench of his hand around his own wrist. They were hovering between half jokes and teases, truth darting like a dragonfly on lilypads, touched upon but never settling.

She froze as he reached over and traced a finger lightly down her cheek, following the contours of her face like she was something precious, something to be understood. The intimacy of it made her think the kiss would have been preferable after all. 'Do you think I woke up this morning thinking it would be fun to wreck someone's wedding?'

'Well, you don't strike me as a sociopath,' she said quietly, not daring to move.

'High praise,' he murmured, his eyes never leaving the angles of her face, as though memorizing them. 'Do you think that when I saw you frozen on that rope bridge, I decided it would be fun to mess with you?'

'No.'

'Do you think that the bride-to-be I rescued not once, but twice, looked to me like a woman running towards her future?'

She sat back suddenly, moving away from his touch and resting her head against the wall. 'I told you, I'm scared of heights.'

He laughed softly. 'You're not, though.' He turned his head to look at her, both of them leaning against the treehouse, their bodies slumped, but between them, taut and quivering, an invisible wire connecting him to her. He shook his head slowly, his face marbled with conflicting emotions.

Was he going to kiss her after all? She watched his gaze drop to her mouth and stay there a moment. Her heart rate spiked but she didn't move. And neither did he. He turned away again, as if banishing her from his sight. He sighed heavily. 'I knew I shouldn't have taken that shift.'

'What do you mean?'

'It was supposed to be my weekend off.'

'But now look, you're partying in a treehouse,' she joked, by way of consolation.

He didn't look consoled as he glanced over again. 'I shouldn't have come here either.'

'Why not?'

'Because it was bad enough just you not wanting to marry him,' he said quietly. 'But now *I* don't want you to marry him either.'

If she hadn't been sitting down already, she was pretty sure she would have slipped to the ground by now. 'I hope you're not going to follow this with a proposal,' she managed.

A half smile spread over his mouth. 'No. But your wedding next weekend really fucks up my plans to take you to dinner.'

Oh God. She went to speak but no words presented themselves. She saw emotion in his eyes that wasn't down to drink, or a dare. Something existed between them, an intimacy that belied their few short hours together. He felt like her best friend, someone she'd known for years. She wanted to put her head on his shoulder and curl into him; she wanted to hear him laugh, talk, sing. She wanted to dance with him again.

As if sensing her thoughts, he reached a hand forward, spreading his fingers into her hair and pulling her towards him, their lips only inches apart now. 'Kiss me.'

'. . . I can't,' she breathed, almost trembling from the effort it took not to lean into him.

'Kiss me.' She felt his fingertips press against her scalp, pulling on her hair gently, frustration growing.

'. . . I can't,' she whispered.

His eyes burned into hers, unblinking. It was like staring into the sun. 'Then we'll never know what this could be.' His hand dropped as he pulled away in the next instant and it was like a cold wind twisted around her. He rose easily, athletically, leaving her sitting on the deck, satin skirts billowing around her legs.

What? 'Where are you going?' she asked, scrambling to stand as he set down the beer bottle and walked towards the treehouse steps.

'Back. I'm not into torturing myself.' He looked back at her and the look in his eyes was the answer to all the questions she hadn't asked him; this was no joke. 'Good luck next weekend. I guess.'

'But . . . You can't be leaving yet.'

'There's nothing more to be said, Nats. There's no time and you won't give me a chance.' He started down the steps.

She felt a desperation to stop him that she couldn't understand. Why would she make him stay? For what? This was good. He should go.

'Please, Tom. Just stay.'

He glanced back but didn't stop, disappearing from sight down the steps in the next breath.

'But if you go, I'll never see you again,' she cried, running over to the veranda.

'Then I guess your fiancé can sleep easy,' he called back, throwing his arms out as he walked across the grass. She watched him move further into the trees, losing sight of his head, then his shoulders, then his legs . . .

'Tom! This is stupid. Just come back!' she called, crouching down on the deck and peering through the veranda, getting as low as she could to keep him in her sights. 'You can't leave yet! It's still early!'

The night blinked back at her, barely stirring.

'Tom!' she cried, her voice splitting into a whisper. '. . . You're not being fair.'

Chapter Fifteen

Nepal, Tuesday 6 December

Seven hundred vertical metres. That was today's job. Left foot. Right foot. He just had to keep going. He tried to keep his mind blank, to be conscious of this moment and this moment only, but his mind was unruly and defiant, wandering freely as his body worked. It scratched at memories that had long sat under scabs and he realized they were no longer ticklish, they no longer hurt in the way they once had – he remembered the lightsabres he and Lottie had received on their sixth birthday and their countless sword fights; he heard their mother's laughter at the Christmas table as they told the jokes from their crackers, her paper crown ripped over her thick brown hair but worn anyway; he saw Crumble, their first dog, learning to roll her own tennis ball from the top of the slope in the garden.

Left foot. Right foot.

He recalled the look in his father's eyes as he saw the 'A' marked in A-level maths that had, for one day at least, made him proud; he could still feel time bend as he hit black ice and knew he would hit the tree, a month after he'd passed his test; he shivered at the prickles that had run up his arm when he'd heard 'Bohemian Rhapsody' for the first time;

heard the snap of his femur as he went over on the roller-blades.

He walked past rice paddies and terraced meadows, through bamboo, rhododendron and oak forests, over hanging bridges, beneath waterfalls. Nature seemed almost to fall over itself in a rush to show its myriad interpretations – thirty thousand different shades of green beneath a stony sky – right on the very boundary where the air grew thin and where, on the other side, nothing could grow at all.

His mind replayed the email he had read over breakfast. He had read it thirty times; there was nothing else to do.

. . . loved the picture of her by the hot spring. I had to run her a hot bath straight afterwards and keep the doors closed so the steam stayed in and we could pretend we were there too . . . that rope bridge looked so dangerous! I trust you didn't actually cross it? You can't have done it, I'm sure it just made for a good photo . . . The winter is so long and bleak here, it's really cheering to get your postcards – that's what we call them. I've been printing them out for Mabes on our printer and then stick them on the back of a Christmas card and laminate them to put on her wall. I know, who actually has a laminator? I am that person . . . Anyway, write back if you can. Take care . . .

She'd gone from 'shame on you' to 'take care' in three easy steps. He could imagine her in person, one of those polished Home Counties women, all armoured confidence and long glossy hair, driving a big shiny SUV.

A man walked past him, overtaking him on the slope, wearing a brocade *topi* and teal down jacket. A world apart.

'*Namaste*,' he said as he passed, head down, walking time

and a half to Duffy's beat. Duffy looked at the large conical woven basket on his back as he went ahead.

'. . . Sir?'

The man stopped. Duffy pulled the toy from the mesh bottle pocket in the side of his pack; he kept the little toy there now for ready access as opportunities presented themselves. He couldn't keep taking off his pack, not even for that little girl. He couldn't trust he would put it back on again. 'May I?'

The man smiled, standing in profile as Duffy set Moodle into the top of the basket – filled with vegetables – his head peeking out, and took the picture.

'*Namaskar.*'

Left foot. Right foot. Time slipped past. The pitch was unremitting now with almost no level sections; he was either going up or going down at all times. He passed a pure white pony on the path. It didn't move as he stepped around it, standing so still and trancelike that Duffy couldn't quite be sure if he was dreaming the beast, or if the beast was dreaming him.

The weather was changing with the altitude. The wind always picked up at three thousand metres and the temperatures dropped; he would have to wear a hat when he fell into his bed in Deurali tonight. He welcomed these indicators of approach, and he could feel the presence of the mountains now. Not the ones he was trekking, though the unremitting inclines made themselves known; but verdant and lush, covered in forests, these Alpine-sized foothills were babies to the giants that lay on the other side. He could feel the sense of suspension growing in his chest, as though his heart was holding itself in a state of contraction, ready for the moment he rounded the corner and the might of the Himalayas fell upon him in an angel's swoop. It was always the same, no matter how often he saw it – like trying to imagine eternity, to fathom an edgeless space, he could never hold in his mind the scale of the place, these mountains that soared and spread and pulled the earth's crust into fine-tipped icy peaks.

Left foot. Right foot.

. . . Lottie singing in the kitchen, making pancakes; their granny teaching 'Chopsticks' on the piano; finishing his Rubik's Cube in under three minutes (never did get to sub-two); kissing *her* in a circle of strangers and friends and knowing what she did not; their twenty-first at Glastonbury and Lottie blagging backstage passes to the Pyramid stage; tasting his first home-grown tomato (too early; the second was better); cycling John O'Groats to Land's End with Ben, for a bet.

No Spitting in the Temple

The sign – recognized, remembered – roused him from his reverie and he knew he was close, that he was nearing the gateway to the next stage. He paid attention, pulling his mind into the present and stopping to look behind him for almost the first time on this journey. So far, he had kept his sights fixed firmly ahead, wholly focused on where he must go. But now, as he approached the straddle point between one landscape and the next, he turned around to see how far he'd come. The mountains folded away behind him in blackish-green vertical pleats, low clouds nudging through the V-shaped gorges like grazing sheep.

He stood there for several minutes, absorbing its beauty as a kind of goodbye, then he turned and continued onwards. He rounded a long bend and a plateau opened up, as he knew it would – a vast plain in an otherwise pinched landscape. It was a core memory, this: the sight of bleached grasses flattened in the wind, brightly coloured prayer flags strung on ribbons and mounted on tall wooden poles, fluttering wildly like birds' wings and streaming out of sight in long lengths, or else criss-crossing one another. The sound of them flapping sharply sparked another memory – his mother shaking out the sheets to dry in the garden. It, like all the other memories, belonged to another Duffy, another lifetime, another world from here.

His gaze rose skywards, to the snow-laden behemoths that showed themselves at last. No more peek-a-boo, they stood unflinching and defiant against his stare as he tried and failed to grasp their magnitude; scale was impossible to quantify, as much at this distance as if he was standing on the summits. They belonged to the land of giants, of gods, of monsters. They were beautiful and cruel, dazzling and merciless. Who could resist them?

The temple lay a short way off the path and he wandered over. He wasn't Hindu or Buddhist; he couldn't even say he was an optimist, not anymore, but he still said a prayer with his eyes closed and his heart open. And when he was done, he ran his hands over the spinning metal prayer wheels for luck and chanted a meditation in a low voice. 'Oṃ maṇi padme hūṃ. Oṃ maṇi padme hūṃ.'

Eventually, he sat on a rock and looked out into the vast-ness. He felt his physical insignificance but his soul felt like it was whistling, every nerve tingling. The shift was happening within him as he became who he needed to be and he realized that these memories playing through his mind were not signs of emotional weakness, but breadcrumbs he was dropping from his pocket and leaving behind him in a trail as he moved on. He was shedding, becoming lighter. When he finally rose again, he realized he was trembling from the cold. It was time to get to the teahouse and rest. Tomorrow would be another big day.

He walked a few paces before he remembered the promise he had made in the dark last night. He pulled the toy from the backpack pocket again and carefully propped Moodle atop one of the wooden poles, the prayer flags stretching away behind her, as if into eternity.

She would like that, he thought, little Mabel from Somerset.

Chapter Sixteen

Frome, Tuesday 6 December

'Rach?'

'Yeah?' The florist looked up from the butler's sink where she was placing bunches of mistletoe into buckets of water.

'. . . Do you have any pheasant feathers?' Natasha asked, picking up another stem of eucalyptus and binding it to the metal ring. It put up a bit of fight and she felt a third hand would have been helpful. Then again, she often thought that – picking up Mabel's toys, doing the ironing, trying to get her sketches down before the memories faded.

'Pheasant feathers?' Rachel echoed with a frown. 'For the wreath?'

'Yeah,' she murmured.

'For a *Christmas* wreath?'

Her tone of disbelief suggested this was highly controversial. 'Yes. Rob was talking about it the other day. He thinks they look really smart.'

'But that's an Autumn palette,' Lauren said, butting in with authority. She was their unofficial leader of All Things Smart.

Rachel thought for a moment. 'Well, if it's feathers you want, I guess I could check out back and see whether there's any pigeon feathers floating about in the yard. It'll depend on whether Breezy has had any kills lately.'

Hels and Lizzie laughed. That tabby cat was a ruthless killer; she could probably stuff a mattress with the feathers out there.

'Ha!' Natasha smiled, sticking out her tongue at the tease. 'It was just a thought.' She picked up another stem of holly and immediately stabbed herself under the thumbnail with one of the leaves again. 'Ouch! Fucker.'

'Language, Nats!' Lauren trilled, her glass of champagne fizzing nicely beside her and her wreath looking fantastically verdant. If Rob had had tree envy at the Tennants' last weekend, he was going to pop a gasket when he saw the wreath of magnificence hanging on their ancient oak door.

Carols were playing in the background.

'By the way, Nats, did you see you're up to seventeen million likes?' Lizzie said.

'Really?' Natasha was surprised. She actually hadn't logged on since she'd received 'proof of life' from Duffy. She couldn't get excited about social media stats. 'God, I can't believe it's still circulating. I put up a post saying she'd been found!'

'Well, these things have a momentum of their own at this scale. It's a juggernaut now. You can't stop it.'

'Mmm, I guess.'

'It's sweet that people are still emotionally investing in it, though. It just goes to show the positive power of social media,' Lauren smiled, looking warmed by the thought.

'Have you heard any more from the guy?' Rachel asked, coming around with the champagne bottle and topping up their glasses. Natasha put a hand over hers. Unlike the others who could walk to their houses from here, she would be collecting Mabel from Rosie's later and driving them both home.

'Yes actually. I think he's getting quite into it. Look.' She reached for her phone and brought up the images – Moolah sitting on a pack mule; Moolah perched on a precarious-looking rope bridge; Moolah half hidden by steam at a hot spring; Moolah peeking out of what looked like a man's laundry basket; Moolah clinging to a wooden pole strung with brightly coloured flags.

'Oh my God,' her friends alternately gasped and cooed. 'So many!' 'God, that's so cool!'

'It's adorable!' Lauren sang. 'He's doing all that for Mabes?'

'You should read the messages. He writes them directly to her.' Natasha wrinkled her nose.

Hels arched an eyebrow. 'Not you?'

'No. He only refers to me as Mabel's mummy,' Natasha grinned. 'I've written to him a couple of times, trying to engage him a bit more, but he never responds to me directly. I don't think he's forgiven me for my first note. To be honest, I did reread it the morning after I sent it and I don't exactly come across as chummy: I wouldn't like me much either. Anyway, whatever. I'm just grateful he's doing this for her. She's *so* excited every time she gets another "postcard".'

'Postcard?'

'Well, that's what we're calling them. I print them up and laminate them for her and put them on her wall.'

'*Laminate*—? Ugh, of course you do,' Hels said with a groan.

'So he's sending them really regularly then,' Rachel said. 'Looks like you got lucky with your world traveller. I bet most people wouldn't bother replying even once.'

'I know, it's amazing. Better than we could have hoped. Rob says he's about six hours ahead of us and he seems to send them at roughly the same time, so it must be once he's back at the hotels in the evenings. I'm guessing he must get wifi at wherever he stays at night.'

'Do they have hotels out there?' Lauren asked.

'Not your sort, I'm sure,' Hels teased, patting her shoulder. 'I can't see you getting on with a long-drop loo!'

'Helena!' Lauren chided as the others laughed.

'So do you have any idea where he actually is out there?' Lizzie asked.

'Nope, none. He just told Mabes that he was going to see mountains that are so high they touch the roof of the world, and that Moolah could jump over the moon from them.'

'He actually said that?' Rachel cooed, her hands folded over her heart and her head tipped to the side.

'So it could be Everest?' Lauren asked.

'I guess. Either way, it's a pretty useful cover story because Mabel is now so invested in the idea of Moolah jumping the moon, that she's no longer asking when she's coming back. I've been showing her pictures of the lunar cycle and as it is, it's the full moon tonight – and no cow can jump a full moon.'

'Oh, clearly,' Hels deadpanned.

'Which buys us two weeks for the moon to wane and become "jumpable" – and for him to trek somewhere closer to a DHL depot!' Natasha laughed.

'I think I love him,' Rachel sighed.

'Have him then,' Natasha grinned.

'Is he married? How old is he? Have you even seen him?'

'No idea and no, he only sends pictures of Moolah. I reckon

it's better that we don't see him. He could be some creepy old bloke and it might freak Mabel out to know he's got her beloved toy.'

'Mmm,' Lauren agreed, looking immediately concerned by that prospect.

Hels frowned. 'Although I don't think you get many old blokes trekking the Himalayas, do you? You've got to be pretty fit and young*ish*.'

'Yeah, maybe,' Natasha said distractedly. 'Here, read this one. This is his most recent.'

She handed over her phone for the others to read at the cutting table, their heads pressed together, champagne glasses in their hands as they read in silence.

Hi Mabel and Mabel's Mummy,

Greetings from the Himalayas. Moolah is having so much fun, I can hardly keep her from galloping up the mountains! I have to keep reminding her it's important we don't ascend too quickly as the air is really fine up here and people can get sick. So that means we're taking our time and having lots of fun along the way. She loved being carried in this porter's basket. The porters help carry food and equipment up to the teahouses and restaurants high up in the mountains where the cars can't go, so it was nice for her to rest her legs for a while . . .

'Awww!' Lauren laughed. 'He's so cute.'

'Don't you think it's sweet he didn't say the air gets *thin* – that might have frightened Mabel. See how he said it got fine?' Natasha said, pointing out the distinction.

'That's really thoughtful,' Rachel said earnestly.

. . . Then we stopped at this temple and Moolah loved the prayer flags so much she wanted you to see them too. Each flag represents a prayer that needs to be answered and they get strung high up like this so they can be carried on the wind. They should never be still as the Nepali people believe that when they flutter, they release positive spiritual vibrations. Moolah really liked that we were moving through air that's filled with so much positivity and I do too. Do you see how some of the flags are really bright? They're the new prayers; the more faded ones show that the wind has carried away the prayers to be answered.

'He could be a Religious Studies teacher?' Lauren mused.
'Or just an old hippy,' Hels quipped.

We're getting quite high up now so it's a lot colder and windier. We can see the snow too but Moolah and I are having lots of hugs to keep ourselves warm. We can see the really big mountains now too. We'll be arriving at one called Machhapuchhre tomorrow. It's known as the fishtail mountain because of the shape of it but I guess it could be a mermaid's tail mountain as well? See if you can see a picture of it and you can decide.

Anyway, we must sleep now so we're strong for tomorrow.

Moolah sends you big cuddles and kisses and says to go to sleep at bedtime.

Your friend, Duffy

'All of this is so . . . extra,' Rachel sighed. 'I mean, he doesn't *have* to do any of it, much less this sweetly.'

'I know, that's what I keep thinking. Maybe it's giving him something to do?'

'Is he out there with anyone?'

'He hasn't mentioned it,' she shrugged. 'But then again, why would he?'

'Mmm. Well, if he is alone, it must be pretty lonely up there. I can't imagine being somewhere like that with no one to talk to.'

'You can hardly go to the loo without someone to talk to!' Hels drawled.

They all laughed as they wandered back to their stools around the cutting table again.

'And how's it going with your hot vet, Hels?' Lizzie asked, pondering on a stem of Baby's Breath.

'Hot and steamy.'

Natasha smiled along as her best friend suggestively waggled her eyebrows to comic effect, but inside she felt an anxious tremor. Even in the Maldives the other week things hadn't been hot and steamy with her and Rob but just pleasingly . . . pleasing. And now they were back to the grind, passing ships in the night, so that even 'pleasingly pleasing' would be a result. Rob had called as she was on her way over here to say he would be home late tonight, which meant another meal for one, a tray on her lap and Netflix on. She started clipping some leaves off the rosehips, determined to stave off the self-pity that seemed only ever a step behind her at the moment.

Hels looked up. 'Oh Nats – Dave said he messaged some former client about a commission for you?'

'I know, I've already been to see her, I meant to tell you. Will you thank him for me? She rang on Saturday morning within minutes of getting his email.'

'Christ, that was quick!'

'She's so desperate to get it done in time for Christmas, she's paying double my fee.'

'Wow!' Lauren said, looking impressed.

'Bet Rob's pleased,' Lizzie said.

'Actually, he doesn't know anything about it. I'm going to keep it a secret and use the money to get him a surprise Christmas present.'

'Like what?' Hels asked.

'Not sure yet. A vintage watch maybe? I need some ideas.' Secretly though, she hoped she would have an even better surprise for him by then too – one that money couldn't buy. She had decided that if she was pregnant, she'd tell him on Christmas Day by getting a Big Sister jumper for Mabel to wear.

'Ugh, you two are so fricking *cute*,' Rachel tutted. 'Surprise presents, tropical holidays. You do know you're not dating anymore, right? This is married life; it's supposed to get dull and a little grey.'

Natasha gave her best smile as she bent the stem gently and pushed the end into the wire cage, but if Rachel's compliment was rooted in the familiar narrative that their lives were perfect, she had also begun to notice what people were beginning *not* to say to her – such as asking whether they were 'trying', when could they expect the pitter patter of tiny feet and did Mabel want to be a big sister? The timeframe between her birth and a subsequent sibling's was beginning to stretch and become, if not suspicious, then certainly sensitive. People were beginning to guess it was an issue. She desperately hoped this would be their last Christmas with just the three of them. She hoped this baby was the answer to filling the emptiness inside her . . .

No. Not hoped. She shook her mind clear, casting out any doubts. It *would* be. Of course it would. She was an optimist and this was going to be their best Christmas ever.

But a question glowed in her mind nonetheless, like a lighthouse beam warning distant ships, refusing to go unseen.

What if it wasn't? What if it wasn't?

What then?

The full moon threw down fat beams upon the carpet, the room glowing a spectral silver. She liked sleeping with the curtains open and she'd seen Rob's headlights swing into the drive as she lay in bed, her body heavy with wine but her mind twitchy. It had been eighteen hours since he'd left this morning; she'd been in bed when he'd left, in bed now he was back and he hadn't seen Mabel at all.

She closed her eyes, trying to stop the stress from taking root in her muscles. This was married life. Everyone had this, or a version of it: conflicting schedules, young kids, the pressures of running a business. They were fortunate in so many ways, she knew that: this house and garden, a smart car, fancy holidays now and then, cashmere jumpers and diamond stud earrings . . . They had good *stuff*, but stuff didn't stop her feeling lonely.

She stared at the shadows climbing the wall. It would be six in the morning in Nepal right now, the sun rising in a fine-aired sky above snow-capped mountains, while here the moon hung like a pendant over foggy fields. Other lives were being lived. Was this really hers?

The question kept presenting itself, impertinent and insistent, refusing to go away . . .

She gave a sigh, just as the door creaked and Rob tiptoed in. He shrugged off his jacket and started pulling off his tie. He stepped out of his trousers and caught them by the hems, dangling them upside down so the front pleat remained crisp. He always draped his clothes over the armchair on his side of the bed. He unfastened his cufflinks and pulled out the brass stiffeners in his shirt collar, then padded across the carpet to his wardrobe, where he dropped them into an open leather trinket box.

Natasha watched him through half-slitted eyes, the duvet tucked high around her shoulders, not sure she wanted him to know she was awake. It would invariably mean sex and she wasn't in the mood. She'd felt her mood flatten throughout the course of the day, even Bella pacing restlessly as they each moved about the too-big house, never quite big enough or loud enough to fill it, and wine o'clock had started early tonight. The wreath-making course with her friends, and carols and champagne, should have been the perfect festive pick-me-up, but even that hadn't quite done the trick and the resulting wreath itself was so sparse and limp – as if reflecting her own wanness – she was tempted to swap it for one from Waitrose. She wondered if he'd even noticed it hanging on the door.

She felt like she was a Stepford Wife, looking great, feeling numb. She'd had a bottle of sauvignon blanc after she'd put Mabel to bed and tried FaceTiming Hels but she was at a gig with Dave, which only reminded Natasha of their 'hot and steamy' status and made her feel more depressed; she hadn't been to any sort of concert – except Glyndebourne, once, which did not count – since uni. There had been no one she could call, all her friends either out or snuggled up with their partners, so she'd written to the only other person she could think of who might also be lonely right now. Probably not her best idea ever.

Duffy wasn't a friend, of course, but he was a friendly presence at the periphery of their lives. She had started out by telling him how much his communications meant to Mabel and how, in making her daughter happy, they made *her* happy too. She wanted him to know how *grateful* she was for his kindness. How, even though they had never met, they felt *connected* to him now and they would never forget what he was doing – he had become part of their story and maybe they were a little part of his, in return? He was sharing moments of his travels with them and that counted, didn't it? She asked him what it was like to be somewhere like Nepal. Did he feel safe there, in the mountains? Did he feel free? Did he feel lonely in such an isolated place, or could people only really feel lonely when they were surrounded by others . . . ? He wouldn't answer her questions, of course. She knew that. He spoke only to Mabel. He and she were not friends and she felt a vague sense of unease at having pressed send.

Rob shrugged off his shirt so that he was standing in just his boxers and socks; he worked as hard for his physique as he did for everything else, and he had looked good in the Maldivian shallows. He liked that they made a beautiful couple, that people turned as they walked past. Well, he always assumed it was because of that, but occasionally Natasha wondered if it was on account of the age difference. There was a light salting to his dark hair now and he was clearly older than her, but she had still been stunned when on a few occasions, he had been mistaken for her father.

Something glinted in the bright, brilliant moonlight, catching her eye – a signet ring on his left-hand little finger. She frowned, peering closer and wondering if she was seeing things. He'd never worn one before. So why start now? And when had he bought it? He seemed to notice it too, looking at it for a moment before pulling it off and dropping it into the trinket box with the other bits. He glanced back at her as if sensing, finally, her bleary-eyed scrutiny. 'Ah . . . You're awake.'

His words startled her as much as her consciousness startled him. '. . . Yes. I was just dozing,' she said. 'What time is it?'

He walked towards the bed. 'Just gone midnight.'

'That's late.'

'I know,' he sighed. 'Doing what needs to be done.'

She felt the mattress shift as he climbed in beside her, his body spooning hers. His skin felt cold beside her slumbering warmth and she gave a shiver. 'It's cold out there tonight. Clear skies,' he murmured, his breath on her neck as he pulled her in close. 'How was your day?'

'Fine.'

'Only fine?'

She paused. '. . . Just quiet. I went to Rachel's workshop for lunch with the girls.' She made no mention of the afternoon spent refining the sketches she'd started at the Lorns'.

'Sounds like a great day,' he murmured, pushing back her hair and beginning to kiss her neck. 'And Mabel was good?'

'Fine. Went straight to sleep.'

'Wow! Is that on account of some more missives from mad McDuff, friend of cows?'

'Yes. We had a few more photos today. They're up on her wall.' Her words ran into one another like toppled dominoes.

'She's getting quite a collection. I'll check them out in the morning,' he murmured. She could feel him warming up, but it was almost as though he was taking the heat from her and she was growing chill. 'I missed you,' he whispered, his hands beginning to wander.

234

'I missed you too.' She closed her eyes and tried to relax as he rolled her over and entwined his body with hers. She reminded herself this was what she had wanted all day – her husband beside her, her companion, lover, friend, hot and steamy – but shadows kept turning over in her mind. He kissed her harder, more urgently, and she tried to lose herself in the sensations, but as she kissed him in return she was realizing something she'd never noticed before.

He was here again. He was back. And she was still lonely.

Chapter Seventeen

Nepal, Wednesday 7 December

'Duff!'

Unaccustomed to being cheered upon arrival, he looked up as he climbed the steps towards the blue-roofed teahouse. Stevie and Jay were sitting on the terrace, their socked feet resting on the stone wall. The place was busy, every table taken, so that it felt more like an après-ski bar in the Alps than a Himalayan base camp. Lines of clothes were strung up at every window and across the terrace, the fast-moving clouds sending shadows racing across the ground. He had ascended hundreds of vertical metres again today and been walking for seven hours.

'Hey,' he grinned, walking over and falling into a sequence of handgrips with them.

'We were beginning to think you were never gonna get here,' Stevie grinned, pulling out a plastic chair for him as Duffy shrugged off his pack.

'I had ten bucks on you having turned back,' Jay laughed.

'Drop by drop is the water pot filled, mate. I've been taking it easy and enjoying the views. I wanted to get here feeling fresh.' Duffy sank into the chair with a deep sigh nonetheless. It felt good to take the weight off his bones.

'Well, we've gone from fresh to overly ripe. We've been stuck here two nights already, just twiddling our thumbs.'

'The avalanche?'

Stevie nodded. 'You heard, then?'

'Met a porter on his way down, near Chhomrong. I thought they'd have had it cleared by now, though.'

'They did. Today.' Stevie rolled his eyes. 'But it's too late now to head out. It'll have to be first light tomorrow.'

Duffy splayed his elbows out and clasped his hands together behind his head as he looked out at the fishtail mountain. Or was it a mermaid tail, he wondered? 'Well, I guess there are worse places to be stranded. It's a good view.'

'Yep,' Jay agreed.

Machhapuchhre Base Camp, or MBC, was only four hundred metres below Annapurna Base Camp – ABC – and nudging four thousand metres in altitude now. He had left the forested valleys behind and moved to the next terrain, almost a moonscape of shattered rocks and frozen ground. The sharp scree slopes were angled only tens of metres away from where they sat in a narrow plateau, the snowline reaching down like a tattered hem, all frozen waterfalls and no sight of a tree. The wooden buildings of the lower, forested slopes were replaced up here with stone huts, and everyone was dressed in fleeces, down jackets and hats, outer layers on.

'Here.' Jay reached down and passed him a beer from a plastic crate.

Duffy took it gratefully, knocking off the cap with the heel of his hand against the side of the table. He didn't usually drink on treks; his body didn't need the handicap, but tomorrow was going to be a light day. Most people trekked to the ABC from here – only a few hours' hike – and then back down to Bamboo village in a day, but he was on a different trajectory. He savoured the cool taste as it slid down his throat. Another simple pleasure he thought he'd left behind. Life, it seemed, was still keeping its hooks into him. He wondered, briefly, where Ophélie was right now. Back in civilization, she would probably never think of him again.

He sighed, feeling his soul somehow stretch and shift in his body as he tipped his head to the sky. His gaze caught on a Steppe Eagle wheeling on the thermals, its fingered wings outstretched, a distant cry tearing through the air. Not much made its home up here; this was the land of moon and stars. He thought of the toy cow stuffed in his side pocket and his hand reached down for it, wanting to feel it was there, his talisman.

'Help!'

A noise – shouts – made them startle. Everyone looked back, searching for the source.

'Help us!'

'There!' Stevie stood first, seeing a couple of coloured dots a hundred metres or so away. A couple of trekkers had collapsed on the path, one getting up and trying to drag the other. People stood as the three of them vaulted the wall and ran over.

It was a young Italian couple in their early twenties. 'Please help us! We need a bed,' the woman cried, almost flattened by the dead weight of her collapsed boyfriend's arm on her shoulders. 'We must stay here!'

'What happened?' Stevie asked, getting his shoulder under one of her boyfriend's arms as Duffy took the other. Jay moved the young woman away. She was trembling violently – as much from fear and exhaustion as the cold – her eyes wide with panic as Duffy and Stevie began carrying the beleaguered trekker towards the camp, his feet dragging between them.

'We just got to ABC when he started hallucinating, not talking any sense. He had been complaining of a headache all day so I said we must come back down. Then he collapsed back there.'

'He's got AMS,' Stevie said quickly.

Acute Mountain Sickness. At four thousand metres, the thin air made legs heavy and heads swim. Simple tasks became difficult as fever, hallucinations, nausea, crippling headaches kicked in. It always took forty-eight hours for the body to start to acclimatize to the conditions here, even for the most experienced trekkers.

'Where did you start from today?' Duffy asked.

'Sinuwa.'

'You did Sinuwa to ABC, in a single *day*?'

The woman's eyes widened in fear at his evident shock. 'The plan was to stop here but there were no beds!' she protested. 'They told us to go back down to Deurali and wait, that the avalanche would be cleared today and we could come back up.'

'So why didn't you?'

'We have flights booked! If we don't stay on the schedule, we'll miss it – and Antonio was insistent. He said we haven't come all this way to miss the ABC by four hundred metres—'

Duffy didn't comment. How many times had he heard this very argument over the years?

'—so we decided to push on to ABC.'

'How did you get past the avalanche?'

'It was hard. We went up to get around but we pushed too much. I think he got dehydrated. I knew as soon as he complained about the headache it was the wrong call. We went too high, too fast, I know that – but we didn't have a choice.'

Duffy looked down at the ground as they staggered onwards, feeling angry about the risks they'd taken. There was always a choice – they had just chosen wrong. This man, her partner, was twice her size; if he'd collapsed further back, she couldn't have dragged him, no way. Daylight would soon be gone and they'd have had a night out in the open air when the temperatures would plunge to minus twenty, if not lower. He took in their clothes – decent, but very much commercial trekking kit. Neither one of them would have survived.

They were almost at the steps now and others began rushing forward to help, the Nepali owners and workers coming out of the building, concern etched on their faces. Duffy knew what they were worried about.

'No beds—'

'Give them mine,' he said quickly. 'Name of Duffy.'

The host nodded gratefully and ran back in.

'Did you book in already?' Jay asked him, panting as they staggered up the steps.

'Yeah.' For once he had pre-booked. Usually it wasn't necessary and the first-come, first-served system worked, but after he had met the porter on the path, he'd figured this might happen – trekkers being turned away and causing bottlenecks all the way down the mountain – and he had booked ahead at that night's teahouse.

The local men took the collapsed trekker from his and Jay's grasp. Duffy rolled his shoulders out, grateful for the immediate relief. The man was heavy and a dead weight. They watched as he was carried through into the warmth, his girlfriend stumbling after them, white-faced with fear.

'Jeez,' Stevie whistled as the medical emergency disappeared indoors and they wandered back to their table. Duffy took his chair again, reaching down for his backpack and pulling out the toy cow. He kissed it lightly, as though the brush with danger was contagious somehow. He set it down on the table, taking a picture of it – his beer bottle pushed out of the frame first – with the precipitous snowy slopes behind.

'What the hell . . . ?' Jay laughed, swigging from his beer again.

'Guys, meet Moodle. My lucky mascot.'

'That thing?'

'We've all gotta have something out here. We need a bit of luck and that just proves it. If that guy had collapsed any earlier than he did . . .' Duffy shook his head.

Jay reached forward and propped the toy on Duffy's shoulder. 'Here.' He reached for Duffy's phone and took a picture.

Duffy laughed as he examined it – a grown man having his picture taken with a grubby kid's toy. 'Ridiculous,' he grinned. There was no way he would send that one on to little Mabel. His beard was growing in now and the look in his eyes was somewhat wild, as if the crisis back there had jangled his own nervous system. Then again, it didn't seem like little Mabel's family was immune to drama either, if the emotional email he'd received from her mother this morning was anything to go by; he didn't claim to like the woman but he also knew you didn't need to be halfway up one of the world's highest mountains to feel lonely – and she had sounded just as alone as he actually was.

'Ridiculous if you think that little toy's gonna save you,' Stevie drawled.

'I have to put my faith in something.'

'Isn't that what religion's for?'

'For many. You?'

KAREN SWAN

There was a short silence. 'I dunno. We're just walking,' Stevie shrugged, resisting the invitation to go any deeper.

Jay took another swig of his beer. 'I'm not out here looking for answers and I sure don't need no mascot to keep me chill. Not when I've got this.'

Duffy turned his head to find Jay holding open his jacket pocket. He peered in at the crushed leaves. His eyebrows shot up in surprise. 'Is that . . . ?' he frowned, hardly able to believe his eyes.

'Yep. Fresh ganja!'

Duffy looked back at him. '. . . Where'd you get that?'

'There was some growing wild just outside one of the villages on the first day.'

Duffy laughed, shaking his head. 'Come on!'

'Naw, I mean it, man. It was growing right there! Fat bunches of the stuff! So we took some. Just a bit, they wouldn't even have noticed. We weren't intending on having any till we got back to Pokhara but . . . We've been sitting here unable to go anywhere, so . . .' He shrugged. 'It's getting cold out here now. We can go back to the room and chill?'

Duffy hesitated. It was true light was fading fast, the sun long since dropped behind the ridges. But the Himalayas were no playground, they were no joke. That incident back there had shown that when things went wrong out here, they went badly wrong. He needed to keep his wits about him, to be sharp and lucid. He knew all that.

He also knew he had a couple of days ahead of him living in this rarefied air and taking things slow. He wasn't going to be pushing himself. It wouldn't hurt to have a puff – just a few puffs – to take the edge off. That scene with the Italians had agitated his spirit, he knew, and he could feel apprehension beginning to nibble at the edges of him. Just being here messed with his head; he had a dread sense of sleeping monsters shifting. He was standing in the shadow of his own destiny, feeling himself – willing himself to – become what he needed to be, to strip himself of all emotion and become just muscle and bone, a hollow vessel. But life was hard to reject. It seduced through myriad tiny temptations: warm water, a hot meal, a soft bed. And now a smoke – a last place of refuge on what really was the final day of his old life.

He looked back at the American, feeling a flash of anger, even defiance. He had everything to lose, and nothing. Mabel's mother had nothing on him when it came to being alone in this world. 'Sure. Why the hell not?'

He reached for the joint and took another long drag. He hadn't done this in a really long time and he felt the drug suffuse through his body, soft and diaphanous, knocking off the hard edges that made this world such a painful place. He could no longer feel the heaviness in his limbs, or his heart; the bleeding blister on his right ankle was forgotten; his father's disappointment; Anya's tears . . . all the people he'd let down and dismayed, their accusing eyes, it all drifted away from his mind, leaving only the good.

'What are you thinking about, Duff?' Jay asked, grinning as Duffy handed back the joint. The three of them were lying on the two narrow beds that were pushed against the walls, below the windows. Stevie had fallen asleep. 'You're looking all . . . dopey.'

Duffy put his hands to his mouth and realized he was grinning too. He let his hands drop down heavily again, as though he couldn't support their weight. '. . . I'm thinking about a girl I met,' he said finally.

Jay raised his eyebrow. 'Here?'

'No. A few years back.'

'Ha, yeah,' Jay sighed, sounding almost wistful, as though he was part of the memory too. 'What was she like?'

'Beautiful.'

'Yeah,' Jay sighed again. 'They're always beautiful.'

Duffy closed his eyes, conjuring her image. It wasn't something he ever usually allowed himself to do. He didn't believe in dwelling in the past, nor on dreaming of the future; rather he concentrated his mind on the present, on this moment and no others. It was a discipline that had shaped the past four years of his life. No looking back. Focus on the next step. But now he allowed himself to drift, his heart pulling him on like a red balloon, back to the memory of her.

'What's her name?'

'Natasha. Everyone called her Nats.'

'Pretty.'

'Yeah. She was.'

'So what happened?'

Duffy was quiet for a moment. 'She married another guy. The wrong guy.'

Jay seemed startled by the news. 'The wrong guy because you were the right guy?'

'. . . Maybe . . . I dunno . . . If I was, I didn't know it back then. I wasn't ready for that. Sure as hell wasn't looking for it.'

'Naw man, I'm still not,' Jay shrugged. 'And I'm thirty-two.'

Duffy inhaled slowly, savouring the ecstasy of allowing his mind to roam freely for once, like an orca released back to the ocean, diving and looping through the deep blue depths. 'I just knew it was right, that was all. Wasn't ready for it, wasn't looking for it – but I still knew it was her or no one.' He stared at the ceiling, conjuring her face so easily. He could still see her standing in that kitchen, in that dress, arguing with him and telling him he was wrong, when she wouldn't face what was obvious – that he'd only met her because her own body was telling her something was off with the other guy. That the thunderbolt between her and him was real. Why couldn't she have just believed him? How might things have been different if she had just trusted him?

'So, you in contact?'

Duffy snorted, feeling the barrier come down, the sea shrinking to a puddle and drying up. 'No. Never saw her again.'

'Nothing?'

He closed his eyes, trying not to remember it. 'She got married and I . . . went my way.'

'But you still think of her.'

'Try not to.' Duffy turned his head and smiled at Jay, reaching his arm out for the joint again. The American handed it over. 'It's precisely why I avoid this stuff. A disciplined mind brings happiness.' He tapped his temple a few times.

'A disciplined . . . ?' Jay cried. 'Aw, man, who comes up with that shit?'

'In this case, Buddha.'

There was a silence, then they burst out laughing.

'So that's why you got that tattoo then, huh?' Jay said, nodding his chin towards Duffy's arm. Duffy stared at the simple black type along his forearm: *The root of suffering is attachment*. ''Cos that's pretty damn bleak.'

Duffy looked back at him. 'It's a good reminder, is all. You never lost anyone you loved?'

Jay paused. '. . . My mom, when I was thirteen. Car accident.'

'So then you know.'

Jay met his gaze. 'Yeah.'

'I'm sorry.'

'Yeah. Me too.'

Duffy squeezed his eyes shut, feeling the pain still push past the anaesthesia. He knew the weed wasn't a solution, just a sticking plaster, a temporary numbing where he might explore the parts of his mind and heart that he ordinarily kept off limits. But it would always wear off and he would always come back to these feelings; he would always come back *here*, because it had started here and it would end here, one way or another.

Not just yet, though. No. He accepted the joint from Jay's fingers and took another determined puff, dragging on it so the tip glowed, feeling himself fall deeper. He wanted to sink back into the last time he'd been happy, he wanted to remember how it had felt – scented hair and soft skin, whispers in the dark of a life that might have been theirs. He wanted to relive those few stolen moments before tomorrow, like the Buddha's prophecy, had indeed come.

When he awoke, his body felt rigid, as if set in concrete, his neck stiff from the awkward angle. He heard some clattering from nearby, felt the cool swish of air brush over him as an outside door swung shut. He lifted his head groggily, his cheek sticking to the cool hard plastic as he tried to get his bearings. What . . . ?

He turned his head the other way and saw there were a couple of people sitting at a table just a few feet behind him, eating bowls of *dhal bat* and *momos* – stuffed dumplings – and he realized he was sleeping on top of a table in the canteen. Not unheard of up here, when all rooms were booked; he'd given his away, of course, and there wasn't enough space in the Americans' room once their roommates had arrived. He was wearing his down jacket on top of his clothes but he was still violently shivering. With a groan, he curled his body inwards like a caterpillar and tried to warm himself up. *Body heat*, his mind yearned, conjuring unwanted memories again of *her*, as though she had become twisted in the smoke that clung to his hair.

He pushed himself up to sitting, every muscle in his body protesting and making him groan. 'Hey,' he muttered to the early risers at the next table as they watched above their breakfast bowls.

'Good morning,' one of them smiled, toasting him with a honey-lemon tea.

He inhaled deeply and looked out the window. It was still dark out there but he could see it was snowing heavily, fat flakes whirling in dizzying dervishes. The nearby slopes might have been miles, not metres, from here, visibility vastly reduced as the low clouds scudded past, enveloping them, then releasing again moments later. He was always struck by the irony of being amid the most dramatic landscape on earth and with weather like this, not actually being able to see any of it. Like the eye of a storm, the drama was elsewhere.

He sat up, stretched out his spine and rolled his arms, swinging them a few times to get the blood flowing. Then he slid off the table and stepped out of the sleeping bag. Apparently he had had the presence of mind to take off his boots before he'd gone to sleep, as they were placed beside the table on the floor – it was just as well; the micro-spikes would have torn the bag to ribbons. He laced them up and stood, feeling gravity bear down on his bones, his body bracing for a new day.

He wandered towards the kitchen, slowly rubbing his hands

in ready anticipation of a hot meal. He felt ravenous, unsurprisingly. He could hear the frantic chatter of voices behind the swing door, metal pans clattering and knives chopping, as the staff prepared for the onslaught of breakfast orders. Trekkers didn't sleep in. It was normal to be awake before sunrise and everyone would be coming through any moment, especially after the few days' hiatus enforced by the avalanche.

He ordered a bowl of *dhal bat* and *momos* too. It cost 500 rupees, a distinct mark-up from the 100 he'd paid in Khande. Market forces, he told himself as he handed over the cash with a tired smile.

They motioned that they would bring the food to his table and he wandered over to the windows, catching sight of something as he went to sit down. He pressed his face to the glass and peered out. A small, hunched figure was sitting on the terrace wall, looking out into the nothingness.

Duffy frowned. He recognized the jacket but for a moment he couldn't quite place it—

'Hey,' he said a moment later, pushing on the door and going over. 'You okay here? It's pretty cold to be sitting out in this.'

The Italian girl looked up at him, her face pale and streaked with tears.

'Oh no,' he whispered, sinking beside her and understanding immediately.

'Antonio didn't wake up,' she said, looking at him with a stunned expression. 'He just didn't wake up!'

Chapter Eighteen

Frome, Thursday 8 December

'Darling, can you pass the butter?'

Natasha looked up to find Rob with an arm outstretched over the breakfast table and a slightly pained look. The prospect of cold toast always stressed him out. That and tepid tea.

She passed the butter, noticing his bare hand. No ring.

'Rob, did I see you wearing a signet ring last night?' she asked him as she poured herself some orange juice. Mabel was sucking on a tube of fromage frais, Bella parked beneath her chair in the well-judged expectation of falling food.

He looked at her. 'Me?'

'Yes.'

He thought for a moment. 'I don't know. Maybe.' He shrugged. 'Why?'

Maybe? It seemed an odd response. Either he had one or he didn't. 'I've never seen you wear one before.'

'Haven't you?' he frowned. 'Huh.'

She waited for a further explanation but nothing appeared to be forthcoming. '. . . Well,' she asked impatiently. 'When did you get it?'

He shrugged. 'I've always had it. An eighteenth birthday gift from my parents.'

'*What?*' She stared at him. How could she not have known that? 'But then, why don't you always wear it? Aren't they supposed to be left on?'

He sighed, sounding irritated. 'Oh, I don't know, Nats. Sometimes it's a bother and I take it off, other times I don't think about it. I don't see why you're making a fuss about it.'

'I wouldn't say I'm making a fuss!' she protested weakly. Perhaps it upset him? If it had been a gift from his parents, perhaps it reminded him of them too much. The wound was still very much open, especially as it had been compounded by the bitter fallout with his siblings. 'I just think it's odd that I've never noticed it before when you're saying you've had it since you were eighteen, that's all.'

'So then it's my fault you don't have an eye for the details?' he asked. His tone was arch and he immediately looked up, taking in her shocked expression. Both of them glanced at Mabel, who was oblivious. 'I'm sorry,' he said quickly. 'I shouldn't take it out on you. I'm so . . .' he sighed wearily. 'You're right. Why *should* you notice when you've always got so much going on, what with chasing after Mabel and whatnot. It's just a ring. I wear it, I don't.' He shrugged. 'Please let's not fight. My bandwidth is already taken up with today's calendar and I don't know how I'm going to get through it. I'm on site in Bristol this morning, then in back-to-back meetings all afternoon till seven.'

Natasha stared at her plate. Meetings till seven meant getting home after eight thirty. It would be another lap tray supper for her tonight.

'. . . Darling, what is it?'

She looked up to find Rob watching her, the piece of toast held in his hand as he chewed. 'What?' she echoed.

'What's wrong? You look . . . distant.'

She swallowed and picked up her spoon, trying to find the appetite for her porridge. 'No, I'm here.'

They both began to eat, the sounds of chewing and cutlery knocking against the china seeming loud in the beautiful kitchen, in contrast to their lovemaking in the bedroom last night, which had been sedate, almost polite. She felt that tremor again – of anxiety, of loneliness, of a sense that all was not as well between them as she was pretending. 'So what are your plans today?'

'Um, well . . .' She thought of the hundred and twenty miles she'd be driving today, in order to earn his Christmas present. 'I've got a dental appointment later,' she fibbed.

'Oh.'

'And I guess I should really make a start on the Christmas shopping. Carol's taking orders for the Christmas puddings today too, so I mustn't forget that.' Her voice was flat.

'Sounds like another nice day,' he nodded. 'I'm glad at least one of us is having them.' The comment was made without any bitterness and Natasha watched as he knocked back the rest of his tea, then pushed his chair back. He stood up, straightening his tie, and leaned down to kiss Mabel on the head. 'You be a good girl for Mummy, okay? Mummy's tired. She needs lots of cuddles.'

'Okay, Daddy,' Mabel replied, puckering up for a wet sloppy kiss.

Rob laughed and gave her a kiss. 'Funny little munchkin. I'll give you a big kiss when I get back tonight, even if you're sleeping, okay?'

'Bye bye Daddy,' Mabel said, turning straight back to her plate. She was used to his absences and didn't question them; he was here when he was here. Natasha just wished *she* could feel so at peace with it.

251

She waited as Rob came round the table to kiss her too, distractedly patting his pockets for his phones. 'Where's my work one?' he muttered, finding only one.

'Hall table,' she said. He always set it down there, along with his keys, when he came in – a way of leaving his working day behind him as he got home. In principle, anyway.

'Of course. Right, must dash. Big day.'

As ever.

'Of course, go, go,' she said wanly.

He hesitated in front of her. 'Take it easy, okay? You look tired.'

'I'm fine . . . Go.'

'Okay.' He rushed from the kitchen and Natasha listened to the sounds of him departing – the jingle of keys, the click of the latch, the whirring of the gates and the unlocking beep of his car. The crunch of footsteps on gravel, the slam of the door and then . . . silence.

Natasha felt something weigh heavily in her chest; she felt like she wanted to cry but she wasn't sure about what, or even why. Something was off, somehow, but she couldn't say what it was. Before the Maldives she'd been adamant it had to be another woman, that he must be having an affair. What else could it be? Women's intuition was real. But quite aside from the fact that this man barely had the energy to eat his own breakfast, much less seduce and sleep with another woman, she knew he loved her wildly; she felt it every time he looked at her. Sometimes she thought he wanted to devour her whole, like he could never quite get enough of her. He loved her with an intensity that she hadn't known was possible and everything he did made her feel cherished and treasured . . . It made absolutely no sense that he would cheat. And yet she was back to being paranoid. Back to being small.

She looked back at her child, pushing her hair back from her face. 'Shall we do bunches today?' she asked.

Mabel didn't reply. She wasn't a fan of anything that involved a hairbrush.

'Come on, let's go and get dressed. It's cold outside, so you'll need your thermals on today.' It had to be blowing a gale or raining a monsoon for the nursery to miss their daily meadow walks. There was a hard frost on the ground, the sky coddling a spectacular red sunrise that always made her nervous. Shepherd's warning. They climbed the stairs and she could see, through the windows, the sheep huddled together in the field.

'Go and do a wee for me, please,' Natasha said, pointing towards the bathroom as Mabel went to toddle past it. 'I'll be through in a moment once I'm dressed.'

Natasha walked into her own bedroom, surveying the unmade bed and Rob's balled-up dirty socks and boxers still on the floor. His suit from last night was still neatly draped over the armchair. She stopped mid-step and stared at it, remembering the midnight scene as he had crept in. She walked across to his wardrobe and peered in at his trinket tray. Collar stiffeners, cufflinks, dozens of coppers . . . she pushed her finger through it . . . But no signet ring.

That made no sense. She remembered clearly seeing his hand just now as she passed the butter and he hadn't been wearing it at breakfast. So why, if he wasn't wearing it, wouldn't it be up here, where she'd watched him put it only last night? Had he moved it somewhere more secure? But where? They didn't have a safe. She opened and closed a few of his drawers – sock drawer, pants drawer, checked through his rolled-up ties compartment. Nothing. She checked his bedside drawer again too. She got down on her hands and knees and checked under the bed. Had it fallen? If it had sentimental value from his parents, the last thing he needed was for it to get sucked up in the hoover.

'Mumma.' She looked up to find Mabel coming through, her toothbrush in her mouth and a stream of foaming toothpaste dribbling down her chin.

'No, no, no, Mabel,' she said, jumping up and scooping her into her arms. 'What have I said about running around with your toothbrush in your mouth? If you were to fall, you would hurt yourself.' Not to mention she really didn't want the toothpaste dripping on the carpet.

She swiped her phone – still charging – from the bedside drawer as she passed, following the toddler to the bathroom for Mabel to spit. Natasha set her down on the toilet seat. 'Now do a wee for Mummy,' she said, taking the toothbrush and wiping the child's mouth clean.

She stood up and clicked on the phone as she waited for the tinkling sound, feeling the small frisson of joy that now accompanied seeing Duffy's name. In the space of a week, it seemed to have become the best part of every day, finding out where Moolah was now and glimpsing some of their adventures. It made Mabel shriek with excitement and she wondered if he could ever understand how important these little missives had become to them both—

. . . Wait. A memory stirred. She had a sense of having done something unwise, the feeling she always got when she drank too much wine . . . Oh lord. It came to her – the email. She'd written to him when she'd been drunk and emotional, lonely and frustrated, reaching out to someone who was doing precisely what she wasn't – *living*. Being free. Chasing adventure.

She pressed a hand to her mouth as she stared at his name in her inbox. What had she said? What had she said? She clicked on the email with a wince, but to her surprise there was no message, only a photograph embedded in the text box. She enlarged it with her fingers, taking in the scene and feeling the very floor tip beneath her feet. Her heart forgot to beat. Moments passed, she had no idea how many.

'. . . Mumma?'

Natasha looked up to find Mabel still stranded on the loo. 'Oh.' Her face was frozen as she struggled to pull herself back into the present moment, seeing the quizzical expression on her beautiful daughter's face. 'Look what the time is,' she swallowed. 'We're going to be late for nursery. We must hurry.'

Her voice sounded curious, even to her own ear, but she couldn't offer any better than that. Her body felt like it had gone into blue light mode – sirens screaming, blood rushing – as she stumbled through to her bedroom and pulled on the nearest clothes she could find.

She did the same for Mabel too, not even attempting to bother to brush her hair, but just slipping an Alice band behind her ears. Within four minutes they were in the car, Bella belted up in the front and already panting happily in anticipation of her day out.

Natasha was so distracted, it took three attempts to successfully leave the house – first she left behind Mabel's packed lunch on the counter; then she forgot the fob for the gate; then she forgot to close the front door.

'So remember, Rosie will collect you from nursery today. You're going to be making some cakes together, okay?' she said tonelessly, the phone sitting idle beside her in the cupholder. She kept looking at it like it was an unexploded bomb, not daring to touch it again.

It couldn't be, she kept telling herself, all the way into the village, in the car park and up the village hall path. Toddlers were running and staggering about, backpacks over their coats and wellies on, mothers congregating by the cars for chats after drop-off.

'Rosie will be collecting again today,' she said quietly.

'Of course . . . Are you okay, Mrs Stoneleigh?' the nursery assistant asked, looking at her with a strange expression.

'Yes. Why wouldn't I be?'

Avoiding the gaggle of mothers around Lauren's Range Rover – it would only lead to coffee at Lizzie's tea rooms – she kept her head down and got back in the car, driving the few streets round the village on autopilot. She was supposed to be heading straight off to Snowshill but as she pulled up outside the dental surgery, she had no sense at all of how she had navigated her way there.

Hels was leaning outside the back door of the stone building, holding a coffee and smoking. Natasha was vaguely aware she was supposed to be holding a vape, not a packet of Marlboro Lights, but right now she didn't care.

Hels almost fell over at the sight of her. 'What the fuck . . . ?' Stubbing out her cigarette, she waited as Natasha let herself in through the back gate and walked up. 'Oh God, what's happened? You're white as a sheet.'

'I need to talk to you.'

'Clearly.'

'Inside.'

Hels didn't need telling twice. 'Follow me.' She pulled open the fire door and led Natasha through to her consulting room. 'Emergency,' she said to her technician, who was walking down the corridor towards her with a bunch of files in her arms. 'Hold my nine fifteen till I come out.'

Hels shut the door and turned back to Natasha, who was holding out her phone. 'What's this?' She took it, looking at the photo. 'Or rather, who?'

'It's Duffy.'

Hels peered a little closer. 'Oh that's him then, is it, Marvellous Mister Duff? He's younger than I thought he'd be. Better-lookin—'

'Look at him more closely. Don't you recognize him?'

Hels arched an eyebrow at the urgency in her voice. 'Should I? You know I'm not a fan of beards.' She looked again anyway. 'Hmm, yeah, there is something familiar.' She pulled a face. 'Oh God, I haven't shagged him, have I?' She put a hand over the lower half of the phone, squinting her eyes.

'What are you doing?'

'Trying to imagine him without a beard.' For several long moments, her expression was blank, then her eyes widened. Her mouth parted as she looked back at Natasha with alarm.

'Oh God, it is him,' Natasha cried, wheeling on her heel, her hands in her hair as Hels's confirmation opened the floodgates. 'Fuck!'

'How can . . . how can it be him? . . . *Him!* . . . I mean, what are the chances . . . ?' she wailed.

'Wait, maybe we're wrong. Just bear with . . .' She peered at the screen so hard Natasha expected it to crack, but she saw how Hels's face fell. 'No, it is. It definitely is.'

'Oh my *God*,' Natasha gasped, clutching her stomach and folding in half.

'Nats, calm down. *Sit* down.' Hels took her by the shoulders and plonked her down on her black leather reclining chair. 'This is an unexpected development, granted, but let's just take a breath and take a proper look together.'

Heads pressed together, they scrutinized the image in silence. It was clearly unposed, a snatched moment, as there was a sense of movement in the image. Duffy was mid-laugh so that his eyes crinkled, Moolah perched precariously on his shoulder. He was holding a beer and she could see people at tables all around them. He might have been skiing in Val Thorens from the looks of this picture. His dark hair was a lot longer than she remembered it and he looked thinner too, though the week-old beard made it difficult to tell properly. But as Natasha allowed herself to meet his gaze properly through the screen, she felt that pitch and swoop in her stomach she'd felt the first time on the tree platform and again in the kitchen as he had told her truths she didn't want to hear.

'It's him. It's Tom.'

'Except this guy is called Duffy. Or Duff. Friend of cows, whatever. But not Tom.' Hels looked more closely at the email address: tduffy@gmail.com. 'Bugger.'

'How can it be him?' Natasha repeated, her voice just a whisper.

Hels gave her a hard look. 'It's a mad coincidence, I agree, but it doesn't mean anything. Look at you – you've moved on.'

Had she, though? She had never told anyone about the dreams she had about him, the ones she wanted never to end. How could she? She was a married woman. A mother. And after what he'd done . . . No. They were her guilty secret, even Hels couldn't know. She never allowed him into her conscious thoughts, she was strict about that, but when she slept she had no control over where her mind roamed and all she knew was that on the nights he came to her, she awoke feeling happy, her soul sated.

'I know that. Of course I have.' She scratched her eyebrow,

trying to recover herself. The initial panic was subsiding now; she was always calmed by Hels. 'The thing is, I think I wrote to him. When I was drunk.'

'You think?'

'Know. I was feeling lonely and I sat down just to tell him how much the postcards mean to Mabel, but also to us, as a family. But then I . . . started rambling.'

'Rambling?'

'I may have mentioned being lonely.'

Hels frowned. '*Are* you lonely?'

Natasha swallowed. '. . . Sometimes.'

Hels seemed to consider this, as though it had never occurred to her before that Natasha could be run off her feet, financially secure *and* lonely too. 'Well, I guess that's to be expected. Rob does work mad hours.' She squeezed her hand affectionately but Natasha remained quiet. She wasn't yet ready to admit that she felt most lonely *with* Rob. That she was lonely within her marriage. It would be a betrayal to admit it to anyone other than him, but with the realization only having hit her last night, she needed to sit with it and work out what to do. It could be dangerous, potentially even destructive, to their marriage.

And now this email had entered the mix, telling her Tom was back in her life, his shadow seeping over the boundaries of their family unit.

Hels looked back at the photo on the phone again. 'So do you think that's why he sent you this photo, then? He's . . . trying to cheer you up? Or *connect* with you by showing his face?'

'Maybe. This isn't like his normal messages.'

'And neither was yours.'

'Exactly.'

Hels's eyes narrowed as a thought came to her. 'Wait . . . you don't think he . . . knows you're *you*, does he?'

'How could he? He wouldn't know my married name and I'm hardly the only Natasha in the world.'

Hels's mind was working fast; Natasha could tell from the way her eyes moved fractionally left to right. 'But there was a picture of you in the Facebook post.'

'And he's in the Himalayas. You can get some level of mobile reception out there but scrolling social media isn't an option.'

'And you haven't sent him anything that could have given him a clue?'

Natasha shook her head. 'I sent him one picture of Mabel but that was it. Nothing with me.'

'Good. Well, just make sure it stays that way. We don't need any complications. He got in your head last time and really messed you up—'

That was an understatement. That final week before the wedding had been a blur and she had almost no memories of the wedding itself. It had only been a tiny ceremony anyway – a luxury elopement, as Rob had phrased it, to cover for the fact that neither of them had family there – but going through the photos afterwards had been like witnessing someone else's nuptials. She'd been in shock.

'—That can't happen again. We just need to focus on getting Moolah back and then he'll be out of your life again, without even knowing he was in it.'

Natasha blinked at her. '. . . Yeah.'

Hels frowned, and Natasha knew her voice was still distorted, but she felt like she'd been pulled inside out. The shock was overwhelming. How could Duffy be Tom? How could any of this have happened?

Neither one of them spoke for several minutes, both trying to wrap their heads around the revelation. Finally Hels bit her lip, a mannerism that always preceded a reluctant truth. '. . . He texted me, you know.'

'What?'

'A few days after the wedding. You guys were on honeymoon and I got this random text.' She sighed. 'I had no idea who it was from at first. I didn't have his number.'

'So then how did he have yours?'

'I'd given it to his mate . . . Jack, was it? James? The one I met in the supermarket. In case they couldn't find us.' She shrugged. 'He must have given it to him.'

'What did it say?'

Hels looked like she didn't want to tell her.

'Hels?' Natasha pressed. 'What did he say?'

'It was just a question: *Did she do it?*'

Did she do it?

Natasha felt her heart catch mid-beat. 'And what did you say?'

'Well, *yes*, of course! Immediately followed by telling him to leave you the fuck alone.'

Which he had done. Natasha stared at her hands, feeling a wave of emotion she couldn't comprehend overwhelm her. Was it rage, anger, despair? Hels was right to have done what she did, she knew that. And yet . . . Her heart thudded, a lead weight in her chest. She jumped up from the chair, unable to remain still.

'What are you gonna do? Now you know it's him.' Hels watched her as she began to circle the room, staring blindly at the shelves and trays lined with equipment.

'There's nothing *to* do.'

'You're not going to send a photo back?'

'Of course not.'

Hels squinted as she watched Natasha pace. 'And you're sure you can do that – communicate with him, even though you know now who he is?'

'This is for Mabel,' she said in a quiet voice. 'It's not about me.'

'Yeah.' Hels watched her walk the room in looping figures of eight, her hands wringing. 'Well, as long as you're sure about that.'

Chapter Nineteen

Nepal, Thursday 8 December

No one spoke much, the mood sombre and detracting from what should have been the climax of the trip. They moved slowly with heavy bodies, all too aware now of what happened when the boundaries were pushed too hard. AMS was more than shortness of breath. It was more than headaches or vomiting. If not addressed, the high risk of fluid build-up in the lungs could escalate into fatal conditions – High Altitude Pulmonary Edema (HAPE) or High Altitude Cerebral Edema (HACE). They didn't know which one Antonio had succumbed to and none of them would ever hear about it, but one thing was certain – he had minimized his symptoms to his partner, he had covered them up and pushed onwards, determined to get to his destination at any cost, never thinking that she would have to walk back down the mountains on her own, behind his body being carried down. She would have to endure days of it before they could be picked up at Khande. They would make their flight after all, but not in a way they could ever have imagined.

Duffy felt his anger grow with every step. Antonio was just another statistic now, another life sacrificed upon these granite temples where the line between life and death flickered and snatched like prayer flags in the wind, one moment fluttering this way, in the next, that. There was no certainty of anything up here. He couldn't rely on oxygen in the air, or the ground beneath his feet. Training helped. Proper gear helped. Medical knowledge helped. Preparation and route planning helped. But at any given moment, all of it could count for nothing. The mountains could stir, the skies could hold their breath and he – any man or woman – would crumple like paper. Tossed away, meaningless. It was Man v Mountain all the way; not till he stuck his thumb up along a roadside and hitched back to Kathmandu could he truly say he'd won and done what he'd come for.

It was still snowing heavily and crunching underfoot as they moved above the four-thousand-metre mark and through the pass. They had been going for five hours, after a delayed start – it had felt wrong to hear a man had died and just carry on, so almost all the trekkers and locals had gathered together first to observe prayers for the lost soul. They were wearing their spikes and every layer of clothing, walking poles leaving a trail of stabbing marks behind them. Duffy had never seen so many people on the trails before as the paths reopened for business and the bottleneck was unclogged, chugging out tourists. Coming towards him were those who'd been stranded at Annapurna; behind, those kept in the holding pen at Machhapuchhre.

He could hear Stevie and Jay a few steps behind him. They had all agreed to walk together to ABC but they were poor company, shaken by the morning's events. Duffy remembered a quote from his boyhood – *Mountains have a way of dealing with overconfidence*. So had said Hermann Buhl, one of the greats, one of his idols, and his American friends' cocksure feeling of mastery over these mountains – Everest! Annapurna! –

had deserted them, not helped either by the comedown from last night. Their heads were woolly, memories of the dumb things they'd said and done pressing forward but not quite breaking the surface of consciousness. Several times, Duffy felt a twitch in his brain of something trying to announce itself, but it was indistinct and uncatchable and he let it fall away each time, his focus on the tragedy.

He tried switching to his trekking mode, the autopilot of *left foot, right foot*, but he was rattled, he couldn't deny it. The Italian's death had shocked him, but it was more than that. Had it been a reminder, a warning shot . . . or worse, an omen? It was hard not to be superstitious when the odds were firmly stacked against them. They were so close now, the camp would come into sight at any moment and they would finally be at the unbeating heart of the Himalayas. The range here was known as the Annapurna Sanctuary, and for good reason, the mountains circling around tightly like a scrum of gods with their backs to the world.

He looked up at the peaks – Machhapuchhre sat behind his right shoulder, Hiunchuli over his left, Annapurna South beside it, Fang, Gangapurna and Annapurna III sweeping round to Machhapuchhre again. In all, the mountains clustered around a ten-mile-diameter circle with a glacier-covered amphitheatre in the middle. The Modi Khola river plunged through to a narrow gorge 3,660 metres deep and which opened up further south into the valley through which he had just trekked.

All of it was majestic, all of it breathtaking, but there was no denying that sitting front and centre, chesting into the valley with three crested peaks, sat the big one: Annapurna I. Duffy's feet stopped moving automatically, his heart holding itself in contraction too as he absorbed the sight of its immense south wall, sitting there as if waiting just for him. It wasn't a storybook mountain with angled slopes and a distinct peak, not like Everest. Not like Fuji. Not like Kilimanjaro. It was better than that – and worse. It was the mountaineer's mountain, the one where only climbers at the top of their game dared to go.

'Shee-it,' Stevie breathed, joining him.

'Yep.'

'She's a monster.'

'Yep.' She was one of fourteen mountains in the world to break past eight thousand metres. The snowfall was beginning to lessen now and passing breaks in the clouds threw down golden shafts of sunlight, setting off her deep contours to dazzling effect, but the scale was still almost impossible to comprehend – even from here, halfway up her immense height.

'You wouldn't think she was the deadliest mountain in the world.' Stevie looked at him. 'One in three who go up there don't make it back again.'

More than that, in fact – 38 per cent, to be precise – but Duffy didn't reply immediately. '. . . Yep. She's a killer.'

Jay came up to them, breathing heavily and leaning on his walking poles.

'You okay?' Duffy asked him. The extreme cold could worsen altitude sickness; no one could take any chances now.

'I'm fine. Just can't believe how slow I'm moving.'

'I know. It's brutal.'

'Want to take a break?'

Jay shook his head. 'No. Let's keep going. The rest will be all the sweeter when we get there.'

'Okay.'

They began walking again. Left foot. Right foot. Spikes and poles speckling the snow.

'Means Goddess of Abundance, you know,' Stevie panted.

'What?' Duffy half turned his head over his shoulder.

'Annapurna. It means Goddess of Abundance.'

'Yeah,' Duffy sniffed, turning his face away. There was nothing abundant about that goddess. She had only ever taken from him.

The day was spent in contemplative mood. No one could quite shrug off the tragedy that had marred the previous stop. Many who had left MBC with them came, saw Base Camp and almost immediately turned around again, eager to drop altitude and return to the relative safety of the valley forests.

Duffy, Stevie and Jay went for a slow walk. The snow was deep and soft but the bracing temperatures cleared their heads and it felt good to be out in it, marvelling at the dramatic sculptures caused by drifts and ice. They passed some climbers coming down from Camp One but few words passed between them; there was a hierarchy, even at the top of the world, and they were different beasts. Trekkers versus climbers; amateurs versus pros; casual versus committed.

At one point they saw a red helicopter circling high up above Annapurna III, the three of them watching as it made several passes over one section, looking for tiny specks of colour amid the blinding white canvas.

'It's a miracle they ever find anyone,' Jay had said. 'Sometimes, all they can find is a rope. How is that possible? It must be like a thread.'

Duffy just watched, his gaze steady on the helicopter as it made one run, then another. He could feel his body and mind hardening in response, as if standing there long enough might turn him into stone too.

Back at Base Camp, they ate early and retired to their rooms. Duffy expected to sleep heavily after his previous night on the table, but after a few hours he stirred awake. His mind felt restless – or was it his spirit? – refusing to release its grip, and he eventually got up, hopping out of his sleeping bag and pulling on his outer layers. Tiptoeing down the long corridor – as much as it's possible to tiptoe in trekking boots – he stepped outside. The wintry skies had cleared, the snow-throwing clouds blown to other lands, and he tipped his face towards the night. It was threaded with a lace of stars, some silver, others gold, dense galaxies twisting playfully above. He didn't care what anyone said – there were no skies in the world like the Himalayan night skies. The Arctic Circle might have the aurora borealis, a different kind of beauty; but there was a purity here that could only be achieved at altitude, as if thinning the skein between this world and the next.

I've never felt as far away from the living and as close to the dead. They weren't his words – they belonged to another idol, Erhard Loretan – but they had found a home in him.

He closed his eyes, trying to feel the dead here, as if their voices or their scent might carry on the wind. He was so close now. Why couldn't he feel them? His heart beat slow and heavy in his chest, he felt the familiar pressure surge in his body any time he opened this door in his soul.

But it was no good.

He might be close. But it was still not close enough.

Everyone woke early, as if prodded by the pink-fingered sun as she tripped over the Himalayan ridge. Duffy looked out of his window to find half the lodge visitors already outside, photographing the sunrise. He dressed quickly and found his American friends sitting on the lodge wall, having a smoke.

'Well, this is what we've been waiting for,' he said, joining them in admiring the view.

'And it's so worth it,' Jay nodded almost reverentially.

They watched in contented silence as wispy clouds drifted overhead like rags, as though they had snagged themselves on the summits, the sky a blazing flamingo pink. The smells of breakfast wafted through as the doors were opened and closed, a buzz of happy chatter rising up that had been conspicuous by its absence yesterday. Duffy's gaze rose to the headwall of Annapurna, unable to make out at this distance whether any climbers were fixing their ropes and trying to get ahead of the winds. Men and women crawled like ants over most of the mountains here, pitching all their strength, will and skill into conquering them while they, the mountains, simply endured. Few climbers tested their luck on Annapurna. They were no more than Lilliputians on Gulliver, deluding themselves into thinking this was a fair fight or that anything had been proved when they did succeed.

'I'll be right back,' Duffy said, remembering something.

He returned a few moments later with Moodle.

Stevie laughed. 'Oh man, you and that cow.'

'My talisman,' Duffy shrugged, propping her on the wall and taking a photograph, the vivid sky and monumental mountain both vying for the eye; but Duffy's own gaze fell to the pale moon, now two days past full and waning softly. Still no time for cow-jumping, he mused.

He frowned.

'What's wrong?' Jay asked.

'. . . I just realized I forgot to do something yesterday.' And the day before that. There had been no signal when he'd stopped in Deurali and with the medical crisis yesterday it had completely fallen from his mind.

'Like what?'

'Send a picture back home.' That meant it had been three days since he had sent anything to Mabel and he felt a lurch of guilt to think of her waiting, because she would be. In allowing himself the indulgence of a penpal – of sorts – he would have created an expectation in her of more communications to come. For all his proclamations of turning his back on the world, he hadn't been able to resist sharing his experiences with strangers. Those closest to him were oblivious but there was a little girl and her mother somewhere in Somerset who knew exactly what he was doing, seeing at least some of what he saw.

'Who were you sending it to?'

Duffy hesitated. He could hardly explain he was sending photographs to a little girl he'd never even met; it sounded dodgy as hell.

'A friend's daughter. This is her toy which I accidentally took.'

'Accidentally?' Stevie queried, a smile hovering on his mouth. 'You just said it's your talisman! You purposely packed that cow, admit it!'

'Fine, I did,' Duffy laughed, holding his hands up. 'But to make up for it, I promised to send her pictures of our "adventure" each day.' He tweaked his fingers to make speech marks.

Jay looked highly sceptical. 'And they go through from here?'

'Seem to. How long it takes I've no idea, but, I keep getting missives from the mother in reply so . . .'

He stopped. He felt that itch in his brain again, a memory flickering and trying to ignite. He tabbed into his phone and checked his emails, bringing up the last one from the mother. *'What's it like there? Is it as awe-inspiring as they say? It's always described as remote but I think there must be beauty in solitude too. Sometimes I think it's even more lonely being in a room full of people . . .'*

No, he'd read this one. It wasn't that which was bothering him.

He stared at the paltry inbox with only two names in it – Anya's and Natasha Stoneleigh's.

Wait . . . He checked the Sent box instead.

08/12/2022 Natasha Stoneleigh 02:12

He'd replied? He didn't remember doing that. He clicked on it, bringing up the photo Jay had taken on the MBC terrace on Wednesday evening – and immediately knew why. He'd been stoned out of his skull.

He stared at the photo. It looked like he was partying at La Folie Douce in Val d'Isère. What the hell had he sent *that* for? It was obnoxious for one thing – him seemingly partying – and there wasn't anything exciting about it for Mabel: no mules, no waterfalls. It was just him and Moolah, and why the hell would she want to see that?

He regarded his own face for a few moments, not sure *he* wanted to see it. He'd not looked in a mirror since he'd left Pokhara and his hand went to his jaw, feeling the thickness of his beard. He'd lost weight too, which wasn't surprising. At least he was laughing, he supposed; he might be dishev-elled and unkempt, but he wasn't completely mad-looking. He looked . . . friendly enough.

Thankfully he hadn't attempted to write anything – he dreaded to think what he might have come up with, writing while stoned – although it also made the solitary image seem an even odder message, with no context. He sat on the wall and wondered what to do. He had sent the image seemingly in response to the mother's lonely letter, but she hadn't responded since. No doubt she was aghast that her daughter's beloved toy was in his possession. He pocketed the phone again, feeling like a fool.

The sky was deepening to a fiery red, setting the snow pink and he stared out into the distance, feeling both discomfited by his own actions and resentful of his discomfiture. A guilt trip out here was the last thing he needed.

'So, what's the plan?' Stevie asked, breaking their reveries. 'Slow breakfast and an explore? I wouldn't mind trekking west and getting a better look at Hiunchuli. It's so underrated.'

'Sounds good to me,' Duffy sighed, pushing Mabel and Mabel's mother out of his mind. He liked the sound of a rest day. No pressures. No guilt.

'Yeah, it's a plan,' Jay sighed, locking his fingers behind his head, still absorbing the view. He glanced at Duffy. 'Why don't you join us on the circuit trek?'

'Thanks, but I'm going to stay here for a day or two.'

'Really?' Jay seemed confounded by the idea. 'I thought you said the journey was the destination?'

'It is. But the destination's the destination too,' Duffy shrugged.

Jay laughed. 'But what are you gonna do up here? Make a snowman? Get a tan?'

'Why not?' Duffy grinned.

'Your call.' Jay shrugged. 'Well, let's get some food first before we think about doing anything.' He pushed his chair back, Stevie too.

Duffy sat there for a moment, regarding the toy staring back at him. It occurred to him that with the Americans heading back down towards civilization tomorrow – and they'd be descending at speed, he knew – this was the opportunity to do what he had said he would. Post it home. Little Mabel could have Moodle – Moolah – back in a matter of days.

And yet . . . and yet . . . this thing was his talisman – the very way it had come into his life told him it was his lucky charm. He couldn't give it up now, could he? He had never needed it more.

If they knew, they would understand.

And even if they didn't, what did it matter? These people weren't his friends. He had acted in good faith and was guilty only of finding something that had been lost. He hadn't stolen it. He hadn't taken it off her. And they would never meet. Their lives had simply bumped together along a rutted path for a few days, but he was already on another road on the other side of the world and they were falling away from one another once more. They hadn't communicated for several days now – technically, Mabel's mother was airing him – so he wouldn't even have to try to lose contact. It would simply happen. It was already happening . . .

He rose and stuffed the toy inside his jacket, turning to go back in. They had been strangers before all this. They could be strangers again.

Chapter Twenty

Frome, Friday 9 December

The fire crackled, spitting out bright sparks onto the stone hearth that wriggled and hissed into blackened silence. Candles flickered at the tables, holly stuffed into jugs, people talking loudly . . . Natasha stared at the pub wall, oblivious. Her eyes were trained upon a print of a horse-drawn carriage, coachmen in red coats, the horses' eyes rolling, nostrils flared.

'Nats? . . . Darling?'

She blinked as she felt a hand on her arm. 'Huh?'

Rob laughed. 'You're a million miles away tonight.' He reached a hand to her thigh and squeezed it.

'Sorry. Sorry.' She sat up straighter, like a schoolgirl caught staring out of the window. 'What were you saying?'

'Dave was saying there's a new line-up at Komedia in Bath. We should go one night, don't you think?'

Them? Go to a comedy club? 'Absolutely.'

'It's a really good laugh,' Dave shrugged. 'Which after a long day sheath-cleaning stallions is generally what I need.'

Hels spluttered with amusement, slapping his arm fondly, and Natasha watched as Dave leaned over to plant a kiss on her forehead. For a woman who styled herself as a hot mess, her life was beginning to look distinctly neat and tidy.

The waitress came over with their meals and they all sat back as the plates were set down – steaming pies for Hels and Dave; steak for Rob; fish and chips and peas for her. Natasha stared at it, trying to summon an appetite as everyone eagerly picked up their cutlery. The pub was packed and they had been waiting for their food for an hour; she should be ravenous. She followed suit, several beats behind, but when she looked up, Hels was watching her.

'I'm so glad we managed to make this happen,' Rob said, glancing across as if noticing the women's unnatural stillness. 'We should do more impromptu nights out.'

'Well, it's easier for us than you,' Hels said, drawing her gaze away. 'We don't have to worry about babysitters.'

'It's Bella who kicks up the stink,' Rob said, rolling his eyes as he sawed his steak. 'But we're lucky, Rosie's very good – reliable, good with last-minute stuff too. And Mabel loves her, of course.'

'Thank heavens you're not still having to bring her out with you everywhere. I imagine that would get exhausting pretty quickly,' Dave said.

'It did,' Rob rolled his eyes. 'Luckily everything calmed down as soon as Moolah was found and she's been sleeping soundly since.'

'Oh yes,' Dave grinned. 'I almost forgot about that. The Harry Styles thing. So is he your new best friend now?' He looked at Natasha, clearly trying to draw her into the conversation.

She drew herself up. 'No! He hasn't even started following me back on Insta,' she replied with mock-indignation. 'It's outrageous. I mean, you'd think he'd be invested in finding out if we got a happy ending!'

'Oh, you definitely did,' Hels said quickly, holding her with a stare. 'You definitely got the happy ending.'

The two women stared at one another across the table. If that was supposed to be subtle . . . Natasha tried to swallow down her fish, but her throat felt closed and she began choking and coughing.

'You okay?' Rob asked, patting her on the back.

'Mm-hmm,' she mumbled, eyes watering.

Dave reached for his wine – a well-bodied pinot noir he'd ordered which Rob was appearing to appreciate very much, his cheeks settling into a gouty rouge. 'Hels told me you've been receiving daily bulletins on Moolah's progress around the Andes.'

'Himalayas,' Hels corrected, without drawing her eyes from Natasha.

'Himalayas, right,' Dave murmured. He looked over at Natasha questioningly when she forgot to reply.

'Huh? Oh . . . Yes . . . He's been . . . very thoughtful. We call them postcards, to make it feel more like an adventure. Mabel's loved it.'

Rob chuckled. 'Nats has printed up all the photos he's sent over and taped them to Mabel's wall so she can see Moolah as she's going to sleep.'

'Laminated them too,' Hels added.

'What did he send over today, by the way?' Rob asked.

Natasha hesitated, her heart rate spiking a little. 'Actually, he didn't.'

'He didn't send anything?'

'Nope.' She watched her husband for his reaction, hoping he could give her the reassurance she couldn't seem to find in herself. The image of Duffy remained on her phone, the email unanswered. She hadn't allowed herself to open it since she had left Hels's clinic yesterday morning but it emitted an almost radioactive hum, making her jittery.

'Huh. He must be out of range. Mabel's okay with it?'

'Well, I tried to explain he's in the middle of nowhere and that he may as well be on the moon, but—'

'Actually, they've connected the astronauts on the ISS to the cloud now, did you hear?' Rob asked Dave.

'Surely not?' Dave replied, looking impressed.

'Oh yes. I mean, the ISS has basically been a floating lab encircling the globe for the past twenty-odd years. The absence of gravity means they research everything from cancer treatments to combustion engines. I'm sure I read somewhere that they've conducted over three thousand experiments in that time, but there were so many competing priorities for the limited connectivity available that—'

Natasha looked at Rob, talking shop. He didn't want to hear then that their daughter had cried pitifully when there had been no postcard at breakfast? That the teachers were having a devil of a job getting her to settle at nursery again? For Mabel, of course, it had counted as the third morning of radio silence, not the second. Natasha had decided against sharing the picture of Duffy – or Tom, as she now knew – not sure if it might upset her daughter to actually put a face to this hitherto anonymous, faceless stranger. For as long as the focus was on Moolah's adventure, it allowed them to sweep over the fact that *that man there* had taken her. They were best off keeping to abstracts and not absolutes, but it meant they were now up to three days without a picture. And Natasha was beginning to panic.

'I'll come with you,' Hels said, throwing down her napkin.

Natasha looked up at her in surprise. 'What?'

'I said I'll come with you. I need to go too,' Hels said, pushing back her chair.

There was a pause, then Natasha rose obediently, following

the girl code; they both knew Natasha hadn't said a word about going to the ladies', but Rob and Dave were deep in conversation now and barely glanced over as they got up.

Natasha felt nervous as she followed Hels across the patterned carpet. A tête-à-tête in the loos always meant she was in trouble. The toilet door swung back as Hels strode in, hitting the cream anaglypta walls. Natasha watched as Hels pushed on all the cubicle doors, making sure they were alone, before she turned back to her with arms crossed over her chest.

'So you *clearly* didn't sleep last night. You look wrecked.'

'Thanks.'

'And as for the permanent thousand-yard stare . . .' Hels arched an eyebrow. 'Talk.'

Natasha looked at her oldest friend, feeling a rush of unsaid words clamour at her. She felt her cheeks flush as repressed anger – no, rage – demanded to be heard. Things she had never told anyone beat in her like a pulse, a drumbeat that moved her out of time to everyone around her.

Hels narrowed her eyes. '. . . What?'

Natasha felt the words surge like a wave, building, rising, toppling. '. . . You should have told me that he texted you.'

She watched as they smashed at Hels's feet. '. . . Huh?'

'After the wedding.'

'Oh. That.'

'*That?*' Natasha flinched. The question *Did she do it?* had been rebounding like a rubber ball in her mind from the moment she had left the dental surgery yesterday morning. She couldn't get free of it, no matter what she did. She'd driven straight afterwards to Diana's with no idea of how she got there; her hand had been on autopilot as she made her sketches, Arty flirting over the stable door at her; and for once she'd been grateful when Rob had rung home to say he'd been held up again at the office. She had kept herself busy with some Christmas shopping online and even made an apple pie while listening to a podcast, but no matter how busy her hands – driving, sketching, bathing or baking – her mind was caught on a loop: Why had he done that? Why had Hels kept it from her? And, more than anything – what would she have done if Hels *had* told her?

Hels frowned. 'Well, what possible good could it have done, telling you that?'

'None! But I still had a right to know. It was about me.'

'Nats! You had just got married and then twenty minutes later you were pregnant. You wanted me to shake that down over a guy you met at your hen weekend?'

Hels looked genuinely shocked that they were having this discussion. Natasha felt the pressure build behind her eyes but she wouldn't cry. She would never let anyone see how it had really been. They didn't know. No one did. She looked away, biting her lip, her fingertips pressing into her arms as she hugged herself tightly.

'Nats, look, I can see why this has rattled your cage. I can. I mean, what were the fricking chances that of all the Airbnbs in all the world, Tom Duffy McDuffduff walked into that one . . . ? But it was just a spooky coincidence, okay?' She watched Natasha through slitted eyes. 'I mean, I hope you're not thinking this was some kind of sign that he was supposed to have ended up in your life again, are you?'

'Of course not!' But Natasha couldn't hold her gaze and she turned away.

'Because if you were thinking that it was a sign,' Hels said quietly, 'then he would have been there, in Vienna, at the same time as you, and not the day after. Wouldn't he?'

Natasha blinked, feeling her heart pounding hard. Had destiny misfired? 'Exactly.' But the tremor had found its way into her voice.

'Look, it was an infatuation, Nats. A last emotional fling before getting married. Feelings were running high, it was intense – but you only knew him for a weekend. You can't love someone in a matter of days. It takes time to get to know someone.'

'He said it can take a moment – a moment to lose someone, a moment to find someone.'

'Yes, well, he would have said that, wouldn't he?' Hels asked drily. How many times had she heard variations on that theme sitting at the bar? 'And fine, yes, *maybe* love at first sight is possible in theory, but Nats, he also buggered off. Didn't he? Whatever he got you to see, or talked you into, he also scarpered before there was any fallout. He wasn't some all-conquering hero. He was a smooth-talking coward. And if you think all this is somehow . . . destiny at work, and you're looking for reasons to ring him in the middle of the Himalayas and tell him you were the hen from four years ago – well I don't want to hurt you, hon, but he probably won't even remember.'

It was like being slugged with a baseball bat. 'Of course. And I'm not thinking about it like that.' Her voice sounded strangled.

'So what then?'

Natasha felt out of words. Her brain felt full of static, her heart made of knives.

'Look.' Hels came over and placed her hands on Natasha's shoulders. 'You were getting a bad case of cold feet and this guy came in as a kind of white knight, I get it. We all got drunk and did things we shouldn't have done – I don't care what Lauren says, I definitely saw her snogging the bike guy in the kitchen. But what happens at Center Parcs stays at Center Parcs, okay? You felt a connection with him, fine. But *this* is real life.' Hels shook her gently. 'Us, here in the loos, while Rob and Dave are talking about astronauts out there. Rob is the one you love. You and him and Mabel are so perfect together it's disgusting. You're like a catalogue family. It makes me want to run screaming into the hills.'

Natasha shook her head. 'You know our life is far from perfect.'

'Of course I do. Whose is? But I also think sometimes you don't realize what a good thing you've got.'

Natasha felt like she'd been slapped. No. *Seen.* Her terrible secret, her most private realization was leaking from her. 'What do you mean?'

Hels held her hands up appeasingly. 'Just that sometimes, from the outside, it looks like poor Rob's forever having to prove himself to you.'

Poor Rob? 'He's not!'

'He is, Nats. It's like you're still playing hard to get, but what more can he do? He busts a gut to give you everything he can, he puts up with me forever in your kitchen, drinking your wine. But he never complains and he's always complimenting you. He adores you—'

'I know that.'

'So then what's wrong?' Hels put her hands on Natasha's shoulders and shook her gently, half joking, half not. 'You don't still think he's having an affair, do you?'

Natasha shook her head. 'No, I know he's not.'

'So then what is it?'

She sighed. How could she possibly explain it when she didn't understand it herself? 'I know this isn't Rob's fault. It's me. *I'm* the problem. I . . . I . . . feel . . . numb.'

Hels dropped her hands down as Natasha pulled back to lean against the vanity counter, feeling ashamed. It was one thing to admit to feeling lonely with her husband, but to feel numb . . . to feel nothing . . . ? After their wonderful holiday, after everything he gave her . . . ?

'Listen, you've been trying to get pregnant for a year, right?' Hels began.

'Eighteen months,' she said quietly, her gaze on the floor.

'Right, yes, eighteen months. That's a huge amount of pressure on any couple. A little numbness is probably to be expected.'

Natasha looked at her hopefully. The worry that she had fallen out of love with her husband was all-consuming; she desperately didn't want Mabel growing up with divorced parents and no siblings. 'You really think so?'

'Of course! That's major pressure. But you just have to remember that it happened for you once before, so it'll happen again.'

'Yes. That's what Rob keeps saying.'

'So then listen to him!'

'I just can't help but feel like something must be wrong. It shouldn't be taking this long.'

'Hon, he is away *a lot*. I bet that doesn't give you that many windows of fertility opportunity.'

'Well no, but even so—'

'Were your dates good for the Maldives?'

'Yes.'

'So then, go buy a test.'

Hels made it sound so easy. 'I don't *feel* pregnant though.'

'What are you? A water diviner? Of course you don't – you'd be two weeks gone! But if you do a test next week, say, and you get the news you're so desperate for, I bet it'll settle you down and all this other . . . *distraction* will be forgotten.'

'Distraction?'

'With Duffy.' Hels was regarding her closely. 'And even if he does drop off the edge of the world and Moolah is never seen again, it won't matter anywhere near as much if Mabes has a little sister or brother to play with. Kids move on, Nats. These obsessions fade.'

Natasha looked away. Seemingly hers hadn't. She had thought she had tucked it up and stitched it tightly shut, locked it in a vault and dropped it to the bottom of the sea. Instead, she had a picture on her phone of the man she needed to forget, enjoying a beer with friends on the other side of the world. It was in her pocket, in her hand, by her pillow, at all times, a Pandora's Box she couldn't escape.

'They're separate things. Moolah is irreplaceable to Mabes. I have to get her back.'

'Hmm. I hope that isn't a euphemism for flying out to Nepal. You're not looking for excuses to see him?'

'Of course not! I have a bad feeling about it, that's all. I think he's gone. This is the third day now with no contact.'

'Only if we're not counting yesterday's offering,' Hels frowned.

'Which we're not. That wasn't something I could share with Mabel. It might have upset her.'

'And Rob? Did you share it with him?'

'Obviously not. Rob no sooner needs to see a picture of the guy than Mabel does.'

Hels arched an eyebrow. 'No, but he also doesn't need *not* to see it. Rob's never met the fella; he has no idea you once had a crush on the guy, that you kissed him on your hen weekend! So what would he care what Duffy looks like? He's just a bloke climbing mountains with his daughter's comforter in his back pocket as far as he's concerned. It's only you it has any resonance for—'

'It has no resonance for me!'

'Why did he send it then?'

'I don't know, I told you. He doesn't even know I'm *me*! He only knows me as Mabel's mum.'

'You don't know that for sure,' Hels argued. 'Maybe he does know and that's why he sent it! He could have scrolled on Insta and seen you—'

'We've talked about this. There is no way he'll have the bandwidth to access social media out there. It's impossible.' She shook her head firmly, certain on this point at least.

'So you think it's completely outside the realms of possibility that he *does* somehow know it's you – and he's gone AWOL because he's making a noble sacrifice by disappearing into the ether?'

Natasha looked at her friend in horror. 'There would be nothing noble about that while he's still got Moolah.'

'So all this *agitation* is just about getting Moolah back? Not because you've found him again?'

Natasha tried to steady her thoughts even though her heart was racing. 'If he goes off-grid and just . . . abandons us . . . how am I supposed to break that to Mabel?' She kept her voice level. 'He has to stay invested in us.'

Hels watched her with an even stare. 'Well, how much longer is he out there for? It's been, what, nearly two weeks already? Surely he's got to be passing a town somewhere along the way soon?'

'That's like saying stop for a Starbucks in the Gobi Desert. He's in the Himalayas! It could be weeks yet.'

'Then email and ask him where the hell he is; don't sit

around waiting for his messages – when is he passing somewhere? Ask him. He must have a route map, he must know. It's not an unreasonable question. Expectations need to be managed at this end. Everyone knows three-year-olds are the most tyrannical and irrational humans on the planet.'

A sudden laugh escaped Natasha, breaking the tension that had her in its grip. 'That is very true.'

'I *only* speak the truth,' Hels said, looking pleased with herself as she saw Natasha relax a little. 'Look – trust me when I say this will just quietly resolve in the fullness of time. Moolah was lost. Moolah has been found. Moolah will be sent home. Duffy will continue on his merry way. You will continue on yours.' She winked. '. . . Got it?'

Natasha sighed. 'Got it.'

Hels looped her arm around hers. 'Come on. We need to go back out there. The boys will think we've climbed out of the window and gone clubbing. You're going to go and flirt with your husband and forget about inappropriate texts and selfies from bearded men with toy fetishes.' Hels laughed out loud at her unflattering description. 'Ha! Honestly, if that doesn't put you off him, nothing will!'

No, Natasha thought, allowing herself to be led out. Nothing will.

Chapter Twenty-One

Whinfell, October 2018

'Oh. My. God.' Hels announced herself with a voice like a drag queen and vertical hair. Her mascara was spooning her eyes and she was wearing her pyjamas inside out. 'Now *that*, my friend, was a send-off!'

Natasha watched as Hels spread her arms wide and launched herself onto the opposite sofa. A bottle of beer popped out from under the cushions as she landed, falling onto the floor and spilling a few last drops onto the rug.

Natasha watched them bleed dispassionately. She had done the tidying up this morning, when the others had still been fast asleep. She'd slept poorly, tossing all night and waking before six, her mind stuck on a loop and her tongue feeling like a carpet. Doing something had felt good. Needed. Moving and keeping busy was her friend, a perfect distraction. She had picked up all the beer, wine, prosecco and vodka bottles, washed the glasses, deconstructed the pizza boxes and taken them – along with the bin bag left abandoned last night on the deck – down to the recycling station. She'd retrieved the bra found down the back of the sofa, put the dishwasher on, plumped the cushions and opened all the doors so the room could air. The family coming in after them would have no idea of the carnage that had happened here last night.

She had put right everything, except the storm still raging in her head.

'Lizzie and Lauren are making bacon sandwiches,' she said, looking up from the magazine she wasn't reading. 'Sara's gone to the shop to get ketchup.'

'Ketchup, God yes,' Hels moaned, her arms crossed above her face. 'Can you *imagine* a bacon sarnie without ketchup?'

'Hmm,' Natasha murmured, able to imagine far worse things than that.

One of Hels's arms dropped down as Natasha sank into silence. '. . . What's wrong?'

'Why would anything be wrong?'

'You're being weird.'

Natasha rolled her eyes. 'I'm hungover. Can I not suffer in peace?'

'Hmmph,' Hels said, but she seemed satisfied with the explanation, bringing her arm back up to hide from the blindingly cruel sunlight.

Lauren walked back through with a tray of mugs. 'Oh, you're up. We were just about to wake you. We weren't sure if Jack was still up there.'

Hels grinned and sighed happily. 'Nah. Booted him out hours ago.'

'Fun night?' Lauren asked, her expression a confused blend of judgemental and jealous.

'Oh yeah,' Hels sighed, sitting up and reaching for one of the mugs of tea.

'Hey, that's for Sara,' Lauren protested, slapping her hand.

'Too bad. You snooze, you lose.'

'But *you* were the one snoozing!'

Hels just beamed unapologetically, closing her eyes and taking a restorative sip of tea. Outside, they heard the sound of feet on the steps and Sara ran through a moment later.

'Got the ketchup,' she panted, going straight to the kitchen.

'Get yourself a tea!' Hels called after her, eyes narrowing as she began to notice their spotless surroundings. '. . . Cleaners were in early.' She was now the messiest thing in the room.

'Nats did it. We came down to her with the Marigolds on, unblocking the sink,' Lauren said.

'Eww!' Hels pulled a face. 'What'd you do that for?'

Natasha shrugged again from behind her magazine.

Lizzie walked through with the plate of sandwiches, Sara still shaking the ketchup. 'There's more if you want it.'

For a few minutes, the room fell quiet as everyone refuelled their battered bodies. Natasha had already downed five glasses of water and was feeling largely past the worst of it. Her night had ended earlier than the others', though no one appeared to have noticed.

'So, did we all have a good night?' Hels asked, her mouth full.

'Some of us better than others,' Lizzie muttered. 'Rach is still up there with whatshisface.'

'Andy,' Lauren supplied.

A slow smile climbed upon Hels's lips as she looked at Lauren intently. Lauren paled. 'Wait . . . did I see you snogging Ben in the kitchen?'

'No!'

Hels's mouth opened into a slow gasp as the memories

became clearer. 'I did! I bloody did! You had him up against the fridge!'

'I did no such thing!'

Hels fell back on the sofa, laughing and drubbing her bare feet on the floor. 'Oh my God! That's so funny!'

'It's not funny, because it didn't happen,' Lauren said hotly. 'And I don't appreciate any stupid rumours starting up. Zach would have a total sense of humour failure over that, I can tell you.'

Hels reached over and slapped her knee. 'Relax, babe. We're not going to drop you in it. Vegas rules. Nothing that happened here officially happened.'

'But I'm telling you, nothing happened.'

'Exactly!' Hels said with a wink, tapping the side of her nose secretively.

'Ugh!'

'Lizzo? Sar? I'm guessing it must have been a bunfight for Hot Tom, thanks to Lauren snaffling the other single man. Which one of you bagged him?'

'Actually, he buggered off,' Lizzie sighed. 'So we ended up doing Musical.ly routines.' She looked at Sara. 'You didn't post them, did you?'

'Course not,' Sara said briskly, only to give a laughing face as soon as Lizzie turned away.

'When?' Hels demanded, looking cross.

'Huh?'

'When did Hot Tom bugger off?'

'Not really sure,' Sara shrugged. 'But it was early. He didn't seem into it.'

'He looked pretty into it when we were playing Spin the Bottle,' Hels said, looking over at Natasha, a dawning suspicion crawling over her features. '. . . And where did *you* go to? You disappeared pretty early too.'

'Uh-uh,' she protested, knowing exactly what her oldest friend was thinking. 'I peaked too early. I was in bed. *On my own.*'

'Can you prove that?'

'Actually, yes. Lizzie walked in and woke me up to check I was still breathing.'

'I was being a good friend! We'd all had a shedload.'

'Thanks, hon,' Natasha smiled. 'I appreciate it.'

'So you had an early night on your own hen night, and then you got up early and did the cleaning?' Hels asked, looking distinctly unimpressed. 'Well, if that doesn't qualify for worst hen do ever, I don't know what does.'

'Actually, *I* loved it and I had a great time, so don't make me feel bad about it.'

'Fine. But you are officially a chicken and not a hen . . .'

Kiss me.

No.

Chicken.

'. . . thank God you only have to do this once.'

Natasha pulled her mind back. 'I have no doubt you'll put me to shame when it's your turn.'

'Uh-uh. I won't ever be so dumb as to put myself in a position where I'm required to be a farmyard animal.'

The others laughed.

I don't think you want to marry him.

'Well, at least we've got a few hours now to recover,' Lauren said, glancing back at the clock in the kitchen. 'We're booked into the spa at noon, then late lunch and checkout at four. Nats, we booked you the deluxe salt scrub and seaweed wrap.'

I don't want you to marry him either.

'Nats?'

'Huh?' She saw the others staring. 'Sorry. Pounding head.'

Lauren leaned forward, looking at her earnestly. 'Salt scrub. Seaweed wrap.'

'They're basically turning you into *maki*,' Hels grinned.

'Excellent. Sounds good,' she replied blankly, not hearing any of it. It was this time yesterday that she'd first met him – frozen on the tree aerials.

Stand on my feet.

Hold me.

Can you waltz?

What were the chances of having met him? And why now? Why not a year ago? Last month? How could this have happened a week before she was getting married? This was her hen party, for chrissakes! Hels had been right; it really was the worst one ever.

She tried to conjure Rob's face. His twinkling eyes, that seductive smile. On the greens right now, playing golf while she . . . flirted with a stranger.

This was madness. She'd lost her mind.

She wanted to be home again, and for all this to be forgotten. As soon as she saw Rob, she knew this infatuation would be dispelled and her life would continue exactly as she knew it should. She put the magazine down with a sigh. She could do this. It was just a few more hours to get through.

But first, they had to make sushi.

The towelling robes were thick, the spa slippers flat and wide like ducks' feet. Natasha pulled tightly on the belt of her dressing gown and looked in the changing room mirror to pull her hair back. She looked how she felt. Swamped.

'Which colour shall I get?' Hels asked, waggling her fingers in her face. 'Pale green, yellow or black?'

'Black?' Natasha cried. 'You're my chief bridesmaid. You can't have black nails.'

Hels laughed throatily. 'I love it when you go full Bridezilla. We've not seen her for a while.' She jogged Natasha with her elbow. 'I'm late. Enjoy your treatment. I'll see you back here in a bit.'

Natasha watched as Hels walked towards the door, somehow managing to rock an attitude even in towelling. She turned back to stare at her own reflection, trying to see the woman who was her but not her – the woman under her skin who was urging her to go and find him, to tell him he was right, she didn't want to go through with it. Something was wrong with her and Rob – she didn't know what, but there wasn't the ease she felt with Tom, a man she'd known only a day. And if it could feel more natural with him – if she had any doubts – she had to be honest, didn't she? This was the rest of their lives they were putting on the line. Rob wouldn't want to live a lie. He wouldn't want to be second best.

But then she blinked and the veil fell away. She saw herself again – conventional, safe, above all things practical. Where would she even find him? She had no way of contacting him, no idea where he lived or even what his full name was.

She pushed herself away from the counter and walked out into the reception area. She could see Hels and Lauren through a glass wall, their feet in footbaths, chatting away. Hels had a colour chart on her lap as she debated which colour to rock with her bridesmaid dress. Natasha realized she really didn't care. Black nails? She was fine with it.

Lizzie, Rachel and Sara were in the swimming pool and jacuzzi, doing a post-mortem of last night.

'Natasha?'

She looked up to find her beauty therapist – Rocco, according to her badge – waiting for her. 'We'll be in the room at the end here,' she said, leading Natasha down the champagne-coloured corridor. 'Do you have any allergies to essential oils?'

'Uh, no, I don't think so,' Natasha murmured, following behind her and looking in as she passed by the nail room at Lauren and Hels deep in conversation.

'It says on your file here that you're getting married next weekend?'

'Uh, yes.'

'Congratulations! You must be so excited!'

'. . . Yes.'

Rocco opened a door and let her in first. The treatment room was double aspect, with vertical slatted blinds set in front of wide double-glazed windows. A massage table covered in towels was positioned in the centre, various bottles of oils and unguents arranged on shelves. It smelled of almonds and roses in there, the temperature warm to increase blood flow and induce blissful feelings of drowsiness.

'Okay, Natasha, if you'd like to take everything off, including all jewellery, and lie under the towels on your tummy, I'll come back in just a few moments.'

Natasha glanced at her, somehow remembering to smile. '. . . Thanks.'

She wandered over to the far side of the room, where a console table sat beneath the window with an empty trinket dish on top. She took out her earrings, staring blankly through the glass as she unclasped her necklace. She wanted to cry. Or scream. Something. She saw a familiar figure cycle past in a black hoodie, black trousers, white headphone wires dangling down . . .

Suddenly the world came alive. *She* came alive.

'Tom!' She reached over and banged on the window with her fist, but the glazing was thick. Only the pigeon strutting on the outside ledge seemed perturbed. 'Oh my God,' she whimpered as he sped along. She felt the same sense of panic she'd had on the treehouse deck last night as he had disappeared through the trees. He was already out of sight. Without a thought in her head, she ran from the room, flat-footed in the one-size-fits-all slippers. 'No. No-no-no,' she muttered as she flew down the corridor, meeting Rocco, who was coming back up with an armful of towels.

'Natasha! Where are you going?' the therapist asked.

'I . . . I forgot something! I'll be right back,' she panted, not stopping as she skidded through the reception area and burst through the double doors. She stood on the path for a moment, looking around for him desperately, but there was no sign. It was busy outside with plenty of families on bikes, groups walking with bags of towels or food, shrieks of delighted children echoing from the various corners of the forest.

He'd gone *that* way, that was all she knew – and she headed left, shuffle-running as fast as she could; she managed a hundred metres before she kicked the slippers off and ran barefoot instead. Her eyes scoured the grounds, looking past every tree, peering through the windows of every building. Where . . . where could he be? At least he was still here, on site, that was something. Unless he'd been heading home? Perhaps he'd been working this morning and finished his shift? Or he'd crashed at Ben's or Andy's or Jack's? She had no idea where the staff accommodation was.

'Fuck,' she cried, still running, still looking, as she realized she was outside the indoor sports plaza. It was so big, it was almost like an airport terminal, conspicuous and blindingly obvious. Almost too obvious. Surely it couldn't be that easy? He was back at the place she'd seen him yesterday?

There was no sign of his bike, but it could be round the back, she told herself, running in and stopping dead. Lines of rope dangled down the grey, blue and purple walls, people pulling and heaving themselves up with various degrees of effort and ease. Life was going on as though nothing had happened, when hers had caught on a nail and pivoted one-eighty, setting her to face an entirely different direction.

Then her eyes caught him, like missiles on laser lock; he was walking across the space, pulling out his headphones and heading towards a PERSONNEL ONLY door. She ran again, weaving and dodging past people as they blocked him from sight momentarily.

'Tom!' she half cried, half whispered, seeing that he was entering a code into a keypad.

'Tom!'

He had a hand to the door but he glanced back, a startled look dawning on his face as he saw her running towards him.

'Nats, what are you doing here?' he asked, holding his hands out as if to catch her. 'What are you . . . why are you dressed like that?'

She looked down at her dressing gown and bare feet. She had forgotten she wasn't fully dressed. She tried to gather her wits. The elation at finding him, at feeling his proximity again . . . 'What? You mean you preferred the wedding dress?' she panted.

He grinned at the unexpected joke. 'Well, no. Nothing could top that.'

She felt her stomach swoop as their gazes locked and her mouth parted as if to say something, but now that she was here she realized she had no idea what to say. She didn't even know why she was here. There was no plan. Her feet had just brought her here.

He looked up and around them, and she could tell he was catching people's eyes from the small smiles he gave. People were looking. 'You'd better come in here,' he said quietly, pushing open the door. 'We're not supposed to house refugees from the spa.'

She stepped into the room, feeling his hand on the small of her back. They were in a store cupboard, with ropes dangling on hooks and shelves of climbing shoes, harnesses and helmets lining the walls.

The heavy fire door swooshed shut behind him, dampening down the noise on the other side as he walked her around a corner. They were hidden by stacked boxes of climbing chalk and the hush enveloped them like a cloud as he looked back at her, questioningly.

The memory of how they had left things last night settled between them.

'. . . I thought you'd have gone by now,' he said.

'Late checkout. I'm supposed to be having a . . . salt wrap and a seaweed scrub. Or . . . something like that. Sushi . . .'

He looked baffled.

'But then I saw you from the window and I wanted to . . .' What? What did she want to do?

'Say goodbye?' he offered into the silence. 'Didn't we do that last night?'

'No. You didn't give me a chance for that. You just left.'

'Yes. What else was I supposed to do? I've never tried to wreck a wedding before. It's not a great feeling.'

'So you just gave up?'

He gave a snort of disbelief. 'I didn't *just* anything, but you've got to meet me halfway. I told you what I think, and what I feel, but if you're not going to be honest about what's going on with you . . .' He gave a hopeless shrug.

She stared at him for what felt like an age, willing her feelings to take a shape, a sound, something she could use to express this feeling of paralysing panic that she might lose him. She had been so steamrollered by loss after her parents died, so terrified of being alone, that it had dictated every move she made since – her degree choice, her career, her sprint down the aisle to Rob (albeit after he had proposed for the fourth time; he had asked her the first time on their one-month anniversary, far too soon even for her). She had thought she had a safety plan in place, that she had carved herself some certainty in this world, but Tom . . . he was all exploding stars and spontaneity, and that frightened her because she'd known that excitement with other guys but it always ended prematurely. Or badly. But there was something else with him too. Something so much more.

He stepped towards her. 'Talk to me.' He took her hands in his. 'Just say it.'

She blinked. It was like trying to push a truck, to turn a ship, to fly a deflated balloon. '. . . I feel like I can't breathe . . .'

'Okay.'

'I'm stuck in a box and I can't get out of it.'

'Okay.' He was watching her, barely stirring.

'And I put myself in the box because it felt safe. It did, for a while. But now . . . now I feel trapped and I can't get out. And everyone's telling me I'm lucky and happy but I don't feel any of those things . . . And you're the only one who seems to see it.'

'I know.'

'. . . And I want to . . . I feel this . . . instinct with you that I've never had with anyone else before, but how do I trust it's not just a way for me to escape? How do I trust you? This could all just be a line.'

'It's not. You know it's not.'

He said it so simply.

'Life's too short for bullshit, Nats. I mean what I say and say what I mean. And I think you should have dinner with me next Saturday.'

She laughed, but she was still fearful. Plans had been made, events set in motion. Everything was already under way. She felt like she was in the Hadron Collider, her future hurtling towards her, wholly unstoppable.

Still holding her hand, he pulled her arm up, drawing her closer to him. 'Come here.'

She stepped forward, her heart hammering, knowing she was getting close to crossing the line. She knew she shouldn't – but then, why else had she chased him in here?

'Your feet must be cold,' he murmured.

Were they? She looked down at the concrete floor. Her feet were the only parts of her body not ringing.

'Stand on my toes.'

She hesitated, then stepped onto his feet, her arms closing around his neck as he wrapped one around her waist, the other behind her head, clasping her close and taking her back to their first ever moments together. Just yesterday. She closed her eyes and felt the world drop away, but this time she wasn't scared. His skin was millimetres from her lips as they stood motionless for a few moments, before he began to move slowly, his muscles moving beneath her fingertips as they danced in silence in the storeroom. She kissed his neck lightly, just once, a soft inevitable touch that stopped him in his tracks again.

'Kiss me,' he whispered.

This time, she did. She reached on her tiptoes and pressed her lips to his. Again. And then again, because she knew for sure now – come next weekend, she wanted this man to take her out to dinner.

Chapter Twenty-Two

Annapurna Base Camp, Saturday 10 December

'So I guess this is goodbye,' Duffy said, holding his hand up for a grab.

'I prefer *hasta mañana*,' Stevie said with a grin, pulling him into a hug.

Their backpacks were loaded, coats and hats on. The winds were picking up, sending clouds scudding across the sky.

'Enjoy the Circuit. Everyone says it's incredible.'

'I'm stoked for it, man,' Jay said, stepping forward and hugging him too.

'Mind yourself at the Thorong La Pass, though,' Duffy said warningly. 'It's five and a half thousand metres there, so you'll need your big boy pants on—'

Stevie laughed.

'Don't hang around for too long. Seriously.'

'Not like you,' Stevie said. 'You're sure you're sure about hanging around up here?'

'Certain. My body's even beginning to like it.'

'You're acclimatizing.'

Duffy shrugged. 'Listen, can you do me a favour?'

'Sure, man,' Stevie said as Duffy pulled a wrapped parcel from his coat.

'First chance you get, *any* chance you get, can you send this abroad for me? It's important.'

'UK?' Stevie read the address, scrawled on the back of a site map Duffy had taken from reception. The wrapping was one of the plastic bags he used for storing wet clothes in his pack, doubled down and secured with duct tape; he just hoped it wouldn't smell too much.

Duffy reached in his pocket and pulled out twenty US dollars. 'That should cover it.' He handed the bills over. 'It's really important, okay? First chance you get. Express post.'

'Sure, man. We'll see to it.'

Duffy nodded, hoping he could trust them to be good to their word. He knew they wouldn't bin it, but would they remember? Would they remember at the right times? He'd spent the past hour in his room, going over the ethics of what he should do, but there was no obvious answer and he couldn't rest easy, whichever way he went with it.

'And you've got our details now, so stay in touch, all right? Be good to hook up again. Maybe see you in Pokhara in a few weeks?'

'Yeah, maybe.'

Jay laughed, patting him on the arm. 'You can't stay up here forever, you know.'

Duffy grinned. 'I agree that would be suboptimal.' He watched as the two Americans shrugged on their packs, groaning slightly as the weight settled upon their wearied, bruised bones.

'Be seeing ya, man,' Jay said, saluting and turning onto the path.

'Stay safe,' Stevie winked.

'And you.' Duffy watched them trudge away, their walking poles and trekking spikes dotting the snow, their warm and waterproof clothes as colourful as the prayer flags that flapped on poles above them, criss-crossing the site.

People were leaving by the dozen; the weather was generally more settled earlier on in the day, and everyone wanted to get going after a hot meal. Duffy turned and headed back to his room – he would do some drills and keep his strength up while he waited – his eyes grazing the mighty Annapurna bluffs. He hesitated for a moment, trying to absorb the colossal mass, as if familiarity would breed nonchalance. It didn't.

He dipped his head and went back inside.

'Mr Duffy!' The voice bowled down the corridor.

Duffy got off the bed and stuck his head out of the doorway. It was the woman who had checked him in when he'd arrived yesterday. 'Hey.'

'Man here.'

He nodded and tapped a hand to his temple in acknowledgement. 'Thanks. I'll be right there.' He went and sat on the bed, pulling on his boots and double-checking his pack one last time. He could feel his heart beating a little harder as he zipped up his jacket.

A contingent of porters had arrived, many of them sitting together at a table, drinking tea and talking with the teahouse owners. But Duffy saw his visitor set apart, standing by the wall beside a conical basket. It was filled to overflowing, so that a bamboo brace had been attached to the upper rim and extended way past his head. He was wearing a matching blue padded jacket and trousers, his skin even more weathered and lined than when last they'd met, a good decade earlier.

'Sanani Sherpa,' Duffy grinned, holding his arms out wide.

The older man took a good look at him, a bright smile softening his features. 'Master Tom Duffy. You grew up.'

They hugged for a long time and when finally they pulled apart, Tom felt emotions pushing up from deep inside him. A few of the other porters looked over, as if intrigued by the evident affection between them.

'So you came back,' Sanani said, resting a fatherly hand on his shoulder.

Duffy nodded. 'How could I not?'

'How could you not,' Sanani agreed – but there was a searching look in his eyes and Duffy knew there would be a conversation between them, at some point, when they would talk about what had happened and the tragedies that couldn't be undone. 'You look good. Fresh.'

'I feel it. I took it really slowly. No pressure, no strain. I treated the trek like a holiday.'

The sherpa laughed. 'That is one way to see it.' He looked straight into Duffy's eyes, making no attempts to hide his scrutiny. 'And in here?' He tapped his own head. 'Are you strong here? Are you prepared for this?'

'I've spent four years preparing. I did Lhotse and Nanga Parbat two years ago. Denali last year.'

'The body, yes. The head. But the heart?' Sanani clasped his head. 'You have sad eyes, my friend.'

'Maybe, but I won't after this. It's what I need to do.' A slight frown puckered the porter's brow. 'Don't worry, Sanani, I'm ready.'

The sherpa smiled broadly again. 'Very well, then.' He patted Duffy on the shoulder, turning towards the woven basket behind him. He pulled out a couple of packs as Duffy lifted his and set it carefully inside the cavity.

'You have taken out what you need?' Sanani asked him.

'Yep,' Duffy said, patting his coat pocket, his hand hitting something hard. 'Oh no, wait, nearly forgot. Great start.' He grinned, pulling out his phone and rolling his eyes. There was no point in taking it with him. There'd be no coverage anyway and no way to charge it; he didn't even want the weight of a solar pack in his bag. He had shut the phone down already, but as he went to put it in the pack, something stopped him. He had screenshotted a single family photo before he'd left for Europe, but till now he hadn't looked at it; the phone conversation at Vienna airport had suffocated any familial longing that might have briefly surfaced as he waited to board his plane. Perhaps if he'd revealed his plans, he and his father might have shared a few honest moments, but any relief for him would have been offset by the stress and worry that would burden his father. It had been easier to let them both retreat to their own comfortable corners, the way they always did. Now though, standing before an uncertain fate, he had a sudden urge to see his father's face one last time.

'Actually . . . I'll just do a final check,' he said, turning it back on. 'Make sure I've not missed anything—'

'No rush, my friend,' Sanani said, seeming to understand and leaning back on the wall.

Duffy waited as the phone powered back up again, whirring gently in his hand as mechanisms were kickstarted out of dormancy and updates automatically downloaded; he could already see the family photo in his mind's eye even before it came up. When it did, he felt momentarily bathed in sunshine – it showed his parents, him and Lottie on a camping trip when he'd been nine, the summer before his mother had died. They were all tanned and long-limbed, easy smiles on their faces as they squinted into the sun. He didn't remember who'd taken the photo. He just remembered that his father had been different then. Before. He'd never taken to the outdoor life like the rest of them but he had always gone along with it for their sakes. He would use green wood for campfires that would never take; he always forgot to pack the milk for his 'vital' teas; he deplored having to walk across campsites with a roll of toilet tissue in his hand. But he had laughed easily and no one could beat his campfire stories. He hadn't been angry back then.

The phone vibrated in his hand. An incoming message. A final word from the world.

'Good timing,' Sanani grinned.

'Typical,' Duffy said, clicking on it and seeing Anya's name.

He sighed, but then he always sighed when he thought of her. He'd put her through so much and hurt her so badly, unable to love her the way she'd deserved. He was damaged goods. What possessed her to continue to want him as a friend? He clicked on the message, frowning as he saw there was no message, just some photos of . . . It was Mabel. She was sitting on the back of a bike in a park somewhere, the greenery looking luscious, Moolah tucked into the front of her jacket and peeking out under her chin, clearly along for the ride.

He closed his eyes, remembering Anya saying she would send him the photos, that night in Khande. *'This little girl is cuter than Bambi. There's not a person in the world who'd deny her her toy.'*

He felt an immediate tightness in his stomach as he clicked on the next photo – Mabel asleep on a beach as a baby, still in a nappy and sleeping in a Superman pose, Moolah clutched in her tiny fist.

Shit.

Mabel sitting in the snow beside a snowman, Moolah tucked into the snowman's scarf.

Double shit.

Mabel blowing out the candles on a birthday cake, helium balloons tied to her chair, Moolah on the table seemingly blowing too.

Fuck. He'd made the wrong call.

God, how many were there? No wonder this had taken days to come through. It must have been buffering in the ether all that time.

He clicked on the next – and immediately staggered back against the wall, as though he'd been shoved. He blinked hard, one, two, three times. He felt a hole open up inside him, a vast crevasse he had never been able to fill with light, only the dark.

'They are beautiful.'

Sanani was standing beside him, looking at the image of Mabel and Nats, their cheeks pressed together, Moolah with them like a third wheel. 'Your family?'

'. . . No,' he whispered. 'Someone else's.'

Sanani's eyes narrowed as he saw Duffy look away, pressing his thumb down hard on the power button and forcibly removing it from his sphere, like Superman to kryptonite.

'You are okay?'

'I'm fine. It's an old photo. Belongs in the past,' Duffy said gruffly, stuffing the phone deep inside the backpack and stepping back for Sanani to take it.

Concern flashed through the older man's eyes. '. . . If you are sure, then.'

'I'm sure,' Duffy said, his chest feeling tight as adrenaline swamped his system. Fight or flight. He struggled to focus, to think straight. 'Everything can go back down. I've . . . I've left some letters in the front pocket here.' He patted it roughly, to show where he meant.

Sanani nodded and lifted the basket on the frame, taking

it over to where the other sherpas were sitting. He spoke to them in Nepali and patted the front of the pack too. A few looked over, vaguely interested, muttering back with hand gestures.

Duffy watched as he returned. 'They will take it back and it will go back to my home as agreed. My wife knows what to do.'

'Thank you,' Duffy said, struggling to keep his composure. He felt like he'd just been jumped. His heart rate had doubled. Why now? After all these years of keeping her out of his mind, why had she stepped back into his life again, at the very moment he was stepping out of it? It felt like a cruel joke, some kind of twisted kismet that she had been there at the very beginning of this journey and now she was here again, at the end. Time – or the lack of it – mocked him, fate's caprice ensuring he was forever on the periphery of her life, never quite in time to catch her, to tell her who he was even . . .

Wait.

He realized he had. Like a broken arrow that misfired from his brain, he remembered that he had sent through the photograph Stevie had taken of him. But there had been no reply, no more manipulatively charming or lonely emails. Had she recognized him? He had changed in the intervening years, of course; his hair was longer and he'd not had the stubble – beard, he corrected, his hand going to his jaw – back then. Or was he flattering himself to think she'd even remember him? She was married now and had a child. She'd moved on a long time ago.

He stood stock still, taking deep breaths and staring into memories only he could see. For four years, he had deplored the timing that had kept them apart, torturing himself with if onlys and what ifs, but now it occurred to him that perhaps everything was actually exactly as it should be. Natasha *wasn't* meant for him, that was why he kept missing her – back then in Cumbria, last month in Vienna, right now . . . The stars never quite lined up.

If things had been even a little bit different – if the timing had changed even by just a few hours, so that Nats had chosen him and not her fiancé – would he be standing here? He knew not. But that would have been a wrong turn. It had always been his destiny to stand on these slopes and to feel the cold shadow of the Goddess of Abundance swoop over him too; he had known that absolutely, even as a ten-year-old boy. Whether he liked it or not, everything had conspired to bring him to *this* moment, and seeing Natasha with her daughter was the final cutting of the ties he'd been searching for. Contrary to the timing being terrible, it was actually spot on, the scales falling away as he understood at last that he had indulged a fantasy, dreamed a dream that had never been his. He could go now into the unknown, untethered and utterly free, to fight his demons and slay his ghosts.

He looked at the sherpa with renewed gratitude and determination. He was ready for the fight that lay ahead. 'Sanani, I couldn't do this with anyone else but you.'

Sanani lifted the red pack and held it out to him easily, even though it weighed nigh-on forty kilos. 'I would not allow anyone else to do it but me. We both have unfinished business here.'

'You're a good friend,' Duffy said, shrugging on the pack. It was twice the size of his trekking one but he embraced the weight.

'You won't be saying that by the end of today,' Sanani grinned, shrugging on his orange pack too. 'There has been a lot of snow. Many avalanches.'

'Yeah, I've been keeping an eye.'

Both men fiddled with the straps and buckles, getting the weight distributions exactly right for each of them. Duffy was a lot taller than Sanani but the sherpa had a compact strength and thirty years of elite altitude experience. He had climbed with the best of the best.

Sanani looked at him. 'Are you ready?'

Duffy inhaled deeply. This would be the most richly oxygenated air he would gulp down for the next three weeks. Possibly ever again. 'As I'll ever be.' His gaze rose skyward again, towards the Goddess of Abundance, imperious and unassailable. 'Camp One, here we come.'

Chapter Twenty-Three

Snowshill, Monday 12 December

Natasha jumped out of the car, Bella already wagging her tail in recognition of where they were. Diana had said she would be out today – her daughter had a cello recital in Oxford – but Artemis was boxed in his stable and Natasha could continue to work on the head detailing without needing anyone to be around. To be honest, she could probably get more done being there on her own. Diana had a tendency to fuss and the endless cups of tea meant the journey home was a race against her bladder.

'Come on then,' Natasha said, opening the car door and going to loop the rope lead over Bella's head – but the dog had other ideas, bursting past her in a spurt of excitement. Natasha whirled on her heel in alarm. 'Bella! Bad girl!' she cried, seeing the dog chase a squirrel over the drive and onto a lawned area. 'Come back here!'

Her hands automatically scrabbled for the whistle that was always around her neck on walks, but it was currently on the footwell floor. She reached back into the car to grab it, catching sight of the fact that the gates were still open. Diana had left them open for her especially – and if Bella was to run out into the road . . .

'Bella! Come!' she cried, jumping up again. She watched as the squirrel took a hard left, scampering over the grass and into the flower bed that abutted the boundary to next door's garden, where an old beech tree stood splayed.

'Oh no-no-no-no-no,' she muttered, running over as she saw Bella get down on her belly and start trying to crawl beneath the shrubbery. 'Bella, *get* back here now!'

In the next moment, the wagging tail was gone from sight.

'Fuck,' Natasha hissed, changing direction and running up the drive instead, through the gates and into next door's garden. She wasn't dressed for chasing dogs. It was Mabel's nativity play later – she was a snowflake – and she would need to travel straight there. The zip tassels swung on her Fairfax leather boots, her olive skinny jeans with not quite enough stretch in them to make running feel easy.

Next door's garden was as manicured as Diana's, albeit with a trampoline, climbing frame and kids' bikes strewn about. Scandi-style Christmas stars twinkled at every window and a luxuriant wreath hung at the door. A muddy Audi 4x4 was parked on the drive, a Save the Polar Bears sticker on the back bumper.

'Bella, for chrissakes, come back here,' Natasha hissed as the dog began barking at the bottom of the tree trunk, apparently being tormented by the squirrel now scampering happily upon a high bough. 'Bella!'

She ran onto the grass and had just got to the errant dog, reopening the loop of the lead and slipping it over her head, when the door of the house opened and a woman looked out. 'Can I help you?' she enquired coolly.

She had long, straight blonde hair and a fine bone structure, her willowy figure draped in a floral dress and slouchy cardigan, thick socks and fleecy Birkenstocks on her feet.

'Oh my God, I'm so sorry!' Natasha said, automatically straightening up. 'My dog escaped into your garden from next door. She was chasing a squirrel, I'm so sorry. I'm just putting her on the lead. She jumped out of the car before I could stop her.'

The woman regarded her suspiciously before stepping out of the house more fully. She glanced towards the hedge. 'Diana's out today.'

Natasha felt taken aback by the woman's evident lack of trust in her account. Did she look like a burglar? Or horse thief? 'Oh yes, I know that. She's at her daughter's cello recital. It's fine. I'm not going into the house. I'll be staying in the garden.'

The woman still looked slightly perplexed.

'I'm painting one of her horses,' Natasha offered further.

At that, the woman's face brightened considerably. 'Oh, you're the artist who's painting Arty!'

'Yes, that's right.' Natasha felt obliged to walk over and show up close that she was of good character and not in fact a criminal mastermind. She stopped a few feet from the woman on the garden path; she was even more striking up close. Like Diana, she was a few years older than Natasha, but she was a vivid beauty with high, rounded cheekbones and light green eyes. She didn't have the exhausted, drawn look Natasha might have expected of a mother to six, although she vaguely recalled mention being made of lots of help.

Bella automatically retreated a few steps, pressing close to Natasha's legs as she always did with strangers.

'Diana's *so* happy to have found you! I've been sworn to secrecy not to breathe a word to Simes,' the woman said in a newly confiding tone, now that kinship had been established.

'She doesn't want him to suspect a thing. He's quite potty about that animal.' The neighbour rolled her eyes.

'Well, he is a handsome specimen.'

Bella was sniffing the air, picking up scents. Squirrels, horses . . . Natasha's hand went to her head, patting it absently.

'Will you get it done in time? She said it's going to be a terrific rush.'

'It is, yes, but we'll get there. I think today will be my last day of on-site sketches and then I can just work in the studio.' Around the clock.

The woman crossed her arms tighter around her chest. 'Do you only do horses?'

'No, pets in general, which mainly means cats and dogs too, but there's been a few more interesting specimens as well. Budgies, a couple of rats, believe it or not.'

She pulled a face as she laughed. 'Heavens! Do you have a card?'

'Oh – I do, but they're in the car.' Natasha thumbed hopelessly towards the hedge.

'I might be interested in getting one of our cat. She's sixteen now; every morning I come down expecting to find her as stiff as sticks, but the kids are devoted and they're going to be devastated when the time comes. A portrait might be a lovely way to capture her memory.' She smiled, looking down. 'Yes, and you're very sweet too, aren't you?' She glanced back at Natasha. 'What's her name?'

Natasha was astonished to realize that Bella had scooted over during the course of their conversation and was now sitting, nose up, by the neighbour's legs, being petted. 'Uh, Bella . . . But she's a rescue so she's usually terrified of people.'

'Hmm, dogs always seem to like me. It's like they know I'm a cat person so they're on a marketing offensive to bring me over to the other side.'

Natasha gave a soft laugh, her attention falling to the door at the woman's back. 'Gosh, that wreath is beautiful.'

The woman gave a half turn. 'Thank you. The florist in the village makes them.'

'Oh really? I need to stop and get some flowers on my way home. They're for my daughter's nursery teacher. Nativity play today.'

'Of course, it's that time of year, isn't it? All the teacher presents.' The woman smiled, giving no indication that she had to buy everything sixfold. 'Well, Florabundance is just around the corner from here – bear left then first right and follow the road round, you can't miss it. Or there's a Tesco on the A44, they always have decent bunches.'

'Great, thanks.' Natasha looked down at Bella fussing at the woman's legs, trying to knock her hand with her muzzle for more cuddles. 'Sorry, she's a pest . . . Well, I'd better start work, I've got to leave sharply today. But it was lovely meeting you, and apologies again about Bella and me haring around your garden.'

The woman shrugged it off. 'I may get your details off Diana, if that's all right.'

'Of course,' Natasha smiled, beginning to walk away.

'I'll just get Christmas out of the way first and then I can think straight.'

'Yes, quite. What's your name, by the way? So I know who I'm talking to if you call.'

'Emily. Emily Richards.'

'Great. I'm Natasha, Diana's got my details.'

'Super.'

'Bye then.' Natasha waved and walked Bella back up the drive, heading around the corner to the drive next door. Her car door was still open, her handbag sitting right there on the passenger seat. Anyone could have taken it.

'Honestly,' Natasha tutted as Bella trotted happily beside her, tongue hanging out. 'Look at the trouble you've caused. What am I going to do with you?'

She sketched for an hour and a half, Bella dozing at her feet, but eventually the cold got to her hands and toes; temperatures were bitter when the wind blew, with wintry flurries gusting, and she wasn't suitably dressed for extended stretches outside. The thought as to what the temperatures might be in the Himalayas right now wandered through her mind but she pushed it straight back out again. Nope. Busy-busy, that was her strategy. She checked the time. The nativity started at three and it was noon now. Rob was in Leeds again this week, so there was no Plan B. If she didn't get there on time, Mabel's rendition of a snowflake was going to be missed by both her parents.

'Come along then,' she said briskly to the dog, getting up off the stool Diana had left out for her and leading Bella back to the car; she didn't want another repeat of this morning's high jinks. Next door, she could hear the sound of a car on the drive, the pull of the handbrake as it stopped.

She walked back to the stable to give Artemis a pat of gratitude. He had enjoyed the salt lick she'd hung at his stable door. She took a few more photographs for good measure too. 'See you soon, big fella,' she murmured. 'You're doing very well.'

'James, can you bring the bird feeder in with you? It needs refilling,' she heard Emily call from over the hedge. A few moments later, she heard the sound of footsteps crunching on the gravel and coming closer, stopping by the beech tree, a blackbird singing from a high perch. 'I think the squirrels keep getting to it. Or the magpies.'

Mundane chatter. Village life. Natasha wondered what it must be like living in such close proximity to the neighbours; she would have liked to have more people closer to them. Far-reaching views were wonderful, but there was a lot to be said for having a friend to chat to over the hedge. Certainly the two women living here appeared close.

She packed up her pencils and zipped up her portfolio, walking back to the car almost in step with the neighbour. She drove out a few moments later, glancing down Emily's drive, but they had gone in again.

She found the florist easily, pulling up outside. 'Stay there. No nonsense,' she said to Bella, reaching over and giving her a kiss on the head.

A bell jangled as she went in.

'Hello,' a friendly woman said, looking up from tying some stems. She had brown frizzy hair and was wearing a duffel coat and yellow fingerless gloves. Profusions of flowers were stuffed into tiered buckets – long-stemmed roses, calla lilies, pussywillow branches, drifts of mistletoe; bunches of berried holly and snowberries, wands of tuberose . . . 'Anything I can help you with?'

'Actually, I'm looking for some flowers for my daughter's teacher.'

'Of course you are. Who isn't? There's some mixed bouquets just to your left there if you like. I made them with the teachers in mind – bigger than a posy but not too silly.'

Natasha looked over and chose an arranged bunch of roses, freesias and tulips. 'Well, that was easy,' she smiled, bringing it to the till. 'You've got a wonderful selection.'

'Thank you.' The florist smiled. 'That'll be . . . eight ninety please.'

'Actually,' Natasha said, looking around the small shop. 'Do you have any more wreaths?'

'Wreaths? Why, yes. I've just been finishing a new batch. They always go so quickly, I can hardly keep up.' She wandered out to the room at the back, her voice growing fainter.

'I just saw one at Emily Richards's house, you see, and it was so beautiful,' Natasha called. 'It was she who told me you were here.'

The florist reappeared again a moment later with several wreaths hooped over her forearms. 'Did she? That was good of her. Are you friends with Emily then?'

'Oh no, not really. I'm working . . .' She caught herself, remembering she mustn't say too much about what she was doing here, in case word somehow got back to Diana's husband. 'Next door. In the Lorns' garden. So we just met briefly.'

'Ah. Well, it's very friendly around here. Everyone knows everyone.' She set the wreaths down. 'There. I try to offer a selection. Well, I have to. In a small village like this, people don't want a row of identical wreaths hanging on the doors!'

Natasha chuckled. 'No. I guess not.' Her gaze drifted over them lightly – some had pinecones twisted in; others sprays of sloe berries and snowberries; and another . . . 'That's the one! It's perfect!'

'Oh yes, that's always very popular. One of my bestsellers. I get the feathers from a local pheasant shoot, so it's local and sustainable too.'

'Yes.' Natasha was just pleased that Rob would like it; it was exactly what he had wanted and after her dismal attempt at Rachel's the other day . . .

'It's twenty-two pounds, that one, so in total that's thirty pounds ninety.'

Natasha tapped her card to the screen.

'Do you need a receipt?' the florist asked as she gathered the bouquet in one arm and the wreath with the other.

'No, I'm fine, thank you so much.'

'Thank you, dear. And merry Christmas.'

It was the first time anyone had wished her that this year. 'Merry Christmas to you too,' she smiled, pulling the door open to a jingle of bells.

Natasha climbed back into the car with a smile. 'Right, well, that was a stroke of luck!' she said to Bella, showing the uncomprehending dog the wreath before sliding it onto the back seat, with the flowers. 'Now we're all set to see our girl.' She turned the ignition on and tapped on Lauren's number, switching the phone to Bluetooth. The sound of the dialtone resounded through the speakers as Natasha put on her seatbelt and indicated to pull out, looking in the wing mirror.

'Hey Nats!' Lauren trilled, picking up almost immediately. 'How are you?'

'I'm fine. Where are you? You sound like you're in a wind tunnel.'

Lauren laughed. 'I'm in with Ros. She's just given me a fresh balayage and it is *so* good. It's taken ten years off me, hasn't it?'

'Ten years!' Ros said dutifully in the background, making Natasha smile.

'You should get one. You'd look amazing.'

'Yeah, maybe,' Natasha said distractedly. A delivery van had parked up behind her, restricting her view somewhat, but she could see two cars coming. 'Listen, I'm driving so I'll be quick. Are you going to the nativity this afternoon?'

'Am I?' Lauren almost choked on the question. 'Nats, it's my babies' first ever nativity! Wild horses couldn't keep me from going!' There was a pause as the hairdryer came particularly close to the phone. 'Why? You're not bailing, are you?'

'No, but I'm just heading back from Gloucestershire now. I'm going to go straight there but in case I get caught up in traffic, can you save me a sea—'

The two cars passed by her.

'. . . Nats?' Lauren asked a moment later. 'Are you still there?'

Natasha stared straight ahead, her brain already on rewind trying to compute what had just happened. Everything was a blur. It had been just a flash of movement. Light had bounced off the windscreen. She'd been looking at the cars but not *at* them. And yet there had been something in the profile, the set of the body . . .

'Nats?'

She pressed disconnect, blood ringing in her ears as with fumbling fingers, she brought up Hels's number instead. Her default panic response. It rang out twice before she picked up.

'Nats, I'm in clinic,' Hels hissed. 'I can't talk—'

'Rob's just driven past me.'

There was a baffled silence. '. . . So?'

'I'm in Gloucestershire.'

'What? I thought he said he's in Leeds again this week?'

'That's what he said, but he's just driven past me – right past me, Hels.' Nats heard her voice travel up through the scales. '. . . Why would he be here? He's a hundred and fifty miles away. Supposed to be. Why would he be here?'

Both women knew Natasha was pleading for an explanation, any explanation but the obvious one. They both knew there was only one reason for a husband to lie to his wife about his whereabouts.

'Where is he now?'

'I told you – he's just driven past.'

'But where's he going? Can you still see him?'

Natasha peered in front but the road had a bend ahead. 'I . . . no . . . But it's a small lane, no turn-offs . . . He'll be just ahead.' Her voice cracked. 'Oh my God, I can't believe this is happening! What am I going to do? Hels! What do I do?'

Hels didn't hesitate, her voice a low growl. 'Follow him.'

Chapter Twenty-Four

Annapurna Camp Three, Tuesday 13 December

The bright dots in the snow were the sight their sore eyes – sore bodies – needed. They had been climbing up the fixed ropes for most of the day; enduring ten, eleven hours of relentless vertical fight for purchase, their crampons hooking into the snow and ice, every single step a feat of tenacity and grit. Camp Three sat in a col at 6,126 metres, eight hundred metres above Camp Two. At these heights, the human body slowly began shutting down. At eight thousand metres, it would start to die. The air was whistlingly thin, forcing muscles to slow and organs to work harder. Gravity redoubled – what had weighed a kilo at Base Camp would feel like ten kilos at the summit.

They had left in the dark and were arriving in the dusk, each camp as lonely as the next. Annapurna was already a notoriously treacherous climb, but much more so at this time of year, when the low temperatures and screaming winds were compounded by low barometric pressure (although no snowfall; above five thousand metres, it would remain 'dry' until March, making the snow firm underfoot). People assumed the elite world of mountain climbing was defined by summiting the highest peaks, but the nuances were much more subtle than that – technical climb gradings meant Annapurna or Nanga Parbat ranked above Everest for difficulty, for example, and winter climbing was a whole other proposition too. K2, one of the fourteen eight-thousanders, had only ever been summited once in winter, and although Annapurna in winter had been cracked, it was still only rarely; some teams arrived, only to see what lay next and head straight back down again. It was important for every climber to recognize their personal limits; there was a famous saying: *In the mountains there are only two grades – you can either do it or you can't.*

But turning back wasn't an option for Duffy. Not this time. He would do it or die trying.

The haunting silence that greeted them at each base was a chilling reminder that this was no game. On Everest, Camp One was like arriving at a party on the moon, the glacial plateau on the frozen landscape dotted with brightly coloured tents. High visibility was the intention but it also lent the place a festival vibe that felt strange considering they were on almost one of the highest points on the planet. Music would be playing, people moving between the tents and holding tin mugs of hot coffee or boiling up pans of dried noodles, chatting like they were in a Soho pub. There would be dozens of tents to support the expedition groups – on Everest it took huge teams of sherpas, porters and commercial crews to get people to the top who couldn't have summited alone.

But Annapurna was for pros only. The architecture of the mountain meant it was covered in huge seracs that could – and did – shear off, and was highly prone to avalanches and ice falls. The fixed ropes that got people to the top of the world's highest mountain couldn't be deployed to anywhere near the same extent on Annapurna. That was why she was the world's deadliest.

And that was why there was only one other tent here.

'*Namaste*,' Sanani called ahead, but there was no reply.

'Hello?' Duffy asked, tapping on the tent, but no reply came. He looked further up the slopes. 'They must still be up there somewhere.' But it was growing dark. It was no time to stay out late.

'This looks good,' Sanani panted, marking their spot beside the other tent with his foot to make the snow compacted and smooth. Duffy looked at the precipitous slopes all around them, checking for fracture lines or overloaded banks. Avalanche was an ever-present risk here.

They got the tent up quickly – as quickly as they could – rolling out their mats and sleeping bags. Sanani set up their tripod and filled the small saucepan with snow. He began to melt it over the small fire, dropping in a water purifying tablet. Duffy just wanted to collapse and sleep, but dehydration was another serious risk at this altitude and they needed to cater to every potential vulnerability in their bodies. He still felt shaken by the Italian trekker's death, even though it had been a wholly avoidable example of the consequences of reckless disregard. He wondered whether the man's girlfriend was back in Khande yet. He wondered whether Stevie and Jay had arrived in Bamboo village. He wondered about Mabel and Natasha and what they would be doing now. He didn't want to guess the time back in the UK but his brain worked it out automatically for him anyway. It was lunchtime.

'Sanani, what day is it?' he murmured.

'Tuesday. Tuesday 13th.'

He wondered what they would be doing on a Tuesday

lunchtime in the middle of December. Was it snowing there? Raining more likely, he knew.

He stepped out of the tent, the shock again of the freezing air purging him of conscious thought and pushing her away, as he had known it would. He took several deep breaths, emptying his head, before he turned his face to the mountain that had haunted most of his life. Finally he was standing upon her with his own feet, his spikes digging into the snow and ice that clung to her. He could pat her with his own hands, like a rider to a horse. He knew he was nothing to her bulk, he knew his entire life counted for less than a second in her ancient existence. It didn't matter. He was within two thousand metres of vanquishing her.

They would rest here for several days at least. They had spent only one night at Camp One and two nights at Camp Two, which was pretty rapid for most teams, but Duffy had prepared his body well by not exerting himself in the run-up to Base Camp and he had acclimatized quickly so far. The altitude was punishing now, though, and although Camp Four was only three hundred and fifty metres above them, the stretch that lay between was especially arduous.

Known as the Ice Ridge, the section had no fixed ropes, and it demanded an elite level of climbing that he had spent the past four years grinding for. He had put in the spadework and crafted a body that could both suspend its own weight on the strength of a hooked finger and fold itself in half. He had eaten well to strip down his body fat so that he didn't expend extra energy on surplus weight; he had studied every route, ascent and ridge and he was ready for this. Now all he needed was to remain fresh and rested and wait for a good weather window. Being caught in a storm up here meant wind speeds of a hundred kilometres an hour; it meant hail the size of golf balls and sleet like knives. Visibility could reduce to the length of his arm, temperatures could plunge to minus thirty within minutes, another twenty off that at night.

It would soon be dark, Sanani's headlight from within making the tent glimmer like a glow-worm on the mountain face. Would anybody see it from down there, in Base Camp? Many of the trekkers – himself included – had sat on the terrace with binoculars, scanning the walls and crevices for signs of human activity.

He searched the sky for signs of any coming storms, but it was clear with very little wind, the temperatures slightly milder than he'd expected. As long as it stayed like that, the team beside them – wherever they were – would be able to head out early and make headway over the ice before sunrise; no one wanted to be caught below a gently warming serac, with the sun beaming on their backs and the glare blinding them. He and Sanani had agreed they would spend at least a couple of nights here acclimatizing, before they pushed on too.

The crunch of snow and the sight of a bouncing flashlight beam coming from around a huge snow boulder caught his attention. Their neighbours were back. 'Hey, how are you?' Duffy said, raising an arm in friendly greeting as the first man approached, his companion a few metres behind and both of them breathing heavily.

'Hey,' the first said in accented English. He sounded surprised. 'Did you just get here?'

'Yes. Fifteen minutes ago. You?'

'Three days now,' he panted. 'We've just been fixing some ropes.'

Duffy nodded. 'How's it looking up there?'

The guy waggled his hand. 'So-so. We're hoping to make the break tomorrow. Forecast is cold but calm.'

Cold but calm. Duffy knew that was how he needed to be, if he was going to summit this monster. He couldn't let himself slide back to a world he'd left behind, a woman who had never been his, but it was easier said than done. All the way up here, his mind had almost playfully, indulgently relived every one of their few moments together so that he scarcely noticed his body screaming for mercy; he saw her frozen, cartoon-style, on the aerial walkway; he remembered the body blow as their eyes had connected on the platform while she still stood on his toes; the way she had clung to him on the wall; he saw her dancing wildly on the sofa in that dress and how she had tried to avoid him in the kitchen; he savoured her look when he'd kissed her and she had known it too; he recalled her evasiveness on the deck when she tried to do the right thing but all the while did it wrong; he remembered the sight of her standing barefoot in a towelling robe in a climbing hall; dancing in a storeroom . . .

'Cold but calm sounds perfect,' Duffy said, drawing himself back.

'Yeah, but it's been unpredictable lately. Flash storms. We met another team at Camp One last week; they got caught by a massive snow dump by the Ice Wall. Had to turn back.'

'All okay?'

'Yeah. But there's a lot of loose surface up there, all sorts of shit coming free.'

'Anyone above us?'

'It's just us up here at the moment,' he shrugged.

'Where are you from?'

'Switzerland. I am Hans Keller and my partner is Juergen

Roth.' Duffy nodded at the other man who had now joined them; his eyelashes were frozen. 'And you? You are British?'

'Yes, but not climbing alone. I'm here with Sanani Sherpa, who is also an old family friend.'

The man smiled a little. 'Then your family has useful friends. I know his name. What is yours?' It was custom to share names with other climbers, in the event of the worst happening.

'Tom.' He swallowed. 'Tom Duffy.'

The climber tilted his head slightly, as if concentrating. As if he'd heard it somewhere before. '. . . Wait . . . you're not—?'

'Yeah,' Tom said quickly. Cold but calm.

There was a moment when no one spoke. Then Hans nodded, as if getting it. He slapped him once on the shoulder. 'Then good luck to you.'

'Thanks.' They both knew he was going to need it.

Chapter Twenty-Five

Whinfell, October 2018

'How was that?' Hels asked as Natasha drifted back into the changing rooms.

'Blissful.'

'Yeah, it looks it! You look incredible. It really worked, huh?'

'I switched to a head massage instead. I wasn't convinced that being rubbed in salt was what I needed.'

'Especially after getting pickled last night,' Hels laughed as Natasha got dressed, her hands trembling, her limbs fizzing with suppressed joy. '. . . Like my nails?' She waggled her fingers.

Natasha forced herself to pay attention. 'Ooh. Mint green. Gorgeous.'

Hels gave her a small frown. 'Wait. You're not going to tell me I look like I have gangrene?'

'Do you want me to tell you that?' Natasha laughed, pulling her jumper over her head.

'I thought you'd say it's the wrong colour to go with the bridesmaid dresses.'

Natasha sat on the bench and pulled on her trainers. 'I just want you to be happy, Hels. Are you happy?'

'I'm not sure now,' Hels said, even more suspiciously.

'Then I'm happy.'

Hels's eyes narrowed to slits. 'What exactly did she give you in there? Are you high?'

Natasha just laughed, picking up her robe and dropping it in the laundry basket. 'Come on. Where are the others?'

'They're holding the table for lunch.'

They walked outside together and Natasha lifted her face to the sky, feeling the October sun's gentle warmth. She felt so light, so untethered, she thought she might fly. The deep feelings of unease that had broken her sleep, dragged on her heart and put lead in her veins had gone. For the first time in months she felt she could see clearly again, the world hard-edged and bright. Rob was a good man, there was no question of that, but a question had been lurking in the shadows of her mind ever since he'd proposed: she loved him, but did she love him enough? Enough to commit her life to him?

She had pushed for a longer engagement and he had pushed back: he had ten years on her and he wanted to start a family. Why wait?

Now she had her answer.

They retrieved their bikes and cycled past the lake to the restaurant in the village centre. Several times, Natasha looked over at Hels as she pedalled and chattered aimlessly, wanting to stop her and tell her everything that had just happened, but for once, she must hold her tongue. She couldn't share her secret. Rob had to be told first; it was the very least she must do for him. She knew she couldn't prevent the hurt and shock she would be unleashing with her decision but she could give him the respect he was due. He didn't deserve what was coming.

The others were already sitting at a large round table,

picking at bread rolls and talking intently as they came in. Lizzie cooed as she and Hels sat down.

'God, you look radiant!' Rachel exclaimed.

Natasha playfully arched an eyebrow. 'What are you saying? That I wasn't before?' she quipped.

'I am *so* booking in for one of those treatments,' Lauren gasped, putting a hand to Natasha's face as if trying to pinpoint the exact source of said radiance. 'What was it again? The Dead Sea salt elixir?'

'Actually I switched to a head massage.'

'You did?' Sara asked, a tinge of disappointment colouring her voice. As with the rest of this hen party, she had been in charge of booking all the spa treatments and this last-minute switch would be seen as another rejection of her best-laid plans. But Natasha could hardly tell them all that she'd missed the first forty minutes of her ninety-minute session.

'Yes and it was incredible, thank you so much.' Natasha smiled brightly. 'And actually, before we go any further, I just want to say a proper thank you to all of you.'

'Aww,' Lizzie cooed.

'Speech!' Hels said, ringing her glass with a fork.

'No. No speech,' Natasha said quickly, dulling the sound by wrapping her hand over the glass and looking around to make sure no one had heard.

She felt her smile become fixed as she looked at her friends. Not telling them the full truth felt like a lie, especially as, when it all came out, they'd find themselves at the centre of the storm with her. But there was simply no other way it could be. Rob had to know first. '. . . I know you had your work cut out with me this weekend. I've been the world's worst hen – I don't like strippers, I went to bed early and I did the bloody cleaning!'

'Uh! Let's not forget the not one, but two panic attacks as well,' Hels said.

'Thank you, yes, those too – huge hen do fail there. But I want you to know that in spite of *all* of that—' She pressed a hand to her chest. 'This *chicken party* has been utterly perfect. You don't know what you've done for me. I know you won't believe me when I say I wouldn't change a thing about it, but please hold onto these words because it's actually true—' She looked at them each, hoping they would remember these words when the fallout came. 'Every single moment of this weekend, I'll treasure forever. I'm so lucky to have you as my friends.'

'Aww, Natser!' Lauren cooed, hands folded above her heart and looking like she was going to cry.

'Jeez, well, talk about victory snatched from the jaws of disaster,' Hels quipped, rolling her eyes, grabbing a water glass and knocking it back like it was a double vodka.

'I will take the images of you rocking out in that dress on the sofa to my dying day,' Rachel laughed beside her, reaching over and hugging her. 'It was hideous and you were such a good sport about it, especially when the boys arrived. I'd have escaped to the bedroom and not come out.'

'You did escape to the bedroom and not come out,' Sara rejoindered. 'With Andy!'

Rachel pressed her hands together and laughed delightedly. 'I know! But so did she with Jack!' she said, pointing at Hels.

Hels merely shrugged. 'It was nothing to what Lauren got up to in the kitchen.'

Lauren's jaw dropped fully open, eyes wide. 'I told you I didn't do *anything*!' she gasped, grabbing a packet of butter from the bowl in the middle of the table and lobbing it at her.

'I know. Vegas,' Hels winked, tapping the side of her nose again.

'Well, we certainly didn't,' Lizzie muttered, glancing at Sara.

They all laughed as the waitress came over to take their orders.

'Ooh, we haven't looked at the menus yet,' Lizzie said.

'I can come back in a few minutes,' the waitress said, making to leave.

'Ah, actually – one thing we'll definitely order is a couple of bottles of champagne,' Natasha said quickly. 'On me.'

'But it can't be on you,' Rachel protested. 'You're the bride.'

She was no longer 'the' anything, but Natasha just smiled. 'It's my way of saying thank you for bringing me here. The taxi's coming at four so we've got a little time to have a last celebratory drink or two, haven't we?'

'To be honest, I do need to retox,' Hels said, looking distinctly queasy. 'I'm beginning to feel quite pure.'

Their bags were packed and sitting in a pile by the door of the arrivals lodge. The taxi was due in half an hour and everyone was lounging on the sofas, caught in that vacuum of not having enough time to do anything else, but restless with waiting.

Natasha glanced at the time on her phone. It was three thirty. 'Oh bugger!'

Everyone looked up in alarm at her tone.

'What is it?' Sara asked.

'I've just realized I've left my bracelet in the spa!' Natasha clutched her wrist as if to make the point.

'What bracelet?' Hels asked.

'My silver one,' she replied in an even voice, even though

she didn't wear a bracelet and hadn't done since catching her Tiffany bean one on a door handle two years ago.

'Well, I'll go get it for you,' Lizzie said, ever helpful, moving to get up.

'No, I'll go,' Natasha said quickly, already on her feet. 'It's quicker if I do it.'

'I can pedal fast,' Lizzie shrugged.

'Yes, but I'll remember which treatment room I was in, won't I?'

'Oh, okay. If you're sure.' Lizzie shrugged and sat back again.

'Well, don't be late,' Sara said sternly. 'The train's at four thirty-six and we do not need any complications. If we miss this one we're stuck for another two hours, and I've got an early start in the morning.'

'Don't worry, I'll be right back,' Natasha said, already running from the building. She jumped on the nearest bike she could pull from the racks and began pedalling furiously, feeling like a heroine in a war film as the wind blew back her hair. It had only been two and a half hours since she'd left him, but she felt the excitement course through her. Tom was supervising in the Indoor Climbing Centre all day but he had another colleague with him who he had said could cover for him for at least a few minutes.

She couldn't bear that she had to get on a train and leave here. Leave him. They'd be three hundred miles apart and it felt like he might as well be in another country, but they both knew that what she had to do, she had to do in person. Staying here wasn't an option yet. They would work out the rest soon enough.

She smiled, almost laughed out loud, as she remembered their stolen moments together, the smell of climbing chalk and how he'd whispered her name in her hair, his casual strength and muffled groans.

She saw the sports plaza up ahead and turned in, almost throwing the bike to the ground and running over to the back door where he'd told her to meet him. It was a staff exit and slightly hidden from the main trails, affording them some privacy. He could only get away for a few minutes, he had warned her; Sunday afternoons were always busy, but anything was better than nothing; the man she'd only met yesterday morning had become her oxygen. He ran through her bloodstream, he was the charge that made her heart beat. She believed in the thunderbolt now.

She went and stood by the door, pacing anxiously, waiting, waiting for him to come out. The door could only be opened from the inside and she tried not to be impatient as the minutes ticked past. He would be helping a child on the ropes, getting someone into a harness . . .

Five minutes went by.

He might be up the wall, rescuing someone who – like her – was stranded at the top. Or a rope had slipped through the carabiner and he was having to climb up to rethread it. It happened . . .

She paced, willing him to come out. Every minute out here waiting was a minute together lost. Should she . . . ? Should she go in? If he couldn't get away after all, if he couldn't leave the hall, she could go over to him. But what if he came out while she ran around to the front? He might think she'd left already, or worse, that she hadn't come at all.

She waited for another few minutes, then checked the time. It was three forty-two. It would take her four minutes to cycle back to the others. No, she couldn't afford to waste any more time.

She ran around to the front of the plaza, wishing she'd just come here in the first place. Eleven minutes had been lost. The noise of shrieking children, amplified by the soaring roof, rebounded and fell upon her like a wave but she tore through regardless, her gaze already fixed upon the climbing walls at the back. She always seemed to arrive or leave here in dramatic fashion.

Tom. Tom. Where was he? Her eyes darted left and right, up, over, down. Where was he? There were so many bodies to see past. She saw a female instructor standing at the bottom of one of the walls, holding onto a rope and calling up to a young girl.

'Excuse me,' Natasha panted. 'Where can I find Tom?'

The instructor glanced at her before putting her attention back on the child again. 'Tom's not here,' she said quickly. 'Very good, Annie! Now move the right foot!'

Natasha looked at the woman with such a shocked stare, the instructor turned back to her. '. . . I'm sorry, what?' Natasha croaked.

'Tom's not here. I've been called in to cover for him. I don't know where he is, I'm sorry.'

'But . . . did he leave a message? Or a number?'

The instructor looked her up and down briefly, as if beginning to get the gist of what was going on between them. This was personal. 'No. He just said he had to leave and he took off. That was it.'

Natasha took a step back. She felt like there was a weight on her chest, the sky beginning to fall down.

'Do you want me to pass on a message?' the instructor asked, seeing how she paled.

Natasha shook her head. She couldn't speak. She couldn't . . . comprehend what was going on. It had all been a game after all? After everything he'd said – finding someone in a moment; seizing opportunity; believing in the thunderbolt . . . he was just a fuckboy on the make? The scales fell away. He'd seduced the bride on her own hen night. *Five times more likely*. And he'd seen her from a mile off.

She turned, stumbling over her own feet, to find Hels watching her.

There wasn't time to hide the tears already skimming down her cheeks as Hels rushed over.

'How did you know . . . ?' she asked, wiping them away.

'You don't need to take a bracelet off for a head massage, for one thing,' Hels said quietly. 'Not to mention you don't wear a bracelet.'

Natasha blinked, but the tears still pooled. She could feel the sobs high up in her chest, wanting to burst from her, but she held them back. If it was the last thing she did, she wouldn't give him the satisfaction of hearing from his workmates that she had fallen apart.

She tried to remain calm. 'He said . . .' But her voice failed her. How could she possibly admit what she'd done? She had jeopardized everything she had with Rob for a handsome hero with a rope and a nice smile.

'I can guess,' Hels said sympathetically, squeezing her arm tightly.

'I'm such an idiot,' she whispered.

'No, you were just scared.'

Cold feet, was that it? She was a cliché. She was pathetic.

Hels looped an arm through hers and squeezed it tightly. Protectively. 'Listen, he's a good-looking guy who's got some moves, but there's no harm done. Not really.'

'But Rob—' She felt gripped by panic, an exploding blackness in her heart.

'Rob will never know. You're not married yet. And he's had ten extra years of sowing his wild oats than you have. You're allowed one last crush—'

Crush. It had felt like so much more than that; it had felt like galaxies colliding, like coming home.

'I promise you, none of this means anything. You'll have forgotten about him in a day or two. Vegas rules, remember?'

Natasha nodded wanly, but she felt like shattered glass; she could never remake herself in the same mould again. '. . . Yeah,' she whispered hoarsely. 'Vegas rules.'

Chapter Twenty-Six

Snowshill, Thursday 15 December

Natasha carried the easel from the car, Bella still belted up on the front seat until she was all set up. It was awkward to carry but she didn't care. Nothing mattered. She was just moving through the motions, doing what had to be done and trying not to feel anything.

Diana had waved from the kitchen window as she'd arrived but Natasha had asked her not to watch as she marked out the fresh canvas this morning. She needed all her powers of concentration to mark the scale, decide on her vanishing point and set her levels before she began sketching the silhouette; but in truth, she wasn't up to the small talk. Her life was crumbling day by day and she seemed powerless to stop it. All her worst fears had been realized – her husband was having an affair. Duffy had gone radio silent for a week now. And she had got her period this morning. The vacuum inside her wasn't just remaining empty, it was getting bigger – and she couldn't even stop to deal with it. To acknowledge even one emotion would be to trigger an avalanche of feelings that would cascade down and bury her. She had to empty herself of emotions if she was going to get through this week – and for Mabel's sake, she had to get through it.

Hels had been over every evening since her emergency call on Monday, bringing curry and wine and talking things over, but there was only so much to say when there was only so much that they knew. Natasha still remained in the dark about the details of her husband's betrayal, Hels arguing there might yet be a plausible explanation.

Following him hadn't ended the way it did in films. She had caught up with him further down the road; he'd been forced to slow for some horses, and a car and van were now positioned between them, hiding her from his sights. She had followed him to a petrol station, where he had unremarkably filled up, before tailing him into Broadway where he had gone into a butcher's, a pet shop and a wine merchants'. He had then headed back in the direction from which he'd come, turning off the A44 back towards Snowshill – but heavy traffic had meant it was over a minute before she too could find a gap to make the turn and by the time she got back to Florabundance, he had gone again. She was right back where she had begun, with no way of knowing where he had gone after there – and no time to look. By then she was already pushing it to get back in time for Mabel's nativity and she'd arrived literally as the curtains opened. Lauren had saved her a seat at the front and she had clapped as though everything was wonderful, her eyes shining with proud tears. No one had been able to tell that she was broken, her tan and smile telling a very different story to the narrative happening inside.

Even Rob didn't know she knew. Not yet. She had managed to avoid speaking to him on the phone, with a litany of excuses – '*Hels is here; curry night. Speak tomorrow,*' she'd texted; '*1% juice left. Speak tomorrow.*' – and she responded to his WhatsApps with emojis that gave communication without revelation. She still didn't know how she was going to play it. Direct confrontation, which was Hels's recommendation? Press him for details about his week until he was backed into a corner? Wait for him to hand Bella a new ball while telling her over a new bottle of burgundy that he'd had an extraordinary meeting with a potential new client in Gloucestershire and had visited in the week?

Hope lingered, refusing to die. She knew she wanted to save their family. She wanted Mabel to grow up with two parents and have her loving father in her life, not on scheduled days. She kept trying to draw her lines. What could she live with and what would she accept? If the worst came to pass and he admitted to an affair, should she let him stay or throw him out? Would he get brownie points for being honest? Could she ever trust him again? Could she ever forgive him?

She set the canvas on the easel, making sure she was out of the wind, then brought Bella over and tied her to the tethering ring. Natasha had put the lead on her before leaving home this time, determined there would be no squirrel-chasing today.

The temperature was hovering at four degrees but the day was crisp and bright and she began working quickly, her eyes sliding between Arty and the canvas, her hand always moving. This was the only time she could lose herself, when her problems sank into a background smudge and she could breathe. Just breathe.

Voices carried over the hedge again; Diana moved around in her peripheral vision hosing the terrace; birds sang on bare branches; the horses snorted and snuffled as they moved restlessly in their stables. Occasional cars trundled past on the lane, the church bells rang out. Natasha felt herself absorbed into all of it like ink into vellum, losing her own edges as her hand moved certain and sure across the canvas. The time she had invested in her preparatory sketches was paying off now as muscle memory rendered the horse's likeness into being and she increasingly felt a power in her own instinct that she hadn't tapped into before. She could do this, and do it well. Better than well.

Natasha stepped back to assess the first marks. Did they have energy? Grace? Proportion? Soul would come later, with the oils, as she layered him up. She smiled, seeing that it was good. Now she needed to see Artemis moving. She needed to capture his lines.

She turned back towards the house but Diana had gone in again.

'Stay there,' she said to Bella, who had lifted her head off her paws in psychic anticipation of her mistress's imminent departure. 'I'll be right back.'

Natasha walked across the drive and up to the house. Like her neighbours, Diana too had one of Florabundance's majestic wreaths, although hers was interwoven with juicy snowberries, holly and sloe. Natasha stepped onto the steps just as Diana came out again, her gardening gloves on and secateurs held up in her hands like a surgeon about to make the first cut.

'Ah, I was just coming to find you,' Natasha smiled weakly. 'Do you need Arty to go in the paddock?'

'If you don't mind. I don't need you to lunge him or anything. It'll be enough for me to just watch him moving freely.'

Diana's eyes were bright with excitement. 'Absolutely! Whatever you need, Natasha. If you want him to tap dance for you, I can make that happen too.'

Natasha laughed as Diana pulled off her gloves and set them down with the secateurs and they walked back towards the stables again.

'It was fascinating watching you, you know. Don't worry, I couldn't see anything – I know you don't want me to see it till it's finished – but my goodness, your absorption is absolute. Did you even notice that rabbit by your feet?'

'What rabbit?' Natasha frowned.

'I rest my case! I thought you were going to stand on it at one point,' Diana laughed as they walked. '. . . Oh! That's very kind, Emily!' she called as they heard the sound of steps on the gravel and Natasha looked up to see the neighbour coming through the gates, carrying a large casserole dish. From the fact she needed two hands to carry it, Natasha could tell it was Le Creuset. '—But I could have come to get it, you know. There was no need for you to trouble yourself.'

'Nonsense,' Emily said, walking briskly in her cosy Birkenstocks again. 'Anything to escape the madhouse for a few minutes. Roops has come down with a severe case of man flu.' She rolled her eyes.

'Oh, poor boy.'

'Nothing poor about it. All he needs is some paracetamol and a Strepsil.' She fell into step with them as they walked towards the stable, the casserole dish hugged comfortably in her arms. 'Hello again,' she said to Natasha, smiling.

Diana reached for a headcollar on a hook as she opened Arty's stable door. 'Emily, this is the lady I was telling you about – Natasha Stoneleigh.'

'Yes, we . . .' Emily stopped mid-flow. 'Wait, Stoneleigh?'

'Yes,' Natasha nodded.

'Huh. My husband's former business partner was a Stoneleigh. Such a nice name. I always liked it. Unlike the man.'

Diana frowned, putting the headcollar on the horse almost absently. 'Oh, I remember him. Didn't he move abroad?'

'Yes, Ibiza. He discovered *yoga*.' Emily's eyes widened. 'Or rather, he discovered that a lot of women do yoga. He always was a player.' She tutted. 'I must say, I was quite pleased when James cut ties.'

'Quite,' Diana murmured.

Natasha didn't stir. She knew it was a coincidence. The name wasn't *that* unusual, and yet, to hear 'player' and 'Stoneleigh' in one sentence, after what she'd discovered this week . . . her antennae weren't so much buzzing as on fire, feeding her irrational but persistent fear that Rob was cheating. All the way here she'd looked out for his car on the other side of the road, parked in villages or in drives . . . She hadn't intended on making another trip out here, but after Monday's dramas, she couldn't stop herself from coming over again to sleuth, snoop. The proverbial jealous wife . . .

'Natasha's doing the portrait for Simes, which you'll remember is very—' Diana tapped the side of her nose. She clicked her tongue and Arty pulled his head back once as Diana opened the stable door and began leading him out.

Natasha and Emily followed a few steps behind as Diana led him the short distance to the paddock and unfastened the gate. 'Yes, I know. We met the other day.'

'Bella chased a squirrel into their garden,' Natasha explained haltingly, struggling to focus her mind. 'I had to crawl through the bushes to get her out and I think poor Emily thought I was casing the joint!'

'Well, you would have been a very chic burglar if that had been the case,' Emily replied as Diana released Arty into the field. 'I loved your boots.'

'Oh. Thank you.'

They all watched as he broke into a canter, giving a few bucks for good measure.

Diana came back out again, closing the gate. 'There. One happy horse.'

'Thanks,' Natasha said again. She would need to move her canvas and easel down here but it felt so hard even just putting one step in front of another. Just being here – smiling, breathing – took such effort.

There was a short silence as the two neighbours watched her for a moment, as if sensing her internal crisis, before Emily held out the casserole pot she was holding. 'Well, there you are, Di. Don't worry if you can't get all the marks off. It's a bloody beggar to clean.'

'You're a lifesaver,' Diana said, taking it with a sigh. 'Christmas shoot dinner for twelve tonight,' she said by way of explanation to Natasha.

'Ah.'

'Time for a coffee?' Diana asked Emily.

'Yes, why not? If you're sure you've time. James can man the fort. He's getting under my feet too. Honestly, what must I do to have the house to myself?'

'Natasha?'

'Oh, that's very kind but I'll make hay while the sun shines.' She gave another wan smile.

'Of course,' Diana smiled, a slight frown at her brow. 'But do say, won't you, if you need a hot drink? It's quite bitter out here.'

Natasha felt her heart beat faster as the two women turned towards the house again. 'Um . . . just out of interest, what was this Mr Stoneleigh's first name?' she asked Emily. She gave what she hoped was a hapless shrug. 'You never know, he could be a relative.'

'Gosh, I do hope not,' Emily said, looking alarmed by the prospect. 'Having said what I just said!' She laughed. 'His name's Robert. Rob Stoneleigh.'

'Oh.' Natasha felt her blood chill in her veins. '. . . No,' she said quietly. 'No relation.'

'Well, thank God for that,' Emily laughed with relief as she turned away again. 'Can you imagine? Honestly, he's dreadful. Once met, that man is never forgotten!'

Natasha opened the front door, stepping back slightly for Mabel and Bella to barge through. The house was shrouded in darkness, looking particularly lonesome on the hill as they had approached, and she switched on the hall and Christmas tree lights before going back to the car to pick up her art materials. She carried the easel and canvas through, then her pens and pencils. She was back on autopilot, trying to stay a step ahead of her emotions by remaining perpetually in motion. If she didn't sit down, she couldn't be caught. Emily's words had been chasing her like missiles all day, but she couldn't let them hit. Not yet. Mabel needed to eat and have her bath, they had storytime to get through. She couldn't do that if she was a hysterical mess on the floor. She also knew, rationally, that there must be plenty of Robert Stoneleighs in the country. Just because he shared her husband's name, didn't mean he was her husband. Just because he was a player and she believed her husband was cheating, it didn't mean they were one and the same man.

The post was sitting on the mat and she swiped it up, flicking through with dead eyes – brochures she never opened, credit card offers she didn't want . . . She caught sight of the postman's distinctive red-bordered card.

Package left in log store.

She went back out and walked over to the small timber structure. Lifting the lid, she found a small, soft parcel on top of the logs, poorly wrapped in a silver plastic bag and secured with duct tape. She frowned. If someone had thrown it at her they couldn't have been more offhand.

Then she saw it wasn't for her. In a flash, her body tensed and she ran inside. 'Mabel!' she cried. 'Mabel, where are you? There's something special here for you! Come and see!'

She ran from room to room, through the kitchen, the pantry, the snug . . .

Her daughter was sitting on the floor, eating a packet of mini crackers swiped from the pantry, Bella sitting beside her, watching, hoping.

'Darling! Look what's come for you! A special surprise! Shall we open it?' Natasha realized her hands were actually trembling as she pointed out the postage stamp – red, with an ornate temple. 'Can you guess which country this has come from?'

Mabel looked at her expectantly.

'Nepal, darling. Where Moolah's been on her holiday, remember?' After the tears that had come back in the first few days of silence, Mabel had stopped asking when Natasha had suddenly started crying too. Duffy's name hadn't been mentioned since.

'Moolah?!' Mabel was on her feet in an instant, mini crackers flying out of her hand and making Bella's dreams come true.

Natasha laughed delightedly, the first time she had even genuinely smiled for days. 'Here, you open it, darling.' She pulled the tape away from one of the corners to get Mabel started. The package had been appallingly secured and it was remarkable that it had made the journey intact. She hated him for his lack of care with something so precious. She hated him for the way he'd dropped off the grid without even so much as a warning for Mabel. After all the effort he'd gone to with his postcards, couldn't he see how devastating it would be for her to suddenly hear nothing again? Didn't he understand anything about children? He hadn't responded to a single one of the emails she had sent.

Still – she watched as her daughter scrabbled excitedly with her parcel – they had Moolah back and that was all that mattered. Everything else might be falling apart, but getting that precious toy back was a small miracle they could be grateful for.

She tried to stay patient as Mabel fumbled with the tape until eventually—

Mabel looked up at her with a dismayed expression and Natasha felt her heart plummet as she saw hot tears gather in her eyes. 'What is it? What . . . ?'

She peered into the package and stared at a brightly coloured cotton square. Squares. Lots of them. They were attached to a tape.

'Mummy, where's Moolah?' Mabel asked, her bottom lip quivering and the first tears already splashing onto her cheek. 'She's not there.'

'Wait—' Natasha desperately rummaged, pulling the cotton bundle out so that the flags fluttered out like wings. There was a distinct lack of toy cow to be found in the bag.

Bastard!

Fucker!

No! Natasha felt the rage spit in her blood. She wanted to scream. To rail. Why couldn't anything go right? What the hell was he doing sending them *this*?

She looked at Mabel, already beginning to sob as the disappointment crashed over her tiny body.

'But darling, these are wonderful,' Natasha said in a strained voice, desperately reaching for the flags. 'Duffy's sent us prayer flags. All the way from Nepal. A present just for you!'

She caught sight of something bright and glossy on the floor and reached for it – a postcard, showing some yaks grazing on a mountain.

'And look, he's written to you too! It's an actual postcard especially for you.'

Natasha turned it over with a flush of relief – a stay of execution? – her gaze falling to his handwriting. It was open and neat and she had the sense he had written carefully, so that it could be read easily. By a child.

Dear Mabel,

Greetings from Nepal!

We are very high up the mountains now so it's getting really cold but the views are very pretty. We met some yaks, which are Moolah's Nepalese cousins, so she was really excited about that. They have two stomachs and they use their horns to break up the snow and ice so they can eat the grass underneath. Isn't that cool? I would have sent you a picture of them like before but we are too far away now and I don't have my phone here. I know by the time you get this, you won't have heard from us for a few days but I hope you haven't been sad. Moolah is missing you so much but she will be able to jump the moon really soon and she's excited about that. It's considered extra good luck to be gifted prayer flags so she asked me to send you these prayer flags in the hope you will send good vibrations for her jump and the wind will carry them to her here, all the way from England.

She sends you a really big kiss and a hug Mabel,

Duffy (friend of cows and fellow moon jumper)

Natasha was quiet for a moment as she digested the message. It wasn't the same as getting Moolah back but . . . it was something. It was better than the previous seven days of nothing! He hadn't completely abandoned them, then? If he didn't have his phone anymore, then that explained why she'd not heard back from him either, although she still didn't understand why he couldn't have returned Moolah to them instead of sending this intricate substitute. *Why* was he holding onto Moolah?

'I can't believe Moolah met *yaks*!' Natasha gasped with wide eyes, trying to convey excitement to her daughter. 'I've always wanted to meet yaks!'

Mabel stared back at her, open-mouthed and bewildered, but her tears no longer falling. She had never heard of yaks before now.

Natasha carried on, holding up the flags. 'And how lucky are *we*, to get to send Moolah our own extra-special, moon-jumping wishes? That's pretty amazing, Mabel! Before we just had to cross our fingers for her.' She crossed her fingers. 'But now we've got prayer flags! And the wind will carry all our hopes and all our wishes and all our love to Moolah on the mountain! With the yaks!'

Mabel's mouth shaped into a smile. 'And with Duffy!'

Natasha's smile faltered. '. . . And with Duffy, that's right.'

'Can we send her my special magic kisses?'

'Yes. You just kiss the flag and the wind will take them!'

'And can we send her the picture I made for her?'

'Yes, we can! We can pin it to the flag and the wind will take all its feelings to her.' She watched as the relief settled over Mabel like a colour wash. She could see the sense of peace trickle down through her daughter's little body.

'We'll have to find somewhere to put the flags up, though,

so the wind can take our kisses. Do you remember what Duffy said about it being bad luck for them to be on the ground?'

At that Mabel jumped up, scooping them in great armfuls, trying to lift them from the floor as though crocodiles were snapping. 'I know where! I know where!' She began running back through to the kitchen, a length of ribbon trailing behind her and exciting Bella, who trotted behind, sensing a game.

She stopped suddenly and turned. 'Mummy.'

'Yes?'

'I love Duffy. He's my friend.'

'Yes, he is.'

'Do you love Duffy too?'

Natasha swallowed, feeling a rush of words that could never be said, fighting to be put out there. She felt stuffed with them. 'How could I not, my darling? Any friend of yours is a friend of mine.'

Chapter Twenty-Seven

Annapurna South Face, Friday 16 December

Duffy lifted his head and stared dully at the next ice tower. It rose just three metres above him, a bulbous, distorted wall of ice and snow; but beyond it would lie another, and another, and another, then another . . . He was standing on the ice ridge, one of the most perilous sections of the ascent. It rose for a thousand feet, a jagged, undulating spine, the towers wind-whipped into a perilous knife edge so that he had no more than half a metre's tolerance either side of him at any time. He didn't know where exactly he was on the ridge, because he couldn't see beyond the wall in front of him; he could only go up and over each one. Down, then up; down then up. It was climbing the ugly way, the hard way and the long way, but it was also the only 'safe' way between Camps Three and Four. At the top of either side of the ridge, three-hundred-metre ice cliffs stood guard over the gullies, intermittently releasing ice boulders the size of houses, sometimes if the sun was out, sometimes after heavy snow, sometimes seemingly just because . . . He and Sanani had already watched an avalanche trigger beside and below them on the west slopes this morning; they had leaned on their ice axes, bent double with exhaustion as they watched, panting heavily. It had been a chilling sight: like watching a bowling ball hurtle down an alley, knowing that if they'd been down there, they'd have been the skittles.

The going was torturously slow. Even without forty-kilo packs on their backs, at an altitude of 6,300 metres they had half the strength they'd had at Base Camp. There was air all around – the wind dancing like a sprite – but no longer enough oxygen to move easily; anyone not acclimatized would lose consciousness within fifteen minutes. Talking was a luxury they couldn't afford, and they climbed in silence to a soundtrack of ice axes sluicing into the frozen snow above them, crampons stabbing below.

There were short sections of fixed ropes, which felt like a mercy. On those, they clipped their harnesses to the rope sections, made stepping slings and used the jumars, metal clamps that could slide up but not release down. Sanani was downhill of Duffy, hidden behind the previous tower, and Duffy waited for a few minutes, blinking back the headache that had started to come on over the past few hours. He pressed on his radio transmitter in his jacket pocket. 'Duffy to Sanani Sherpa, just checking in, over.'

A minute went by before his receiver crackled back. 'Sanani Sherpa to Duffy, all good. Coming over the top in five, over.'

Duffy looked down upon the massif, seeing how the monster mountains rippled around and away, the earth's very crust beneath his feet. At these heights, the weather lay below them and he could see clouds beginning to rise up and the spindrift whistling off the peaks of Gangapurna and Annapurna III, telling him the winds were strengthening. A strong storm was coming. Sanani was an expert on the glacial architecture of the mountains, but the weather was every bit as much the enemy here as the forty-five-degree ice walls.

They could not afford to get caught out on the ridge and they had only two options: get to their destination quickly, or turn back. He looked up at the next tower and steeled himself. They had been climbing for six hours and he knew the end, Camp Four, was somewhere close, even if he couldn't yet see it. He swung the axe above his head and hauled himself up, doing what had to be done. His idol Ed Viesturs had famously said, *Getting to the summit is optional. Getting down is mandatory*, but Duffy disagreed. For him, the opposite was true now. All that mattered was getting to the top. Standing on that summit would be his revenge, at last. He didn't give a damn what happened to him after that.

The wind was beginning to howl, whipping up the snow and whistling past the tents like racing demons, making them shudder and flex. Duffy lay on his mat and sleeping bag, trying to keep warm as he listened to the ripstop nylon flap sharply. He and Sanani had spoken briefly on the radios to the Swiss guys, who were nine hundred metres higher up, in Camp Six. There the temperatures were even lower, the winds approaching hurricane strength, and their voices had been bowed with strain as they shared information about conditions.

It doesn't have to be fun to be fun. Lottie's voice carried to him on the wind. He could hear her perfectly, as though she was right there. It had been her favourite quote, the one she would throw down on him as he struggled on a boulder or missed a finger grip, cursing and yelling as he fell back on the ropes and was left swinging while she climbed. She had always been better than him.

He closed his eyes, trying to empty his mind. This was no time for reminiscences. Sanani was asleep beside him, looking at peace as the storm picked up. Although fierce, it was forecast to blow through quickly; this was just a mini tyrant toying with them, but it was the other one, already on its heels and blowing in from the east, that the Swiss were worried about. They wanted to make their push for the summit, having already been forced to turn back once by the high winds and sit out this tempest. It was always a bitter blow having to drop hard-won altitude and many had died from not listening to the mountain, wanting to pitch their wills against Annapurna's might. The Swiss guys knew better, and he did too. Climbing was as much a waiting game as a feat of endurance, and he was here for the long haul if need be. He had planned for weather delays and acclimatization setbacks. He had made sure he was coming here with money and time, keeping his team minimal and his loads light precisely so that he could be nimble and reactive, unencumbered by the concerns and demands of an expedition pack.

But even with all that, he had a bad feeling that twitched in his guts, spreading slowly. He squeezed his eyes harder, willing sleep to come, but though his body was spent, his spirit was restless. It had been six days since he'd been confronted with seeing *her* again and although the initial shock and anger had spurred him on, every time he stopped moving, she filled his mind like smoke. He was rattled, he couldn't pretend otherwise, all the preparations he had undergone in the months and years leading up to this feeling shaken loose. There had been no way to prepare himself for suddenly seeing her again – just as nothing could have forewarned him the first time either. It had been like standing on the fault line of an earthquake; nothing could have readied him for the moment their eyes had first met.

He knew distraction could kill him, and yet the images of

her swam through his mind's eye anyway – only an ice ridge could push her out, an avalanche, a precipitous serac that threatened to release and sweep him away. If it did, would she be his last thought?

It was always her face after their first kiss that he remembered: that look of desire marbled with fear as she had been confronted with the truth of what he'd been telling her – or trying to. Kneeling in a wedding dress on the floor of a tree-house, she had finally understood she was marrying the wrong man.

She'd still gone and done it.

And now . . . now she had a family: a beautiful daughter who looked just like her. He had heard for himself in her first fierce email just how protective she was of her; fighting for her child's happiness, she would take on anyone. She was a good mother, he could tell that, but was she a good wife too? Was she living the life he had predicted for her: set up in a big house, spending her days painting, sleeping beside a man she hadn't wanted to marry? Was she happy? Happy enough? Or was she empty, like him?

He opened his eyes, staring into the blackness, trying to find escape there. He sat up and let his head hang for a moment. The headache wasn't going away and he'd thrown up twice on arriving here. He wasn't yet operating at his limits, but he was on the approach. Sanani was watching him closely and had said they would spend three nights here minimum. If he didn't improve by then, they'd drop back to Camp Three. Duffy desperately didn't want to have to drop height. He wasn't sure he could ever face the ice ridge again.

The wind howled, an airy wolf chasing its tail around their tent, circling them tightly. He switched on his head torch and watched it draw its claws over the walls. There were so many things that could kill them up here, the wind chief among them, and it sometimes amazed him that such a thin plastic skin – which he knew would be covered, inside, with a thick frost come the morning – could provide any meaningful protection in temperatures of minus forty. Then again, he thought the same of the light, narrow ropes from which they dangled when a foot slipped, the slim pegs that could pierce a mountain's hide; the single blade of an ice axe that could halt a fall down sheet ice. Life hung on the tiniest margins up here, sometimes just a single inch of stainless steel.

It occurred to him that if he did die, she wouldn't even know. She already didn't care, but she wouldn't know. She would continue living in this world, with no awareness that he – a man she had only known for twenty-four hours – had gone. Probably she had forgotten him already so that even if she were to be told, his name would mean nothing anyway, the memory failing to register. Why would it? It hadn't been for her what it had been for him. She didn't believe in the thunderbolt—

Fuck. He realized she was in his brain again. The irony wasn't lost on him that he should go so high, only to feel so low.

His gaze fell to Sanani's satellite phone, lying in the space between their ground mats. The sherpa kept it by his side at all times, but at $6 a minute – in a country where the average annual income was $830 – he only ever used it in emergencies. Duffy reached for it. He would give Sanani the money for the call, he would give him all his money – he just needed to speak to the one person left in this world who still cared about him. His soul felt troubled, the sense of foreboding inching closer.

He stepped out of the tent and half zipped it shut. He knew

the number by heart, listening to the dial tone as it rang. He wasn't sure what time it was here, much less in Europe. It had been dark since five. Was it eight in the evening? Two in the morning?

'Hello?' a female voice asked, sounding distracted.

'Anya?'

There was a time lag, then an audible gasp. 'Duffy! Oh my God, I didn't recognize the number! It's so good to hear from you. I've been thinking of you so much. How are you?'

He smiled at the onslaught of questions, feeling some of the tension leave his body. 'I'm good, yeah. A bit tired. You?'

'Ugh,' she groaned. 'We've got a new IT system that's completely mucked up the personnel records so I've spent the past two weeks trying to get that sorted.'

He smiled, trying to imagine office life – days spent sitting in front of a screen, subject to air conditioning or central heating and where lunch came wrapped in plastic. It had never been for him. 'Well, if anyone can get it sorted, it's you.'

'Where are you?'

Her voice was a little distorted – satellite phones had to tread a line between bandwidth and power capabilities – stretching the time lag further. He bit his lip. '. . . Well, I'm up a mountain.'

There was a pause, one that had nothing to do with satellites. Her silences were always concerning. 'You never said anything about climbing. You said you were trekking out there.'

'Don't worry, it's all good,' he said quickly. 'I'm fine. Nearly there, actually.' Sort of. Just the height of a European Alp to climb and he'd be there.

There was still a pause. 'Which mountain? . . . Duffy?'

He sighed, knowing he couldn't avoid telling her; knowing

that perhaps he didn't want to. Otherwise, if the worst did happen, he would just disappear and no one would know. Not till his letters were sent. 'Annapurna.'

'Annapurna Three?'

She was giving him a get-out clause to lie. She was hoping against hope. 'No . . . One.'

There was another long silence. A costly silence. It felt like a twelve-dollar silence to him – but she had a right to be angry with him, he accepted that.

'And you didn't tell me.' Hurt inflected her voice.

'I didn't tell anyone.'

'Not even your father?'

Him least of all. Duffy scrunched his eyes shut. 'Only you.'

'I should have known it wasn't just a trek!' she cried.

'I'm sorry. I didn't want to lie, but—' They both knew that if she'd known, she would have raised merry hell to stop him; she would have told his father, told the press, anyone who would listen, to prevent him getting on the plane. 'This is something I have to do. Please understand.' He tried to keep the emotion from his voice. 'I can't go forward without doing this. You know better than anyone that I can't.'

'But if you die—'

'Then I was never supposed to go forward.'

He heard the horror in her gasp. 'You can't believe that!'

He didn't respond for a moment. '. . . I do believe I can do it.'

'Duffy, I'm not doubting in *your* abilities! You're a prodigious climber, it's in your blood, but it's not going to come down to what you can do. It's the weather! The avalanches! The falling seracs! All those things you spent years telling me about. None of those are within your control!'

'I know, but we're mitigating risk wherever we can.'

'We?'

'I'm with Sanani Sherpa.'

'Sanani? I thought he retired after—?'

'He did. But when I asked him, he agreed. It's unfinished business for him too.'

Anya exhaled, expensive seconds ticking past in silent contemplation. '. . . Well, I suppose that's something,' she said finally, her voice small. 'If anyone can keep you safe up there, it's him.' Her voice was brittle with worry and he knew she would be biting her nails.

'Stop biting your nails,' he said quietly.

'How did—?'

'I just know.'

There was another six-dollar silence. '. . . So how far up are you?'

'Camp Four. Six and a half thousand metres.'

'What does that mean?'

'It means we've crossed the ice ridge. It was brutal but we could see a storm was coming in, so we had to get ahead. We'll probably stay here for a few days now.' There was no chance of him mentioning his headache. 'Another squall's coming in almost immediately, so we'll stay put and recover for a bit.'

'And then what?'

'We've got the traverse to do—'

'The Terrible Traverse?' she clarified.

He hesitated; she really had been listening, all those years. At the top of the ice ridge was the ice wall, which no one had ever scaled. The only way past, first achieved by Bonington's expedition in May 1970, was a perilous traverse. It was fixed ropes all the way and was so dangerous, no porters or load carriers could cross it. They remained stuck at Camp Four.

'Yes, but once we're past that it's just a trek through the snowfields up to Camp Five, and then we're at the foot of the rock band, quick climb and we're at the summit.'

'Oh well then . . . You make it sound easy.'

'If the weather is on our side, it'll be manageable.'

'That's assuming there are no avalanches from the serac at the top of those snowfields.'

There really was no fooling her. She was a climber too; she had loved him and his obsessions had become hers. She had read the maps with him, discussed the merits of the different routes, never once thinking he would be so mad as to actually do them himself. She knew the serac was within a hundred metres of Camp Five and that until they got to it – the camp itself just tucked into a crack at the foot of the rock band – they were fully exposed. He closed his eyes, pinching his temples. 'Anya, I won't take any unnecessary risks.'

'Every climber says that, till they're within sight of the summit. Then it's death or glory.'

The rock wall extended up for half a mile, leading to another stretch of snowfields and, finally, the elusive 8,091-metre peak. 'Not for me.'

'*Especially* for you! Don't bullshit me, Duffy. We both know why you're up there at all.'

He didn't bother to deny it. 'Listen, if anything happens—'

'Duffy, don't! Don't even talk like that!' she cried, as if even just by saying the words he was tempting fate.

'Anya, I have to say it!' His voice cracked. 'I have to, okay?' He waited for a few moments, but she was silent now. Obedient, for once, as if she'd heard something in his voice and understood the stakes. 'If the worst happens, my trekking pack has been taken back to Sanani's home. He lives in a village called Muna. Remember that, okay? Muna. There are some letters in it. One for you, one for Dad.'

'You're wrong to do this, Duffy,' she said, and he could hear she was crying now. 'He deserved to know! We all did!'

'I didn't want you to worry.'

'No, you didn't want us to stop you!' she cried.

He swallowed, knowing it had been selfish to ring her. He'd done what he always did – used her for support, giving her nothing but heartache in return. 'Anya . . . I promise I'll do everything I can to come back.' There was a 38 per cent chance he might not. He knew she knew that too, but she didn't articulate the fact; she wouldn't tempt fate. 'Just know that I love you. And I'm sorry I was never better than I am. You're the best friend I've ever had—'

A sudden whip-crack, like a clap of thunder, made him turn. He froze, waiting for the flash of lightning. One . . . two . . . three . . .

'Duffy? What was that?'

Four . . . Five . . .

No lightning, but the sound had been close – which meant it hadn't been thunder. He felt the ground tremble, saw the tent begin to shiver and shake . . .

'Duffy?' Anya screamed as the rumble exploded into a roar. 'Duffy!'

Chapter Twenty-Eight

Frome, Friday 16 December

Natasha sat in the armchair, staring into the Christmas tree lights. They were mesmeric, transporting. The fire was crackling and she was already half a bottle of sauvignon down. Bella was lying in her favourite spot, but she kept lifting her head off her paws as if checking on her; as if somehow sensing that something was wrong. Or about to be.

Rob was on his way back. He had texted to say he was leaving three hours ago and she was braced for the sound of his car on the drive any moment. She had decided on her plan of action – which was that there wasn't one. Hels was right; there were myriad reasons he might have been in Gloucestershire. Her work had taken her there, so why not his? A meeting too inconsequential to mention. Why should she assume a worst-case scenario? What kind of wife was so ready to believe the worst of her husband?

Besides, coming home the other evening, after she had settled Mabel from the excitement of Duffy's parcel, she had spent hours sleuthing online for Robert Stoneleighs, finding dozens before hitting upon the correct one. Seemingly settled on the north coast of Ibiza, he was a 500-hours qualified yoga instructor and 'intimacy coach'; he was attractive enough but with a look that suggested he knew it, confirming everything Emily and Diana had said about him. There was nothing to find online about 'her' Rob, of course; he always said it was the very definition of irony to have a data security expert with a lax social media habit but it was a running joke that she'd barely been able to get him in their wedding photos, much less onto Instagram.

She took another large sip of wine, willing herself to relax. She had wound herself up all week, and for what? Things weren't as cataclysmic as she'd made out. So she wasn't pregnant? At least now they would see the specialist, like he'd promised, to start proper investigations. And Mabel was *so* excited about her prayer flags and Moolah's upcoming prospects for moon-jumping that that was more important than anything right now. And the portrait was coming along far better than she could have hoped. She had never tested herself in this way before, never dared commit to the next level in her work, but she was surprising herself with what she was producing.

She had spent all day yesterday and today working on Artemis's portrait, losing herself as she developed the sketches she had set down. She had decided upon a blackish-green background, with umber smudged through it to create pockets of golden light. Arty was captured mid-trot, his head turned slightly to the side in his signature way, and she was already beginning work on his hide, layering up the dappling on his hindquarters and bringing up the silver sheen. All being well, and assuming Rob could take Mabel out for a bit this weekend, she anticipated finishing early next week and delivering to Diana on Wednesday the twenty-first. She had seen a vintage Rolex in the window of the antique jewellers' on the high street that she had thought Rob would like.

Another sip of wine. The television was playing on mute and she realized it was still set to Disney. She grabbed the remote and began scanning the myriad options – too many to choose, so she switched it to BBC One. Bella jumped up and Natasha looked up in time to see full beams swing past the windows, washing the house with light as he parked, before switching off again. She listened for the cut of the engine. Then his footsteps on the drive. The key in the door.

He was home again.

She anticipated the relief in her body that always accompanied this soundtrack – the sounds of a happy home – but this time, she felt her brain seize like a cog jammed on a pebble, unable to move past . . .

Move past what? What was it?

'Hey!' he called through, dropping his keys in the trinket dish, his leather-soled shoes echoing on the wooden floors. 'Anyone miss me?'

He peered his head round the door, taking in the sight of her drinking wine by the fire, watching . . . *EastEnders*? 'Oh I see,' he grinned, seeming pleased by the sight. 'This is what happens in my absence, is it? Feet up, wine in hand.'

'Ha ha.'

He came over, bending down over the chair to kiss her. 'I missed you,' he said, lingering for a moment.

Natasha felt her smile waver. *I saw you*, she wanted to say. 'Me too. How was your week?' she asked instead, getting up and following him towards the kitchen.

'Oh, fine,' he sighed, shrugging off his jacket. 'Tiring.' He hung it over the back of the kitchen stool and reached for the wine glass in her hand, taking a deep glug. 'Mmm,' he nodded, closing his eyes with satisfaction. 'I need some more of that.'

She wandered over to the fridge and took out the bottle as he loosened his tie. 'Mabel down already?'

'Yes. I could scarcely keep her awake.' She poured him a glass and handed it over.

'That makes a nice change.'

'Well, she's been sleeping like the proverbial ever since she received a nice parcel in the post yesterday. From Nepal.'

Rob's eyes widened, his mouth dropping open. 'Moolah's back?'

'Oh, no – not quite,' she said quickly. 'But Duffy has sent her some prayer flags.'

Rob frowned. 'He's sent her *what*?'

Natasha walked over to the back doors and switched on the terrace lights. The garden was illuminated, the washing line that ran the entire length of the lawn now adorned with brightly coloured flags fluttering in the breeze.

'What the hell . . . ?' Rob pressed his face to the glass, one hand framing his face as he tried to get a better look. 'Did the circus come to town?'

Natasha felt a jolt of irritation at his snobbishness. She had thought they looked rather beautiful. 'Remember what he said in his postcard – about the wind carrying their prayers, creating good vibrations? Well, he sent Mabel these so she could send prayers and good vibrations to Moolah for jumping the moon.'

Rob turned back to her. 'But that makes no sense! Why not just send back the damned cow?' he asked incredulously. 'I thought the whole point of this charade was to cover for the fact that he's in the middle of nowhere with her toy, which – let's just remind ourselves – he, a grown man, had no right taking in the first place. If he could send *those* over, why not just send Moolah?'

Natasha had wondered exactly the same. 'It would have been simpler, I agree . . . but this is still very sweet. And Mabel's beside herself with excitement; she won't let me take them down. She can't talk about anything else but Moolah jumping the moon.'

Rob walked back towards the kitchen island, draining his glass and pouring himself another. 'And what's going to happen when Moolah *doesn't* jump the moon?'

'What do you mean?'

'Well, our eccentric friend Duffy McDuff of Clan McDuff has created an expectation now that he can't possibly fulfil. He clearly doesn't have kids or he would know better than to promise something he can't deliver. Who's going to be picking up the pieces when she's in floods of tears? We are! And he'll just swan off to Tibet. Or Timbuktu. Or wherever the hell people like him go.'

People like him. Natasha stared at the floor.

Rob took another sip of wine, looking over at her as if detecting something of her tension, like a low-frequency hum. 'You look tired, darling. Have *you* been sleeping okay?'

'I never sleep as well when you're not here, you know that,' she said, turning away, not wanting the scrutiny. She opened the fridge and stared into it, pretending to consider what to make for dinner.

'Well, I'm back now,' he said, coming over and placing one hand on her hip, sweeping her hair back with the other to kiss the crook of her neck. 'I missed you, you know. More than usual. You've been . . . elusive.'

'Elusive? Don't be silly,' she demurred, feeling her pulse skyrocket. 'I've just been busy.'

'What? With *all* those coffee mornings and playdates?'

'Oh for heaven's sake, Rob! It's the week before

366

Christmas!' she said, irritated by his condescension. 'I've not stopped!'

He drew back, sensing her edgy mood. 'No, you're right, of course you haven't. I was just teasing. You must be shattered. You've had Mabes on your own all week. Why don't you go and run yourself a bath and I'll make sups?'

'It's fine.' Why did he always think a bath was the answer to her problems?

'No, I insist,' he said, taking the bottle and refilling her glass. 'I want you to take some time for yourself. You mustn't overdo it—'

She watched his gaze drop fleetingly to her belly. 'No . . .' she said flatly. 'I got my period.'

'Ah.' He set the bottle down with a dismayed look, as if understanding now the reason behind her bad mood. '. . . Oh darling, I'm sorry. Are you okay?'

'Fine,' she said in a brittle voice, nodding a bit too hard.

'No, you're not. It's why you've not been sleeping, I know it is.' He came towards her again and clasped her face in his hands. 'Listen, I don't want you getting stressed about telling me. It's fine. There's always next month. And the month after that. It will happen. We'll just keep trying and keep believing.'

It was her opportunity to remind him of his promise that they would see a specialist in the new year to double-check nothing was wrong and put their minds at rest. But now wasn't the time for that conversation; how could they plan for another baby when their very marriage teetered on the brink?

He took her silence as tacit agreement to his 'wait and see' plan. 'Good. Now I insist that you have that bath while I cook, then we'll watch a film in front of the fire. I'm going to light your favourite candles and make everything feel special for when you come back down. Do you want a hot water bottle?'

She stared at him, knowing he was thinking about the stomach cramps that accompanied her monthlies. He was so considerate she wanted to scream. 'No. Thanks.' She turned and headed for the hallway, feeling herself trembling with suppressed emotions, hearing Hels's words echo in her head: *'You don't realize what a good thing you've got.'*

She heard him open a drawer. 'Darling . . . where are the matches?'

'In the second drawer,' she mumbled back. The second drawer of the dresser in the kitchen was where everything that didn't have a rightful home was placed: matches, torch, rubber bands, radiator and allen keys . . . She was turning the taps when she remembered she'd used them to light the woodburning stove in her studio—

'Rob, wait! Don't go in! I'll fetch them for you—'

She ran straight back down to stop him from entering the room, but it was too late. On seeing they weren't in the drawer, he must have reckoned upon her warming up her studio during the cold days, for he was already in there, standing by the easel, the box of matches in his hand. The embers were still glowing in the grate from when she'd been working in here earlier, the canvas sitting on the easel; she hadn't been able to put it away or cover it while the oils were wet. She had taken the gamble he would have no reason to come in here tonight and that she could hide it tomorrow.

'Jesus Christ, Tasha! This is incredible!' His eyes were alive and dancing as he met hers. She hadn't seen him so animated in a long time. 'You never told me you were doing this!'

Natasha stopped by the door, wishing he hadn't seen it. The entire commission was supposed to be a secret so that he knew nothing at all of her extra earnings for his present, but she supposed it didn't matter, not really; it wasn't like the portrait was for him, and she was so pleased by his reaction . . . 'Really? You like it?'

'Like it? Darling, I knew you were good, but I never knew you could . . . do *that*! You're a proper artist!'

Natasha gave him a funny look. What had he thought she was before? She went over and stood beside him, staring at the canvas afresh. Her gaze went straight to everything that wasn't right – yet – or that still needed doing, but she couldn't deny she was already prouder of this than anything she'd ever done.

'No wonder you're tired! I hope you've upped your prices!'

She smiled. She'd never earned this much money before. It was her old monthly wage – but for a week's work.

'God, you really have got him.' Rob stared at the painting, engrossed. 'His tail, the markings on the backs of his legs there, that funny toss he does with his head. It's all absolutely spot on.' He reached over and kissed her on the cheek. 'I'm so proud of you, I really am. Well done.'

Natasha watched him go out. The hairs on the back of her neck were standing up. The world seemed to have slowed down, but her brain had sped up . . . *That funny toss he does* . .

How could he possibly know that was a thing this specific horse habitually did – unless he knew Arty?

She didn't stir. She mustn't . . . she mustn't panic . . . She had promised herself – and Hels – she would be rational. No paranoia. But those words, his reaction . . . And she had seen him in the very village where Artemis was stabled . . .

She sank into her thoughts, looking for the most plausible explanation, but as she began to think . . . to really concentrate . . . she felt memories stir; they were still fresh; like the oils on the canvas, they hadn't yet dried . . . Eyes closing, she remembered standing at the stable, the wind cold as she

KAREN SWAN

sketched. She'd barely felt it, she'd been so absorbed in her work, utterly lost in concentration and yet . . . thinking back now, she could remember the chill on her bare hands. And she recalled, now, a light scrabbling by her feet, scarcely audible. It wasn't Bella. She was sitting in front, tethered to the ring . . . She thought harder. Scrabbling . . . Rabbit. A bunny nearby, nibbling on a dandelion.

More than that, too. Birds had been singing, a plane flying overhead. Voices in the garden. Over the hedge. Low murmurings. Background sounds. Innocuous . . . *Let me do it. I can reach better.* Innocuous by familiarity. Heard every day, they hadn't registered as something new. Only now did she process that they were new *there*. She had heard *him*, *there*.

Her eyes opened. She felt a wave of nausea surge up inside her. Emily . . . ?

She clapped a hand to her mouth as the realization hit her, she felt her knees buckle and she staggered to her desk, falling onto the chair. He was having an affair with Emily Richards?

That couldn't . . . it couldn't be. Tears welled in her eyes as she stared through the stove's glass door at the glowing ashes. No. But also, yes. Something told her yes.

She inhaled sharply, moving suddenly, feeling her brain move through the gears again, the jammed pebble pushed out and cogs turning once more.

She went onto Instagram. Emily Richards . . . Emily Richards . . . There must be a thousand women with that name, she despaired, scrolling through, her eyes scanning for an avatar that matched up to the woman she had briefly met.

One looked possible but it was difficult to tell, the images were so small and oblique. She clicked on it – private account. 'Fuck,' she hissed, scrolling through again and trying others.

But none of them were right – too young, too dark, private account.

She sat back. Her body was ringing with alarm. There would be no hiding her accusations from him now; she wasn't that good an actress. She knew what she knew – Emily was his mistress – even if she couldn't prove it.

Diana. Her name popped into Natasha's head. Lorn was a distinctive surname. There couldn't be too many of them about, surely? She entered 'Diana Lorn' and leaned in closer as the first result yielded a bay horse avatar. She clicked on it – public account.

It was the Diana she knew, no question about it – almost every photograph was of a horse or pony at a hunt, eventing, Badminton . . . Natasha scrolled down, looking for humans, not equines. Diana and Emily were good friends. Perhaps there was something . . . ?

She moved down through the weeks, the months . . . stopping at an image of the garden last summer. It appeared to be hosting a village fête – there was a marquee on the lawn, bunting and hay bales in the background. Ten images posted. She flicked through, seeing pictures of children playing whack-a-mole, a candyfloss stall, pony rides . . .

Natasha's heart forgot to beat as she found exactly what she had been looking for. Diana and Emily were standing together, wearing floral dresses and sunhats and holding a glass of Pimms each. But beside Emily was Rob . . . his hand placed intimately on her hip, his head tipped towards her. They were all laughing, looking at ease. Natasha's gaze fell to the caption, to the people tagged. She clicked on Rob's image—

'Darling, your bath . . . ?'

She looked up to find him standing by the door. He had

his Simpsons Piccadilly apron on and was chopping up herbs in a cup with a pair of scissors.

'Just coming,' she whispered as he turned to leave again and her gaze fell back to the tagged photograph.

She saw her world fall apart. She understood immediately how completely it was all over. She stared at his back.

'Oh, James . . .'

'Yes?' He turned.

It was another moment before he understood what had just happened.

Footsteps on the drive. A familiar sound, too familiar to clock. Filling a birdfeeder in humdrum domesticity. The signet ring, the door wreath . . . articles from another life, telling her this was no affair.

Emily wasn't his mistress, nor even the other woman.

Natasha saw, four years too late, *she* was.

Chapter Twenty-Nine

'Natasha, listen to me – I love you.'

She stepped back, trembling. 'No.'

'Yes!' His eyes were wide, burning black with fear. 'From the very first moment you got out of the car, I knew I couldn't be without you! I drove away and I was shaking – *shaking* – with terror that I would never see you again! I knew I had to do something.'

'And bigamy felt like the answer?' she spat, half crying, half laughing with incredulity. She couldn't believe it. She actually could not make her brain believe it. 'How could you?' Her voice sounded degloved and she pressed a hand to her heart, as if trying to hold it up or press it in. Her whole psyche was going into shock. It was too much to process. She couldn't . . . she couldn't . . . 'Oh my God,' she whimpered, sinking to the ground, her legs unable to bear the weight. The air felt heavy and leaden, sinking in her lungs, pushing her earthwards.

He rushed over, enveloping her, wanting her to slump upon him, to depend upon him. 'My darling,' he hushed, his chest against her face. She had never been able to breathe easily against him, she realized. Something in her had always needed more air. More space. 'You have to believe me when I say you are the love of my life. I know it was wrong. Don't you think

I know that? But what was I to do? You would have left me. I had no choice.'

'No choice?' She pushed against him, though her arms were feeble. She felt drugged, beaten, numbed by shock, her body and mind shutting down, unable to absorb the enormity of what was happening. 'You had a family! Your *choice* was to be with the wife and children waiting at home for you.'

'I know.' His face twisted and he hid it in his hands, shaking his head. 'I know. I know they deserve better than me—'

'You think?' she cried, the sarcasm refuelling her. 'You think Emily deserves a husband who's married just to her? You think your kids deserve a father who's satisfied with just one family? You have six children with her! Six!'

His hands dropped, his eyes red-rimmed. 'I know, but I panicked, Nats, okay? I wasn't thinking straight. None of it was planned. I had gone out to buy a fucking cauliflower! I wasn't expecting you to literally crash into my life!'

Her eyes widened. 'So it's *my* fault?'

'Of course not. No. No.' He shook his head vehemently. 'But the way it happened, suddenly you were just there . . . it was like it was fated.'

She stared at him. He was her fate? It was her life's destiny to be married to a man with a whole other life and another family? He even had another name to the one she knew him by! How could *this* be her fate? Surely she deserved more than half a husband, half a home, half a life?

All these years he had told her how much he loved her, but she had never *felt* loved by him; there had always been something possessive, insular, to his actions, as if she was a trophy, something for him to own. Look how he had dictated the terms of their life together: buying this house as a wedding present, already decorated for them to move into – him coming and going at will while she and Mabel remained here, unaware they were locked inside a gilded cage. No, what lay behind his extraordinary gestures and overt consideration wasn't love, but self-love. He was a narcissist, plain and simple.

She watched as he got himself to standing again, running his hands through his hair, his elbows pinched forwards in front of his face.

She felt a tear slide down her cheek. 'You,' she whispered. 'It's all about you, isn't it? But what about Emily? What about me? You had no right to come into my life and say all the things you said to me. To do all this!' She swept a hand around, indicating their beautiful, sterile home, the empty life they had built together. 'You were a married man who already had his family! If I had meant anything to you, you never would have done this to me! I deserved to find someone who would be truly mine!'

Duffy. His face flashed in front of her, kneeling in the tree-house having just kissed her. Both of them knowing, without knowing why . . . just that it *was*.

A sob escaped her, wracking her body so that she slumped again. 'I deserved that chance and you took it from me!' she wept. 'You knew I didn't want to get married so quickly. I said no.' She looked up at him. 'I said no!'

'But then you said yes.'

'Because you pushed and pushed and you overwhelmed me! You wouldn't accept it! You made it seem romantic but you were just gaslighting me.' She stared at him, his image blurry beyond her tears. She felt so weak, like her body had no bones. A sob escaped her. '. . . Why did you take it so far? . . . Huh? We could have just had a fling! I would never have known about Emily; you would have got what you wanted and we could have moved on. It would have been a fling and no one else would have got hurt.'

He shook his head, coming to crouch beside her. 'That was what I thought too, at first,' he said urgently. 'I thought I'd get you out of my system. I'd never cheated before—'

She gave a snort of disbelief.

'I swear to you, on my children's lives.'

'Don't do that!' she said harshly, pointing a finger at him that sent him retreating from her personal space again. 'Don't you dare! Not when your word doesn't count for anything anymore!'

He swallowed. 'Look, I watched my partner bedding all these women—'

'Oh – you mean Rob? Rob Stoneleigh?'

He hesitated, then nodded. 'He was everything I wasn't. I never wanted to be like him. I pitied him, he was a slave to his own lust. He couldn't help himself. Every woman was a challenge.'

'But not you, huh?' Contempt dripped from her words.

'No. Never . . . Not till you.' He looked down. 'I thought . . . yeah, I admit it, I thought an affair would be enough. I thought we'd go on a few dates, fall into bed and then we would . . . move on.' He raised his gaze to hers, those sincere grey eyes trying to work their magic on her. 'But I couldn't. Instead I fell for you. I fell in love again and I realized I couldn't let you go, even though you didn't feel the same. I loved you more, I knew that, and I knew that you might end things, if not sooner, then later. If I hadn't married you, I knew you'd leave me.'

'So you married me to *trap* me?'

'I married you to spend a life with you.'

'Half a life!' she snapped.

He winced, holding his hands up defensively again, as if he was the wounded party. 'Please. Please, Nats. I couldn't risk losing you.' His voice cracked on the words; like a broken record, saying the same thing over and over, they were beginning to sound worn.

'I was never yours to lose!' She stared at him hatefully, trying to believe it all, but the scale of his lies was overwhelming. Their marriage, this home . . . Even just on a legal level, what did it all mean? '. . . Where does she think you are now?'

He looked away, as if bringing Emily into the conversation, as if saying her name here, in their home, was somehow painful to him.

'Tell me!'

'Here . . . Somerset.'

'What do you tell her?'

His mouth drooped at the corners, making him look older. Old. '. . . That we have an office here.'

She gave a small snort of derision. 'Does she have any suspicions about me and Mabel?' The very question seemed ridiculous. How could his wife possibly imagine this? And yet, Natasha had sensed *something* was amiss; no matter how much she had tried to sink into the illusion of their life together, her instincts always quivered as if strung too tightly – an affair, or affairs, she had assumed because . . . well, that was the obvious thing, wasn't it? God, how pedestrian it seemed now. He had been capable of so much grander a deception than that. '. . . Well, does she?' She watched the ball of his jaw clench at her anger.

'No. She doesn't think about much beyond the kids.'

'So you're blaming *her* now?'

'No, I didn't mean—'

'Are you surprised she's too busy for you? I'd be pretty tied up looking after six children too! And you're gone half the time? That poor woman! God that poor, poor woman being stuck married to you – what have you done?' She stared at him with disgust, seeing that this entire life together was a mirage, that he was a complete stranger. Five years of her life had been spent with this man and he'd been hidden that whole time. Standing there, he seemed to recede before her, becoming smaller. Weaker.

Her eyes narrowed. '. . . I saw you, you know.'

'What?' He frowned. 'Where? When?'

'In Snowshill, on Monday. You drove right past me.'

'What were you doing there?' He sounded confused.

She motioned towards the easel. 'Working. Clearly. At your neighbours'.'

She saw him make the connections. It had been his unthinking mistake recognizing Artemis that had unmasked him, after all.

'I had just come out of the florist's. I'd bought a wreath, one with pheasant feathers – just like the one you were looking for the other week, remember?'

If she had never stopped in there, he would never have passed by her in the car; they would have driven along the same road, separated only by a five-minute window.

He swallowed. 'I wasn't . . . I wasn't thinking. I got . . . confused.'

'Oh, I'm sure. It must have been incredibly confusing – not to mention tiring – maintaining a double life.' She watched him fall very still. He couldn't meet her eyes but from what – shame? Guilt? Her gaze fell to his hand. 'What about the signet ring? Why did you have to take that off when you came over here?'

He didn't reply. But she guessed anyway.

'Oh. It has your initials on it, right? J? Or J. R.?'

'Look, Nats—'

'And what about your partner – Rob? What does he make of all this? Is he aware he's a married man and living in Somerset?'

He looked pained as she pronounced the truth to him. 'Of course not. Rob's in Ibiza. The day I met you, he'd just told me he was jacking in the business and basically running away with the fucking circus. He'd lost the plot. He'd done years of cocaine benders and now he'd found a new high – he sold his flat, all his clothes, his possessions and basically went to live in a tent on some rocks. He gave me some bank details and told me to buy him out or dissolve the business, whichever. Either way, I had to deal with the mess and sort out all the paperwork.'

'So you bought him out?' *Family money*, Diana had said about Emily. She saw the mechanics, the means, of his fraud fall into place. '. . . You kept his business credit cards, his phone and used his identity as an alias for your life with me.'

'I'm not proud of it.'

'Oh I don't know!' she said, unable to stop the sarcasm from flowing; all she could feel was rage. Rage and disbelief. 'A deception on this scale? I think you probably should be! Precious few could pull off something like this! You're a rare beast, Rob! Sorry, *James*.'

'Don't!' He looked pained, hearing the name fall from her lips.

She got to her feet suddenly. 'Why not? It's who you are! Rob doesn't exist. Not as your version.' She walked away, running her hands through her hair, her fingers gripping at her scalp. It helped to move; it dislodged her thoughts and

379

gave the adrenaline somewhere to go as her heart beat on, her brain oiled with information. What was she going to do now? Oh God, how was she going to tell Mabel? It was all too much. Her entire world was a lie. Her marriage illegal. Nothing was real. She felt like this house, stone and mortar, would dissolve into dust . . .

'Who was that man you called James at our wedding? The best man?' She realized she had never seen him since. Rob had told her he had taken a new job in Sydney, his conversations with him always by WhatsApp.

He looked down. 'He was begging outside Bristol station. I bought him a new suit and paid him to pretend to be my friend.'

'You paid a complete stranger?' she whispered. 'Your parents . . . ? Are they even dead?'

He hesitated, then shook his head. 'They live near Oxford.'

She felt the sobs wrack her as lie after lie was exposed, as her brain started to predict the further fallout of his actions. It wouldn't just end with the unravelling of her life; everyone would hear about it, the gossip in the village . . . Would it get into the press?

He was standing too now, watching her, his face contorted with fear and pain. 'Nats, we can work this out. I know we can.'

She threw her head back and laughed. 'Really?' she cried. 'How's that, then? Are you going to leave her for me?' Her voice had raised, a bloom of anger in her cheeks.

He hesitated. 'Yes.'

She stopped walking. '. . . What?'

'I'll leave her. I'll tell her I've fallen in love with someone else; she doesn't need to know who. And we'll . . . we'll get married – again – you and I. We'll do it properly this time, as Natasha and James. We'll move somewhere new where no one knows us and all this will just blow over.'

She blinked. '. . . Blow over?'

'No one will ever know.'

She stared at him, feeling herself begin to shake again. 'You'd leave Emily and your children . . . ?'

'I love you, Nats! I should have made the choice years ago, I see that now. Let me make this right.'

Her jaw fell open. 'You think leaving your children for me and Mabel will make this right?' She stepped back, away from him. 'I don't think you understand what's happening here. I don't *want* you – James, Rob, whoever the fuck you are! You disgust me!'

'Nats, no—' He reached for her.

'Don't touch me! I don't even want to look at you!'

'No.' Tears were falling down his cheeks now, his head shaking from side to side at her words.

'Yes. There's no coming back from this! Can't you see the carnage you've caused? That accident wasn't the car crash! This is!' she shouted. 'How could you possibly think we can move on from this? You want to destroy Emily's life – and those of your *six children* – just to save your life with us? You actually think I *want* a man like you as Mabel's father?' Her voice cracked. '. . . You're a liar and a cheat and I don't believe a word that comes out of your mouth,' she sneered. 'I could never love you. I don't think I ever did!'

He froze. 'What? . . . What are you saying?'

'You heard me. You were right, I didn't ever love you enough,' she cried. 'There was someone else – and I loved him more in one day than I could love you over a lifetime—'

'Stop it!' His voice had changed. 'You're lying. Take that back.'

But she had fallen still, remembering something else – a tiny detail that had been lost in the avalanche of information which had snowed upon her head. 'Oh my God,' she whispered. Her heart pounded so hard in her chest she felt it would burst past her ribs. She began to laugh, her eyes bright with sudden delight.

'Why are you laughing?' he demanded, moving towards her. 'Natasha, stop it! Tell me who he was!'

But she couldn't stop laughing. She felt wholly released, like she'd found the ejector button on a jet that was in flames and plummeting towards the ground.

'Tell me!' Rob slammed her against the wall, his hands suddenly at her throat. There was a glazed look in his eyes, his face twisted in a grotesque mask of jealousy and rage as he began to throttle her. 'Tell me who he is!'

Natasha felt terror instantly suffuse her as she tried pushing against his straightened arms, slapping desperately at him as thoughts of Mabel, sleeping upstairs, filled her head.

No. No—

The pressure in her head was unbearable. She would have only moments until she lost consciousness. She kept trying to prise his fingers from her neck, kicking at him with her legs . . . His eyes connected with hers and she saw something click back in again, just as she brought her knee up, kicking him hard in the groin and he released, doubling over and staggering back. He was sobbing, huge wracking cries of anguish releasing from his body like a wolf's howls. 'Forgive me! You have to forgive me!'

Natasha gasped for air, her whole body shaking violently, fat teardrops falling from her lashes onto the floor. She watched them crash like crystal balls. How had they come to this?

'Hey! What's going o—?'

The sudden voice made Natasha cry out and whirl around. Hels was standing in the kitchen doorway, holding up a bottle of wine and a bag of Maltesers – looking first bewildered, then fierce.

Her eyes narrowed to slits. '. . . What the fuck is going on?'

The fire was almost out. Hels threw on another few logs and stirred the ashes with a poker. Natasha watched the flames leap, flickering into vivid beauty again, the wood crackling and spitting up glowing embers that twisted and arched in the heat.

Natasha felt the sofa cushion deflate as Hels sank back down beside her again, fussily rearranging the blanket she had thrown over Natasha's legs. They had been talking for hours. Rob – James – had packed and left. He wouldn't be coming back; Natasha had told him she would call the police if she ever saw him again.

Hels was urging her to call the police regardless, but Natasha felt paralysed by the weight of the decision now facing her. To report him for bigamy or fraud, or whatever other charges he might face, would be to deprive six children of their father. If he was arrested and imprisoned, she and Mabel would have justice, but Emily and her children were just as much victims in this too – six children would lose their father. Hels kept arguing they would be better off without him. She was probably right; but how could Natasha choose?

'What if you let Emily decide?' Hels said, cradling her glass. 'If you're so worried about the impact on them, let her choose whether to get his lying arse thrown into the slammer.'

'But that still involves telling her what he's done. It will destroy their lives as they know it. Whether she stays with him, whether she reports him . . . the life they know now, right this minute, will be gone.'

'Like yours is,' Hels reminded her. 'Stop worrying so much about everyone else.'

'Mabel and I will be fine,' Natasha murmured, pressing her lips against the rim of her glass as she stared into the flames.

Hels watched her, before giving a sigh. 'Well, I don't know, Nats. All I can tell you is if I were married to a lying snake, I would want to know about it. You've only got his word that he's never done this before, but how do you know he doesn't have another wife, or another mistress somewhere else too? If he's done it once, why not again? He could have been a serial shagger for years. Doesn't this poor woman deserve to know the kind of man she's married to? At least then she can make her own decision.' She shrugged. 'And you never know, she might decide to stand by him. Stranger things have happened.'

Was that an option? Might Emily even accuse her of lying? People denied the truth – indisputable fact – all the time; they saw the reality they wanted to see. Natasha knew she was guilty of it herself. Her instincts had known something was wrong, somehow the vibrations had been off and yet she had overridden them, ploughing on with her ambition of a happy family life and the charade of a successful marriage. She had played her own part in the deception, hiding from herself.

She was devastated by what had unfolded here tonight – how could she ever trust anyone again? – but for someone whose life had just fallen apart, she also felt somehow *intact*. Sitting here now, knowing he wasn't coming back, it was disconcerting to find that her overwhelming feeling was one of relief. The door of the gilded cage had swung fully open, releasing her. The hysterical laughter that had gripped her in their final moments together had been the realization that she was free of him – fully, wholly and completely. He had no claims here. Their break would be clean and elegant. A small mercy amid the mess. She didn't yet know how she would explain it all to Mabel – how did she break this down to a toddler's comprehension? – but it was a blessing now that they were so used to his absences. It had never been him that she had cried for at night, never his knee she sat upon when she needed a cuddle. She and her daughter had been a duo from the start; in all reality, not that much would change in their day-to-day lives.

'What do you think will happen to all this if you do go to the police? Will they confiscate your assets? Isn't that what they do in cases of fraud?'

'I'm not sure.' Natasha felt frightened by the very thought. To be without Rob was one thing, but to lose their home . . . 'Everything's in his name – the house, the cars.' Her eyes widened as something occurred to her. 'Do you think Emily could make a claim? He probably bought it with her money. Apparently she has family money.'

Hels could only offer a pitying look. 'You really need to speak to a lawyer.'

'But I can't. I can't risk anyone hearing—'

Hels patted her knee, calming her. 'Client–attorney privilege. Anything you tell them, they're bound to confidentiality.'

Natasha dropped her head to her hands. 'I don't know. I just don't know what to do.'

'You don't need to know tonight. You've been through enough.' Hels thought for a moment. '. . . Although I guess one option could be that you come to an agreement with him – get him to transfer it all into your name – the house, the car, all the money in the bank account he used as Rob Stoneleigh – in return for *not* going to the police?'

'But isn't that blackmail?'

'I don't think so. It's just an . . . agreement between consenting adults. He has options; he can always refuse it. And you can always go to the press.'

'But I'd never do that.' Natasha felt horrified.

'He doesn't know that.'

'Yes he does.'

Hels shook her head. 'All bets are off. He can't assume anything anymore. He's the one with most to lose here. You're in a strong position, Nats. You can agree to keep this private – no police or press involvement in return for all the assets as a settlement. You're trading keeping him out of prison in return for financial stability for you and Mabes, that's the straight swap.'

'But that would mean not telling Emily, and surely I have a moral obligation to let her know what kind of man she's married to?'

'What Emily is due is a separate matter to what *you* are due, and that's your call. It's your choice as to whether or not you give his wife a choice too. But for what it's worth *I'd* want to know – and I think you would too.'

'Yeah, maybe,' she said quietly. She looked across at Hels, who was watching her with a concerned expression. She gave a sad smile, resting her head back on the cushions. 'I don't know what I'd do without you, Hels. I've felt like I've been unravelling in one way or another for the last few weeks and you're the only person who's kept me together.'

Hels winked at her. 'Just thank God you're *not* pregnant, right? You might think this couldn't get any worse but, honey, there's *always* further to fall.' She rolled her eyes.

Natasha didn't respond. Hels was right – it all could have been a lot worse. This wasn't even rock bottom.

'What? What is it?' Hels leaned forward.

Natasha glanced across. 'Thank God you walked in when you did,' she said quietly. She could still feel the heat at her neck, her skin bruised and tender from his squeezing hands.

'You don't think he'd actually have . . . ?' Hels couldn't say the words out loud.

Natasha couldn't respond immediately. The terror she had felt as his hands had closed around her neck and the air had stopped in her throat, the thought of leaving Mabel . . . 'No . . . I don't think so,' she whispered. 'He lost control for a few moments but . . . when he realized what he was doing—' She could vividly recall the look that had come into his eyes as he had come to again; but she couldn't be sure. She never would have thought he could have laid a hand upon her before tonight, but he had. Did Emily know she was sleeping beside a man capable of that? Didn't she deserve to know?

Natasha looked around the room, at the family photographs in frames and on the walls. Her entire world had fallen apart but everything looked as perfect as ever. She had arranged for several professional shoots after Mabel was born; they were supposed to be timeless images, with her and Rob dressed neutrally in jeans and white shirts, their cheeks pressed together, smiling brightly as they clasped Mabel between them. For reasons she had never been able to pinpoint, the results had left her cold. They were a photogenic family, she could see that, and everyone always admired the photos when they entered the room, but there was something hollow about them. She had been trying to convince herself there was a beating heart to their life together and that an image showing it would surely make it true; but Rob hadn't been the only pretender in their marriage. She had been a fraud too. Their life may have been a lie, but it was a lie they had both lived.

She looked back at Hels as something occurred to her. 'Wait – what made you come over tonight? Did we have plans?'

'Oh, uh, no.' Hels looked uneasy, scratching her head.

'Where's Dave? . . . Oh God, has something happened between you and him?'

'No, no – it's nothing like that. He's asleep on the sofa.'

'So then, why did you come over here?'

'I was just concerned when you didn't respond to my texts so I popped over to check you were all right, but it's fine, we don't need to do it now—'

'What texts?'

'Honestly, it's nothing. It can wait.'

Natasha's eyes narrowed. Hels wasn't one to leave a sofa with a hot man on it without good reason. 'Tell me what's going on.'

'Honestly, it can wait till tomorrow. You've had enough to deal with and there's nothing that can be done anyway. I don't think you should overload—'

'Done? Hels, what's going on? Just tell me!'

Hels sighed. '. . . It was just something I heard on the news, that was all.'

'The *news*?'

'Yes, but it's nothing,' Hels said quickly.

'It's nothing but you still texted me about it and when I didn't answer you got into your car and came over here to *check* on me?'

The two women stared at one another for a moment, as if trying to read each other's minds. With a small gasp, Natasha grabbed the remote, bringing up BBC News 24. 'What could possibly be on here that involves me?' she asked, a tremor in her voice.

Hels reached forward trying to take the remote from her. '*Please* just leave this till tomorrow, Nats. You've been through enough tonight and nothing can be done from here anyway. It won't help him. Just get some sleep and we can discuss it in the morning.'

'Him? Who are you talking about?' Natasha asked, looking back at the TV screen, but fear was still swimming through her blood, her nervous system stuck on high alert. The anchor was interviewing a politician about the social care system – but it was to the red ticker tape running along the bottom of the screen that Natasha's gaze fell.

'. . . *British climber Tom Duffy missing, feared dead, in Himalayas* . . .'

This was rock bottom.

Chapter Thirty

Annapurna Camp Four,
Friday 16 December

He came to on his stomach, his body twisted awkwardly and his face pressed into the snow. What had happened? He blinked once, twice. He couldn't see anything. Everything was black. Was he dead?

No, he couldn't be dead – he could feel immense pressure on his body, a burning heat, an urge to pull off his clothes. He blinked again, twitched his fingers, then his toes. He could move them, it seemed. He pressed his palms into the burning cold surface – cold? – and gingerly lifted his head. The wind whip-cracked at his cheeks as he broke cover and he dully realized where he was. The storm was still raging. He remembered the roar of the mountain shifting off the snow, like a wet dog shaking its coat.

Avalanche.

How long had he been out cold for? A minute? Ten? An hour? No, he'd definitely be dead if it was that.

The snow was heavy on his back, pinning him down, and it took several attempts of sweeping snow angels before he could push up enough to free himself from the snowy tomb encasing him and get onto his knees. He automatically reached for his head torch but it wasn't on his head; his eyes were adapting slowly to the darkness but the moon, only a week off being new, had nothing to offer him. His hands patted the ground blindly around him, searching for detritus – light, warmth – and he felt the roughness of a huge boulder right before him. Had that protected him? He remembered diving forward, pitching himself as best he could behind something solid. There had been less than a second to think or act. It was a miracle he hadn't been buried. The avalanche must have been largely diverted. Was this a stray offshoot from the serac, as the rest whistled past in the gullies? Certainly, if the full force of it had been coming straight for him, he wouldn't still be here, blinking in the night. He—

Sanani!

The realization that he hadn't been alone hit him like a bullet, spinning him around. He got unsteadily to his feet and turned on the spot, feeling the wind grab at him as though he had made himself a target; there were no good vibrations here. He realized he was in his thermal layers but no jacket, that he was violently shivering, his body jerking spasmodically. He needed to get his jacket, find the tent . . . one, or ideally both, of those options. What the avalanche had started, hypothermia would finish off.

'Sanani!' he yelled, the wind spiriting his voice away. 'Sanani!'

He squinted into the blackness, his hands up to his face as he tried to protect himself from the frozen snow cruds that were whipped back up by the wind. Something – not a colour exactly, but a small breach in the all-black vacuum – caught his eye, thirty metres down the slope.

'Sanani!' He ran, his legs sinking knee deep into the newly sown snow. It hadn't yet compacted but it wasn't as deep as it might have been and it confirmed for him that they had been 'lucky' with this; a mere side-swipe from the Goddess of Abundance, a flick of her hair. The tent seemed to have surfed along with the crud, rather than been buried by the snow, its progress stopped by another massive boulder. The frame was buckled beneath the weight of a block of ice and frozen snow the size of a washing machine. It was just as heavy, too, having settled over the opening face of the tent. Duffy remembered he had zipped it closed – almost closed – as he'd gone out, to keep the wind from whistling through and waking his friend.

'Sanani Sherpa, can you hear me?' he yelled, getting down low and putting his shoulder to the block. It was sharp, jagged and immediately achingly cold to his skin without his water-proof layers on, but he used all the strength he had, powering through his legs to roll it a few metres to the left. Momentum took over but he didn't wait to watch it lumber out of sight. The tent had popped back up now that it was released from its pinnings and he tore at the zip.

'Sanani,' he panted, looking in at the kaleidoscopic sight. Remarkably, the structure appeared to be intact, but everything was scattered to the far end, Sanani lying beneath the packs.

'My . . . chest,' the sherpa gasped.

Had he been thrown full-throttle against the rocks outside? Or had the rucksacks crushed him? They weighed forty kilos each. Duffy scrambled in, pushing them off him. Sanani cried out with a sharp yelp as the pressure was relieved. It wasn't a good sound – or sign.

'Where?' Duffy panted. 'Where's the pain?'

Sanani pointed to his breastbone but kept his hand up, as if guarding the area. 'I heard . . . the crack.'

Duffy stared at him, feeling again the fear he'd felt in that split second when he'd seen the snow bear down upon him in a solid wave. A broken sternum was catastrophic at an altitude where breathing alone was difficult. If there was a bone break, Sanani wouldn't be able to tolerate the jolts of even walking downhill; there was no question of him being able to get back over the ice ridge . . . to carry any supplies . . . to risk knocking it against the rocks. He wouldn't have the strength to pull up on the jumar, to bear a harness that could lower him . . .

'Okay. Okay,' Duffy said in a low voice, trying to gather his wits and not betray his panic. But Sanani was a lifelong sherpa and he knew perfectly well what this meant. There was no chance he would be getting himself off the mountain. And very, very little chance he would get off the mountain full stop. Duffy covered his face in his hands. The odds were overwhelmingly against them. 'Fuck!' he cried into his cupped palms.

'It's okay,' Sanani breathed, lightly touching his arm, comforting *him*, and Duffy felt his composure desert him.

'No. It's not. It's happening again.' His voice broke on the words and he sounded, to his own ear, like his ten-year-old self again. A small boy, lost.

'I know the . . . risks . . . I made . . . the choice.'

'But you wouldn't be here if it wasn't for me! I did this! I've made this happen!'

'No.'

'Yes! I never should have asked you!' He pressed his fingers hard against his skull.

'It was not you . . . who made me come . . . It was a promise . . .' He gasped with pain. 'I made a long time . . . before.'

Tom stared at him, tears pooling in his eyes. '. . . To Mum?'

Sanani nodded. 'To always protect . . . you . . . up here . . . She knew you . . . would come . . . and so did I . . . I accept what comes.'

Duffy looked at his friend, seeing his calm acceptance, dignity in the face of inevitable death. Another death. Another loved one lost. How many did there have to be? . . . Who said this death was inevitable?

He felt a sudden surge of rage. 'Well, I don't!' He wasn't prepared to accept this fate without a fight. 'No. To hell with that. You are not dying up here, you hear me? No!'

He pulled back, looking around the tent wildly. If he was going to act, he needed to do it decisively and fast. With his arms, he began sweeping out what he could of the snowdrift that had chased into the tent through the opening; the first thing was to keep Sanani warm and dry. He reached round for the packs, emptying them both on the ground and scanning the contents. 'I'll need your head torch,' he said, finding Sanani's and holding it up. 'I'm sorry, mate, you know I don't want to leave you in the dark but I'll be quicker with it. Mine came off. And the sat phone's gone too. I was on it when the avalanche hit.' Buried under God-knows-how-many tons of snow, or swept off the mountain altogether.

'Not . . . the ridge,' Sanani rasped. Talking clearly hurt.

Tom hesitated. The sherpa was right. The ice ridge was difficult even with a sun in the sky. There was no way he could navigate such a narrow span in the dark, with these winds, post-avalanche. 'I'll go up to Camp Six and use the Swiss team's comms to send help.'

'No.'

'Yes.'

'No . . . Too far . . . Too long.'

'I'll go quickly.'

'Dangerous . . . Too fast.'

'I'm fine,' he lied, ignoring the headache.

'No . . . moon.'

'It's fine. I only need to see a few metres ahead of me. It won't be the first time I've climbed in the dark. I love a sunrise,' he said, forgetting to add a smile to the comment. In truth, they were only a few hours past sundown – he didn't think it was yet midnight – but if he was going to leapfrog Camp Five and ascend nine hundred vertical metres, then he needed to get started. What might be possible in a few hours at sea level was quadrupled in effort level up here. The altitude would fight him for every step; every breath would have to be snatched, but he had no other choice. Sanani couldn't stay up here, stationary, for any period of time. He would be hypothermic within hours.

Duffy knew he would need to climb fast and light, carrying no unnecessary weight. Changing out of his wet thermals, he pulled on his other set – they were stiff with dried perspiration – and shrugged on the jacket that had been left on his sleeping bag. He slipped the sling across his body, counting out the carabiners and checking his jumars. He looped the coil of rope over his other shoulder. He pulled his spikes onto his climbing boots and grabbed two pickaxes and the collapsible ladder; it was bulky, but if he encountered a crevasse . . . He fastened his helmet. Falling rocks or ice were missiles up here – he'd had one split clean in half by a falling rock in Yosemite once. He hesitated over the bivouac sheet, then packed it anyway. If something should befall him as well, it would be his only shelter. He brought a few shots of dexamethasone, too; he would be nearing the death zone at speed and without oxygen. He needed every aid he could get.

He looked down at the sherpa. Sanani was lying flat, his

arms folded protectively above his chest, his face held in a permanent grimace. 'Are you comfortable? Can I move you? Sit you up?'

'No . . . This is . . . good.'

It categorically wasn't good. It was the very definition of *not good*. Duffy got the rest of their clothes and draped them over the sherpa to keep him warm. Sanani's only stroke of luck had been to be asleep in his bag when the avalanche struck, the thermal down wrapped around his core and inserting a protective layer between his body and the tent's single-wall floor on the snow. Duffy moved their food to his side – dry packs of noodles, some energy gels . . . He propped up the water bottle inside Sanani's crampons and set it within easy reach. He rearranged the woollen hat on the sherpa's head. Warmth and hydration would be critical in the coming hours.

He felt the adrenaline coursing through him. 'We were lucky, Sanani. It looks like we just caught the sidewind of a serac drop and those boulders did a great job of buffering for you. We got lucky and we're going to stay lucky, you hear me?'

Sanani nodded, recognizing the bravado in his voice.

'. . . Oh, radios,' Duffy said, talking in a stream of consciousness, his mind going into overdrive now with what had to be done. He couldn't overlook any details; they could make the difference between success and failure. Life and death. He checked his radio was still zipped in his jacket pocket; thankfully it was. He checked in Sanani's coat – now draped over him – and placed the radio in his hands too. 'You buzz me if there's anything, you hear? Even if you just want to hear my voice. You buzz me. If you feel worse, you buzz me.'

Sanani watched him, saying nothing, and yet speaking with

his eyes. Duffy crouched down beside him. 'I'll be quick, I promise. I'll come back. I won't desert you.'

With effort, the sherpa moved his arm to touch Duffy's hand. 'Victory is living,' he whispered. They were the words of famed mountaineer Jean Troillet, but every climber knew them. Every climber faced a moment where he had to choose: was a dream worth dying for? Was life worth living without a dream? Duffy knew exactly what he was saying. The sherpa had seen a variation on this scenario before, the one Duffy wouldn't let himself think about.

He just nodded.

The two men clasped hands and Sanani whispered a few words of a prayer. He was no monk but he recited the words of the *puja*, asking for blessings, that Duffy might climb with the permission of the goddess Annapurna herself. They locked eyes and souls one last time; then Duffy headed out into the night.

The going was slow on the traverse – the Terrible Traverse, as Anya had reminded him – the frozen rock face poor company in the dark. As a horizontal rather than vertical manoeuvre, it was harder to find footholds and finger grabs and several times he slipped, finding himself hanging in the solid blackness by just the clip on his harness to the fixed ropes. The winds howled as he hugged the headwall, inching across by feeling his way. He felt as if he were in a fight with Mother Nature herself; she gave him nothing, no respite for a single yard as he battled ice and snow, frozen rocks and perilous drops, thin air and hurricane-force winds.

Was she after him too? Like Annapurna, did she want him to join the 38 per cent club?

He gripped the rock face more tightly but it seemed only to make the winds blow harder and by the time he put a foot to the snowfield, he felt he'd been blown inside out, his legs trembling just to stand. He ducked his head down, tucking his chin right down to his chest as he planted one foot, then another. He knew that the serac which had disgorged part of its load onto them only a few hours earlier stood right above him now. If she did it again, he would be directly in the line of fire; he was the skittle in the bowling alley, but it was a risk he had to take. Do this, he might die. Don't do it, Sanani definitely would die.

The winds continued whipping up the snow's frozen crust, stinging his cheeks. There was so much blowing snow, he felt snowblind – ironic for a man walking in the pitch dark. He had just the narrow cone of light from his head torch to see by but the snowflakes whirled dizzyingly in front of him, frenzied and vicious. This was far from the playstuff of his boyhood, this was the land of yetis and not snowmen; of avalanches, not snowball fights. Snowfields was a misnomer, too. It implied smooth plains – even if they were angled at sixty-five degrees – but in truth, this was a landscape of bulbous and grotesque shapes, layered snow whipped and carved by the winds, creating obstacles that stopped sight lines and making him walk twice as far as the eagles had to fly.

By his best estimate, he had been going for five or six hours when he saw the narrow dark entrance to Camp Five at the foot of the rock wall. His body slumped at the sight. Even with a light pack, he felt like he was trudging with a gorilla on his back. His lungs pulled for every breath, his heart pounding so hard and fast it was louder than the winds, the handles of his axes plunging deep into the snow with every step, checking for hidden chasms. Danger lay above, around and below.

It was another ninety minutes before he made it into the low cave, the sound of silence almost deafening as he stepped out of the winds. His head splitting open, he retched but could only bring up bile, his stomach empty now. He fell to the ground, which was unyielding but dry, and without even removing his pack he rolled onto his side and fell asleep.

Natasha paced. It was midnight and she had finally convinced Hels to go to bed – that she would be all right – but she couldn't do the same herself. There was no chance of sleeping through something like this. Her entire body was ringing with klaxons; she felt the cold chill of fear on her skin. He couldn't be dead. No. She didn't believe it. He was . . . That man was *aliveness* personified. It ran through him like a river of liquid sunshine: it shone in his eyes, beamed from his smile. She remembered how it had felt to be seen by him, touched by him. She had felt golden in his gaze.

No. He was alive, she knew he was. No one with that much life force would die so young. He was too determined to live well and to live happily. There was nothing aimless or indifferent about him. He had known what he wanted and he went for it. He had wanted *her*. She could still remember his words in that kitchen that night. *When life gives you something, you have to take it. Because there will be other days when it takes away. You have to recognize the opportunities to be happy and take them, even if on paper it doesn't make sense.*

It didn't make sense that four years later she still thought about him. It didn't make sense that on the night her life had crumbled, she was more worried about his. There had to be someone who knew something, someone with more information than *missing, feared dead*. Was there a British consulate in Nepal? They might have some information—

399

She stopped. No.

She suddenly realized she knew exactly who to call. She picked up her phone and opened the app, texting quickly: *Please call me on this number as soon as you see this. Please, any time of the day or night. It's urgent. Please. Please. PLEASE.*

She threw the phone back on the sofa, chewing on her thumbnail and continued to pace.

The storm had passed and the sun was rising when he opened his eyes again. Had two hours gone by? Four? An entire day? He felt more exhausted than he could ever have imagined it was possible to feel and still be alive. He stared out motionless across the range, white jagged peaks piercing a blue sky. Their scale felt galactic, their immensity in converse relation to his own insignificance, for he was wholly invisible to anyone on those other mountains looking back at him. How many eyes were upon Annapurna right now? He thought of the hearty trekkers in base camp, of Stevie and Jay, the Italian couple . . . all had looked or were looking upon this face in awe, with no inkling he was tucked into a fold of it. The Goddess of Abundance had swallowed him whole – but then, she'd done that long before today.

He lay there at 6,984 metres, knowing that Camp Six was at 7,315 metres and willing himself to move. All that lay between here and rescue for Sanani was a half-mile band of rock. Sheer metamorphic rock. If getting over the ridge had been an exercise in utilizing his ice axes and crampons, this section was technical rope climbing. He could do this in his sleep. He just had to do it at extreme altitude.

With a groan, he pushed himself up to sitting and shrugged off the pack, before uncoiling the six-millimetre rope and quickly – well, as quickly as he could with frozen limbs –

making two different-sized loops. Even out of the wind and with the sun up the temperatures were bitter, at least minus twenty; he couldn't have his gloves off for more than a few moments, his skin burning. With fumbling fingers, he secured the loops with prusik knots and attached them to his chest and seat harness. It would have taken him five minutes at sea level. Up here, it took fifty.

He took a couple of packs of caffeinated gel from the rucksack and swallowed them quickly, grimacing; he had always hated the taste and he retched violently again, his stomach protesting against the enforced fuel, but he kept it down. He needed calories and electrolytes; he couldn't help Sanani if he allowed himself to weaken. The headache was worsening and he debated giving himself one of the dexamethasone shots. It was the emergency treatment for AMS, with nasty side effects – sleep disturbance, psychosis, dangerous blood pressure drops . . . but he decided he could go on. He still felt lucid and in control. For now at least.

Gloves back on, gaiters straightened, he stepped out of the cave into the elements once more – and began to climb.

Natasha stared at the ringing phone, her breath held, heart thudding. She might get answers if she picked up, but were they the answers she wanted to hear? What if the worst was confirmed? Wouldn't it be better to remain in ignorance for as long as possible?

'Hello?' she whispered, as if tiptoeing into the conversation might mitigate what was coming.

There was a pause. 'Hello. Is that Natasha?'

She closed her eyes. The woman's voice was lightly accented. 'Yes, hi Anya, thank you for calling me back so quickly.'

'It is no problem. I was awake.' There was another pause. 'I think . . . I think you must have heard about Duffy, yes? That is why you are awake too?'

Natasha squeezed her eyes shut harder. *Heard about Duffy*. The words had an ominous ring to them. 'Mm-hmm,' she said, pressing a finger to her lips as if that could hold back her tears. 'Is he okay, do you know?' It was an idiotic question. He was *missing, feared dead*. Euphemism wasn't going to save him! But she couldn't . . . she couldn't allow herself to believe the report. Her brain wouldn't go there.

Natasha heard the other woman sigh. It was a tremulous, defeated sound. 'I do not know. I was on the phone to him when the avalanche hit.'

'Avalanche?' The word, just a breath, drew blood like a blade.

'I have been trying to call him since, but nothing. Sometimes it rings, other times no, although that can just mean the satellite has dropped out of range—'

Satellites . . . avalanches . . . what was this world he belonged to? But of course she knew – it was the world of adventure, the one he'd chosen. Just as she had chosen security. They had both got what they'd said they wanted, standing in the kitchen that night, four years ago.

'—But it is ringing, so I am holding onto that. If the phone is still receiving signal then it means it cannot be buried too deep. He was holding it when it happened, so . . .'

Her voice trailed off. Both women knew that was no guarantee of anything. There was nothing to say *he* wasn't in deeper snow, or that he hadn't been slammed into rocks, or swept off the cliffs—

Natasha heard a moan fall from her own body as she sank to the floor, denial giving way to instant, overwhelming grief. She felt herself dissolving, losing her edges and becoming nothing. How could he survive an avalanche? And how could she survive without him? There hadn't been a day in the past four years when she hadn't thought of him, she would admit it now – he had always been there, a whisper from the corner of her mind, a shadow upon her heart.

'Does he . . .' Anya cleared her voice; she sounded cool in the face of Natasha's distress. 'Does he still have your daughter's toy?'

Natasha caught a sob mid-breath. Did Anya think that was why she was calling? That she was on here, pressing for her daughter's toy, when a man's life hung in the balance?

'I . . . I don't care about that,' Natasha said, her voice juddering.

'No?'

'No! I'm worried about him.' Had the roles reversed? Did Anya think she was the media groupie now? 'I . . . I knew him, once.'

'You knew Duffy?' Surprise inflected Anya's voice.

'Only briefly.' And yet, fully. Wholly. *Souls connecting*, he'd said.

There was another silence and she heard Anya exhale slowly. '. . . Oh.'

'I knew him as Tom though, I never knew his surname.'

'I thought everyone called him Duffy.'

There was something possessive in the way she said it. 'Well, he was working when we met. I guess he was being professional maybe.'

'When was this?'

'Four years ago, just before I got married. He was a climbing instructor at Center Parcs.'

'Wait.' There was another pause. '. . . Natasha? . . . Oh my God, are you *Nats*?'

'. . . Yes?'

She heard a gasp down the line, followed by a low groan. '*You're* Nats? You're *the* Nats?'

Natasha wasn't sure what that meant. She wasn't 'the' anything. 'Um . . .'

'You're the reason he and I broke up.'

'I'm sorry?'

'It's fine. I'm married now and he's my best friend. We're good. But . . . you really messed him up for the rest of us.'

'Me?' Natasha felt her heart beginning to pound.

A sigh whistled down the line. 'How could you do that to him? After everything that happened, he had to lose you too?'

Natasha felt the ground lurch beneath her prone form. What did she mean – *lose you too*? He was the one who'd abandoned her! 'I don't . . . I don't understand.'

'No? You're sure?' Sarcasm inflected the words. 'Because I remember sitting in Yosemite campsite with him, watching the sun set on El Cap and it was all pretty straightforward. We were telling each other our life stories and our romantic histories – as you do when you're about to kiss someone for the first time.' There was a pause. 'I was pretty bummed when he said it was love at first sight with you, that he tried to stop you from marrying your husband. He didn't sugar-coat it for me either; he made no pretence that he was okay about it. You were the straw that broke his back, Natasha.'

Natasha couldn't reply. It didn't add up, this story of him pining for her – as if she had left him. She'd gone back to say goodbye, exactly as agreed as they had wrenched themselves apart in the store room. *He* was the one who'd left her!

'Ach, maybe I'm being harsh,' Anya muttered into the silence. 'I guess I should have seen the red flags, but he had that air of the wounded soldier about him and I just couldn't resist.' She sighed. 'I made the mistake every woman makes, thinking she can fix the man she loves.'

'What had happened to him?' Natasha asked.

'What do you mean?'

'You just said after everything that happened, he had to lose you too. What had happened?'

A small snort of disbelief came down the line. 'But surely you know?'

'I don't.'

'. . . His sister died.'

What? Natasha couldn't find her voice. Words crumbled like ashes in her mouth.

'You must have known that?' Anya pressed, sounding incredulous.

'. . . N-no,' Natasha stumbled. '. . . When?'

'October 2018.'

Four years ago. 'Do you know when in October?'

'The twenty-first. It's really hard for him . . . You really didn't know?'

Natasha closed her eyes. She and Rob had married on 27 October; her hen party had been the weekend before . . .

He's gone.

He must have heard the news and left. He would have been distraught. Lottie had been his twin, his big sister; Natasha had seen just from the way he talked about her how close they were. And she . . . she'd shown no faith in him. In spite of everything he'd said and done, she'd believed the worst about him – just a player, just a fuckboy.

And she had ploughed on, becoming Mrs Robert Stoneleigh without missing a beat.

Did she do it?

Natasha felt her head spin. What had she done? 'What happened to her?' she whispered.

'She was killed by a falling rock. Tom said she would have known nothing about it, that was the only saving grace.'

'A falling rock?'

'Yes, it was dislodged by some climbers just above them.'

'So it was a climbing accident?'

'Of course.' She sounded perplexed again, as though this should be obvious. 'I'm surprised you didn't hear about it. Tom got on the first plane out but he said it was all over the news at the time.'

Natasha tried to think back, but the week before the wedding had been a blur; devastated by what she'd thought was his casual betrayal, she'd been in no fit state to watch TV. Instead she had lurched into a bridezilla mania, painting every room in her flat and exhausting herself so that she had no energy to think or feel, getting ready for the estate agents to sell it while they were on honeymoon. She'd married Rob with paint under her nails, but it wasn't the sort of paint Tom had glimpsed on her, the paint that had revealed her true passions and her true self.

'Like it is now again too. The papers get one whiff of their name and they're all over it.'

She switched back to what Anya was saying. 'Sorry – what about his name?'

'Well, because of his mother, Steph Gilmour – Steph Gilmour Duffy.'

Natasha gasped. 'Steph Gilmour was his mother?' Natasha knew of her, even though the impressions were grainy; she had been a young girl when Gilmour was hitting the headlines, maybe eight or nine? Steph had been the mountaineering world's poster girl back in the late nineties and early noughties, but the press had had a love–hate relationship with her.

On the one hand, her striking looks – piercing blue eyes, short dark boy-cut hair and long, tanned, supple limbs – sold covers; people were intrigued by her ability and sheer daring. On the other, she was publicly lambasted and shamed for taking what many saw as unacceptable risks now she was a mother.

Tom's mother.

Have you ever lost someone? You can lose them in an instant.

Natasha frowned, trying to remember those headlines. 'Didn't she die trying to rescue someone?'

'Yes. An injured climber got caught in a storm higher up the mountain and was in a bad way. Her sherpas talked her out of going up to him, but Steph left the camp in the night to help him. She never got there. Avalanche, they think. Her sherpas spent weeks looking for her but her body was never recovered.'

Natasha pressed a hand to her mouth. 'My God, poor Tom. So he lost both his mother and his sister . . .'

'Yes. And on the same mountain.'

'. . . What?'

'Annapurna. They both died on Annapurna. That's why he's up there.'

Tom was climbing the very mountain on which his mother and twin sister had died? Natasha felt her blood chill. Every sentence revealed a new horror. *Missing, feared dead* had been replaced with *avalanche*; that was terrifying enough. But to learn he was there – what, as a pilgrimage? A sacrifice?

'He said he was going trekking,' Anya said defensively as a silence opened up, Natasha lost in horrors. 'He'd been out there a few times before – his father took him and Lottie after their mother died so that they could say goodbye; and he went again a few years ago, on his and Lottie's birthday – but always just trekking. He said it brought him peace to sit in

Base Camp and just look up at the mountain that holds them; it made him feel close to them both there. He said it was the only place where he didn't feel alone. Only . . . this time, when he said he was going out there, he lied by omission. He lied so I wouldn't stop him.'

Natasha felt the blood slow in her veins. 'Stop him from what?'

'"Finishing the job" – that's how he always puts it. He wants to finish what his mum and Lottie had started. Steph was obsessed with being the first woman to climb all eight-thousanders without oxygen. She'd done ten of them, but after she died, Lottie and Tom wanted to finish the quest on her behalf. I think they felt like they were honouring her memory when they were on the mountains.'

'But then Lottie died too.'

'Yeah. They'd done two together and there was just Annapurna and Denali left. Tom felt like Annapurna should be left till last, seeing as that was where their mum's body was; he thought they should finish there as a way of saying goodbye. But Lottie didn't want to give the mountain any more of a "special" status – as far as she was concerned it had killed her mother. They argued about it, her and Tom, and they stopped speaking for a while. The first he knew of her even being on Annapurna was when the news came in. He can't forgive himself for not being there with her; that's part of his trauma. He thinks he deserves to be alone now, that he doesn't deserve to be happy.'

Natasha closed her eyes. 'Is he alone? What about his father?'

'They're pretty much estranged. Things were bad after Steph died anyway. His dad's response was to stop them from climbing at all – he'd refuse to drive them, so they'd hitchhike;

he'd cut their ropes that they paid for with their own Saturday job earnings. Tom would get so angry when he talked about it but I guess I can understand where his dad was coming from. He was terrified he was going to lose his entire family, but he handled it badly and his fear just drove Tom and Lottie further away.'

Natasha closed her eyes and saw again that happy-go-lucky smile that had hidden so much.

'He really never told you any of this?' Anya's voice was quizzical.

'He touched on it but . . . there wasn't enough time.' Natasha's voice was small, flat. 'And he hadn't heard about Lottie when I was with him.'

'So then you knew a different man.'

'Maybe.'

'The one I met was so angry and lost. He felt the world kept taking from him – his mother, his sister . . . You.'

'But I didn't know—'

'No. But he still lost you.'

Natasha felt physical pain at her words. Did he hate her now, then? Did he think she'd just turned her back? She pinched her temples between her fingers, a dull throb beginning to pound in her skull. It had been a night full of trauma. '. . . What was he like with you?'

'Oh, my soulmate – I thought.' Anya's voice tremored on the words. 'We had so much in common. I was a keen climber myself when I met him in California. I had this fantasy that we would spend our lives just camping and climbing faces together. But I soon realized he'd got his demons. He was always a class above in terms of his climbing skills anyway; he'd been climbing practically since birth. I tried my best to keep up with him but he kept pushing himself harder, increasing the gap, like he didn't want us to do it *together*, like he wanted to pull away. He would tell me he wanted to be with me but his actions said different and I realized, though he was with me physically, his heart and head were always somewhere else.'

'So what happened between you?'

'We broke up when I wouldn't go to Alaska with him. He was attempting Denali. It was difficult for him of course – he was supposed to have done it with Lottie – and he was stressed, distant. I couldn't reach him, no matter what I tried. When I finally told him I was leaving, he said he needed me but the truth was, he had never needed me. He was walking this path alone, and I had just been a companion for a little while.'

She stopped talking for a moment, as if to compose herself; Natasha heard her take a deep breath. 'It was very hard having to face facts. I loved him very much and I wanted to help him but the truth was it had been one-sided from the start. I never had his heart and never could, not while it was still with you . . .'

Natasha pressed her hand to her mouth, feeling her tears fall. She had never known any of this.

'I wanted to shut him out of my life completely, but that would have been too hard on both of us. It wasn't his fault he couldn't love me the way I loved him and he was so alone.' She was quiet for a moment. '. . . As it was, we found we were better suited to being friends anyway. I met my husband and moved here to Vienna, and Duffy would call me every now and then, just to check in and let me know he was still alive. I think he thought I was the only person who cared. He had this sadness he could never quite throw off, even when he was laughing and joking; but he seemed to settle down a bit too. He did. After Denali, which seemed to give him some sort of closure, he went down to South America and he liked it there. He stopped talking about Annapurna and I thought he was reconciled with his past. But now . . .' A sudden sob broke through. 'Now I think he was just getting his plan into place. I think it calmed him to know he was going to do this thing that had been haunting him for most of his life. He's made peace with it.' She sobbed again. '. . . I should have known better when he told me he was going out there trekking . . . I was stupid to believe him.'

Natasha was quiet for several moments. A question was poised on her lips but she didn't think she could ask it. She didn't think she could hear the answer. 'When you say he's made peace with it . . . Are you saying you think he's gone there . . . to die?'

There was a heavy silence. Natasha could hear the other woman struggling to control her emotions. 'Suicide? No . . . But I think . . . I do think he is very *prepared* to die,' she said finally. 'I don't think he thinks he has much to live for . . . I don't think he expects to come back, no.'

Natasha dropped her head onto the sofa seat cushion again, tears streaming down her cheeks. She couldn't bear that he had thought he was unloved. If he had only known that he walked through her dreams at night, that his name was branded on her heart . . .

Neither of them spoke for several moments, both of them strangers united in grief.

'I was supposed to see him in Vienna, you know,' Anya said finally, her voice choked. 'That was why he was there, the other week. He was on his way over from Buenos Aires and he flew up from Paris especially to see me. I thought it was a little odd, him diverting like that, but I was so excited to see him, I didn't think too much about it. But then my husband's mother got sick and we had to visit her in the countryside. I couldn't get back in time so it was a wasted journey for him. He was disappointed, but fine about it. I tried to get him to stay another night, but he said he would miss his other connections otherwise . . .' She sobbed again. 'If I had only seen him . . . if I had, I would have known what he was planning, I know I would. I'd have seen it in his eyes. He could never lie to me; even when it hurt me, he couldn't lie. And I'd have been able to stop him getting on that plane. Just like when he rang last night, I knew – I knew straight away something was wrong.'

Natasha felt her heart catch. 'Wrong how?'

'His voice was off; he sounded tired, obviously, but . . . strained too. I got this feeling he was calling to . . . make arrangements. A sort of goodbye. He told me he'd written a letter for me and where to find it if anything happened to him.' Natasha could scarcely understand her through the tears. 'It was like he had this intuition that something bad was going to happen. And then I heard it – I heard the avalanche coming—'

Natasha whipped her head away from the phone as though that would help her not to 'see' the image, but it was in her head, her body.

'I screamed and called out his name, but the sound . . . it made me drop the phone here in Vienna! When he didn't respond, I rang the Nepal Mountaineering Association in Annapurna and they sent up a rescue team. Duffy had mentioned they were at Camp Four while we were talking so at least they will know where to look. They can get the helicopter up too, when it's light, although it will be too high up for them to land. The air's too thin.'

'Right . . .' Natasha took a deep breath, trying to rally herself as they circled back to the emergency unfolding right now. It didn't help him to have them wallowing in pain. He needed their action and their hope. Right now there was a rescue team on the way and no firm proof, yet, that he had died. People did survive avalanches. Sometimes. 'Well, that's good,' she said in a wobbly voice. 'Imagine if he hadn't called. We wouldn't know where he was up there.'

Anya gave a moan. 'We wouldn't even know he was *up* there. The first anyone would have known of it would be when his father and I got his letters several weeks, if not months, from now. *If* we got them.'

Natasha closed her eyes. She likely would never have known. She would have just continued writing emails into the ether. 'How long will it take the rescue team to get to Camp Four?'

'From Base Camp, probably a couple of days. It's over two thousand vertical metres, so acclimatization is the biggest obstacle. The altitude sickness can kill you.'

It seemed everything could up there. 'Is there . . . is there anything *I* can do?'

'No. We're all helpless. I'll keep trying him on the satellite phone for as long as the battery holds out. If we're lucky, his phone might have a geotracker on it which will help the rescue team when they get there.'

But would they be looking for bodies by then? 'Good . . . Good.' Natasha bit her lip, wishing she could do something more than just wait. She pinched her temples between her thumb and forefinger again; the headache was taking root. 'Have you slept at all? You sound exhausted.'

'No, I have to keep ringing.' Vienna was an hour ahead of the UK – it was half three in the morning there.

'Well, do you want me to take over ringing for a bit? You can sleep, then I'll hand over to you in a few hours?'

'I can't ask you to do that.'

'Why not? We both love him.' She said the words simply. Honestly.

There was a hesitation but they both knew they weren't rivals. 'Okay . . . yes. This will be a long haul, I think. We both must rest at some point.'

'Exactly, and you've been dealing with this for hours now. Let me take over. It's half past three with you, yes? So I'll go to half seven, your time? Then you can pick it up again?'

'You're sure?'

'Absolutely. Four-hour shifts.'

'Okay, I'll send you the number of the satellite phone, along with the contact details for the search coordinators. If you do get hold of Duffy, you must try to let them know. He will likely be injured or in shock or hypothermic, so it is no time for reminiscences. As quickly as possible you must get him to tell you any identifying characteristics, anything they can head towards, in case you lose the connection again. That is how you can help him, okay?'

'Okay.' She couldn't imagine hearing his voice again in her ear; the last time had been in the store cupboard, as he'd whispered into her hair.

'And don't be alarmed if the connection does drop out. It's just the satellites orbiting; another will come up in a few moments; you'll get used to it.'

'Okay.' Natasha bit her lip. '. . . Anya, before you go. Can I ask you something?'

'Go on.'

'I know it's an odd question to ask at a time like this but . . . *why* did Tom take Moolah with him? If he's climbing up one of the tallest mountains in the world . . . well, even *I* know weight is critical. Why bother with a child's toy?'

A sigh whistled down the line. 'I was on FaceTime with him when he found it. He said it was a sign.'

'A sign?'

'Yes. He said Lottie had one just like it when they were little; she took it everywhere. She called it . . . Moo . . . Moodle? Something like that. He looked so happy when he found it. Like a little boy. He said it would be his talisman, the second best thing to having her with him.'

And now he was climbing the very mountain where she had died? And their mother too.

She remembered him standing in that kitchen, so determined, so charismatic, so right. He had almost predicted his own future: *Do today what must be done, for who knows? Tomorrow, death comes.*

Chapter Thirty-One

Was it lunchtime? The sun looked to be high in the sky – at least, as high as it ever was at this time in the year. Duffy rested against the rocks, one leg extended, the other bent in the stairsteps prusiks. One more haul-up and Camp Six would surely be within his sights. With a cry of effort, he crested the ridge, falling onto his stomach like a landed eel. He had moved beyond exhaustion into another realm. His body moved without any conscious instruction, the pain of the cold and effort now just an overwhelming numbness. He lay there for several moments, gasping for breath.

'Hello?' he croaked, trying to get up off all fours. He didn't think he had it in him to stand. He lifted his head, panting. He could see the Swiss climbers' orange tent. It was pitched on a small plateau that pressed back against the cliff face: a meagre home in such a hostile environment, but he'd never been so pleased by the sight. Here was safety. Here was rest. Here was contact with the rest of the world. With what felt like superhuman effort, he got to his feet and staggered over. 'Hey,' he called weakly, stumbling forward. 'Hey.'

He patted a gloved hand to the nylon, sweeping his arm

across it in uncoordinated, clumsy movement. 'Anybody . . . home?'

There was no reply. Were they sleeping? He unzipped the tent, taking in the sight of rolled-up sleeping bags, the backpacks almost full in the corners. '. . . Fuck,' he whispered.

He put a hand to the small pan on the tripod – it was cold. It hadn't been used in the last few hours. 'No.'

He sank to his knees, dragged the packs towards him and began breathlessly ransacking them. It went against the climber's code, but a man's life was hanging in the balance. If he didn't raise the alarm and get help sent up to Sanani, his friend would die up here; he couldn't get himself down, he needed to be stretchered off. And all of that could happen if he could just use a phone. Where was it? Where were they?

But he already knew. He'd known it from the silence that had whistled over the ridge. He'd known it from the clear skies at his back and the way the storm winds had dropped.

He was too late. This was the weather window they had needed and they were making hay before the next storm blew in. They were charging up to the summit.

The phone rang on loudspeaker through the kitchen. It would ring for twenty-nine rings, then cut out. Natasha was allowing six-minute breaks in between, worried that incessant ringing might drain the battery; ten-minute spaces felt too long, five not enough.

She and Anya had each done a four-hour shift and Natasha was back on duty, grateful she had something to keep her occupied. Hels had given Mabel breakfast and taken her down to the swings while Natasha tried to sleep during her 'off' shift, but she'd kept startling herself awake every forty minutes or so; now she felt no more rested than if she hadn't bothered.

She made another coffee and sat back down at the laptop. She had been googling Tom's family for the past hour as the phone rang out on the counter beside her. She had brought up pictures of his mother, and of Lottie – not identical, clearly, but she was the feminine version of him and she looked bright and confident, dynamic, brilliant. She had read interviews Steph had given after her ascents up Lhotse, Everest and K2; she had won a Piolet d'Or for her solo route up Nanga Parbat; vitality sparkled from her as if she was somehow *more alive* than everyone else. Tom had told her, in that treehouse, that he had lost someone, though he hadn't said who – but to have had Steph as his mother, and then to have lost her . . . Natasha could only imagine the impact it must have had on both him and Lottie. And so the two of them had kept on trying to reach her by being like her. Trying to reach her by being *there*.

There were very few direct references to Tom. She had found, in some newspaper archives, some early family photographs of the twins aged seven or eight, also in climbing harnesses and ropes as Steph prepared for her ascent of Lhotse; and there were a few passing mentions of Tom's name on blogs on specialist mountaineering sites, but he seemed to actively avoid making public that he was Steph Gilmour's son. Was that because he felt it would create even more pressure on him – or did he just not want to share his pain with strangers? The fact was, he hadn't told *her* either, even while he'd argued they should be together. He had told her they instinctively knew each other, but didn't this show there was so much they didn't know? Stories and histories, motivations, ambitions and fears . . . ? Time had been against them. Then again, it had been the one thing she did have with Rob – but she'd spent five years with him, and it had turned out she didn't even know his name.

It hardly seemed possible that that life was suddenly shattered, that he had left here only last night. His clothes were still hanging in the wardrobe, his face smiling back at them from photographs, his running shoes by the back door . . . It had been the worst and longest night of her life, but the nightmare wasn't over yet. It was just after eleven in the morning here, but five in the evening there . . . growing dark again. Another night was coming.

The phone cut out, and Natasha pressed the timer again as she tried to swallow her coffee. Six minutes till retry . . .

He moved slowly; the splitting pain in his head made any sudden movements impossible. He was into the last snowfield before the official peak but a fresh dump in last night's storm meant he sank to his thighs with every step, making everything so much harder still. He knew he was in the death zone now; he had breached the eight-thousand-metre mark. He could feel the spectral air, that whipped around him like fighting dogs, hollowing out; his lungs could never fill, his heart was beating too hard and fast, his field of sight was shimmering with bright rings, his fingers still burning up from when he'd taken his gloves off earlier to make the stairstep slings. At a molecular level, his body was already beginning to die. He had to get up here and go straight back again. Lingering wasn't an option; no one could survive more than a few hours up here without oxygen. Most would never even *get* here without oxygen, but his mother hadn't used it, and Lottie hadn't, so when planning this climb, it hadn't crossed his mind to even try. He had been doing this as they had wanted to do it themselves. He had been doing it for them, finishing what they had started. But it shouldn't have been like this – so fast. Too fast. Searching for strangers with a phone on top of one of the highest mountains in the world.

His eyes scanned the desolate landscape, looking for dark shapes that would prove to be the two Swiss men. There were tracks in the snow to follow but the unremitting winds were constantly blowing at the surface, eroding the footprints from the outside in. He consoled himself that even if they were to disappear, there were no hiding places on a mountain like this, especially not at the top. There was one way up and one way down, so they must be either enjoying the view from the top or already on their way back. He would see them any minute and intercept them, raise the alarm . . . Any minute now.

Vaguely, it crossed his mind that this was late in the day to still be up there. Climbers liked to summit early – often in the dark to catch the sunrise, and usually before the sun warmed the slopes, making snow and ice slowly melt, making it heavy. They should have been down long ago, but there were countless reasons why they might have been delayed going up or coming back again: trouble with the ropes, acclimatization, a slip or fall . . .

He stopped moving for a moment and radioed back to his old friend. 'Sanani, you there, over?' he panted, leaning heavily on his ice axe.

It was almost a minute before he heard back.

'. . . Sanani here . . . over.' The sherpa's voice was weak, his breathing laboured.

Duffy frowned. 'All good, mate, over?'

'. . . Good . . . here . . . Over.' But there was no colour to his voice. No power.

'Okay, that's good . . . I'm nearly at Camp Six,' Duffy lied.

There was no point in telling him the camp was empty. 'Just hang in there . . . Help is coming . . . Hang in there.'

There was a long pause, static crackling between them. Almost two thousand vertical metres separated them now, a distance so vast they might as well not be on the same mountain – they weren't even experiencing the same weather conditions. Temperatures here were well below minus thirty. Sanani would have at least a ten-degree advantage, which was crucial.

'Hanging . . . in . . . over and . . . out.'

Duffy felt a quiver of fear as he stowed the radio. What if he *couldn't* get there in time to save his friend? His spirit was willing but the flesh felt so, so weak. Or what if the Swiss didn't even have a satellite phone? It wasn't unheard of. Not all climbers used them – as with oxygen bottles, some felt any sort of remote 'assistance' undermined the integrity of the expedition.

He willed his body to move with some sort of urgency. Left foot . . . Right foot . . . Left . . . He remembered his leisurely, almost playful, trek up here, striding out on paths through the forests, leaping across rope bridges like he was in a playground, beers and smokes with new friends, even the brief comfort of sex with a stranger. It had all been so easy, back in that 'other world' where a full breath was a given, where bodies were warm and sensual, not brittle and burning and stiff.

Something caught his eye and he stopped moving – it glistened, catching the light as the sun moved out briefly from behind the gathering night clouds. What . . . ? He reached for the small binoculars hanging at his neck, frowning as he tried to make his fingers work to adjust the focus, but it was too hard in gloves and too cold to risk taking them off again. He tried to speed up his legs but couldn't do that either; he could only keep going. That was the very most he could achieve now.

He didn't know how long it took to approach the site. Forty minutes? It was hard to tell. The day was almost done and the sun had been swallowed by a growing, thick haze. The light became flat, making it hard to gauge its exact position in the sky. Time, like everything else, was becoming blurry. He had no references left from which to work and his world felt like it was narrowing down to just the small bright white field of sight directly ahead of him.

He stopped and stared at the thing that had glinted in the sun half a mile back. It was an ice axe, embedded in the far edge of a deep, gaping hole that had opened up in the snow like a scar. Duffy felt a liquid fear course through his veins at the sight of it left hanging on the lip of the chasm, swung too late. The Swiss might have plunged six hours ago or six minutes, but Death felt close, like it was surfing the wind.

'No!' With a sudden cry of despair, he fell to his knees and stomach, inching his way across, spreading his weight. Where there was one crevasse, there were often many. He squinted as best he could, scanning the snow's surface for signs of lightly sagging trenches or changes in the sheen and texture, but the flat light was against him – just as the brightness of the mid-afternoon sun would have been against the Swiss if they had been passing here then.

He moved slowly, carefully, listening for sounds of the snow creaking below the surface; the crevasse might extend beneath him and he wouldn't know till he was falling through air.

'Hello?' he tried shouting, but his voice no longer had any power. He couldn't have blown out the candles on a baby's birthday cake right now. He crawled with excruciating slowness, finally getting to the edge and peering in. It scared him to the depths of his soul to see the bottomless drop, blue ice stretching earthwards in infinite ripples. It would be like falling to the very centre of the planet.

'*Hello?*' he yelled, the echoes carrying his voice downwards to a place where no human had, or could, ever exist. '*Is anybody down there?*' Only silence spiralled back up. The Swiss climbers were gone, and with them, his only hope for saving Sanani.

He rolled onto his back, tearing his gaze away from the ice chasm, and crying out soundlessly. It had all been futile. He had been chasing ghosts up here. He would have been better going back down over the Ice Ridge and back to Base Camp after all. He had just climbed for nineteen hours, too hard, too fast, too high – for nothing! How could he radio Sanani and tell him there was no help coming? There was no saving him now. Death would crawl over him in a black-fingered creep.

He wasn't . . . he wasn't even sure he could save himself. He knew he had to get back to Camp Six. He could take shelter in the Swiss climbers' tent before the storm blew in and ride it out in there. He would be just below the death zone there, too; breathing would be easier. It had taken Bonington's 1970 expedition two months to make the first successful ascent up here – and only a day to get back down.

Get down. That was what he knew he had to do. It was the new plan – but as he lay panting in the snow, feeling the winds whip over him, he felt another pull. To finish this.

He turned his head uphill. Even lying flat out, he could see the summit. It was maybe a hundred and fifty metres away, spindrift shooting into the sky so that the mountain looked like she was smoking.

He turned his head away again.

He needed to get back to Camp Six. It was the only way he would survive this. The two Swiss men were dead; Sanani was dying – the Goddess of Abundance was already claiming three of the four men standing upon her slopes. Was Duffy going to make it a full tally for her? The sun was dropping quickly and the winds would soon pick up; he couldn't afford to get caught out up here in a storm. He needed to move back down.

He rolled back onto his stomach and with excruciating slowness, got himself up. He swayed as the winds snapped at him, testing him like fighting dogs. He could see the first night clouds beginning to thicken from the north. He heard his mother's laugh. His sister's teases. Finally, he could hear them! Feel them! They were in the winds up here, he realized. They were part of the mountain now.

. . . But they'd never been to *that* part.

He looked back at the summit, knowing the enormity of his next decision. It was life or death. Victory is living, Sanani had said. But was it? What really did he have to live for? Surely winning was victory? Winning for his mother's sake. His sister's. Had he really come this far, to only come this far?

He could hear his father's voice in his head as he took a step uphill – *Why?* – and his mother and sister's voices answered back on the wind: *Because it's there.*

It was right there.

Mabel was on the floor doing a puzzle as Natasha stood at her easel, staring blankly at the canvas. She was trying to stay active, to keep her body and mind occupied, but she found herself zoning out for long periods of time. She felt weak with tiredness, but there was no rest to be found in sleep.

The phone was on the desk behind her, still ringing to cut-off every six minutes, though no longer on loudspeaker so as not to clash with the TV playing cartoons in the background. It was a cold day and the fire had been going since breakfast, Bella snoring in front of the flames, her paws still muddy from her yomp across the fields . . . From the kitchen every few minutes came a loud clatter, usually followed by a curse. Hels was preparing supper, which was always a scary prospect.

To a stranger looking in through the windows, it was a typical domestic scene; but the worst nightmares were often disguised as something ordinary – an attentive husband, for example.

The timer on her phone buzzed and she stopped it, ringing the number again that she now knew by heart. The distant ringtone began to echo through the receiver as she turned back to the canvas and stared at Artemis's likeness. She had achieved in three hours what she typically would do in one. She raised the brush to the canvas again, trying to focus on the stippling on his hindquarters. The background had an unfinished impasto quality to it that she liked and had already decided not to overly work.

It was a moment before she realized the ringtone had stopped ringing.

With a gasp, she grabbed the phone.

'Tom?'

There was a long pause. The time-delay Anya had told her about?

'. . . No,' a voice rasped, so weak she could barely make it out.

'Tom? Is that you?'

Another pause. '. . . Gone.'

Gone? What did that mean? This man sounded barely alive.

'Who . . . who is this?' she cried, pressing her fingers to her lips to hold the tears back. Was he saying Tom was dead? Was this it?

'. . . Sanani . . . sherpa.'

A sherpa? 'Where are you?'

'. . . Camp . . . Four.'

'Camp Four Annapurna?' That was where Anya had said Tom was when she had spoken to him.

'. . . Ye . . .'

She tried to focus her thoughts. What had Anya told her? 'Okay, look – help is coming. A rescue team is coming up from base camp. They were alerted as soon as the avalanche hit. They should be with you soon, okay?'

'. . . Okay . . .' Every word sounded painful, as though an elephant was sitting on his chest.

'Are you hurt?'

'. . . Yes . . . Chest broken.'

She winced. 'But you got the phone now? You didn't hear it ringing before?'

Between them, she and Anya had been calling every six minutes for twenty-two hours.

'Under . . . bag . . . in snow.'

It took a moment to understand what he meant. She knew the bags in question would be heavy packs, not handbags. And if he had a broken breastbone, how easily could he use his arms? . . . And if he was there alone, could he reach, pull, dig . . . ?

Gone. She closed her eyes as she braced to ask the next question. '. . . When you said Tom was gone, what did you mean? . . . Where is he now?'

She held her breath waiting for the one word that would undo her.

'. . . Up . . .'

Her eyes opened. 'Up?'

'. . . To . . . get . . . help.'

Tom was alive? A laugh of relief escaped her. He was still alive? He wasn't dead? . . . Almost immediately the laughter died on her lips. Or was it that he wasn't dead *yet*? Wasn't going further up the mountain like running into a house that was on fire?

Distantly she heard noises – a commotion – in the background.

'What's that?' she asked as they grew closer and suddenly louder. There was no reply but she distinctly heard voices. They were speaking in a language she couldn't understand, the words sharp and hurried. 'Hello? Sanani?' she cried. 'Are you still there?'

The man didn't respond. All she could hear was the sound of zips and shouts, of frantic voices, a muffled cry.

'Hello?' she cried again. 'Can anybody hear me?'

There was more background kerfuffle. It sounded like they were being ambushed by bandits, but it had to be the rescue team. It had to be.

'Hello?' she called into the noise. There was a sound of rustling and of static, as if the phone was being wrapped up.

'*Namaste, yo ko ho*?' A new voice suddenly came on – strong, younger, fresh.

'. . . Hello? Do you speak English?'

'. . . Yes. Who is this?'

'I . . .' Who she was, was irrelevant. 'My friend was speaking to Tom Duffy when the avalanche hit. She was the one who called you.'

'Tom Duffy? He is not here.'

'No, he's gone up the mountain, apparently. To get help.'

'. . . Camp Five?'

'I don't know, I'm sorry. I just know he's gone up.'

'Is he injured?'

'I don't know.'

There was another cacophony in the background, more voices moving around. She tried to imagine the scene – a post-avalanche site on a Himalayan mountain – but all she saw was a jagged mess of rocks and snow and ice, and Tom somewhere amid it all.

A voice in the background said something that caused another conflation of voices. The man came back to her at the other end of the line. 'You are wife?'

'What?' The question took her by surprise. How could she possibly respond to that?

'You are Tom Duffy wife?'

'Yes,' she said quickly. 'I am.' They would tell her more if they thought she was his next of kin.

'Wait—'

The snow hole was too shallow to keep more than the worst of the wind off but it was all he had been able to dig as the storm caught up with him, his limbs leaden and no longer doing what he asked of them; coordination was all but gone, along with his strength. Duffy lay curled up, looking out at the night sky. The moon dangled as if on a string, elegantly spare and still a few days away from being wholly new, when she would seemingly turn her back on the world and slip into serene obsolescence for a night.

Everything was happening in slow motion, it seemed. His blinks, his breaths. The headache hadn't improved, but the glare off the snow was now gone and he could rest his gritty

428

eyes, if nothing else. *I've never felt as far away from the living and as close to the dead* – Erhard Loretan had said that, and now Duffy was living it. Or rather, dying it.

The radio crackled suddenly, a jarring burst of static that outgunned even the wind. 'Tom Duffy? Are you there, over?'

In the fog of delirium, Duffy frowned. The voice did not belong to Sanani.

'This is Annapurna Mountain Rescue. We are at Camp Four with Sanani Sherpa. Where are you, over?'

Duffy gave a small smile as his brain made the connection – Anya. Of course. He should have known. Always. So. Efficient.

'. . . Tom Duffy, do you read me, over?'

With agonizing slowness, his arm reached for the radio and pressed the button. '. . . Tom Duffy . . . speaking . . . I'm at the top.'

There was an ominous pause, filled with crackles. He knew what it meant; he heard the dread it contained. 'You are *on* the summit?'

'Just below now . . . Top of . . . rock wall.' His eyes closed. He could feel the life force trickling out of him. If he was bleeding to death, there would be something to see, staining the snow . . . But he would be found simply looking like a man asleep.

'Are you injured, over?'

'F-f-frostbite to fingers . . . Hypo . . . th-thermic . . . Headache . . . AMS,' Duffy sighed wearily, knowing what that spelled. Was it oedema of the lungs or brain, though? Again, he would never know.

'Have you got shelter?'

But they both knew a tent on the summit wouldn't withstand a storm. He would be blown off *in* it. '. . . Snowhole . . . bivvy.'

'Can you get down to Camp Six?'

'. . . No.'

'You are certain?'

His eyes were still closed. He didn't have the energy to keep them open now. 'Yes . . . Take Sanani . . . Broken . . . sternum.'

'He is being made comfortable by medic. Do you have dexamethasone?'

Duffy frowned. 'Yes . . . but . . .' It was in his rucksack and the energy that would be required to take it off, to find it, to administer it . . . 'No.'

'If you have medication, now is time to take it. You must get to Camp Six.'

'. . . No.' The word escaped like a wish. 'Too late for me . . . I . . . belong here . . .'

There was a long pause. He could hear voices, garbled and indistinct, though raised and alarmed. 'Tom Duffy, your wife is on phone.'

'. . . My . . . ?'

'I patch through . . . Wait . . .'

He clasped the radio to his jaw. The winds were howling, trying to rip off the plastic sheet, his clothes, his skin . . .

'. . . Tom?'

Her voice sounded soft and warm. It made him think of apples and roses. He closed his eyes and saw a cottage garden, he heard children laughing, a dog barking . . . all traces of another world, security; a life that had never been his. He had had another destiny – of rocks and ice, of sweat and pain and loneliness. 'Anya.'

The static crackled between the two radios and he looked up at the night sky, wondering where the satellite was that was bouncing the signal from here to Vienna.

'No. It's Natasha . . . Nats.'

His eyes opened, his head reflexively lifting off the compacted snow – a mistake, the wind forced him back down again.

He could hear the tremor in her voice. She was scared of something. 'Tom . . . I know it's been a long time and . . . we should have talked before now . . . but I really need you to do something for me first, okay?'

Was he hallucinating? Was this the start of it? His brain shutting down, chemicals shorting? '. . . Okay.' He should have known she would be his last thought.

'I need you to get down to Camp Six, you hear me? You have to go down.'

'. . . I . . . can't.'

'Yes, Tom,' she said firmly; quickly. 'You can. And you must. You must go down . . .'

'No—'

'Yes. You told me once that getting to the top is optional but getting down again is mandatory. Remember?'

He gave a feeble smile, seeing her now in that terrible dress, her cheeks flushed, her eyes distrustful, her lips kissable. '. . . I . . . I did say that . . . didn't I?'

'You said a lot of very wise things to me. And I should have listened to you . . . But right now, I need you to listen to me.' Her voice had a firmness to it he hadn't heard before. She had grown up, become a woman. A wife. A mother. 'They tell me you want to stay up there but that's just not possible. You have to get up and go down.'

He was quiet for several moments, understanding. 'Because Moolah . . . Mabel.'

'No. Mabel doesn't need Moolah . . . She needs *you*. We both do.'

He frowned, trying to make sense of the words. 'Me?'

There was another burst of crackles and a sob. 'She's yours, Tom. Mabel is yours . . .'

The headache exploded inside his skull, all the pressure dissipating into a confetti of colours, stars dancing behind his eyes.

'. . . Please . . . please don't leave us!' Her voice broke. 'Get up and come down.'

His brain was reigniting, synapses firing against the icy anaesthetic, trying to understand these words that made no sense. 'Mabel . . . ?'

'Yes! Come down and meet her . . . I'll explain everything. She loves you already, Tom.'

'But . . . ?' Was she crying? Her voice sounded different. '. . . I can't . . . move.' He heard the note of frustration break through his voice too. It was too late, this. It was all too late. Always too late. He could feel himself being pulled under.

'Do you remember I said that to you, that I couldn't move? And you helped me.'

He felt emotions prickle like spring buds, rousing from their numbing sleep. He remembered every moment of her standing there – the smell of her hair, the tension in her hands around his neck, the warmth of her breath . . .

'Close your eyes and tell me what you see. Three things.'

Memories were flashing through his mind like fireworks, colour bleeding into his frozen world of white and black. '. . . I see you and Mabel in the photograph . . . I can see Lottie . . .' He gave a small shocked sound. 'I can see Mum . . .'

There was a pause and he had a sense he had got it wrong. Said something wrong. 'Tell me three things you can hear.'

'I hear you . . . I hear Lottie . . . I can hear Mum . . .' His

432

voice broke on the last word, as though it was being tugged from him, pulling him on.

'Now tell me three things you can feel.'

He could feel himself dying. '. . . Wind . . . Cold . . .'

'Can you feel Moolah?'

He pressed his arm gingerly against his body, feeling the soft squishiness in his jacket pocket. 'Yes.'

'And she's your lucky charm, right?'

'. . . Yes.'

'Yes she is. It's why she's with you. It's why you found her and why you took her. She'll get you down. She's your talisman. But you have to choose us, Tom,' she cried, openly now. But her voice was fading. 'Not your mum. Not Lottie. They wouldn't want this for you . . . Tom, do you hear me? You have to choose us.'

He heard the wind kick up, trying to carry her words away. Or was it him that was leaving? He could no longer feel his body. He felt as if the wind was peeling at his edges, freeing his spirit to forever lilt like a feather in the mountain spindrift.

'Tom.'

The word brushed his skin like an angel's whisper.

Natasha.

Mabel.

Us.

But it was all too late. They really were out of time, this time.

Chapter Thirty-Two

Vienna, Friday 23 December

Snow was falling, the soft flakes whirling through a velvet sky. Mabel turned her face upwards to catch them on her tongue and Natasha did the same, wholly unconcerned by how strange they might look.

'They taste sweet,' Mabel laughed.

'Of course they do. They're made of sugar, you know.' Natasha smiled, making Mabel laugh and open her mouth again for more.

Natasha was carrying her on her hip as they walked slowly through the Christmas market, weaving through the throng, music playing. The baroque white 'wedding cake' splendour of Karlskirche sat as an opulent backdrop to the humble wooden stalls set up on Karlsplatz, lights threaded across and around the square, with avenues of Christmas trees bringing something of the forests to the city. It was all significantly more low-key than the giant glitzy headliner Christkindlmarkt on Rathausplatz, which drew in crowds in their thousands from other countries. Natasha knew she couldn't cope with a throng right now. Her mind needed calm, her nervous system still jangled and ringing from the traumas of the past week.

The crowds were beginning to thin and it was well past Mabel's bedtime, but they had both needed to stretch their legs and get some air after the flight. Tomorrow would be a big day and they needed to walk off some nerves. At least, Natasha did.

Mabel hadn't remembered the apartment, even though they had stayed there only a month previously. Then again, she had been carried in asleep and carried out again in full flight. For Natasha, though, revisiting the very point at which her life had strayed from its path, it had felt almost like a pilgrimage. She had gone to the curtain where Anya had told her Tom had found Moolah and she had looked behind it as though it was a sacred site. Her hands had brushed over the sofa where he had stretched out in comfort for the last time, and as she had stood in the bedroom, she had stared at the bed trying to imagine her own sleeping form in it, and then Tom's only twelve hours later.

Time. It had never been their friend. They'd always been running out of it or against it, the stars never quite lining up for them. So many near-misses, so many if onlys. She had been running from family trauma while he had been running towards it, facing it head on, refusing to back down. What was it he'd said to her that time in the kitchen? Security is an illusion?

He'd been right. She had looked to Rob to be the family she had lost. Watching her parents die, waiting for the moment when she was truly alone in this world, had been terrifying. As an only child, her sense of safety had always been fragile, she always had a feeling of there being just paper walls to protect her from the storms. Becoming an orphan, all her worst fears had been realized – and she retreated. Instead of moving to London where her new job awaited, she had moved back

435

to her childhood village straight after graduation, surrounding herself with comfort and familiarity where she could. Old friends became her walls instead. Then Rob. And when Mabel had come along, her desperation to give her siblings – to give her the safety and companionship she had never known – had been overwhelming. Almost obsessive. She didn't want Mabel to grow up like her, always alone, somehow apart even in groups.

Now they were alone, together.

Rob didn't figure in the story anymore. It had been a week since his lies had unravelled but he was already fading from her mind; like a celluloid roll exposed too quickly, only faint impressions remained.

She knew her composure – the few times they had spoken in the days since – had unsettled her husband. She knew he must have envisaged his secret one day becoming known, but could he have ever seen it going like this? She was supposed to fall apart, surely? Or rage and rail? But she didn't want revenge or even justice, she just wanted him gone.

For the first few days after he went, she kept life small. There was so much to unpick that she could scarcely match her socks, much less make any life decisions. She couldn't yet find an answer to Mabel's question – where has Daddy gone? – not a real one anyway. 'Working' had done up till now and would do for a little longer. In the meantime, they did the simple things – walking Bella across the fields, washing her down with the hose, going to the swings. In the afternoons, they made mince pies and paper chains and tissue angels. Hels was forever buzzing in and out, checking in on them and fussing over whether they had enough firewood and if they needed an oil delivery.

In the quiet hours, mainly through the night, she painted.

It was a balm to her soul, allowing her to process everything that had happened. She applied oil to the canvas with an intensity of focus she'd never known before. She stippled and dabbed, she swept and brushed and sparred and jabbed with the brush, making marks. Making her mark. Finding herself, so that by the time she eventually stepped back and knew it was done, she had decided on her course of action.

She had delivered the canvas to Diana yesterday, on time, and she had watched in quiet delight as she saw her client's genuine joy. It was a triumph, but she hadn't lingered in the glory. Thirty minutes later she was in a cafe in the next village, sitting at a table opposite Emily and apologizing for the secrecy, warning her to prepare for a shock. Natasha didn't say much to begin with. What words could convey the enormity of what he'd done? She had simply started by showing a photograph of her and Rob on their so-called wedding day; she then showed images of their family portrait with Mabel and Bella (understanding now why Bella had been so excited to meet Emily – she had recognized her smell whenever Rob came back to them); finally she had showed her the bruises on her neck. 'I never knew until last week,' she had said quietly, apologetically, as tears silently slid down the other wife's cheek.

Emily had suspected affairs too, but this was – as for Natasha – an inconceivable fear; its sheer audacity meant it had never crossed either of their minds. It was, of course, all far worse for Emily. He really was the love of her life; they really did have children together. That he wasn't Mabel's father helped simplify things for Natasha, but it posed inescapable questions for his wife: did Emily want a man who had chased and 'married' another woman? Did she want as her children's father a man who had happily believed he had another family, even though he had – as Diana had unthinkingly once mentioned in passing – had 'the snip'? Emily told her in a crushed voice that it had been shortly after their youngest, Rupert, now five, was born; around the time he had crashed his car into Natasha's. 'Mistakes' were still possible within the first year of the vasectomy, which was why he'd accepted Mabel as his. Of all his deceptions, Natasha would never forgive the way he had lied to her as she cried, month after month, longing for a baby he knew damn well he would never give her.

And thank God. Thank God for it now.

Emily and Natasha were agreed neither one of them wanted publicity, for their children's sakes. Natasha just wanted a simple extrication, keeping the house and their 'married assets' made that a given. She need never step into their lives again and no one – not even the neighbours on the other side of the hedge – need know. *If* that was what Emily wanted. It wasn't about protecting Rob, but his family. Natasha had no idea which way Emily would go with it; she would need time to process it but she wouldn't be wholly surprised if, for the sake of their children and the life they had built together, Emily chose to save her marriage. Six children, six hearts broken? Could any mother do that? Could she not? But whatever she decided, at least it would be an informed choice. Emily's own choice.

They had parted, if not as friends, not as enemies either. Natasha had driven back home, crying the whole way for everything that had been lost, but as she pulled into the drive, she wiped her cheeks dry, knowing she would never shed another tear for him.

Was it timing or perspective that had turned this tragedy into mere farce? If Tom hadn't been dying on a mountain, if she hadn't learned he'd come back into her life – however lightly – would Rob's deception have undone her? Because she didn't feel undone. She felt utterly, gloriously free. She felt how she had that afternoon in October four years ago when for a few hours she had thought her future lay with Tom. Not because she had needed *someone*, but because something in her had recognized something in him. Spirits colliding. Hearts and minds, as well as bodies. It had been love at first sight and love until the last.

She had dropped Bella over to Hels and Dave's – he had unofficially moved in, 'with half a drawer and everything', he'd said wryly from the sofa – before, with Mabel in her arms, she'd bought two plane tickets to Vienna with the cash for Arty's portrait still in a roll in her coat pocket.

Now they were here and it felt good to be back where it had all begun, closing the circle. Anya had arranged everything, booking the apartment and having the fridge stocked up with provisions for them. They would be meeting for lunch tomorrow and it felt funny to think that – for a woman Natasha now felt so intimately connected to – she had had to ask how she would recognize her!

'Look, Mummy!' Mabel squealed, seeing a wooden toy stall and somehow propelling Natasha towards it by a strange but highly effective jerking motion of her body. Natasha laughed, kissing her on the cheek and allowing herself to be steered. The crowd absorbed them, just two more snowflakes landing in the snow, no different to anyone else. Their secrets couldn't be read. They were just like any other mother and daughter, excited about Christmas and all the days to come.

*

He watched from a distance, allowing himself the luxury of soaking them in, unobserved. They moved as one, almost still connected to one another, and he saw for himself the bond between them that had driven Natasha to scour the planet for a lost ragged toy. Was it luck or serendipity that had made the impossible happen, bringing them back into each other's orbits after all this time, connected by such a fragile thread? And if he hadn't met her again this time, would there have been another chance? Or another? Until they got it right?

They were standing at a toy stall, looking at a collection of wooden farmyard animals. The stallholder was holding up a pig and saying the word in German for Mabel. He looked enchanted by the child; everyone did. She was exquisite. Could she really be his?

He still couldn't believe that the mountain that had taken his family had given him one back. It had been the thought that had propelled him as he somehow released the bag from his back and found the dexamethasone shot. That had given him the biochemistry to get back down the rock wall and out of the death zone, into the Swiss men's tent. And it had been the hope for this moment, when he would see them both with his own eyes, that had kept him going through that gale-force storm as he waited for sunrise and the rescue team.

The journey down had been hard and painful, but not as hard and painful as it had been on the way up when he had trekked and climbed with the world at his back; back then he had given up on finding peace or happiness, shutting everyone out with a smile. He hadn't expected to ever come back. He had thought the world had nothing left for him – too much love had been lost. The irony wasn't lost on him that he'd found life in the death zone. The margins for survival had been thin, his life force flickering when her call had been patched through, and he knew very well that, but for her voice and her words, he would still be lying up there now, perpetually.

He had saved her once. Now she had saved him. Not everyone was so lucky. Sanani had been sedated and safely, slowly, transferred to Base Camp where a helicopter had taken him to hospital; Duffy had been put in the bed next to him the day after, when he'd gathered enough strength to be assisted down too. But Hans and Juergen, the Swiss climbers he had searched for and never found, would remain up there. The rescue team had seen their bodies in the daylight the next morning – unreachable, at the bottom of the crevasse.

Though he might be down again, the mountain had left her mark on him, inside and out – his core temperature had dropped to eighty-three degrees by the time the rescue team had arrived and he was battered with severe windburn, third-degree frostbite in four fingers, a cracked rib. He had been put on oxygen for two days and an intravenous drip, discharging himself before his doctors wanted, but he had planes to catch. He wouldn't be stopped. He was no picture right now, he knew that, but he would wear the scars like a tattoo, something by which to remember the Goddess of Abundance. If she had taken from him, she had also given back. They were all square as far as he was concerned.

He watched again as mother and daughter laughed by the toy stall, both of them so beautiful they made his heart ache, and he felt again those traces of the man he'd been once, in a treehouse, trying to woo a woman in a wedding dress.

He stepped forward, out of the shadows and walked towards them.

* * *

'Hey diddle-diddle . . . the cat and the fiddle . . .'

Natasha jumped at the low voice, at the discrepancy of English words in an Austrian market. That rhyme? She whirled around, to find Tom standing there. Or rather, to find Tom standing there – with Moolah, perched on his shoulder.

Mabel stared at him for a moment, seeming to freeze as surprise and shock overwhelmed her, before her whole body went stiff and her arms shot out. 'Moolah!'

Natasha had to keep from dropping her as she almost lunged at Tom, her little hands grabbing the toy and bringing him to her face, her body immediately going limp. 'Moolah,' she murmured.

Tom caught her gaze as Mabel sat slumped between them, her legs in Natasha's arms, her head against his chest. She saw as his eyes closed instinctively at the child's weight against him, one arm coming up to cup her head and stroke her hair.

Natasha felt the tears spring to her eyes, completely unbidden and unstoppable. 'Hi,' she whispered.

'. . . Hi.'

Never had so much emotion been carried in such a small word. It held a world, three hearts, a new life. Their eyes roamed one another, taking in the changes of the past four years. He had lost weight, clearly; his hair longer, eyes brighter, newly shaven with severe windburn lines. The smile was still the same though. She recognized it in their daughter now. It took everything she had not to walk into his arms and lay her head upon his chest too but they had waited this long; they could wait a few minutes more.

'I didn't think you landed till tomorrow,' she said quietly.

'I caught an earlier connection. I was on my way over to the apartment when I saw you coming in here.'

'So you were spying on us?' she smiled.

'Absolutely. I thought I'd better do a risk assessment before I just jumped in, you know?'

'Quite right,' she grinned. 'We're quite a proposition, she and I.'

'You're incredible together.' His voice was hoarse with emotion, though his eyes never left her.

Mabel stirred from her reverie, sitting up again and seeing that she was hugging a stranger.

'Mabel, this is Duffy,' Natasha said carefully. 'What do you say to him for being so careful to keep Moolah safe and bring her back to you?'

'Ank oo uffy.'

Natasha pulled her thumb out of her mouth. 'Again, please.'

'Thank you Duffy.'

'That's better.'

His eyes sparkled as Mabel made curious, guileless eye contact with him for the first time and Natasha saw how he caught his breath. Could he see himself in her too? 'You're most welcome, Mabel. She is an excellent travelling companion.' Natasha could see the emotion in him, the strain in his own body not to reach and draw her – them – to him too. But timings still had to be navigated. They weren't quite there yet.

'Did she jump the moon?'

Natasha felt her stomach drop at the question. Rob had been right about one thing – Tom had made a promise he couldn't keep. 'Let's not worry about that just now—'

Duffy tipped his head to the side as he looked at Mabel. 'Well, did you put up the prayer flags and send her good vibrations?'

Mabel nodded her head vigorously.

He looked surprised, and so happy. 'You did?' he laughed.

'They're still flying on the washing line in the garden,' Natasha said with a roll of her eyes. 'The postman is very confused.'

He laughed. 'Ah, well, thank you. Mabel, tell me the rhyme, I can't quite remember it all – *Hey diddle-diddle, the cat and the fiddle, the . . .*'

'Cow jumped over the moon!' Mabel cried as he reached into his pocket and pulled out a large glossy photograph, so freshly printed the ink was still sticky. It showed a starry night that seemed to belong to another world than this one. It was as though entire other galaxies could be seen, twisting in helixes, through a crystalline atmosphere, as many stars in the sky as there were grains of sand on the beaches. The gibbous moon – seeming so much closer, so much finer, than she had ever seen it – lay tipped on its back and there was Moolah, leaping over it. On the back were written two words: *Mission Accomplished!*

Natasha's gaze fell to the bandage on his hand, the one he was mainly keeping in his jacket pocket. He would have had to deglove to take the image, surely? To toss the toy at just the right moment as he clicked the shutter? What had he risked for that photo, keeping a promise for a little girl? His little girl.

'It took her a few goes, because even all the way up there, the moon is still a long way away – but she loved it and she said it was worth all the hard work,' Tom said quietly, seeing how Mabel's eyes shone as she looked at the image. 'That's for you to keep.'

'Will you go to the top of the world again?' Mabel asked him.

His gaze fluttered towards Natasha. 'No.'

'Why not?'

'Because I like it down here more.'

'Were you scared you might fall off?'

'Yes, a little bit. But Moolah's very good at giving cuddles, isn't she?'

Mabel nodded earnestly.

'Mm. She made me feel safe. No wonder you love her so much.'

'Do you love her?'

'Yes, I do. Very much.'

Mabel blinked, hearing the crack in his voice, as she looked at him, then at Moolah, then at him again. 'We can share her.'

His eyes widened, tears pooling. '. . . Really?'

She nodded earnestly again. 'But I think she should sleep with me at nights because she doesn't like the dark.'

'Yes, I noticed that. I think that's a very good idea.'

Natasha watched them talk, seeing how something in him melted as Mabel held Moolah out to his cheek and he nuzzled against it. They had agreed, during the couple of phone calls they had managed over the past week, not to mention anything about fathers; no public displays of affection, or anything that might confuse her. Not yet. There was so much to say and she still hadn't told him the full story yet. He had been so weak when they got him back down, she had just wanted him to recover. But they had time now; for once, it was on their side.

'It's cold out here,' she murmured, wanting to go somewhere warm with strong walls, where they could hide and be alone at last; where she could stand on his toes and dance with him, her head against his chest.

'Perishing,' he replied, meeting her gaze.

She smiled at the irony. This man knew a thing or two about the cold. 'Let's go home, shall we?'

Home. 'Yes.'

They turned and she felt his hand reach for hers, squeezing it tightly as they walked, Mabel and Moolah between them, just another family in the Christmas crowds.

Read on for an extract of

The Last Summer

The start of a major new series by Karen Swan

'Powerful writing and a wonderful premise make this a novel you'll simultaneously want to savour and race through'
Jill Mansell

Summer 1930 on St Kilda – a wild, remote Scottish island. Two strangers from drastically different worlds meet . . .

Wild-spirited Effie Gillies has lived all her life on the small island of St Kilda, but when Lord Sholto, heir to the Earl of Dumfries, visits, the attraction between them is instant. For one glorious week she guides the handsome young visitor around the isle, falling in love for the first time – until a storm hits and her world falls apart.

Three months later, St Kilda falls silent as the islanders are evacuated for a better life on the mainland. Effie is surprised to be offered a position working on the Earl's estate. Sholto is back in her life but their differences now seem insurmountable, even as the simmering tension between them grows. And when a shocking discovery is made back on St Kilda, all her dreams for this bright new life are threatened by the dark secrets Effie and her friends thought they had left behind.

Available now

Chapter One

13 May 1930

The dogs were barking on the beach. The old women came to stand at their doors, looking out with hard frowns across the curve of the bay. The tide was going out and there'd been a testy wind all day, whipping up the waves and making the birds wheel with delight.

Effie didn't move from her position on the milking stone. She had her cheek to Iona's belly and was filling the pail with relaxed indifference. She knew it could be another twenty minutes before a boat nosed around the headland, though it would probably be sooner today, given these winds. Her collie Poppit – brown-faced, with a white patch over one eye – sat beside her, ears up and looking out over the water, already awaiting the far-off sea intruders, though she wouldn't leave Effie's side.

She watched the movements of the villagers from her elevated perch. The milking enclosure was a good third of the way up the hill and she always enjoyed the view. It was a Tuesday, which meant washing day, and she could see the younger women standing in the burns, skirts tucked up and scrubbing the linens as they talked. They wouldn't like having their sheets flying in the wind if visitors were coming. None of the tourist boats were scheduled to come this week, but if it was a trawler, it wouldn't be so bad; most of the captains were friends.

The indignity of airing their linens before strangers was taken seriously in a village where privacy was merely a concept. The layout alone meant anyone could see the comings and goings of the villagers from almost any point in the glen; it was shaped like a cone with smooth but steep slopes two-thirds of the way round, leading up to towering cliffs that dropped sharply and precipitously on the other sides to the crashing sea below. The cliffs only dipped, like a dairy bowl's lip, on the south-easterly corner, skimming down to a shingle beach. There was nowhere else to land on the isle but here. The seas were heavy and torrid all around but by a stroke of luck, the neighbouring isle, Dun – no more than a bony finger of rock – almost abutted the shores of Hirta, creating a natural breakwater and rendering Village Bay as a safe haven in the churning grey waters of the North Atlantic. During some storms they had as many as twenty ships taking refuge there.

Trawlermen, whalers, navy men, they all rhapsodized, as they took shelter, about the welcoming and cosy sight of the village tucked beneath the high-shouldered ellipse, chimneys puffing, oil lamps twinkling. The grey stone cottages – interspersed with the older traditional blackhouses, which had been steadily abandoned since the 1860s – sat shoulder to shoulder and fanned around the east side of the bay, bordered by a strong stone dyke. Looking down from the ridges on high, they were like teeth in a jaw. Giant's teeth, Effie's mother used to say.

The village's position afforded the best protection from winds that would funnel down the slopes at speeds that lifted rocks and tore the steel roofs from the stone walls (at least until the landlord, Sir John MacLeod of MacLeod, had had them strapped down with metal ties).

The Street – and there was only one – was a wide grassy path, set between the cottages and a thick low wall that topped the allotments. It was the beating heart of island life. Everyone congregated there, protected further from the wind by their own homes and able to bask in the sun on fine days. The old women sat knitting and spinning by their front doors; the children ran along the wall, cows occasionally nodding over it. Every morning, the men would meet outside number 5 and number 6 for their daily parliament to decide upon and allocate chores; and after tea, the villagers would amble down it to pick up from their neighbours 'the evening news'.

In front of each cottage, across the Street, was a long, narrow walled plot that ran down towards the beach. It was here that the villagers planted their potatoes in lazybeds, hung their washing and allowed their few cattle to overwinter. During the summer months, the cows were kept behind the head dyke, whilst the many sheep were grazed on the pastures of Glen Bay, on the other side of the island. Separated from Village Bay by a high ridge, Am Blaid, Glen Bay spiralled down to a sharply shelved cove. There was no beach to speak of over there, for the northerly waves were relentless and though the villagers kept a skiff there for emergencies, heading out and coming ashore were only possible on the rare occasions when the prevailing wind switched and the sea lay fully at rest.

Iona stopped munching and moved with a twitch of irritation. Unperturbed, Effie reached down for the pile of dock leaves she had picked on her way up and wordlessly passed her another few. The cow gave a sigh of contentment and

Effie resumed milking. This was their usual morning routine and both were accustomed to its gentle rhythms.

A few minutes later, the pail was almost full and Effie sat up, patting Iona on the flank. 'Good girl,' she murmured, standing up off the milking stone and looking down the slope. As predicted, the prow of a sloop was just nosing round the headland of Dun.

She watched keenly as the ship slipped silently into the embrace of the bay and threw out an anchor, sails drawing down. Not a trawler, then. The women would be displeased. This vessel with its slim-fingered triple masts and low curved hull was a finessed creature, more likely found in the azure waters off France than the outermost Hebrides.

'Friend or foe?!'

The question echoed around the caldera.

The crew were just black dots from here but she could see the locals already readying the dinghy; the men would need to row powerfully against waves that were pounding the shore. The passengers aboard the sloop had chosen a bad day to sail. The open water would have tossed them like a cork and although Dun's presence granted mercy, it was no free pass; a south-easterly made the bay's usually sheltered water froth and roil like a witch's cauldron and there was no guarantee they would be able to disembark.

Only one thing was certain: if the men were able to land them, no one would be coming back dry, and the villagers knew it. Already faint twists of grey smoke were beginning to twirl from the chimneys, people rushing in and out of the arc of low cottages that smiled around the bay and taking in their washing, sweeping floors, putting on shoes, moving the spinning wheels to their prominent positions so that their visitors might watch.

They all knew the drill. Catering to the tourists had become a quietly profitable sideline. It couldn't help feed them – with not a single shop on the isle, they had little use for money on Hirta itself – but it was useful for asking the more familiar captains to bring back treats when they were next passing, or to give as extra credit to the factor when he came wanting the rents. Or in Flora's case, to purchase a brightly coloured lipstick she'd once seen on one of the well-heeled lady visitors – even though it would be wasted on the three hundred sheep she was currently herding in Glen Bay for the summer.

None of the villagers understood quite why the world at large took an interest in them, but the postmaster, Mhairi's father, Ian McKinnon, had been told by colleagues on the mainland that a St Kilda-stamped postcard was now considered desirable, if not valuable. Their way of life, they were told, was being rapidly left behind by the rest of the world. Industrialization meant society was changing at a more rapid pace than any other time in centuries and they were becoming living relics, curiosities from a bygone age. Some people pitied them, perhaps, but the St Kildans cared naught for sympathy. They had learnt to play the game to their advantage – Effie chief among them.

She lifted the pail and began to walk down the slope, her eyes never fixing off the black dots as they transferred from one heaving vessel to the other. Once they'd dried off and recovered from the swell, she knew they were going to want a show. And she was going to give it to them.

'Where'll they do it?' her father asked gruffly as she finished with churning the butter. He was standing by the window, looking out, his pipe dangling from his bottom lip.

'Sgeir nan Sgarbh, I should say,' she replied, closing the lid of the churn and going to stand beside him. 'It'll be more protected from the wind round there.'

'Over the top, aye, but will they get the dinghies round on the water?'

'Archie MacQueen's got the arms on him,' she murmured. 'Just not the legs.'

'No, not the legs.' She watched a trio of men walking down the Street. One she recognized by his distinctive gait – Frank Mathieson, the factor, their landlord's representative and the islanders' de facto ruler – but the other men were strangers. They were wearing well-cut dark brown suits and wool hats, but from beneath one of them she caught the gleam of golden blonde hair and a tanned neck. She willed him to turn around, wanting just to glimpse the face that went with that hair and elegant physique; but the path curved, taking them out of sight.

The group that had come ashore had been disappointingly small – a private contingent, Ian McKinnon had said with his usual authority. It meant the tips would be meagre. If the women were to take their sheets in, there had to be good reason for it and two men alone could hardly reward everyone. The captain had been put up in her Uncle Hamish's cottage and the other two men would stay at the factor's house, for it was the largest on the isle. She didn't envy them having to endure Mathieson's hospitality.

'I'm just going to put this in the cool,' she said, lifting the churn onto her shoulder and walking out, Poppit trotting at her heels. She could see the visitors further down placing pennies into the palm of Mad Annie as she sat carding the wool and telling stories about broomstick marriages and snaring puffins. Unlike most of the village elders her English was good, but that didn't mean the others couldn't communicate, and Effie gave a small grin as she saw Ma Peg make a play of bustling and hiding from their camera, even though those days of shock at the new technologies were long past. More coins crossed palms.

She went round the back of the cottage and a short way up the slope that led to the plateau of An Lag, where they herded the sheep into stone fanks in bad weather. Beyond it, Connachair – the island's tallest mountain – rose majestically like a stepping stone to heaven. For some it was. Many had met their fate over the precipice, tricked into distraction by the summit's rounded hummock on the village side and caught unaware by the sheer cliffs – 1,400 feet high – that dropped suddenly and vertically to the sea, as if cleaved.

The lush grass was speckled with buttercups and thrift and felt springy underfoot as she moved past the countless identical stone cleits to the one where she and her father stored their butter and cream. She ducked down as she stepped inside and set down the churn. It was the very store her family had been using for this purpose for over three hundred years. There may have been over 1,400 of the hump-topped, stacked-stone huts on the island, but she could identify every single one that belonged to her family – this one below An Lag for the dairy; that one on Ruival for the bird feathers; that on Oiseval for the fulmar oil; that on Connachair for the salted carcasses, that for the peats . . . There were plenty that lay empty, too, but they also had their uses as emergency larders, rain and wind shelters, hiding places for courting lovers . . .

She came back down the slope again, jumping nimbly over the rocks nestled in the grass and seeing over the rooftops that everyone was beginning to gather on the beach, preparing for the visitors' exhibition.

'Are you joining them, Effie?' a voice called.

KAREN SWAN

She looked over to find Lorna MacDonald coming out of the postmaster's hut, fixing her auburn hair. She worked there sometimes with the postmaster.

Effie skipped over, Poppit beating her by two lengths. 'Aye,' she grinned. 'You never know, there might be some pennies in it for me.'

'And more besides,' Lorna said with a wink.

'What do you mean?'

'He's a fine-looking fellow, the young one. A smile from him would be payment in itself,' Lorna laughed, her brown eyes twinkling with merriment.

Effie gave a bemused shrug. 'I only caught the back of him.'

'That's pretty enough too, I should guess.'

Effie chuckled. It was a wonder to her that Lorna was their resident old maid – all of thirty-three years old and still unmarried – for she was a terrible flirt. Alas, the visiting men never stayed for long and the St Kildan bachelor nearest in age to her was Donnie Ferguson, who had no interest in a wife seven years older than him, cleverer than him and almost through her child-bearing years.

'Who are they, anyway?'

'Rich,' Lorna shrugged. 'If that ship's anything to go by.'

Lorna knew about such things. She wasn't a St Kildan by birth but a registered nurse from Stornoway who had chosen to make her life here; she had seen another world to this one and what money bought.

'Good,' Effie sighed, catching sight of the men beginning to head up the hill with their ropes, the dogs running ahead in a pack. 'Well, then I'll still aim for some pennies from them and you can have the young gentleman's smile. What do you say?'

'Deal,' Lorna winked as Effie took off again and darted back into the cottage to grab their rope. It was thickly plaited from horsehair, supple and rough in her hand. Her father was sitting in his chair by the hearth now – he could never stand for long – tamping his black twist tobacco.

'Well, I'll be off then.'

He looked back at her. His eyes had a rheumy look, the whites yellowing with age, but they still revealed a strong man within an infirm body. He gave a nod. He wasn't one for sentimental farewells. 'Hold fast, lass.'

'Aye.' She nodded back, knowing those had been his last words to her brother too.

For a moment she thought he might say something else; the way he held himself, it was as if an energy for more words lay coiled within him. But the moment passed and she left again with just a nod.

Some of the men were already walking the slopes, ropes slung over their shoulders too. As she'd predicted, they were heading for the easterly cliffs. A small rock stack just out in the water provided enough of a break from the broadside waves for the dinghy to rope up in relative comfort whilst the show was put on.

She ran and caught them up, listening in as they chatted about the visitors and the news from 'abroad', meaning Skye.

'. . . friends of the landlord,' David MacQueen, Flora's eldest brother, was saying. 'So we're to make it good.'

'Shame the wind's up or we could have gone further round,' her cousin Euan said.

'There'll be no tips if they're sick as dogs,' Ian McKinnon replied.

'But the cliffs are lower here.'

'This will do them fine. It will all be high to the likes of them.'

She fell into step with Mhairi's older brothers, Angus and Finlay.

'What are *you* doing here?' Angus asked with his usual sneer.

'Same as you,' she shrugged, slightly breathless as their longer legs covered more ground than hers.

'We're not fowling. This is just for display.'

'Aye, so there'll be tips.'

'Then knit them some socks!'

'You know I'd get a fraction of what I can get up here and the agreement is whenever you're all on the rocks, I'm allowed to be too.'

'You're a pain in my side, Effie Gillies,' Finlay groaned.

'And you're a pain in mine,' she shot back.

They rolled their eyes but she didn't care. Her brother's friends, her friend's brothers, they had been teasing her all her life and she knew to give as good as she got. They had all grown up playing hide and seek in the cleits as children, learnt to read together in the schoolroom beside the kirk, and kicked each other during the minister's sermons.

But she couldn't ignore that things were changing. Or had already changed. A tension existed now, a low-level hum, that hadn't been there before. Her brother's death had profoundly affected them all and she was no longer John's little sister to them – or anyone but herself; sometimes she caught them looking at her in a new way that made her nervous. Finlay's eyes seemed to follow her wherever she went and Angus had tried to kiss her as she cut the peats one evening; he hadn't yet forgiven her for laughing.

For visitors wanting to take in the view – and they always did – this would be a forty-minute to hour-long walk, but she and the men did it in under thirty and were already spread across the top and looping out the coils of rope by the time the dinghy appeared around the cliffs. Birds whirled and screeched around them, feathers lilting on the updrafts. From this height, the boat looked no bigger than a bird either. Effie glanced down a few times, scanning the rock face for the line she wanted to take, then casting about for a rock with which to drive in her peg.

Looping the rope around the peg, she leant back, checking its firmness and tension. It vibrated with pleasing freshness and she wrapped it around her waist in the St Kildan style.

She looked down the drop once more. Cousin Euan had been right; it really wasn't so high here. Seven hundred feet? Half the height of Connachair. A single drop of the ropes would take them maybe a third of the way down. Still, they were merely going to be playing up here today. No bird hunting, no egg collecting, no saving stranded sheep. Just playing.

'You're looking peely-wally there, Eff,' Angus drawled. 'Sure you're up to it?'

She looked back at him with scorn. Angus prided himself on being the fastest climber on the island. He had won last year's Old Trial, a climbing race among the young men to prove they were worthy of providing for their families – and future wives. If he had wanted to prove anything to her, the point had been well and truly lost. Effie was certain she could have beaten him (and the rest) had she only been allowed to enter too. But as a girl . . . 'Actually, I was just wondering how quickly I could get down there.'

A smirk grew. 'You think you can do it *fast*?'

'Faster than you.' She pulled her fair hair back, tying it away from her face in a balled knot. The last thing she needed was a gust of wind blowing it about and blinding her on the route.

'Ha! You're all talk and no trousers, Effie Gillies.'

It was her turn to smirk. 'Well, yes, even I won't deny

there's not much in *my* trews.' Angus McKinnon might be the fastest man on the isle, but he wasn't the brightest. As if to make the point, she hitched up her breeches at the waist; they had been John's and were the only suitable attire for climbing, but she didn't wear them purely for reasons of practicality.

Finlay blushed furiously. 'Ignore her,' he said. 'You know she's only trying to rile you. Everyone knows you're the fastest, brother. Just give the rich people a show. This is an exhibition, not a race.'

Effie shrugged as if she couldn't care less either way, but they all knew the gauntlet had been thrown down. She – a girl! – was challenging Angus for his crown; the competition could happen here between the two of them. Why not? It was as good a chance as any. She watched him looking down the cliff as the islanders did final checks on their ropes and took their positions on the cliff edge.

Effie kept her eyes ahead, her hands already around the rope. Waiting. Hoping—

'H'away then!' Archie MacQueen cried. Flora's father, he had been an experienced cragger himself, but he left these shows to the younger ones these days; already lame in one leg, his grip wasn't what it used to be either. Besides, someone had to stay up top in case anyone needed hauling up.

It was the cue to go, to perform, to show off their derring-do and the skills that made the St Kildans famous around the world as they all but skipped and danced over the cliffs. Without hesitation, Effie leant back and stepped over. She felt the swoop of her stomach as her body angled into open space and the rope tightened. She pushed off, allowing the rope to swing on a pendulum, her bare feet already braced for contact with the rock face, ready to caper across it in a bold defiance of gravity. A visitor had once told them it was like watching spiders drop from the top of a wall. She herself loved the sound of the ropes under tension – a *huzzahing* – as she and the men scampered and sprang from side to side.

'First to the boat then?'

She looked across to find Angus on his rope, staring straight at her. She smiled at his tactic – finishing the race at the boat, not the bottom, when neither one of them could swim . . . 'Aye. But I'll wait for you, don't worry.'

Angus's eyes narrowed at her insult, but she was already off. Abandoning the acrobatics, her foot found a toehold and she brought her weight to bear on it as the other foot searched. The St Kildans never climbed in boots, always bare feet. The cliffs were too unyielding to give any more than a half inch to grab and there was nothing that compared to skin on rock. Shoes and boots – the hallmarks of civilization – had no place on a granite cliff.

She left the older men to the games, their powerful arms and legs flexed as they made a point of playing on the rock faces, bouncing off with their feet, reaching up for a fingerhold and pulling themselves up like lizards, before repeating again. Others scrambled sideways, scuttling like crabs over the rocks.

Effie just focused on going down. She could see the boat between her legs, far below her, as she descended on the rope, her arms braced as she lowered herself, hand over hand. She didn't have biceps the size of boulders to help her, but as she always said to her father, she didn't need them. She was wiry and light, skinny even, but that didn't mean she was weak. The less there was of her, the less she had to support. She wouldn't tire so quickly. She was more nimble, more flexible . . .

From her peripheral vision, she sensed she was already ahead of Angus, but only just. He had power, height and gravity on his side.

Soon enough she was out of rope. Balancing on a narrow ledge, she unwound the rope's end from her torso.

'What are you doing?' Ian McKinnon called sharply down to her as she began to free climb.

'Winning! Don't worry. It was Angus's idea.'

It always felt different scaling without the rope and she knew it was reckless, but there was something about the intensity it brought – her brain and eyes seemed to tune into hyper-focus, the adrenaline refreshed her muscles – that meant she could remember her mother's eyes and smile, hear again her brother's ready laugh. Somehow, by thinning the skein of life, it seemed she could almost reach the dead.

Down she went, agile and sharp until the horizon drew level, then hovered above her, and the crash of the waves began to intrude on her concentration. White splashes of cold sea were beginning to reach towards her, spraying her bare brown calves, but she didn't care about getting wet or cold. She just had to win. She had to know – and crucially, Angus had to know – that she was the fastest and the best.

She saw the dark sea, ominously close. She was less than thirty feet above the waves now, but the cliffs just sliced into the ocean depths, and as she scaled ever downwards, she realized that the only place where she could stand and pivot was a narrow ledge perhaps six feet above the surface, no wider than her hand's span.

For a moment, she felt a visceral spasm of fear. This was madness! If her father was to hear of the carelessness with which she was treating her life . . . Or maybe that was the point of it. Maybe she wanted him to hear of it. His heart had been broken by death too many times, and she was the only one left. He couldn't – or wouldn't – love her in case he lost her too. Was that it? If she was to slip, to go straight down, under the waves . . . would he weep? Would she be mourned like the others? On the other hand, if she won, would he be proud? Would he see that she could be enough?

There was no time to think. Everything was instinct. Her feet touched down and her arms splayed wide as she hugged the wall, gripping its surface with her fingertips, her cheek pressed to the cold, wet granite. Breath coming fast, she gave her muscles a moment to rest. They were burning, but she knew she wasn't there yet.

She glanced up. Angus was only a few feet above her. What he lacked in nimbleness, he made up for in power. In a few more seconds . . . She looked carefully back over her shoulder and saw the dinghy tied to a rock just a short distance away. Her Uncle Hamish, skippering, was frowning and watching her intently, the way Poppit had watched for the boat earlier. He saw her movement and seemed to understand she wanted in; that she was going to launch herself towards it, one way or another. If he was alarmed, he didn't hesitate nonetheless. Not in front of the guests. Quickly he pulled in on the rope, hauling the small dinghy as close as he dared to the cliff wall, knowing that if he went too far, the swell risked tossing them against the rocks.

A nervous flinch inside the boat betrayed someone's nerves as her intentions became commonly understood. Effie knew she would have to time the next wave and then leap. She hugged the wall as she watched and braced for the next break – just as Angus landed beside her.

A blast of white water broke upon them both, making them gasp with the shocking cold as they were soaked. She didn't care. As she felt the draft pull back, she twisted and leapt blind. Death or glory then!

For one stunning, protracted moment, she felt almost as if she could fly, like the very birds that soared and wheeled and sliced around her in this island sky. Then gravity took hold, and she landed – half in the dinghy, half in the water. She took a hard knock to her chest but her arms gripped the prow as the boat rocked wildly, water slopping over the sides. But it was flat-bottomed and made for heavy weather; it righted itself almost immediately, and she laughed victoriously as her uncle Hamish hastily got a hand to her waistband and dragged her aboard in one swift movement like a landed salmon.

'I didna' know you had decided to make it a race to the bottom,' Uncle Hamish said to her with a stern, disapproving look. It was the most he would reveal in front of the tourists, but she already knew he'd be telling her father about this. There would be trouble to come, most likely a hiding; but it was worth it. Effie's eyes were bright. She'd beaten Angus McKinnon! The fastest cragger on the isle. Not just that – he could make no further claims now of providing for her when she herself had beaten him.

'It was Angus's idea,' she panted, scrambling to her knees and looking back to find him still clinging to the ledge. With her leap to victory, he now stood frozen in place and was becoming more soaked with every breaking wave. He either had to jump too or climb back up, but he couldn't stay there.

With an angry sigh, he jerked his thumb upwards, indicating the latter. He had lost. What good was there in riding back with them now? She would only crow her victory at him.

Uncle Hamish nodded, understanding perfectly what had just happened between them. It was a man's look, the kind that cut her out, but what did she care? With a satisfied smile, Effie sat on the bench, pulling out her hair tie and wringing her long hair. Seawater puddled in the dinghy floor.

'Heavens above!' a voice said. 'It's a *girl*?'

She twisted back to face the visitors properly at last. In all her ambition to beat Angus, she'd forgotten who they were trying to impress in the first place. The three men seated towards the back were staring at her in wide-eyed amazement: Frank Mathieson, the factor, and the two men she'd glimpsed from behind earlier.

'Well, I can't climb in a skirt, sir,' she grinned, wringing out her tweed breeches as best she could.

'It wasn't just your clothes that fooled me. The speed! I've never seen a spectacle like it. You scaled that cliff like a squirrel down a tree!' It was the older man speaking. He was portly, with a dark moustache, lightly salted. Spectacles made it difficult to see his eyes past the reflection, but he appeared friendly as well as impressed. 'Do you mean to say females climb here, too?' he asked their skipper.

'Only this one,' Uncle Hamish said with a resigned tone, untying the rope from the mooring rock and beginning to row. 'This is my niece, Euphemia Gillies.'

'Effie is Robert Gillies's daughter. They live at number nine,' the factor added, as if that information was somehow enlightening. 'How are you, Effie?'

'Aye, well, sir, thank you for asking.'

'Becoming bolder, I see.'

'If by bolder you mean faster.'

He laughed. 'Allow me to present the Earl of Dumfries and his son, Lord Sholto,' he said. 'I'm sure you will be aware that they are great friends of Lord MacLeod.'

'Ah,' she said blandly, although she was aware of nothing of the sort. Who their landlord kept as friends was no business of hers, though it confirmed Lorna's observation that the visitors were rich.

'They were visiting his lordship at Dunvegan when they heard I was planning on making the voyage here—'

'It's been something of an ambition of mine to get over here,' the earl said brightly, interrupting. 'I'm a keen birder, you see, and Sir John very kindly agreed to my proposal that we might sail Mr Mathieson here ourselves. Two birds, one stone and all that.'

'Aye.' She could feel the younger man watching her keenly as she talked, but for as long as the others spoke, she had no such opportunity to cast her gaze openly over him. 'So will you be staying for long, then?'

The factor inhaled. 'Well, a lot will depend upon the wea—'

'Certainly a week,' Lord Sholto said suddenly, allowing a dazzling smile to enliven his features as she finally met his eyes.

'A week?' Effie smiled back at the blue-eyed, golden-haired man. Finally she could see his face at last. And she liked it.

'Miss Gillies.'

She turned to find the factor hurrying up the beach after her. Uncle Hamish was tying up the boat, the distinguished guests having been appropriated by the minister again the moment they'd set foot on shore.

'Mr Mathieson.' She tried not to show her impatience, but her tweed breeches were soaked from her half-swim and she wanted to get back and change. Their progress round the headland had been slow as they'd met the headwinds and she was shivering now.

He stopped in front of her, slightly downhill from where

she stood, so that she was aware of standing taller than him. He wasn't a tall man, stocky but not conspicuously short either, and the consequence of not standing out in any way seemed to work to his advantage; many times an islander had been caught saying things they shouldn't, not realizing he was within earshot. His relationship with the St Kildans was highly taut, for as the bringer of supplies every spring, and the collector of rents every autumn, he was both carrot and stick to the island community. He could smile and be charming when it suited him, but no one could ever quite forget that the power he wielded over them was almost absolute, and few – apart from Mad Annie – would clash with him. He wore finer suits than the village men and affected the manners of his employer, but reddened, pitted cheeks and the forearms of a wrestler betrayed him as a fighter first.

'Well, that was quite a display,' he said.

Effie wasn't sure this was intended as a compliment. 'That's the idea,' she replied vaguely. 'They always like it.' A sudden gust blew her long, wet hair forward and she had to use both hands to pin it back. The sky was growing ominously dark.

'Indeed.' He gave what she had come to learn over the years was his customary pause. It preceded a direct contradiction of what came after it. 'Although I'm not sure such daredevil antics require the added *novelty* factor.'

It took a moment to understand his meaning. 'Of a girl climbing, you mean?'

He shrugged. 'I understand your obligations to your father impel you to undertake men's work in a regular capacity, but when it comes to making a good impression on visitors . . . '

'But they seemed to like it.'

'Well, they're polite, of course, but things are quite different in the wider world. I know it's not your fault that you don't know any differently – why should you? – but decorum and good taste are held in high regard. Women scrambling over cliffs like monkeys . . . ' He pulled a face. 'No. It's important to think about the impression you make on these visitors and how you and your neighbours will be conveyed in their onward conversations. I'm sure you wouldn't want to embarrass Sir John, would you?'

She had never met Sir John. '. . . Of course not.'

'Very well, then. So we're agreed there'll be no more fits of vanity on the ropes. We must strive to make sure the guests are not made to feel uncomfortable by what they witness here. Best foot forward, yes?'

She stared back at him, shivering with cold and anger. '. . . Aye, sir.'

He looked over her shoulder, along the Street. 'How is your father, anyway? Still lame?'

Her eyes narrowed. 'And always will be.'

'Which only makes him all the luckier to have you,' he nodded, oblivious to her terse tone. 'But please tell him I shall need to find him later and discuss the rent arrears.'

'Arrears?' Alarm shot through the word.

'As I recall, you were short thirteen Scotch ells of tweed last year. Your uncle picked up some of the slack, but you were also down nine gallons of oil and seven sacks of black feathers.'

'It'll be fine this year,' she said quickly. 'We were only short because I twisted my ankle and couldn't walk for ten days. It was just bad luck that it happened when we were fowling.'

The factor looked unconvinced. 'I'll need to reappraise the quota with him. You will remember I extended a great kindness in not reducing the oatmeal bolls after your brother's accident and as a result you have enjoyed more than your share for nigh-on four years now—'

Effie looked at him with wild panic. What he said was true, but it still wasn't enough. The past few winters had been hard ones and their harvests had all but failed, save for a half-dozen potatoes and those oats that were only half blackened by frost.

'—I have been both generous and patient, but it's not fair to expect others to compensate for your shortfalls. Accidents will always happen, Miss Gillies. You cannot expect to be fit and well every day of the year.'

'But I do. And I will,' she said urgently. The factor didn't know it yet, but she and her father had lost four of their sheep over the top this year already, so they were already down on their wool yield. Her father had bartered 100 extra fulmars instead with Donald McKinnon and it had been a rare endorsement of Effie's climbing skills that both men believed she was capable of bagging the extra haul, on top of the usual harvest.

'Miss Gillies, you don't need me to remind you that you are a girl doing a man's job. The odds are already grossly stacked against you.'

'But I'm eighteen now, and I've grown this last year. I can do anything they can and I'll prove it to you. I'll show you, sir.'

The factor looked at her keenly. 'You receive more than you are due and you deliver less than you owe. You see my predicament? I must be fair, Miss Gillies. Why should I ma[?] – and keep making – exceptions for you? If the othe[?] to know—'

'But they won't. I'll make sure we're squar[?] this September.'

'So you're saying you want me t[?]

'Secret . . . ?' Behind him, the reverend and the two gentlemen guests walked past on the path back to the village, the minister holding forth on the repairs made to the manse. Lord Sholto glanced across at them talking as he passed by and she found herself smiling back at him, as though he'd pulled it from her on a string.

'From your neighbours? And your father too?'

She looked back at the factor in confusion. He was watching her intently. '. . . No, please don't tell him. I don't want him to worry. I can make the quota this year, I know I can.'

He tutted. 'I don't know why I allow you to manipulate me, Miss Gillies—'

She frowned. *Did* she manipulate him?

'A "thank you" doesn't pay the fiddler, now, does it?' he sighed. 'Still, I have sympathy for your predicament and although I have a job to do, I believe in being a friend in the hour of need.'

Effie bit her lip – she had to – to keep from laughing out loud. What? There wasn't a person on the isle who would have considered the factor a friend. He bought their feathers at five shillings a stone and sold them at fifteen, and the supplies he brought over – oatmeal, flour, sugar, tea and tobacco – cost them three times what he paid. Was it any wonder the villagers tried to bypass him with money they earnt from the tourists and could spend directly themselves?

'Talking of which, I have brought you something, again.'

'For our studies?' She had finished her schooling four years ago, but he never seemed to remember this.

'I've left it in the usual spot. Just . . . be discreet, please. I can't oblige these sorts of favours for everyone.'

ours? Secrets? 'But—'

Miss Gillies,' he said briskly, assuming his usual

manner as he noticed the three men now ahead of him on the path. 'I must get on. Our visitors will be requiring some refreshments after the afternoon's . . . excitement. Just remember what we discussed. We shall have to hope first impressions don't stick.'